Miriya Greer

First published by Miriya Greer 2025
Morgantown, West Virginia

First edition

Ebook: 979-8-9891065-3-0
Hardcover: 979-8-9891065-4-7
Paperback: 979-8-9891065-5-4
Library of Congress Control Number: 2025919290

Cover art by Elanor Greer

To my friends,
Fueling my enthusiasm
And waiting eagerly for this release

I

Breach

Prologue

He had heard the stories of Korodon, but seeing it for himself is by far much different and *much* more nerve wracking. The dark clouds, the dead land, the lack of beings. Even the biting chill of the air makes him tense, always wary of his surroundings.

The only light he has to keep himself company in this dreary place is his lightning, which arcs from his clothes in bright flashes. The white beams scorch the barren dirt path he walks alone and off the trunks of the leafless trees that line the empty road forward.

Ahead of him looms Korodon's ancient castle, its sheer size appearing more as a painting come to life than an actual building. Its tallest spire touches the dark sky above, the point of origin for the swirling black clouds. Its age is slowly starting to show; crumbling stones and cracked balconies stand out on the large structure. What isn't slowly falling into physical decay is becoming dirty. Dark water streaks run down from the undersides of windows and at the points where the blocks of stone join together, making it appear as though the structure itself were weeping.

If the theory he had been given proves to be correct, what

he's looking for should be somewhere in there.

Yet doubts grow in his mind with each step. His very being rejects wandering through such a dismal land, crying for him to turn around. He knows he shouldn't be here in the first place with the travel ban in effect. If he returns to Asandra now he might not get into any trouble…

A jolt of lightning sparks against something that stops it mid-air, creating a small pinprick of pain on the back of his hand as the energy rebounds back to him. He stops in his tracks and turns, staring deep into the shadow of a nearby tree.

"Who's there?!" he demands.

No response. No movement. Nothing.

But his guard remains high. He knows that there's *something* there, something he can't see but that his lightning can touch. His magic has never steered him wrong before.

He raises a hand and releases a massive bolt of energy, lighting the land with its grandeur. When the beam fizzles out, the tree he targeted is now scorched.

"Impressive, for an Electromancer."

The voice makes him jump and turn fully. Now standing in the path behind him is a boy dressed in black robes, a ragged cape hanging from his shoulders and an old, wide-brimmed hat adorning his head. While appearing as alive as him, the boy's soulless stare sends a shiver down his spine.

"Who are you?" the boy asks. "And why on Astria are you in a land you don't belong in?"

"I should be the one asking *you*," he replies. "This isn't a place for a student to be." The boy just narrows his eyes in response.

The two stare at each other silently as a gust of wind washes over them, making the hairs on his arm bristle. The boy's eyes are glassy and lifeless, regarding him as if he were nothing but a small animal in the way.

"What's your name?" he is then asked.

"Electro."

"How very creative," the boy scoffs.

Electro's right eye twitches as the urge to punch the boy grows in his gut, hot and twisting. He thought he was finally done with the name-mocking after graduation.

"You're not supposed to be here, Electro," the boy continues. "Though, now that you *are* here, I'm afraid I can't let you leave."

Electro lets out an amused huff, a grin spreading across his lips. Is this going to be a fight now? While he doesn't enjoy beating up students, he's not afraid to put *this one* in his place. "What on Astria could you possibly do to stop me from doing what I want?"

The boy stares on, the long dark shadows of the trees stretching across the ground towards him. The darkness pools at his feet and a blast of cold air batters Electro's face. The stinging chill of magic lingers on his cheeks as the atmosphere grows heavy on his body. His cocky confidence is replaced with dread magnified tenfold. The lightning that sparks from his body ceases instantly upon sensing the superior magical prowess standing before him.

"I would suggest you start walking," the boy speaks, raising a hand to point in the direction of the distant castle. As he moves the shadows underneath him warp and stretch, forming shadowy claws and needles along the ground. "I'd rather not have to drag you to the Lady myself."

Seeing no other option, Electro turns and starts walking toward the castle again, this time shadowed by his new companion. The boy's cold gaze causes the hairs on Electro's neck to stand straight, tingling with static.

What have I gotten myself into? Electro thinks in the quietness of the island. If he wasn't already regretting coming to Korodon before, he certainly is now.

"Why are you on Korodon, Electro?" the boy asks again

from behind.

"That's none of your business," Electro replies.

No sooner do the words leave his lips than something cold presses against his back, poking through his jacket and shirt to sting his skin. Eyes wide, he glances over his shoulder. A long black needle is jabbing at him, risen from the pool of shadow that continues to follow under the boy's shoes. The boy's stare bores into his own, his lips parted to reveal his gritted teeth.

"Only a fool would come to Korodon without a mission."

Electro clenches his jaw. He can't simply tell any old being what he's here for, let alone *this* kid, whoever he is. It's too important for any being to know about. Too powerful. If this boy wants an answer out of him, he better be ready to brawl for it.

"Good luck beating it out of me."

Chapter 1

The doorbell chimes merrily as the cycle slowly comes to a close, painting Asandra in vibrant yellows and oranges. Jake, flicking a speck of ice cream off his freshly-shined golden shoulder pads, turns to greet the latecomer with a wide smile.

"Kimberly!" he booms, arms outstretched as if he were going to receive a hug from his girlfriend at that very moment, though the countertop that stands between the two wizards often gets in the way of such immediate loving embraces.

The Cryomancer looks up at him, her icy blue eyes dull as she holds her textbook down at her side. She tugs at the white shawl that hangs over her shoulders, the large blue snowflake of Ice magic adorning either side, as she readjusts the sapphire string that holds it in place. "Hi, Jake."

She lets herself behind the counter and Jake wraps his arms around her. She raises her free hand to half-reciprocate his gesture with a tired pat on his back.

"You look exhausted," Jake comments at last as he steps away.

Kimberly gives him a weak smile in return. "Our teacher has been pushing us hard lately. I've not had to make so much ice before in my life!"

"Then go on upstairs and take a rest. Let us worry about cleaning up."

Kimberly nods. "It better be spotless for next cycle."

"Yes, boss!" Jake salutes.

Kimberly chuckles and makes her way into the back of the shop as Jake sets about closing up for the cycle. As he steps out from behind the counter to flip the store's "Open" sign to "Closed", he hears, "Hi, Kim-Star! You look–"

"Exhausted? Yeah, Jake told me that already. You should help him clean up."

"I know, I'm going to. Take it easy, Kim, okay?"

"Don't worry, Amber, I know what I'm doing. Thank you for all your hard work."

"No problem!"

Jake turns back to the counter to see Amber emerge from the back of the store. She flicks a part of her bright pink hair over her shoulder and gives him an energetic wave. "I'm going to wash the empty containers."

"Don't forget the ones under the counter," Jake reminds her.

"I won't."

"Can you throw me the broom?"

"Sure." Amber picks up the broom leaning against the wall near the store's back doorway and tosses it over the glass display. Jake just narrowly misses the wooden stick and it clatters to the ground at his feet.

Much has changed around the shop since the midterm projects. Amber is a full-time employee, bringing the place some much-needed positive energy. Though that doesn't mean running the shop has gotten any easier. With Blaze gone and Ethan all tied up with the Council in the wake of Korodon's "mysterious and sudden" restoration, the shop is always low on hands for three quarters of the cycle.

The clatter of metal rings throughout the shop as Amber

goes about rounding up the nearly-empty to empty ice cream tubs to be cleaned out. Even if the beings have changed, the duties haven't.

Just as Jake begins to sweep the floor a being raps on the door, rattling the tiny bell. With a small sigh, Jake turns to the door prepared to shoo away whatever wizard it may be. Though to his surprise, it's Ethan standing on the other side with a thin, apologetic grin across his lips, the wide brim of his hat casting his face in light shadow.

Jake opens the door but still blocks the Spiritist's way inside. It's been almost half a season since Jake has seen him. Staring at him now, he never realized just how scruffy Ethan had looked before. The ragged piece of cloth that used to cling to his back is now a vibrant, flowing cape. The little frays in his hat are gone, smoothed over and rich with new color. Even the silver-stitched runes that run along the edges of his robes seem much more neat and orderly now.

"Hey, Eth. Long time, no see," he greets his friend.

"Yeah," Ethan forces a chuckle. "I was passing through so I thought I'd drop by. How's the store?"

"It's been a little busier but the three of us have been making the most of it."

Ethan nods and the two fall into an awkward silence as Jake still holds the broom in hand, itching to get back to sweeping.

"Did you just start cleaning?" the Spiritist inquires.

"Yes," Jake replies with a soft eye roll.

"Need any help?"

"No, we're fine. Thanks."

"Come on, it'll go faster–"

"Eth, I appreciate the offer," Jake sighs, "but you're not employed here anymore. Besides, letting beings in right now would be… setting the wrong expectation." His gaze passes over Ethan's shoulder and at a small group of wizards who have gathered behind the Spiritist, standing around nervously as they wait for a chance to slip inside and demand a cone. He's seen these types countless times before.

He hates to turn his friend away right now. If anything, if he had come later towards the end of cleaning time, Jake might have invited him in to hang out for a bit. But right now he's got a job to perform and he's not looking to break any of the store rules – or Kimberly's trust – just because it's Ethan at the door. There's cleaning to do and wizards to shoo.

As if sensing the beings behind him, Ethan half-turns to the small group and tells them sharply, "They're closed."

The group stands rigid, staring at the Spiritist with wide eyes. Then, slowly, they frown and grumble among themselves as they trudge away from the storefront, shooting the Spiritist glares of disappointment.

"If you come back later–" Jake starts.

Ethan shakes his head, cutting Jake off as he lets out a tired sigh. "I've got a lot going on later."

"Still stuck in all that red ribbon, are you?"

"Sadly."

It's not terribly surprising to hear that. After the "dead island" Korodon was restored to its former liveliness and the travel ban was lifted, Ethan has been available less and less. He already dropped out of school and quit working for Kimberly to consult with the Council of Asandra and help the Feni on Korodon get back on their feet. He felt it only appropriate being not just a Fragment Shadow – Jake can still hardly believe he's been friends with a *god* this entire time – but also taking responsibility for his past shortcomings. If Jake were in his position, he'd most likely do the exact same thing.

On a more personal level, however, Kimberly is graduating soon and both Jake and Amber will be moving on to their next terms. It's almost strange to think that his senior year is coming up, and then he'll have all the time on Astria to spend with Kimberly after that.

"Hey," Jake speaks again, "don't push yourself too hard. We'd all like to see you more."

Ethan flashes him a weak grin and replies, "I'll see if I can make some time to hang out. I should be going now…"

"Have a good night, Eth."

Jake stands in the doorway and watches his friend stride away from the shop, his cape billowing behind him as if it were waving him goodbye.

Finally, Jake turns back to the interior of the store and begins his end-of-cycle sweeping. The bristles of the broom brush along the ground rhythmically as he makes his way from one corner to the other, dragging around shards of ice cream cones and sprinkles as he does so. It's probably the most relaxing thing he gets to do all cycle when it comes to running the shop.

"I'm done with the washing," Amber announces, emerging from the back room. "Did some being stop by earlier?"

"It was just Ethan."

Jake glances up from his work to see disappointment flash in the Healer's silver eyes. "Oh. How is he?"

"The Council still has him by the neck. He didn't stay very long."

Still, Amber's shoulders slump. Jake can't really blame her for being so deflated. After their adventure to Korodon, Amber's seemed to grow quite attached to the Spiritist. But she hasn't seen him at all since they've returned.

"So long as he's okay," she sighs at last.

"He's resilient," Jake tries to reassure her. After all that Ethan's supposedly been through from all the bits and pieces of his story that Amber has shared with Jake and Kimberly over time, he sort of has to be.

Amber just shrugs. "I'm going to go if that's alright."

"Yup. Rest well."

"Thanks. Enjoy your class trip."

Jake only half-smiles back at her, a tight ball of panic slamming into his chest. Oh no. That's next cycle, isn't it? He completely forgot to tell Kimberly about it!

He gives Amber a stiff wave goodbye as she leaves the store. As much as he trusts Kimberly to run the store by herself for at least part of the cycle, he worries what it'll be like when she has to go to class and Amber is all alone serving customers. Will Kimberly decide to close for the cycle? Can they eat the lost revenue?

He lets out a frustrated sigh. It's not like he can skip the trip. It's for history, after all, which is taken *extremely* seriously at the Asandra School of Magic, or ASM for short.

He looks down at the small pile of food bits and trash next to the bristles of his broom. All of a sudden, the thought of finishing his simple chore brings along with it the sharp sting of anxiety.

***

"All done, boss!" Jake announces as he strides triumphantly into the living room.

Kimberly looks up from her textbook as she sits on the sofa and musters a thin grin. "Thanks, Jake. Is Amber gone?"

"She left a little while ago," Jake nods.

Kimberly shifts on the sofa, closing her book and setting it aside to give her boyfriend her undivided attention. It's been a long couple of cycles for sure. Business is as booming as ever, and it doesn't help that she's still associated with the now-revered Ethan Nightshade, resident Fragment Shadow and expert Spiritist. She doesn't mind the new customers, but the amount of work on top of preparing for graduation is really starting to take its toll on her.

"I've been thinking about hiring some more help,"

Kimberly says as Jake takes a seat next to her.

He wraps a warm arm around her shoulders and leans in close. "More help is always appreciated."

"I just don't have the time to make fliers or anything," Kimberly continues. "Maybe if we can hold out until I graduate..." That way she'll not be dividing her attention between her schoolwork and running her store, and she'll be able to focus on other things. Like hiring.

Jake, in response, lets out a nervous chuckle. "Right. Until you graduate. About that..."

Kimberly turns to him and furrows her brow. "Jake...?"

"Well..." he lifts his arm off her shoulders and laces his fingers together, "it's not *that* important. I'm just... not going to be around next cycle."

"What's going on?" she presses.

"My class is going on a trip."

"Oh." Well *that* certainly complicates things.

"I'm sorry," he continues, "I meant to mention it but it slipped my mind until now."

Kimberly just sighs with disappointment. "Jake..."

How is she going to run the shop *now*? It'll just be her for half of the cycle, then she'll have Amber for the lunch rush, *then* she'll need to leave for class right after! She's not leaving Amber all alone at the shop, and with the number of wizards they've been serving lately it's not like Kimberly can handle them all by herself anymore, either. She hates to close the shop for a whole cycle, but it seems like it's her only option if she doesn't want to drive herself insane. Now she's got to let Amber know what's going on or else she might begin to worry about Kimberly's safety and well-being.

"Are you going to close?" Jake asks sheepishly.

"Might as well," Kimberly replies. "There's no point in working myself half to death all alone."

"Are you sure about this?"

"Yes, Jake. It's okay if we close for one cycle."

Jake's worried frown isn't phased by her reassurance, his eyes haunted by the past. Haunted with leaving Kimberly alone, with the shop closing for any length of time, with panic and uselessness and pain. Before when the store closed, it was alright. Maybe she needed to take some time off. Maybe she was short staffed like she will be next cycle. But after *the Shadow Incident*, closing has taken on a new meaning.

"Jake…" she hums, placing a hand on his nearest leg, "it'll be okay. *I'll* be okay."

"I know," he replies quietly, a hint of disbelief in his voice. He knows and he can't push past it. She doesn't blame him.

"If it'll make you feel any better, I can have Amber over until you're back."

Jake presses his lips together, contemplating her suggestion. He stares intensely at the table in front of the sofa, almost as if he were trying to light it on fire with his eyes alone. Eventually, he nods. It's a slow, reluctant nod, but an agreement nonetheless. Kimberly musters a smile.

"I just don't want anything to happen to you," Jake says, turning back to her.

"I know," she replies softly. There's more she wants to say to him – how that era is over, how that *maniac* is gone, how that the only other being who could cause such pain to happen again is their close friend who means them no harm – but she decides to keep her mouth shut. Nothing said by even her would affect his thoughts.

"So, what's for dinner?" she asks instead in an effort to take their minds off of *the Shadow Incident* for the time being.

"I thought *you* were cooking," Jake replies with a halfhearted chuckle.

"I could, but you *will* be getting meat."

Her boyfriend lets out a sigh and stands. "I'll cook then." In response, Kimberly kicks her legs up onto the sofa, taking up the rest of the sitting space.

"Thanks, Jake," she sings after him as he disappears into the dining room and, ultimately, the kitchen.

She doesn't know *why*, but Jake's been much more fussy about eating meat since *the Shadow Incident*. She's had to buy almost double the fruit she used to get before just to keep his appetite satiated.

She doesn't mind eating only fruit for dinner, even with the limited ways that they can be prepared. Afterwards, she sometimes cooks up some meat for herself to complement his meals. Eating a balanced meal is still important to her. Though she'll always enjoy the sweet aroma that lingers in the air long after they dine, making her long for more.

She turns back to her textbook to pass the time, flicking to the last chapter of the text. *Methods to Push Limits and Grow Beyond* is its title, and what she was working on in class that cycle. It is what it says, a variety of different strategies for how Cryomancers can further their own magical power beyond the Hall. While the chapter is in every textbook, the methods and advice for each branch is different for obvious reasons.

Methods to Push Limits and Grow Beyond

As your time at the Asandra School of Magic comes to an end and you look towards your future career, the uses of Cryomancy in our lives may seem limiting at first. However, from waterworkers to simple ice-makers, the role of a Cryomancer is highly integral to the continuing survival of all the known islands of Astria.

The learning and growth of one's power does not end with graduation. Throughout this text, the concept of passive power has been lightly discussed. The concept of passive power stems from that of the General of Ice himself; known to not favor his magic, the General was still able to accumulate a great wealth of magical prowess. It is not always the active use of a wizard's magic that allows it to grow in strength, but rather our active use is a form of control over our endlessly-growing internal power.

The extent of our passive power – how it accumulates and how it affects us, physically and mentally – has not yet been explored in full. It is advised that the active use of magic is never fully ceased, as it is the primary, if only, way you can keep your magic healthy alongside yourself. This continuous use will also help you to adjust to your passive magic as it accumulates over the course of your life.

The sugary smell of sizzling fruit slices wafts into the living room. She inhales the scent with deep breaths, savoring the sweet sensation. She can hear Jake banging something against a metal pan as he cooks the freshly-cut fruit slices.

Slowly, she closes her textbook and lays on the sofa, waiting for the call to eat.

***

Knock, knock, knock!

With a heavy sigh, Blaze stands from his desk and hauls his tired body over to the door of his dorm, wondering who on Astria would ever come knocking.

It's probably a mistake, he automatically assumes. No being has come to explicitly see *him* since… Well, he would rather not think about *that time* too much.

He throws the door open with his most dead-inside glare only to be surprised by the sight of his ex-best friend. Ethan stands in the doorway awkwardly, clearly unprepared to be there as his hands fiddle with the edges of his cape with his hat tipped forward, letting its wide brim partially hide his eyes from view.

For a long moment, neither being speaks. Blaze pulls a deeply confused expression. Why is Ethan suddenly at his door, this night of all nights? Didn't he make it clear that he doesn't want to see him again? He doesn't want to talk. He doesn't want to try and figure himself out. He doesn't want to be experimented on, especially not by *him*.

"Hey," Ethan finally says.

"What do you want?" Blaze demands.

The harsh question stuns Ethan for a spell. "To... see how you were doing."

"I'm doing just fine, *thanks*."

Blaze moves to shut the door but Ethan holds a hand out to stop him. The timidness has left his face, replaced by what he reads to be frustrated concern.

"Liar," he states.

"*Tch,*" Blaze replies. "What does the Council's *pet* know about his former friend?"

"It helps to be friends with one of the most well-connected beings in all of Astria," Ethan retorts. "I'm worried about you."

Blaze rolls his eyes. "*Sure* you are."

It's easy to not believe him. Since dropping out of school, Ethan has just been... *missing*. Not actually missing, but largely gone from the public. Eating with the powerful, walking and talking with the influential, sitting atop his new heroic pedestal. Blaze hates everything about it. Everything about *him*.

"I've heard a lot–" Ethan starts.

Blaze shakes his head furiously. "Whatever you've 'heard', they're just rumors."

Ethan's gaze instantly goes sharp, sending a chill down his spine.

"When was the last time you socialized?" Ethan asks.

"What's it to you?" Blaze snaps back.

"Blaze..."

"Don't patronize me," he growls. With a single swipe of his hand, he gets Ethan out of his way and finally slams the door shut in his face.

Silence. It's a sound he has grown accustomed to. It's hard to tell sometimes if it's comforting or maddening, but he likes it all the same. It brings him away from the rest of the world and the beings in it and allows him to do what he wants. Silence doesn't judge.

He returns to his desk, his textbook wide open and painted in black ink with annotations both helpful and unrelated. He wasn't annotating anything he was currently learning but rather rereading old lessons he has already forgotten, wasting his time.

In the candlelight, he sighs, looking to his small pot of dirt that sits on his right. With hardly a thought, a small green vine rises from the dark soil and waves at him.

Secretly, part of him is thankful that Ethan showed up, even if it was only for a short time before he pushed him away again. Even though he has hardly been outside – unheard of for a wizard of his type – he has heard the whispers about himself, too.

He has become a shut-in and he knows it. After his eight-cycle absence during his midterm, he hasn't been able to handle the new air of Asandra. He's been a wizard with few friends for the longest time, originally with a reason. Now he has no excuse for his abrasiveness, yet he has failed time and again to shake it. His old reputation hangs over his head like a dark cloud. Instead of uneasy gazes, he's met with nothing but disgust from his peers. What's the point in putting in the effort to change when you've already burned down all your bridges?

He runs a finger along the small vine, and similarly a small cold spot forms on his side, moving at the same speed his finger moves.

He is lonely, yes, but it's better than being in the public eye.

Chapter 2

Early in the cycle, Jake makes his way to his Hall as ready as he'll ever be for his class trip. He even remembered to bring a scabbard for his sword so he doesn't seem weird for carrying around such a long weapon without a place to properly store it. Summoning it in the middle of the trip would be too much of a hassle but he didn't just want to leave it at home, either.

He walks around the dorms, his Hall coming into view, flames bursting from between the cracks of the stone walls and dancing across the roof in an endlessly mysterious dance. He also sees other third term Pyromancers already huddled together in small friend groups, injecting a soft drone to the air on top of the usual buzz of magic against one's skin. He stands towards the edge of the crowd and folds his arms uncomfortably, staring silently at his peers.

He has no urge to mingle with them. Instead, he lets his thoughts drift to Kimberly. It's hard not to think of her. She was still sleeping when he left; he had been extra quiet not to disturb her. Is she awake now? What will she eat when she wakes? What else will she do this early in the cycle, waiting for first term classes to end and for Amber to join her? His hands firmly grips his arms. The urge to abandon his *required* class trip just to check on her slowly builds in the back of his mind.

Eventually, his teacher emerges from the Hall and claps her hands to grab the students' attention. All conversion ceases in an instant. With a reluctant sigh, Jake approaches the rest of his class to listen in.

"Alright, class," she says with a warm smile, "I hope you all are excited to see the Great Pyramid of Solari!" There's a small murmur of tired enthusiasm from the students. Jake, however, grins to himself. He's been looking forward to it ever since the trip was first announced. It's one of the oldest standing structures that was built long before the Great War, alongside the old royal castle on Korodon.

"Now, before we go, I must set some ground rules," his teacher continues, unfazed by her unenthused students. "The use of magic inside the Pyramid is strictly prohibited. We don't want to ruin anything inside. A lot of the things on the walls are *very important* to the history of Astria and the Serperas of Mirage.

"Stay with the group at all times while we're inside the Pyramid. We still don't know what *exactly* is inside the Pyramid, as we've not had access to it for a very long time, and there are still many rooms that have traps and other protections within them. I don't want any being to get hurt or accidentally bring the Pyramid down." She lets out an amused chuckle at the thought of the Pyramid collapsing on top of them as unease settles over the students as a thick blanket of silent dread.

"As always, the punishment will fit the individual. I implore you all to be on your best behavior while we're there. We're guests in a work zone, after all!" His teacher beams, as she always does, and holds up a pale yellow stone in the air. "Now, let's go see the Pyramid. Follow me."

She starts off towards the campus Archway, a small crowd of red-dressed wizards in tow.

Jake has met a Serperas before, beings akin to wizards capable of changing their legs into long scaled tails, which is an astronomically lucky thing to happen in this era. Not to mention that the Serperas was *royalty*. What was his name again? Luke, right? He doesn't really know if he's right, but he feels close enough. It's been a while since Jake's seen him, but he seemed like a decent being when they met. He spoke really well, too, for a Serperas. He didn't think they still practiced that, being an isolated nation and all.

The Archway, a series of gray stones covered in white runes in the shape of a large arch, stands open, a large rip revealing a flat sandy plateau leading up to a large sandstone building, probably the Pyramid. Around the opening of the Pyramid is a series of colorful tents with a variety of beings rushing between them with papers, tools, jugs of water, and other various ancient knickknacks.

With Jake being at the back of the group, it takes a while for him to feel the warm desert air blowing through the rip, but when it hits him it fills him with this strange glow of comfort. His prior worries over Kimberly dull as he finally steps through the Archway and plants his armored boots onto the packed sand on the other side.

While the fragment of Solari City he and his class stand on is small enough for them to be completely surrounded by Void on nearly every side, the Pyramid stands at its center tall and proud, its point to the sky as the large Mirage sun rises from the black abyss. However, it still *feels* and *smells* like a desert, hot and arid. These sensations are really the only way to tell that there once was an entire city built in the middle of sandy dunes. What's left over, however, is only a small collection of buildings and the Great Pyramid itself.

"Alright, class, this way!" his teacher calls, raising her hand like a flag for the class to follow. She leads her red cluster closer towards the Pyramid's opening where most of the tents are situated.

The packed sand under his boots lightly shifts as he

follows behind his class, a slight crunch reaching his ears. It's surreal how much Void he can see from this little chunk of floating land. ASM is built next to the edge of Asandra so he sees the Void nearly every cycle, but it's only a small sliver of the black expanse. Farther into the island, all sight of the Void disappears, and it takes a while to walk to another public edge point. Here, however, the island is ringed with a single thigh-high rope. It's so scarily easy to push a being over the edge here, never to be seen again.

The group stops just outside the entrance to the Pyramid and stands around murmuring among themselves as the teacher briefly disappears into a nearby tent colored a bright red with silver trim, larger than most others around it.

Jake looks around the camp from where he stands as they all wait for the tour to begin. A Shask half-dressed in a dusty beige outfit steps from a different smaller tent nearby, a long brush attached to the end of one of his arms with a small handkerchief held by a metal hand screwed onto his other arm. He run the handkerchief under his fuzzy chin as he makes his way from one side of the camp to the other, briefly casting a glance at the group of students with disinterested mechanical eyes. From a different tent on the other side, a wizard in bright blue robes sets out a large bucket and waves her hands over its opening. The sharp snap of ice meeting warm air crackles faintly as Jake watches the bucket fill to the brim with solid ice. With that, the Cryomancer steps back into the tent she came from.

"Alright, class!" his teacher's voice rings out once more, drawing his attention back to the front of the collection of students. She emerges from the large tent with two more beings. One is a Shask with his chest covered in a stiff-looking red coat, buttoned up to mostly hide the clacking gears beneath it, with his legs a mixture of metal framework, pistons, wires, and patches of dead, gray fur left behind. The other being, shockingly, is *Ethan Nightshade*.

As much as he's happy to see his friend again, he frowns. What's Ethan doing here? Solari is the last place Jake expected to see the Fragment Shadow.

"I'm sure you all know Ethan Nightshade by now," his teacher continues, gesturing to Ethan, who just half-smiles at the students and nods, his gaze somewhat removed from reality. "And *this* is Sir Dalton Taylor, leader of the Solari expedition and Astria's greatest historian of Serperan culture."

The Shask salutes the students, the stiff metal fingers of his right hand raised to his brow. "Salutations, students! It is my utmost pleasure to be taking you all through this wondrous monument this cycle. Me and my team have been hard at work here for just over two years now, uncovering the secrets of one of the oldest remaining structures on Astria."

"For those that don't already know, Solari used to be a large city connected to the rest of Mirage," Ethan picks up for Sir Taylor. "The cause of the collapse is still speculated upon, but needless to say, it's a miracle that the Great Pyramid is still standing in this era. And now with it finally open we are able to access its records for the first time in many millennia."

Now it's no wonder why he's here on Solari. He's a Fragment Shadow, after all, older than any being present by a long shot, so spouting the history of Astria to a group of young students is right up his alley.

"Shall we go inside?" Ethan asks Sir Taylor.

The Shask nods in approval. "Yes, there is much to explore within the Pyramid. As we walk through the Pyramid's halls, please do not disturb any of the workers. They are trying to preserve the Pyramid's many wonders and aren't available for answering questions."

"If there *are* any questions, please feel free to ask either one of us," Ethan grins. "You may stop and look at the walls but don't fall too far behind the group. The place is big and we don't want any being getting lost."

With that, the group begins their trek into the Great Pyramid.

The entryway is breathtaking. The paint on the pillars is rather vibrant for being sealed away and uncared for for many millennia, depicting the Serperan belief of the beginnings of Astria. At the top of each of the eight entryway pillars is a large tree, with the painted canopies stretching up and over the ceiling, connecting them all together. From the tree falls dark purple fruits, fruits that slowly morph into the various races of Astria, many of which have either evolved far from their birth roots or that wizards haven't seen since the Great War ended. The tree roots fade into thin blue rivers, and the brown trunks become green grass. It's truly a masterwork of artistry.

The small entryway opens up to a large hall leading far into the distance, lit by small electric bulbs hanging on a long length of copper wire. A handful of Electromancers huddle together in a small corner near the entryway, chatting among themselves as lightning sparks from their figures, the bolts landing on the large metal pads that they sit on to provide power to this temporary lighting system.

The walls of the hallway are large and long, engraved with images of all shapes and sizes. Many are of crops and rivers. Some are of the sky, painted either void black or brilliant white wherever they appear. Serperas, with their long tails ranging from blues and greens to reds and browns, make up the majority of beings depicted, which is understandable since they had curated the Pyramid up until Solari's collapse. Along these walls stand or crouch various Shasks and wizards holding tools like brushes and chisels. Some have pots of paint beside them, carefully tracing the images and revitalizing their faded colors. Others carve out shallow lines, redefining figures nearly lost to time altogether.

Ethan raises his hands, gesturing to the walls on their left and right. "To the Serperas, the Great Pyramid was known as the Pyramid of Prophecy. At the peak of their magical powers, it was said that the sands of Mirage gave them visions of the future, which they etched into the sandstone walls for future generations to heed. Of course, they also treated this place like a library, storing all their important records in the many chambers throughout the structure."

"Some of these chambers are heavily protected by ancient enchantments," Sir Taylor adds, folding his hands behind his back. "We have been able to gain access to some of the earlier chambers thus far. We are working on others as we speak. However, I must advise you students to keep to this hall here lest some being gets hurt."

They keep walking down the hallway, students letting out occasional gasps and pointing to images they find awe-inspiring. Jake stares as well, watching each scene pass him by slowly. There's one that appears to be a prediction about a food shortage, with woven baskets tipped sideways with orange grains of sand pouring from them and Serperas scooping them up as if they were drinking water. There's another with a large column of sand stretching from floor to ceiling with tiny beings running away from it. There's a smaller depiction of a feast, the table covered in mounds of what appears to be different kinds of fruits. At the head of this table is a Serperas being crowned with a silver circlet.

"...lived by water way back when," Jake's ears pick up Ethan's voice. He's not speaking too loudly, probably just answering a question asked by some being in his class. "Now, that's not saying that there weren't Serperas with brown and red tails in Solari, but generally if a Serperas was from the city their tails would be more water colored, and if they were from the desert they would be more sandy colored."

A warm draft blows through the hallway, dry and stiff. The heat he doesn't mind, but breathing it in makes him suddenly feel like he's stuck in a dusty attic.

"Any other questions?" he hears his friend ask. In an instant, he raises his hand to try and catch his attention.

He doesn't see any other being raise a hand nor shout out a question, yet still he doubts Ethan sees him in the very back. But then the crowd parts and he strides his way up to him with a wide grin.

"Jake!" he says. "It didn't even occur to me this was your class."

Jake lowers his hand and smiles back. "Didn't expect to see you here."

The Spiritist laughs in response as the two walk side-by-side. "I wasn't expecting to be here, either. Well, not this cycle, anyway. I was asked pretty late to come and give my historical insight."

"Why? Are you helping with the expedition?"

Ethan's smile strains. "No, not really. It's... not something I want to talk about. Not... Not *now*." He nods to the group of students before them. "But it's more for personal reasons. Nothing to do with the Council."

"Stars, you're so busy."

"I know. It can't be helped. Did you have a question or did you just want to say hello?" Jake gives him a look and Ethan can't help but shrug back. "Sorry. I'm supposed to be working right now."

"Uh..." Jake takes a wild look around him, then points to the feast. "That. What's that about?"

Ethan takes one look at the scene and lets out a small snort. "I shouldn't interpret Serperan carvings, though if I were to hazard a guess, it's a crowning ceremony."

"Do they often eat so much fruit?"

"Yes," Ethan nods. "Even now, the Serperas that still survive on Mirage exclusively consume fruit for their diet."

"Do they have cattle?"

The Spiritist shakes his head. "It's too hot throughout the

cycle, too cold during the night, and they have limited space and resources to grow the variety of plants needed to keep both the cattle and Serperas properly fed. It's why they evolved to survive only on fruit."

Jake nods along, licking his dry lips. Interesting.

He opens his mouth to ask another pointless question, just to keep Ethan talking a little longer to retain some familiar company, but is interrupted by a deep rumble and a booming, echoey laugh. A laugh full of unhinged malice.

As one, the group of students, Jake's teacher, Sir Taylor, and Ethan all stop walking, frozen by the ruckus. If anything, the edges of the hallway grow slightly darker as a large burst of magic fills the air, making Jake's skin crawl uncomfortably with its buzz.

"*I'M FREEEEEEEEEEEEE!*" the voice that laughed cries in triumph. The sound of popping glass follows not long after, casting a portion of the hallway ahead of the group into darkness. There's a dark figure fast approaching them, blowing out the small light bulbs as it goes with bright bolts of lightning, leaving the broken bulbs sparking hopelessly in their wake. Small burn marks also appear on the floor, ceiling, and even walls, sadly, as the entity flies forward.

The flash of crimson eyes catches Jake's attention, making him reach for his sword in an instant. It's a Shadow. Whose Shadow it is he doesn't know, nor does he care to know. There shouldn't be any more Shadows simply wandering around. Not since Korodon's restoration.

Next to him, the temperature sharply drops and, casting Ethan a quick glance, Jake sees cold white mist rolling from his hands and wrists.

He looks at the Pyromancer. "Don't. Just get out of here."

Jake grits his teeth, wanting to reply, to say he can help, but Ethan turns away from him and jumps into the air, yelling to the class, "Out of the Pyramid, *now*! Go!"

The students do just that, turning tail and running back the way they had come, some of the workers joining them as they go. Jake, however, remains planted where he stands, watching Ethan with his sword in hand. There's no frantic screaming. There's no fear in the air. Just running feet and quiet murmuring, unsure as to whether or not they're truly in any sort of danger. With Ethan present, that might have given many a false sense of security. He's a Fragment Shadow, child of the Spirit of Shadow above. Of course whatever danger there may be, he can solve it within moments. That's the theory.

Speaking of every being's favorite Fragment Shadow, Ethan floats in the air, putting himself between the approaching Shadow and the Pyramid's exit. He extends his hands to his sides, releasing a burst of ice that spreads across the surfaces of the hallway, covering the carvings in an attempt to protect them.

"Jake," a firm hand lands on his shoulder. It's his teacher, her smile completely gone and replaced with a worried frown. "Let the Fragment deal with this."

"Sorry, miss," Jake replies, shaking her off, "I've fought Shadows before."

The Shadow lets out another maniacal laugh, drawing Jake's attention back to the situation at hand. The Shadow Electromancer wears a short sleeved shirt, torn in some places as if it had been in battle, with cloth strips wrapped around its arms. The same with its pants, half-ripped to shreds and covered with more tied cloth strips. Its boots rise to just below its knees, decorated with all sorts of buckles in various states of functionality. Some of the straps are hanging on by a sliver of thread. Others are outright missing from their buckles. To top it all off, in usual Electromancer fashion, its spiky hair crackles with electricity.

The Shadow doesn't look that much older than himself. If Jake were to hazard a guess, it appears like a wizard only a handful of years freshly graduated. Still, the Shadow appears to be nearly a head and a half taller than the average adult wizard, its clothes and skin cast in heavy shades of dark gray and void black, the only ounce of color to its brutish figure being its bright blood-red eyes and wild, white-toothed grin.

"*My, look who it is,*" the Shadow says. "*The Lady's favorite shell.*"

"I've always wondered where *you* went," Ethan replies through gritted teeth. "Riona's dead, Electro."

It's not shocking that Ethan knows this Shadow already, nor the fact that they both used to work for the same insane Spiritist. The Spiritst who stole Ethan's magic, took Jake's and Kimberly's Shadows, and ruled over Korodon with an iron fist for centuries.

Now faced with the news that its leader is gone, Electro does something that catches Jake off-guard: It smiles *wider.*

"*I know,*" it replies, its grin turning into a gleeful sneer. "*I felt it. But I stopped caring about her years ago.*"

Ethan raises a hand, pointing at Electro with confidence and booms, "*Return to your body, Shadow.*"

Once again, a massive burst of magic fills the hallway, cold and oppressive, sending a rare shiver down Jake's back.

And... Electro explodes into its third crazed laughing fit as Ethan's hand lowers hesitantly. A flurry of lightning leaps from Electro's figure and strikes the ice around it, leaving behind wisps of smoke and small indentations in the bright blue protective coating.

"*WHAT MADE YOU THINK I'D STILL LISTEN TO* YOU, *HUH?!*" Electro roars. Its false smile snaps into a scowl of pure, unbridled rage. "*AFTER ALL THIS TIME, HAVING BEEN ABANDONED FOR* YEARS, *LEFT TO ROT IN THE SAME DARKNESS THAT CREATED ME! GET OUT OF MY WAY, PUPPET!*"

Electro propels himself forward with a release of lightning behind it, its hands balled into fists as it rushes at Ethan. In response, a mass of black mist rises from the Spiritist, swirling to form a dark copy of himself, holding a long needle-like sword in its hands and ready to strike back.

Electro turns its forward momentum into sideways propulsion with a second burst of lightning from its side, narrowly missing the swing of the sword. It plants a single foot against the hallway's left wall, and with a third jolt of lightning it flies forward at an even greater speed than before.

"Watch–!" Jake starts, but he only manages to speak the one word before the blur that is Electro's shin comes into contact with Ethan's side. The Spiritist is flung into the hallway's right wall, sending thin spidering cracks across the ice layer from the impact.

Ethan's Shadow spins around, its red eyes shining with deadly focus as it raises its sword once more. With how close it is to Electro, there shouldn't be a way the Electromancer could possibly dodge or counter the strike in time. Yet expertly and seemingly without a care, Electro pushes aside the oncoming sword with its left arm and throwing a punch with its right, knocking its second opponent right out of the air as the sword flies free and plants itself tip-first into the floor.

Jake's heart sinks. In one fell swoop, this random Electromancer took down one of the most powerful beings currently alive on Astria. It doesn't even look hurt from deflecting such a sharp-looking blade.

"*And* you," Electro speaks, turning to face Jake. It's smiling again, fists still clenched, eyes wide and wild. Jake holds his sword up in front of him reflexively and sucks in a nervous breath. "*Are you going to get in my way, too?*"

Jake can feel his heartbeat pounding against his chest like a heavy hammer. He's nervous, yes. How could he not be? The last time he fought any sort of Shadow, being Shadow itself, he *lost*, even with it being greatly magically weakened at the time. He has no hope facing a fully-powered, rage-filled Shadow of an Electromancer that can *fly*. The technique of using the power of lightning bolts to suspend a being in the air for any length of time is extremely complex. Only a few Electromancers have ever learned and perfected the technique, let alone expanded on it to make themselves ostensibly *fly*. Electro is either extremely gifted or *far* older than it appears to be. Jake, meanwhile, is still a student, bound to the use of an aid for all eternity!

Yet he somehow finds it in himself to plant his feet firm and level his blade at the Shadow above him. He's not going to let it leave this Pyramid without a fight.

"*Kch*," Electro snickers, "*They were just my warm-up.*"

The Shadow bursts forward, its left arm drawn back in anticipation to strike. Flames curling around his blade, Jake slashes at the air, sending a long wave of fire at the incoming threat. Like it did with Shadow's sword, Electro quickly redirects its momentum to avoid the fire, once again positioning itself to spring off of the hallway's wall. Jake shifts his weight in anticipation.

All he sees is a streak of black hurtling towards him as he springs to his left, sword outstretched in his wake to try and strike Electro, believing that it's moving too fast to avoid his extended blade.

To his surprise, Electro grabs the fiery blade without an ounce of hesitation and uses it as a pivot to swing its body around to face Jake once more, yanking on the blade as it does so. Electro swings itself under the blade, and as it comes back up on the other side, it brings its knees close to its chest and kicks at Jake's head with all its might.

Unprepared to take such a blow, Jake stumbles over himself and falls to the ground hard, his head pounding. Before he can even attempt to sit up, Electro plants its heavy boot on his chest and looks down at him with eager eyes, clearly basking in its superior fighting prowess.

"*Pathetic,*" it spits on Jake, which surprises him as he didn't think a Shadow was capable of producing spit in the first place. Electro lifts itself into the air once more, lightning swirling around its figure, and with that it zooms off, laughing the entire way to the Pyramid's only exit. Jake can only lay there in the darkness of broken light bulbs and listen to the fading crackle of electricity, his vision swimming with his sword growing cold in his hand and his heart heavy with helplessness.

"Jake," he hears Ethan call his name. His friend slowly trudges into his view, his hat crooked on his head as a weird black substance runs from the bottom of the thin slit that is the scar across his left eye, elongating it to his cheek. His injured expression is painted with undertones of disappointment. "You should have left."

Jake just shakes his head, unable to reply. He knows he probably should have and yet he didn't. He couldn't bring himself to run away. Not from a Shadow.

The Spiritist lets out a sigh and bends down, firmly taking Jake's arm. "Stand up."

With Ethan's help, Jake manages to sit up, letting the blood in his head even out before standing.

As Jake tries to steady himself, Ethan turns to look over his shoulder at his dark double. He says nothing as he watches it stagger to its feet, though his face is stiff as if he were chastising it. Jake, too, can't help but drink in its presence as well. He's only ever seen Shadow twice before. The first time it was a black knight without an ounce of free will to act upon. The second time was a much friendlier interaction as it was formally introduced to Jake, Kimberly, and Blaze. Even so, he's not quite sure what to even *make* of it. Jake has a Shadow of his own, too, but he couldn't be conscious without it. Ethan, on the other hand, can exist separately from his. It could just be a Fragment Shadow thing. That's the only thing he can think of to explain this weird situation he is bearing witness to.

Shadow's face is deformed and misty, mostly around its nose. Seeing a near-exact copy of Ethan, hat and cap aside, standing not too far from him and his friend is certainly eerie. Its crimson eyes land on Jake, something regretful glimmering in its gaze, alongside a bit of shock from the sudden strike it sustained from Electro.

Ethan finally wraps Jake's right arm around his shoulders to support him as he sways on his feet. "We should get you to a Healer."

"Yeah…" Jake breathes in agreement. He closes his eyes, which helps his pounding head a little bit. A Healer would make him feel *much* better.

***

"My," Sir Taylor grumbles, "what a mess."

"Indeed."

Ethan folds his arms as he stares at the rubble before him. The chamber is rather sizable, one smaller room attached to the main space, with the Serperan carvings desecrated with all sorts of crazed runes. "Detainment", "prison", and "anti-magic" galore, among others similar to them. Across the ground rubble is strewn about, smooth beige sandstone for half of it and black char for the other. Worse, the chamber practically reeks of the suffocating smell of burned sandstone, and the walls are so electrified that anything any being touches zaps them.

"A stone tablet used to be there," Sir Taylor says, pointing to a rather sizable rectangular patch on the ground in front of the smaller room. While the rest of the floor is gray and orange from tracked-in sand, that one rectangular spot remains a somewhat pristine beige. "Rather large, floor to ceiling, wall to wall, unlike anything we had seen so far. We were wondering for the longest time what would drive any being to create this chaos."

"Now we know," Ethan hums sadly. To think that Electro's

Shadow had been here the entire time, right under his nose, and only last cycle did he hear anything about this place. The price he pays for being as busy as he was.

"Respectfully, Fragment," Sir Taylor says, turning to look at the Husk, "I thought it was said all the Shadows were gone."

Ethan just nods back, his mouth pressed tightly closed. He had thought so, too, and only after he had made that statement he was proven wrong. He thought he could correct it before the accidental lie grew into a problem, but he was simply too slow.

"Nothing happened here when it was still detained?" he asks instead.

"No. Nothing I or the crew knew of."

"Any idea as to how this chamber in particular would be used for such a thing? Who did it?"

Sir Taylor shakes his head. "As far as we're aware, we're the first beings to have stepped into the Pyramid after it opened."

"How did it open, then?"

"We're still trying to figure that out ourselves," the Shask huffs.

He bites his tongue and retreats into his own thoughts. Sir Taylor is wrong in saying that the Kendon archaeologists have been the first to set foot inside the Pyramid after its opening. Electro's Shadow wouldn't have put itself in this sort of makeshift prison for all this time and come out of it *that* vengeful. It's impossible. Other beings were here long before the entrance was found open. But who…?

{*They're here,*} Shadow's dull voice rings in his ears.

"Ah, please excuse me, Sir Taylor," Ethan speaks. "I have other business to tend to."

"Of course. Leave the tidying up to us."

With a single nod of his head, Ethan turns away from the Shask and steps into the nearest shadow, willing himself to the infirmary back on Asandra. If Kimberly has arrived, then he should inform Azna.

"...repeat his third term," a female voice cuts through the darkness, making Ethan pause. Azna's office melts into view before him as he hides himself in the corner, staring at the scene silently. Azna stands in front of his desk, conversing with the Fire teacher from ASM. The Feni's gray ears droop as he wears a troubled scowl, one hand to his chest. Beneath it, Ethan can make out a flash of regal blue and the sparkle of white iron between the folds of his white robe.

"It's clear he has a natural affinity for the Fire branch and he's a good student," the teacher continues with a disappointed huff. "But... well... he's just not a *Pyromancer*."

"What is it that he's lacking?" Azna inquires.

"He's not *lacking* in anything. Rather, he's been having a hard time... ah, *expressing* himself with his magic–"

Ethan turns away from the office, willing himself to Shadow's side instead, feeling incredibly awkward. Azna's clearly busy right now. Besides, Ethan doesn't want to be eavesdropping on private conversations like *that*.

He steps from the dark corner of the medical room where Jake rests, giving Shadow a pat on its shoulder as it watches over his friends. Kimberly sits by her boyfriend's side as he lies in a plain medical bed. Amber lingers nearby as well, twirling a strand of her long pink hair between her fingers idly. When Ethan appears, her bright silver eyes instantly snap to him, a smile spreading across her face. She must have been with Kimberly when the Healer showed up to bring Jake's girlfriend to his bedside. Whatever the case may be as to why she's here, Ethan's still grateful for her presence.

"Hey," she says with a small grin.

Ethan tries to give her a somewhat comforting smile. "Been a while, hasn't it?" Amber just nods back at him, her eyes drinking in his presence as if he were to disappear forever the instant she looks away. Ethan shifts his weight. He has never been a fan of uneasy silence, especially when he's at a loss for words.

He is disappointed that nearly all of them have been reunited like this. Blaze is the only one who isn't here, obviously. Ethan thought about sending for him but decided against it. This situation doesn't involve him as much as this doesn't involve Amber, yet she just happened to be in the right place at the right time and he wasn't. A part of him feels like Blaze wouldn't have even come if Ethan had sent for him anyway.

The door to the room opens and in strides Azna, the head Healer of the infirmary and long-standing member of the Council of Asandra. The air around his figure shimmers and sparkles, leaving in his wake an atmosphere of calmness and ease. The old Feni's ears now stand stiffly perked, making it clear that he's here to conduct some serious business.

Upon seeing Amber, the Feni lets out a small sigh. "You just can't stay away from this sort of stuff, can you, Amber?"

Amber smiles awkwardly back at her old boss. "I survived last time, didn't I?"

"You did," Azna nods, approaching Jake's bed. The Pyromancer's eyes open ever so slightly, his eyelids fluttering. Azna places a hand on Jake's forehead and a small glow of green light flashes from under his fingertips.

"He's doing just fine," he announces. "He should be able to leave before nightfall." The old Healer shakes his head. "I asked for his teacher to stay his punishment just this once."

"I told him to leave," Ethan says.

"Do you mind sharing what happened, then?"

Ethan's hands reach for his cape as all the eyes in the room turn to him. A swirl of anxiety rises in his chest, coming more from Shadow than himself, and yet he shares in its concern. It's something he's never talked about to any being – not even Azna knows the full story – but that was almost eighteen years ago by now…

He takes a deep breath. "Inside the Great Pyramid of Solari… there was a Shadow."

Kimberly sucks in a breath and Amber's eyes widen. He can probably guess what they're thinking right now. *A Shadow? They should all be gone!*

From the dark corner of the room, Shadow floats out into the light, its hands clasped in front of it nervously as it looks down at the floor, avoiding eye contact with any of the wizards.

Riona liked to experiment with ways to control Shadows, Shadow says. *Once she came up with the idea about changing a Shadow's form, but none of us knew what that outcome would have been. Ethan managed to convince her not to experiment with any of the Feni Shadows in case the process... killed them.* A sickening unease grows within Ethan as it reflects.

"The first Twisted Shadow was a Storm wizard called Electro," he continues. "He went to Korodon–" A wave of anxiousness washes over him, making him pause and look to Shadow. Its body is tense as it continues to linger in the darkness, shaking its head furiously.

{*They don't need to know,*} its voice whispers in the back of Ethan's mind.

[*I didn't want them to get involved again, either, but… friends support each other,*] Ethan replies gently, attempting to reassure it. Still, doubt swirls between their connection, and Shadow visibly scowls.

{*I don't know, Eth…*}

[*Shadow, please. They've helped us already. They can help us again.*]

Shadow remains tense, but reluctantly it gives him an approving nod.

"He went to Korodon because he had been asked to," Ethan speaks again, turning back to the wizards. "I was forced to bring him to the castle and *he* became her test subject… It– He– I–" He has to take a breath and right himself. "After it was over, I brought his body here, to the infirmary, and his Shadow disappeared soon after that. When Korodon was restored I thought his Shadow would have returned, too, but… Well, imagine my shock when I found out it didn't.

"I've not been as involved with the Council as much as I may have let on, and I'm sorry. Most of my time was spent looking for his Shadow so I could put the last of Riona's insanity to rest. But… it didn't go well. I couldn't stop it, and Jake got hurt as a result."

We *couldn't stop it*, Shadow corrects lightly. Ethan just presses his lips together and nods reluctantly. He doesn't want to acknowledge how fast Electro's Shadow knocked *both* of them out. Ethan is one thing; as a Husk, he's not as strong as Shadow. Shadow, however, is a different story.

Kimberly frowns in confusion and asks, "Why was he asked to go to Korodon? I thought the travel ban was put in place nearly half a century ago or so."

We don't know– Shadow attempts to lie.

"Riona didn't ask?" Amber interrupts.

Ethan doesn't reply immediately, but he can't stop himself from appearing greatly perturbed. He doesn't want to think about that moment, and yet it springs to mind so easily, so sharply, as if it just happened. How Electro's Shadow rose up surrounded in a strange new air that made even Ethan scared, even as screams of pain still echoed throughout the castle's derelict walls.

Riona asked alright.

Two hands clamp down on Ethan's shoulders, warm and firm yet comforting all the same, bringing the Husk back to reality. He sucks in a sharp breath and looks up at Azna towering over him. Sympathy paints the Feni's face as he says, "No more secrets, Ethan. No being can help you if you don't say what's going on."

But his hesitation is coming from Shadow this time.

{*We shouldn't,*} it says.

[*It's not new to them,*] Ethan replies. [*Other beings have looked in the past.*]

{*No,*} Shadow answers firmly.

He understands why it's so insistent. To be friends with beings is one thing, but to place trust in these friends is another. It trusted Riona and look at what happened. She was the last being it grew close to. But Ethan has had more time to himself to think. It's not necessarily the trust that leads to mishaps, but the beings they befriend in the first place.

Ethan clears his throat. This is something even Azna doesn't know all the details of. As much as he doesn't want them all to be put back into danger related to his past, they've already done so much to help him try and escape it. He *needs* their help again, no matter what Shadow might think.

"He was looking for the Font of Magic," he reveals.

Amber's brow furrows. Kimberly, however, gasps as Azna's eyebrows shoot up in an instant.

"Really?" Kimberly mutters under her breath.

"What is that?" Amber asks, clearly not feeling the gravity of the situation at hand. Ethan can't help but let his face fall momentarily into concern. Her memories still haven't returned yet? Or did she simply never hear the stories?

"Your parents never told you the…" Kimberly trails off, the surprise in her eyes turning to a hollow sympathy instead. "I'm sorry, I–"

Amber shakes her head and musters a weak smile. "It's okay. I just… need a refresher."

"A surprising number of the stories about the Font of Magic that have survived are, for the most part, extremely accurate," Ethan says. "It's the heart of Astria, a localization of much of the power the Spirits of Light and Shadow used to create not only our world but the whole universe. It's also the origin point of all of our magic. It once resided far below our islands, beyond a mass of water and a thick layer of bedrock, but it was moved in the wake of the Great War. I… don't know who moved it or why, but what I *do* know is that our Father eventually split it into three Shards and hid them away among our civilization. It has always existed, but many have searched for the Shards before and found no traces of them. That is, until recently.

"Electro was friends with a Shard Hunter. This Hunter and another friend of his, amazingly, actually *found* two of the three Shards, almost eighteen years ago now. Though even Electro didn't know exactly why he was sent to Korodon, either. He had just been told to go and look and that he would 'feel it eventually' if he ever found it."

Riona thought that she could use the Font to further her power, Shadow timidly adds, *so she sent his Shadow away when she was done with her experiments on it to collect the other two Shards. That was the last we saw of it… until this cycle.*

The room is silent as the information sinks in. To Kimberly and Azna, the reveal of the Font's true existence must be a shock. For all they knew, it was always a myth told to young children as bedtime stories.

"Do you know where his Shadow is now?" Azna finally asks.

Both Shadow and Ethan shake their heads sadly.

"What about his friends? Did he reveal anything about them?"

[*Did he?*]

{*I… don't remember.*}

[*…Me neither.*]

It's almost maddening how selective their combined memories are. How vivid some moments feel, and how hazy others have become. Ethan spent quite a lot of time with Electro before his Shadow was taken from him, down in the dark and decaying dungeons of the castle, but everything he can recall is nothing but worthless bits of idle chitchat.

[*Even if he did, it's been almost twenty years. They've had plenty of time to change their names and relocate.*]

{*But they don't have many places to hide. If only we had a name to start with…*}

[*It's not like we can ask him. His body's been in the infirmary since–*]

An idea strikes Ethan. A crazy idea, one that might not even work, but an idea nonetheless.

"No," he says aloud, "but I might be able to find out. Azna, I need to see his body."

The Healer scowls. "What good would that do you?"

But Shadow already knows what he wants to do, and its eyes widen in panic. *Eth, I don't think I–*

"You're both going to have to trust me on this," Ethan interrupts. "*Please*."

Chapter 3

Shadow cowers behind Amber, its cold hands on her shoulders as she descends the stairs that lead into the infirmary's basement. Azna leads the way, with Ethan only two steps behind the old Feni. Kimberly stayed behind to keep an eye on Jake. Amber's only here with them because Shadow won't let her go.

Amber pats one of Shadow's hands awkwardly, trying to give it some reassurance. "Hey, it's going to be okay."

Shadow tightens its grip on her in response, whispering, *But I don't want to…*

"It's not going to be forever, right? We don't even know what will happen."

Ethan is one thing, Shadow says. *We're one in the same. But to inhabit another being's Husk? That's... so...* wrong. It blasts a strong wave of cold that makes Amber shudder.

Yes, Ethan's crazy plan is to have Shadow enter Electro's body. In theory, it should be able to do that as if Electro's body were Ethan's. But no being knows if it will awaken Electro's consciousness or if it will simply be Shadow controlling his body like a puppet.

“I don't know what would cause the spirit to be attached to the Husk over the Shadow, but if Electro is like Blaze, his personality *should* awaken,” Ethan had explained earlier.

Well, there's only one way to find out.

The basement of the infirmary is where the Electromancers work, providing the building with the power it needs to function. They walk down a long hallway, rooms with iceglass walls on either side. All the surfaces of the room, minus the wall of viewing glass, are covered with large metal plates that the Storm wizards' lightning bolts spark against, converting their magical energy into usable electricity. Naturally, from a Healer's perspective, it seems like such a boring job to be stuck with, sitting in semi-darkness all cycle, save for the lights from the hallway, pouring all of one's energy into powering the building above one's head. But, at the same time, if they did not perform such a boring and dreary task on the regular, then their technology would never have been allowed to progress as much as it has.

And yet Amber sees Storm wizards huddled together playing board games amidst the lightning around them, or simply chatting away as they suck water from their iceglass-capped cups through small tubes, somehow finding some enjoyment in their mundane job. It's nice to see that it's not always so miserable for them.

At the end of the long hallway is a single solid metal door. It has no viewing port on it and is sealed by three large metal bolts. Azna slides these bolts out of their locks and opens the seemingly heavy door with little effort, waving the two wizards and one very nervous Shadow inside.

They enter a rather small viewing dome along the edge of a large circular chamber made of iceglass much thicker than that of the walls of the rooms they passed on their way here, and another bolted door that leads to the chamber's interior. Suspended in the center of this chamber, static flaring all over his clothes, is a single wizard Amber can only assume is Electro. His eyes are closed, his brown hair matted and hanging heavy with oil, his clothes wrinkled. Occasionally, her eyes pick up on a brief flash of lightning leap from his body and strike against the curved metal walls around him, but otherwise the only thing that crackles with electricity is the fabric that hangs from his thin frame.

"Keeping him nourished has only grown more dangerous as time has passed," Azna says, shutting the door behind him. "His magic has grown wild. It's nigh impossible to get close to him now without coming close to being electrocuted, even with my magic."

"How is he floating?" Amber asks in awe. She has heard the stories of wizards growing so powerful that they can use their magic to propel themselves through the air, getting as close to true flight as possible. But she doesn't see anything that may be keeping Electro suspended.

"I believe he must be releasing hundreds of bolts that we simply cannot comprehend," Azna replies. "And with his magic expelling in every direction, he's producing enough energy to keep himself fixed in place like that."

"But doesn't he not have his Shadow?"

"A Shadowless body still accumulates magic," Ethan replies with a thoughtful hum, "but without a Shadow there's nothing in the body to store and regulate it, so the body will naturally reject it in its own way."

"I've been trying not to rely on him too much," Azna admits. "The amount of electricity he's been generating alone the last couple of years is enough to keep most of the infirmary powered all cycle."

Ethan nods lazily as he turns to Shadow, completely disregarding the Feni. "Ready?"

Must I? Shadow asks in a small whisper.

"We won't know if we don't try."

Once again, Amber pats Shadow's hand encouragingly. "It won't be for very long."

But Eth–

"Don't worry about me, Shadow. I survived Riona just fine on my own."

A flare of great unease fills the small enclosure, but Shadow finally floats forward, its expression hard to read beyond its nervousness. The three wizards watch it wordlessly as it passes through the iceglass like a ghost and approaches the unconscious Electromancer. It circles the suspended body anxiously, clearly mustering the courage to carry out Ethan's plan.

Finally, after what feels like an age, Shadow's form bursts into black smoke and wraps itself around the wizard's figure. Amber holds her breath, bracing herself for whatever is going to happen next…

***

A blossom of warmth grows in Electro's chest, chasing away the icy chill that he had slowly grown accustomed to. He doesn't know how long it's been since he's felt anything, being left in the numbing dark with his thoughts as his only company. It could have been cycles. It could have been centuries.

Like an old machine coming back to life, he flexes his fingers first, his stiff muscles and bones creaking. His heavy head fights his aching neck to stand up straight. As he does, his mouth hangs open.

Breathe…!

A rush of sharp, cold air enters his mouth and stings the back of his throat as it flows into his chest. As his chest bulges, his ribs ache as his joints do, and his head tilts backwards. He forces his heavy eyelids open, breaking their crusty seals.

Bleary-eyed, he watches his world pitch as an

overwhelmingly heavy force pushes down on his figure, sending him to his hands and knees. Power comes back to his jaw and it trembles as he gasps for more air. His arms shudder, threatening to give out under his own body weight. His heart pounds throughout his body as the blood rushes to his head in an instant.

What's going on? What's happening to me?

His head throbs as the magic inside him swirls violently, only expanding with each breath he takes. His arms and legs feel increasingly bloated, bulging with bottled-up energy. It feels like he's going to explode at any moment.

{*C-Calm down!*} a new voice stammers in his head, a voice he recognizes but can't place his finger on where he remembers it from. No sooner does it finish speaking then his frantic breathing evens out to a more stable rhythm, and the expanding energy within him recedes, replaced by the calm, cold flow he's more accustomed to as a new surge of strength fills him.

His vision finally sharpens. He sees bony fingers beneath him attached to two weak arms. Was he always this thin? Where did his ring go?

Slowly, he raises his head to look around. He's in a small room covered in metal. In front of him is a small section of iceglass, and behind it three wizards. He doesn't recognize the pink-haired girl. Azna isn't an easily-forgettable face, though he seems to have aged ever so slightly since last he saw him. But the boy…

Rage fills his chest, and he balls his hands into fists. He takes a long, deep breath and roars, "*YOOOOOUUUUUUU!*" His throat aches as he screams, but he doesn't care.

Something foreign lurches inside his chest, a cold ball of dense energy. It presses against the inside of his skin, agitated by his outburst, as the boy behind the iceglass takes a step back, fear plastered on his face. He *better* be scared.

Slowly, he rises to his feet, swaying unsteadily. He hasn't stood in… a long time by the feel of it, but he can still stand nonetheless. And if he can stand, he can teach that little *jerk* a lesson.

{*Wait– No!*} the second voice rings in his ears, and the agitated ball of energy pushes against his chest harder. His right eye only twitches uncomfortably in response. He must be crazy or in a dream. If he ignores it, it might go away.

He takes a shaky step towards the iceglass. Oh, how he's thought of all the ways he's going to torture that *jerk*. His hands crackle with the buzz of electricity in anticipation. How about he takes him to the brink of electrocution first? Then he can see how long it will take for his head to explode.

He takes his second step. He probably looks ridiculous, his whole body hunched over as he tries to waddle his way towards the wizards, his arms hanging limp beside him, but he doesn't care. He doesn't need to stand up straight to throw a decent punch.

On his third step the wizards finally seem to react. Azna throws a door open and enters the chamber, wrapping an arm around Electro to help support him.

"Don't push yourself too hard," the old Feni tells him as he slowly guides Electro towards the exit. "You need to take it slow."

"Do you know," Electro croaks, nodding to the *jerk*, "who *he* is?"

"Of course I do," Azna replies flatly. "He's a friend."

Electro opens his mouth to retort, but when he tries to speak his throat goes deathly cold. His eyes widen as he moves his jaw and sucks in breath after short breath, trying to speak and failing.

He's in shock, a new voice rings from his mouth instead, sounding just like the new one in his head. Only now does he notice that it *also* sounds suspiciously like the voice of that *jerk*, too.

The Feni's eyes shift to look into his, his expression straight and serious. "You have been in a coma for eighteen years, Electro. Much has changed since then. I'd advise you to stay your hand until we can properly explain."

Electro just stares back at the Feni in utter disbelief, his unforgiving words ringing in his ears. Eighteen *years*? Oh no… Oh *no*…

***

Electro is placed in a room by himself, giving him some space to breathe while Azna fetches him a meal. He slumps in his chair feeling more tired than he's ever felt before in his life. Mentally. Physically. Emotionally.

{*I'm sorry,*} the voice in his head says as shame swirls in his gut.

"What are you?" Electro mumbles.

{*Shadow. That's my name and what I am. We… We met before.*}

"When?"

{*The castle. I was the knight.*}

Electro presses his lips together. He remembers that knight, its tall and imposing figure looming over him as he stood frozen before it, helpless, staring into its cold red eyes as the darkness closed in around him.

{*And that* jerk,} Shadow continues, {*his name is Ethan.*}

Electro just lets out an uncaring grunt in response. He doesn't care for his name. He *might* care for his name after he gives him a good thrashing, though.

{*I know this is all a lot to take in right now. I'm… surprised that you still have your consciousness.*}

"I still don't even know what's going on," Electro grumbles.

{*I'll explain when Azna comes back,*} Shadow promises gently.

Staring up at the ceiling, weak and frail, he mulls over what his life has come to. He never should have agreed to go to Korodon. He was starting to build a life, a proper one. He was healthy and strong. Things were looking bright. Then he let *him* get to his head. Now he's lost eighteen years and has some strange entity living inside his head.

"Ryan…" he growls aloud. When he finds him, he'll–

The door opens, and Electro shifts in his chair. Azna enters holding a small steaming bowl of soup.

"It's fresh," the Healer warns, holding the bowl out to the Electromancer. Electro takes the bowl and cradles it in his hands, cherishing its warmth. The heat enters his fingers, making them tingle, but the cold void that now sits inside him consumes whatever warmth that manages to travel down past his wrists.

"You know," Azna continues, "I was surprised when Ethan brought you here."

"That *jerk*?"

"Yes, him."

{*He felt bad,*} Shadow chimes in weakly, though Electro gets the feeling that his anger has made it feel intimidated, {*and didn't want your body to sit abandoned in the castle.*}

"You're lucky," Azna continues. "In the time you've been in your coma, Korodon was restored. But the Feni are struggling to get back on their feet. Many haven't been nourished like you were. If it weren't for Ethan, Spirits only know how much worse you would be doing right now."

Electro takes the metal spoon, also warm from the soup, and stirs the dull yellow broth. "He was also the one who put me *in* my coma." It's mostly hyperbole but still somewhat true. If it weren't for that *jerk*, he wouldn't have been put before that knight and that Spiritist.

Azna nods. "I know."

Electro scowls at the Healer's lack of care for what he's

trying to tell him, that that *jerk* is dangerous and shouldn't be trusted.

"You won't be back to brawling strength any time soon," Azna tells him. "However, if you eat well and do some light workouts, you should build back the muscle you've lost in a year or so. Until then, *try* not to get into any fights."

"No promises," Electro replies with a small amused huff, finally shoving a bite of hot soup into his mouth. He sloshes the warm liquid around his mouth, absorbing its heat as much as he can before swallowing. The Healer stands before him silently a little while longer before turning to leave.

"Can I get a stick of arcane?" he asks as the Feni reaches the door.

Azna lets out a disappointed sigh. "You've already gone through withdrawal."

"I've still got the craving."

"Arcane gold isn't allowed in the infirmary. You can buy a pack yourself when you leave."

With that he is gone, leaving Electro alone with his soup and Shadow. Oh well. It was worth a try.

"You promised to explain," he says.

Shadow stiffens, making Electro briefly feel breathless as his chest tightens. {*Me and Ethan are a Fragment Shadow, forced to serve Riona, that Spiritist you saw. But we were freed not long ago, along with the rest of Korodon. We were trying to reunite you with your Shadow, but... it didn't go well. Now it's somewhere on Astria hunting for the Shards. Your friends are in danger.*}

"*Tch*," Electro huffs. "They can fall into the Void for all I care. Ryan, anyway. Kelsy..." Just thinking about Kelsy makes his rage subside. He wonders how she's doing. He wonders *what* she's doing. "I don't have many thoughts about Kelsy yet."

{*Is that their names?*}

"Yeah. Ryan Ashblade and Kelsy Skyshield. Ryan got me

into this mess in the first place."

{*What about Kelsy?*}

"Well, she..." He sighs into his soup. Eighteen years... Maybe she gave up. "...we had a fling, but otherwise we were all just school friends."

{*They each have a Shard?*}

"As far as I know, but I could be eighteen years out-of-date."

He takes another bite of soup. He wants to find Ryan and beat him up for what he did. He wants to get his hands on that *jerk* and beat him up, too. But most of all, he just wants some arcane gold to chew on. Is all of that too much for him to ask for?

{*I can ask Ethan to get you some,*} Shadow offers, referring to the arcane gold. A small yet sharp shiver worms its way down his back. Did it just... *read* his mind?

Cold fingers unwrap themselves from around his head almost instantly, relieving him of a great and oppressive pressure he didn't even realize was there. With it, his muddled thoughts slowly begin to clear.

"He can do what he likes, it won't change my mind," Electro grumbles back. "But I would appreciate it..."

{*What is it, by the way?*} Shadow asks.

"Arcane? You don't know what it is?"

His neck goes numb as his head briefly shakes side to side.

{*I know Ethan doesn't like it...*}

"And you two have been on Astria for *how long*?"

A flare of anger erupts in his gut. {*Just because we've been on Astria doesn't mean we know everything you wizards have and do.*}

"Especially Shadow," a new voice fills the quiet room, making Electro jump in surprise. In one of the room's dark corners, the shadows shift and warp to form the figure of that *jerk*, who stares at him with a hard scowl as he holds a long blue box in one of his hands. He approaches Electro and holds the box out to him. While he's not happy to see this *jerk*, he accepts the box wordlessly. "It's been isolated from the rest of Astria for a large part of its time here, and I'm just like you are right now, a Husk. I'm far from being omnipotent."

Electro pops the top of the box open and takes out a stick of arcane gold, a thin golden rod that shimmers in the light of the room. He pops one end of the stick into his mouth and lets out a relieved sigh as his teeth clamp down on the stick's familiar chill. Almost instantly, a sugary taste fills his mouth as he sucks on the gold. Its taste is sweet and potent. Even though he still vaguely remembers the taste, it's clear he hasn't experienced it in a *long* time.

"A Husk, hm?" he hums.

"A body without its Shadow. Or, in your case, a body with a Shadow that isn't yours. Now, ah, don't let Azna know I brought you that."

Electro just rolls his eyes. If he did say anything, he'd get his new box taken away, and he doesn't want *that* to happen. "Just this once."

"I've got a friend willing to give you a place to stay for the time being as well. Housing around here has only worsened, and even though Korodon has been restored it'll take some time for the hostels to open up again."

"Thanks."

"It's already getting late so there's not much we can do right now. But next cycle we can start looking for your friends."

***

"Kelsy?" Kimberly hums to herself. Ethan just nods back at her. "Skyshield?"

"Yes."

"That's my mother," she says.

"Really?" Ethan asks.

"Well, that's what my father always told me," she corrects. Her mother left when Kimberly was only one, but Kimberly has been told many stories about her growing up. Kimberly's amazed that Electro knows her mother despite his name never being mentioned once. "Maybe he knows where she went. Where she is. Or has an idea."

To the side, she sees Amber emerge from the kitchen with a cup of water. "Did he say anything else?"

"No," Ethan sighs disappointingly. "Aside from the other friend being called Ryan Ashblade, that's about all we have to work with for now. There will be time to properly question him next cycle. He's tired and still getting used to Shadow. You don't mind him biting arcane gold, do you?"

Kimberly laces her fingers together. "No, not really. Arcane is mostly harmless." To this, Ethan quietly rolls his eyes. "I know it's addictive. If he doesn't try and get me or Jake on it then it's fine."

"Where do you want the mattress?"

"Just along the wall behind you."

The Husk snaps his fingers, and a long mattress appears in a puff of black smoke, along with a single pillow and a sheet.

"Isn't that…?" Amber starts, pointing to the mattress.

"The one you slept on, too, yes. Now, Kim will pick up Jake and Electro later this cycle, and next cycle Kim can go talk to her dad about Kelsy while I can try and get more information out of Electro regarding Ryan and where the two Shards were originally found. Electro's Shadow probably knows as much as we do so we have to get to them first to warn them."

"Will you need my help again?" Amber asks, approaching Ethan's side. The two stare at each other for a spell, Amber's face full of silent longing and Ethan's only that of reluctant concern.

"Probably," Ethan finally says, "but don't let all of this get in the way of your schooling."

"Right..." she mutters, taking a sip of her water. She shifts her weight anxiously, her eyes searching the room for somewhere else to look besides him.

"I should go update Azna and see if he might have any information we can use," Ethan then announces. "Have a good night you two."

The two girls watch him melt into a nearby shadow, leaving a strong buzz of magic in his wake.

Amber sets the cup down on the table between her and Kimberly, her hair covering her face. "Thanks for the drink."

"Amber, I know you just want to be helpful, but you're just a–"

"Save it, Kim," Amber sighs. She runs a hand through her hair, revealing a troubled scowl. "I just don't want... School is great and all but I..." In frustration, she grits her teeth and shakes her head. "On one hand, I'm happy to stay out of your way, but on the other... I don't want to just sit by and watch. I want to put myself to good use."

"Right now that good use is studying," Kimberly tells her calmly.

"*Is it*?" the Healer exasperates, holding her arms out wide. "Right now it doesn't feel like it! I don't even remember why I'm going to school in the first place!"

"It'll come back to you," Kimberly tries to reassure her, but her words only seem to send Amber into more of a frenzy. She presses her hands to the sides of her head and falls to her knees, hyperventilating as she rocks back and forth on the floor of the living room.

Watching her breakdown, Kimberly isn't sure if she should get up and comfort her or let her get over it herself. It's hard to tell sometimes which strategy will work, which makes standing by and waiting to see what will happen even more agonizing. Then again, she's not looking to make Amber cry. She's been through enough as it is.

Does Ethan even know of her meltdowns? Even though he's not been around much until now, he still has Shadow to use as his eyes and ears. Maybe that's why he doesn't want her to get involved in this sort of adventure. Or maybe he doesn't know and he's only thinking of her schooling.

Slowly, Amber's breathing stabilizes and she calms down bit by bit. Kimberly keeps back a thankful sigh as she watches on, waiting for her to come back to her senses properly before she says anything to her that could possibly send her spiraling again.

Finally, Amber stands once more, her expression devoid of emotion. "Sorry."

"It's alright," Kimberly only replies.

"I think… I want to go," she continues timidly. "Tell Jake I'm sorry."

"It's okay. Thanks for being here as long as you were. And… take care of yourself."

Amber just nods, then walks out of the living room with light footsteps and a rigid posture. The only way Kimberly knows Amber made it to the front door is the chime of the store's bell, which rings as the Healer leaves.

As much as she hates to admit it sometimes, *the Shadow Incident* has left a deep scar on Amber, too. Kimberly is lucky she even remembers her parents in the first place.

***

Amber feels small and alone as she walks down the Straightway, her hands clasped in front of her, her fingers tightly interlocked, as she glides through the thin crowd with deft ease.

They don't know what you're going through, the tiny voice in her head says. *Just keep your head down and act normal. Act normal.*

She bites her bottom lip and picks up her pace, avoiding eye contact with any being she happens to pass. Her heart is tight with panic and confusion. She had forced herself to stand and leave in the middle of her panic attack. She didn't want Kimberly to suffer through another one. She just wants to get back to her dorm where she can be confused in peace.

Just keep it together and act normal…

Her brisk walk breaks into a trot the moment she reaches the end of the Straightway, dashing up the street as fast as she can while still trying to not appear in any sort of distress.

Still, tears of frustration sting her eyes. What's the point in school anymore if she's forgotten why she wanted to go there in the first place? Her adventure to Korodon took away that meaning, but gave her a new one. To help those in need, not just those injured or sickly but suffering silently in other ways in other situations as well. She's been itching to leave behind her schooling and head off to do something new and… *exhilarating*.

Still, as she reflects on who she had been before, why, *why* can't she remember anything else? Why hasn't her childhood come back to her? What made her so quiet and timid? What's holding her back from breaking out of that and being herself? Who *is* she?

Amber stops dead in her tracks as her knees buckle, dropping her to her hands and knees. Her head pounds, the void of absent knowledge overwhelming. There's something there, she *knows* it, deep down, but she can't see it. Something is keeping that history from her. A history that has shaped her. A history that she desperately wants to know, so that she can figure out where she came from and how to move on from that. To move on from that timid and shy wizard she once was.

Why must this be so *hard*?

Tears roll down her cheeks and drip off of her chin, and her ears roar with her rapid heartbeat. The cobblestone street is rough on her legs, making her knees ache as she rocks herself back and forth on the ground. She squeezes her eyes shut in an attempt to stop her tears, only for them to flow even faster.

You're in the middle of the street! Get it together!

She opens her eyes again, wet and aching, to darkness. Heart in her throat, she raises her head and blinks. No, her eyes *are* open. Where did this darkness come from then? *Ethan…?*

Then there's a shift, a slight tremor in the ground around her, and a small hole of light opens up above her.

"The *one time* I step outside my dorm," comes a tired sigh. Blaze leans into view, the glare of the light on his goggles hiding his eyes. Amber's mouth opens wordlessly, trying to find something to say in response. *Blaze*? What is *he* doing here?

"Why don't you clean yourself up first."

Using her sleeves, Amber wipes her cheeks dry.

"When did you…?" she tries to ask, though her words get caught in her throat.

"I've been here for a while," he replies flatly. "You're welcome."

Now she can see it. The darkness was brought about by a dome of vines, shielding her from the outside world.

Blaze looks around, then he disappears and the vines that surround her retreat back into the ground, replacing any cobblestones they happened to displace when they emerged, leaving behind a ring of dark brown dirt in their wake. The Naturist no longer stands by her. Instead, she spots him walking away from the street and toward the willow tree in the distance. She didn't even realize that she had made it to the lake just outside of the ASM grounds before collapsing.

Quickly she stands, though she still stares after Blaze with mild confusion. She can't help but appreciate his kind gesture, yet her mind notes that this is the first time he's been even remotely *nice* to her since she met his Shadow.

She finally turns away from him. She's almost back at her dorm. She should get there before anything else happens.

Chapter 4

Kimberly gestures to the storefront. “This is where we live.”

Electro tilts his head, staring at the storefront curiously. “What sort of business is this?”

“Ice cream,” Kimberly replies with a proud grin. Jake nods next to her as he half-leans on her shoulder for support.

The Cryomancer leads the way inside, the three passing through the neat store and into the back room where the stairs are.

Electro finds it impressive for a fourth term to not only have such a successful business with a storefront on the Straightway, but for her to also own so much equipment, too. The large coolers, the cauldron-like mixing bowls, and a sink so deep it could fit an entire wizard in it. It all must have been quite the expensive investment.

He raises a hand to twist the stick of arcane gold that hangs from his mouth, staring at the back room for a moment longer before following the students upstairs.

“Ethan brought a mattress for you,” Kimberly tells him as he emerges from the stairwell and is met with a narrow hallway.

Kimberly stands by an open doorway, gesturing to it expectantly.

The living room he enters only contains a single sofa and a table, with the dining room in full view at the other end. Pushed up against a bare right wall is a single mattress.

"Thanks for letting me stay here," he says to her.

"Of course," she replies with a warm smile. "After all, I'm the one with a proper house of any kind."

{*Even* we *still live in Ethan's dorm…*} Shadow mumbles, making his head buzz uncomfortably.

"Feel free to sit and relax. I'll start on dinner. Do you have any allergies?"

"To what?"

"Fruit, really, but anything."

Electro once again twists the stick of arcane gold. "Nothing I can think of."

"Then it should be ready soon."

Kimberly disappears into the dining room, leaving Electro alone with Jake on the sofa and Shadow in his head.

"This is just wonderful…" he mutters aloud to himself.

"What is?" Jake asks. Electro turns to the lounging wizard, his feet propped up on one arm rest and his head resting on the other.

"Just…" he shakes his head and throws his arms out wide, "…*this*… this *thing*. Ah." He sits down on the mattress and presses his back up against the wall. "Shadows and Fonts and all this missing time…"

"How much did you miss?"

"Eighteen years."

"Stars…" Jake shifts on the sofa, turning on his side to face Electro. "I'm turning nineteen this year."

Electro raises a hand to his hair, where a greasy brown strand hangs just in front of his eye. He pinches its tip and lets his mind's eye see it how he wants it to look. A burst of color rushes from his fingertips, turning the brown to a much more familiar rich amethyst color, while at the same time chasing away the rather dirty appearance. He still feels dirty, but at least no other being will know upon first glance. Thank the stars for glamour.

“This is all Ryan’s fault,” he huffs at last. “If I just shut that door...”

“Ryan?”

“Ryan Ashblade. Pyromancer. Massive jerk. Always had his head in a history book. He had… crazy ideas back then. The Font of Magic was one of them.”

“Have you seen them? The Shards?”

“Of *course* I have. When Ryan found the first one he practically paraded it around to us.”

“What did they look like?” the Pyromancer asks out of curiosity.

Electro licks his dry lips. What *did* they look like again? He remembers being in complete shock and awe, totally and utterly enraptured by their mystical majesty, but he can’t quite recall what either of the Shards actually looked like. Even with his hazy memory, those moments involving the Shards are even blurrier, as if the Shards themselves don’t want him to recall their existences before his very eyes.

“White… Shiny… Glowy… They looked like… stars. Little stars you could hold in your hand. They were… warm, too. Warm with magic.”

“Why did Ryan want to find them so bad?”

“Same reason as any other Shard Hunter. To ‘reunite’ them. But…” Electro just shakes his head. In hindsight, it didn’t really seem like *Ryan* wanted to reunite the Shards. If he did then he could have just done it all himself. But Electro's not Ryan. He doesn’t truly know why Ryan got him and Kelsy involved with his insane schemes, sending the two of them on their own little adventures. But when Electro finds Ryan he’ll *certainly* not forget to ask. With his fists.

"I don't know," he admits aloud. "I just… I don't. Really. Sorry my Shadow gave you a concussion."

Jake smiles weakly back at him. "It's not that bad. I just can't stand. Your fighting was impressive, though."

A small bloom of pride fills his cold chest. "Thanks. It's not every cycle a wizard decides to fight foot and fist. *I* like it."

"I'm stuck using an aid," Jake comments sadly.

"Wand or staff?" Electro asks.

"Sword," Jake replies.

"Ah. Ryan used a sword, too."

The Fire wizard perks up at the news, his eyes widening eagerly. "He did?"

"Yeah, though it's not like he used it much," Electro sighs in disappointment. "He just liked the look of it. He didn't treat it like the weapon it was."

"Oh…" Jake deflates.

"Look. You want a wand? Get a stick. You want a weapon? Then you better learn how to swing it." He pauses to take a breath and notices Jake's dark expression staring back at him. "What?"

"At least *you* don't need an aid," he states.

Electro frowns back in confusion. "That's not the point. A wand isn't a weapon any more than a weapon is a wand. Swords cut. Staffs don't. So if you got a sword, treat it – *use* it – like a sword! It's not that hard, *Ryan*!" He runs his hands down his face. "Stars above… 'But Electro, you don't need an aid! Why do you care? Why don't you just use your magic like every other being?' Yeah, well, I know mixed martial arts! I don't *need* a stick or fancy hand gestures or *whatever*. The only weapons *I* need are these!" He holds up his fists in front of him triumphantly, showing them off to his completely made-up opponent. Usually he'd flex, too, although with his current skeletal frame it'd just make him feel stupid if he tried.

Jake's pout turns to a slight frown as his eyes shift back to

Electro. "Mixed... Mixed *what*?"

"Mixed martial arts."

"What's that?"

"It's..." he trails off, confused himself, though he tries not to show it. Mixed martial arts... What *is* that, exactly? He knows the words. He *should* know what they mean! "Ah... you know, um, punching and kicking." He shrugs, lost for a proper explanation himself. "Do you at least understand what I'm trying to say?"

The young Fire wizard just rolls his eyes and turns his gaze to the ceiling.

{*I understand,*} Shadow chimes. {*I also use a sword.*}

"Gee, that's nice," Electro sighs.

"What?" Jake asks.

"Nothing. Shadow."

"Oh."

{*Though... I don't think wizards have used weapons since the Great War,*} Shadow continues. {*I just... don't use my magic a lot.*}

"Why not? Go on and talk. I don't want to look crazy."

Of course, in an instant, his lips go numb, and Shadow speaks its answer, *I just... don't? Ethan's the magic expert of us two. Well, I... I also didn't have my magic for a long time, so that might also be why.*

He waits for his lips to return to his control. When they don't, he frowns and has to slap his mouth to get Shadow's attention.

Oh! Sorry...

"Thank you," he sighs. "You know, I had a similar conversation with Ryan way back when. It's not necessarily that if you use a weapon you can't use magic and vice versa. It's more about finding that balance between the two that you're comfortable with." Recalling the old argument, he chuckles. "He wasn't having any of it though. 'Well *you* don't use a weapon',

‘What kind of wizard *are* you, anti-magic?’” he mocks. He tries to keep it playful, but rage builds in his stomach regardless. He forces a shrug to try and move past it. “But I can also see how not having magic for an extended period of time also has some effect. How did that happen?”

Riona.

Ah. She must have been far stronger than what he saw of her to steal *any* being’s magic, let alone that of a Fragment Shadow.

A sweet, sugary smell fills the air, and Kimberly calls, “Dinner’s almost ready! Electro, can you come help me for a spell?”

“Yep.” Electro stands from the mattress and wanders into the dining room, instantly noticing the opening leading into the kitchen, where Kimberly stands at the stove. On the counter next to her is a set of plates, forks, and cups, enough for the three of them to eat off of.

Kimberly briefly gestures to the dining ware with one hand. “Could you set the table? Any seats are fine, but Jake usually sits across from me.”

“Got it.”

He takes the items and sets them out on the table, two across from each other and one at the head of the table. It’d feel a little weird for him to sit right next to only one of his hosts in his opinion.

“Can you get to the table, Jake?” Kimberly asks.

“Yeah. Just let me know when you’re serving,” he replies tiredly.

“Well, it’s practically done now…”

Jake shifts on the sofa and stands, swaying on his feet. Slowly, he staggers over to the table, gripping one of the chairs as soon as it’s within his reach for support. As he sits, Kimberly emerges from the kitchen with a steaming plate of fried fruits.

“No meat?” Electro asks upon laying eyes on the meal.

"Would you like some?" Kimberly replies. "I can make you some if you want."

"No, it's fine, just..."

"I know," she nods. "Jake consumes fruit almost exclusively during these cycles so I pay a little extra so we can both eat properly, and cooking two meals every night is just... exhausting."

"I see."

With that, he sits at the table as Kimberly serves herself before she sits as well. Jake takes the spoon next, scooping a heap of caramelized fruit chunks onto his plate. When he's done, he slides the plate down to Electro.

The dish smells *wonderful*, especially since the last thing he's smelled that's anywhere this good was probably the soup that Azna gave him earlier. He takes the arcane gold out of his mouth and carefully props the end that he was chewing on up onto his plate, the metal stick already covered in teeth marks. Serving spoon in hand, he fills his plate with what remains of the cooked food, an amalgamation of half-firm, half-squishy fruit cubes and an ooze of thickened fruit juices.

He takes a bite. The fruit is still warm as it lands on his tongue, gushing with juice still trapped within the pieces that squirt as they are crushed between his teeth. The sugar and flavors swirl together into a storm of deliciousness. He has to pause and let out a hum of delight before swallowing.

Kimberly lets out a light chuckle. "Is it *that* good?"

Electro nods back. To him, her cooking is to the stars and back again. But the happiness doesn't last long before turning to a twisted sorrow. The only other wizard he'd trust with cooking excellent meals would be Kelsy. Even if she always brought down the temperature of any room she stood in, whatever hot dish she made would always bring a little joy to his cycle.

His second bite lingers halfway between his plate and his mouth, his smile straining.

“So, how are you doing?” Kimberly asks Jake, the two not paying Electro any mind.

“Still a bit dizzy,” Jake replies with a heavy sigh. “Azna said it should go away at first light, but that still doesn’t make me feel better.”

“Healing isn’t a completely painless process,” Kimberly comments with a half-smile of sympathy.

“I wish it was,” Jake grumbles.

“Don’t be in such a foul mood, Jake. We’ve got a guest.”

“Sure, boss…”

Kimberly, seeing that she’s mostly failed at trying to get Jake to perk up, runs her free hand through one of her bright blue pigtails. “Well, just eat as fast as you can and then you can go rest.”

“Right,” Jake mutters between bites.

The room descends into silence as the three wizards return to their meal. Exhaustion hangs heavy in the air. It’s been a long cycle, after all, for every being.

Finally taking his second bite, Electro's thoughts still fixate on Kelsy. When was the last time he saw her? He was leaving a house. She was clawing at his arm, trying to get him to stay. But once she realized that he wasn’t going to listen, she gave him a hug, a tight one, her cold hands pressed against his back, not wanting to let him go. He knows there was a short conversation but he can’t recall their words. Then he left, and that was that.

The longer he thinks, trying to recall that moment, his head slowly begins to pound with a growing headache. He sets his fork down to rub his temples.

“Are you alright?” Kimberly asks, noticing his movements.

“Yes,” he replies automatically, lowering his hands. Jake is gone from the table now, though his plate still remains. He left so silently, Electro didn’t even notice. He forces a small smile and picks up his fork again, waving it over his plate. “It’s really good.”

Kimberly nods back at him. “Thank you.”

“Does he not have a bed?” Electro asks, nodding in the vague direction of the sofa.

“No, not yet,” Kimberly replies. “I don’t have an extra room for him and we’re not ready for sleeping together yet.”

“Oh, are you two dating?”

“Yeah.”

“How long?”

“Three years now,” Kimberly beams. “We’re planning to marry some time after he graduates.”

Electro smiles along with her. “You know, I was married after three years.”

“You’re *married*?” Kimberly’s eyes instantly darted to his hands.

“Well,” he sighs, holding up his right hand, revealing his absent ring, “I guess I’m not anymore.”

Kimberly’s eyes widen with shock. “*What*? Why? Who was it?”

Electro just shakes his head back at her. “I don’t want to talk about it too much right now. I don’t know if she really broke it off or not yet. But… I think you found a good match.”

“That’s… good to hear.” Kimberly looks down at the table, lacing her fingers together as a tinge of anxiety flashes across her face. “I haven't introduced him to my family yet. They’re the ‘date within your own magic branch’ types. I know Ethan wants to interrogate you more next cycle, but… I think my family can help, too, so I’m a little nervous.”

“Yeah, my wife’s family was that way, too. I get it.”

“Did they like you?”

“Of course they did! But, you know, accepting me as marriage material was a different story. That’s kind of how things go in this case. Just don’t try and push them too much and they'll get used to him soon enough.” A weak chuckle escapes his mouth. “That’s what I did and it did *not* go very well.”

Kimberly lets out an amused snort. “Thanks for the advice.”

“I’m just brimming with it,” he laughs. He finishes his dinner and stands from the table. “Need help cleaning up?”

“No, thank you, I’ll be fine. You should be resting, too.”

{*Kim’s right,*} Shadow buzzes in Electro’s ear. {*You might feel fine right now, but that’s only because I’m here. When you get your Shadow back you’ll need to carry yourself. Rest and exercise should be your priority.*}

“Gee, thanks,” he grumbles under his breath, turning back to Kimberly. “Have a good night, then.”

“Sleep well,” Kimberly replies.

Chapter 5

The narrow side streets of Asandra leave little side-by-side walking room as Kimberly guides the way to her family home. With first light having just broken, many windows are still dark and homes silent.

Jake is somewhat eager. This will be his first time meeting his girlfriend's family. They did talk about them long ago, about their expectations for her to find a Cryomancer, so as much as he is excited he is also nervous.

"I hope they're awake," Kimberly mutters, an anxious frown plastered on her face.

Jake wraps an arm around her shoulders in an attempt to comfort her. "One of them should be."

"I know, but…"

"Hey, it'll be fine. How can they *not* like me?"

"Well…" Kimberly trails off, shaking her head.

They eventually reach a crossroad, and Kimberly points to a nearby house on the corners, one made of gray brick and a bright blue door adorned with a white snowflake symbol.

"There it is," she says, a hint of joy in her voice. Even if she's nervous, she's still somewhat eager to see her parents again.

The pair approach the door, and Kimberly gives it a good knock. Looking up and down the street, Jake takes note of the empty, sleeping street. He gets the feeling that not a lot of students live in this part of the neighborhood.

Eventually, the lock of the front door clicks, and it swings open to reveal a bleary-eyed wizard dressed in a soft blue robe and white slippers. The wizard's eyes widen in an instant when he sees Kimberly at the doorstep.

"Kim-Star!" he exclaims with a smile. "So nice to see you!"

"Hi, dad," she replies, mirroring his smile.

"And who's this with you?" her dad asks, turning to Jake. "A friend?"

"My name is Jake," Jake replies, "and I'm her… boyfriend."

The wizard's smile strains as he slowly nods. "I see."

"Can we come in?" Kimberly asks. "I have some questions for you."

"Of course." Her dad steps aside and waves the two students inside. Kimberly enters first, wiping her shoes on the carpet laid in front of the door, then quickly takes them off and sets them on a small shoe rack on the left. Once she's out of the way, Jake steps inside and does the same, unbuckling his armored boots and setting them next to the rack as they're a bit big for it.

There's a set of stairs in front of him, with a small hallway leading deeper into the house, and a doorway to his right where he spots Kimberly standing, watching him, probably waiting. She waves him into the room before disappearing.

"Would you two like something to drink?" Kimberly's dad calls as Jake enters the room. It's a small living room, with another doorway leading into a dining room.

"What do you have?" Kimberly asks.

"Warm drinks. Cold drinks. Water."

Kimberly just rolls her eyes. “I’m good.”

“I’ll take some water, thanks,” Jake replies.

Kimberly takes a seat on the sofa, pressed up against the rightmost wall of the room, and waves for Jake to join her. He sits on her left, the two now facing a small table and two armchairs draped in blue. As a matter of fact, the entire house – floors, walls, ceiling, furniture – is shaded in different blues and whites, accented with Ice magic iconography.

“I can’t believe you grew up here,” Jake mutters, looking around.

“I *told* you they were die-hard Cryomancers,” she replies.

“Yeah, but…”

“I know, Jake. I know.”

Kimberly’s dad emerges from the dining room, a clear cup in one hand and a steaming mug in the other. He sets the cup down on the table in front of Jake, then takes a seat in one of the armchairs across from the two students.

“Kim, why don’t you go wake up Ian,” her dad suggests with a light smile. “I’m sure he’d appreciate having you jump on him like you used to.”

“Uh, sure…” she replies. She stands slowly, casting Jake a small glance of sympathy before leaving him alone with her dad.

The two quietly listen to her tromp up the staircase.

“Boyfriend,” her dad eventually hums, taking a sip from his mug.

“Yes,” Jake nods. He looks at the cup of water before him, unsure if he should bury his face in it or leave it where it stands.

“I’m sure she mentioned our expectations for her,” he continues.

“She did.”

Her dad takes another slow sip of whatever he made for himself, his expression unreadable. “With our lineage, this family cares more for carrying on our legacy first and foremost.”

"That… being?"

"She never told you?"

"No…?" Kimberly hasn't talked a whole lot about her family life, aside from her funny childhood memories. Anything beyond that she's been vague or cagey about. He never pushed it, though. If she didn't want to share, that's her decision.

"Our family roots trace all the way back to the sister of the General of Ice," her dad reveals. "Ice magic runs in our blood."

Jake nods, finally reaching for his cup of water. That certainly explains why Kimberly's parents want her to marry another Cryomancer at the very least.

"She never mentioned anything like that," Jake comments.

"That's understandable," her dad sighs into his mug. "She was never all that interested in our legacy. You could say we live on the less influential side of the family tree."

"Isn't the Ice Representative for the Council also related to the General's sister?" Jake asks.

"Yes, he's a distant relative," her dad nods.

Jake's shoulders sag as he takes a long sip of his water. No wonder Kimberly omitted such details of her life. She's already super strong, being a Blessed wizard and all, but also having such an extensive and powerful family lineage…

Laughter rings from the hallway as footsteps descend the stairs. Kimberly enters the room again, followed by a second man also in the same blue robe as her dad wears.

"Jake, this is Ian Stonebreaker," Kimberly introduces the second wizard, "my step-dad. And Jay Starsong, my actual dad."

"Step-dad?" Jake hums as she sits on the sofa again, Ian taking his place in the other armchair.

"Dad remarried when I was three," Kimberly replies with a small shrug.

"You're the boyfriend I hear," Ian remarks with a jovial laugh. Jay attempts a weak smile and sips from his mug once more.

"Ah, our little snowflake is all grown up," Ian continues merrily. "When's the wedding?"

"Ian," Jay mumbles.

"Come, now," Ian replies with an eye roll, "if they have children–"

"That's assuming they *want* children."

"If they don't then what's the point in fretting over who she dates?"

The two adults turn to the pair expectantly.

Jake, nervousness erupting in his gut, buries his face in his water reflexively. Kimberly musters a weak grin back at her parents.

"We've not talked about kids yet," she admits.

"So there's still a chance," Ian says to Jay. "Let her be happy." Jay doesn't reply, his expression seeming to darken.

"I hope he wasn't hard on you," Kimberly says to Jake. "Dad is a bit of a stick in the snow."

"It's fine," Jake replies weakly. "He just… told me about the family legacy."

Kimberly's expression wilts instantly. "Oh. I…"

"It's okay, Kim," Jake reassures her. "I get why you didn't want to mention it."

Still, Kimberly shoots Jay a sharp glare. She probably wanted to be the one to tell him, not her dad.

"I'm sorry, snowflake," Jay says flatly.

Kimberly, in response, folds her hands on her lap and dons her business face. "I didn't come here to talk about Jake. I came to ask about mom."

The smile on Ian's face strains as Jay shifts in his seat, unease descending on the two adults.

"What about her?" Jay asks.

"Did she mention any being by the name of Electro?"

Ian shakes his head definitively. "Never heard that name before."

Jay, however, takes a long sip from his mug and stares down at the table that separates him from his daughter.

"She did," he finally speaks. "Though that was... decades ago by now. How do you know of him?"

"We're housing him," Kimberly replies, "and he wants to know where she is."

"Excuse me?" Jay leans forward in his seat, eyes wide with panic. "He's *where*?"

"It'd take too long for me to explain everything, and time is the one thing we don't have a lot of right now. Do you know where mom might be?"

"Jay, who is *that*?" Ian asks.

"One of Kelsy's old friends," Jay replies with a heavy sigh, sitting back in his chair again. He cradles his mug in his hands, staring into it long and hard, thinking to himself. "Do you remember Ryan?"

"That Voidterror?" Ian spits. "How can I not?"

"You know Ryan, too?" Jake breathes.

"I was a term below," Ian replies, "and Jay was two terms above."

Jay nods. "Sadly, we attended ASM with Ryan, that troublemaker, though it helped that we were studying different magics. He also was the one that broke your mother's heart."

"How?" Kimberly inquires.

"The Electromancer's failed quest," Jay replies. "One that Ryan pressured him into taking. Kelsy didn't agree, but Ryan persisted. It tore them all apart, and she felt like she couldn't forgive herself if she stayed on Asandra. I... wasn't willing to move with her, so you and I stayed here. And I'm glad we did." He turns to Ian with a warm grin.

"He really *was* a Voidterror," Ian only sighs, shaking his head disappointingly.

"What was Ryan like?" Kimberly asks.

"Vain," the two parents say at once, though Ian continues

with, “That’s all I remember about him. I never met Electro, though.”

“He wasn’t very social,” Jay replies. “He usually went to the training grounds after his class finished.”

“Ah, one of *those* types.”

“Well, he was certainly a vindictive one with an *odd* sense of humor.”

“How’d he ever come to associate with Ryan, then?”

“The two were sparring partners, I believe.”

“So where did mom go?” Kimberly steps in, steering the conversation back on track.

“I wouldn’t be surprised if she wound up on Gardall,” Jay answers. “She often talked about building a cabin up on the side of Frostfall. Maybe she did that. Although,” he pauses, licks his lips, and inhales slowly, “if you go searching for her, don’t… don’t bring Electro with you.”

“Why?”

A haunted look befalls Jay, and he replies with a stiff voice, “That’s for her to tell you. Or *him*, for that matter.”

“He doesn’t remember anything, though.”

“Good for *him*, then,” Jay spits. Ian gives his husband a sideways glance, his eyes full of questions and his face one of worry.

“You haven't told me any of this…” he says quietly.

“I promised her not to speak of the matter,” Jay replies. “It… was a hard time for all of us.”

A heavy silence descends on the group, Jay’s words still ringing in the air. Jake takes a cautious sip of water, his eyes darting between the two parents.

Out of the corner of his eye, he sees Kimberly turn towards him, and so he turns to look back at her. Her expression is flat, and he doesn’t know if what is in her eyes is confusion or annoyance. If it’s annoyance, he understands. They’re so close to getting a straight answer, only to fall short. Whatever Jay promised to keep silent about, he sure is sticking to it. Which only makes him more curious as to what happened.

"Thanks, dad," Kimberly finally speaks, turning back to her parents. "That's… I think all we needed."

Jay nods. "If and when you find her… maybe we can talk about it."

"Right." Kimberly stands stiffly, gesturing for Jake to follow her. "We'll see ourselves out."

"Well, it was great to see you again, snowflake!" Ian chirps. "It was nice to meet your boyfriend, too."

"I'll be sure to visit again," Kimberly nods, a small smile managing to slip through her stony exterior.

"Thanks for the water," Jake nods, placing his cup down and standing. The two parents nod back at him as he turns to leave with his girlfriend, each wearing different smiles. One is genuinely happy and the other tense and haunted.

***

"We're back!" comes Kimberly's call as the bell to the store jingles below. Electro lets out a thankful sigh and sinks into the sofa, clearly weary from all of Ethan's questions. He couldn't help it. The more information they have, the better.

"Well?" he calls over his shoulder as he hears Kimberly and Jake tromp up the stairs. When they appear, Kimberly also appears drained as Jake pats her shoulder.

"We got what we could," Jake is the one to speak. "She might be living on Frostfall Mountain or probably near it."

"Makes sense for her to return there," Ethan nods. "That was where one of the Shards was found."

"Frostfall?" Kimberly breathes, perking up. "Really?"

"Yep," Electro nods. "I was shocked to hear, too. The other one was inside the Solari pyramid."

"So close…" Jake mutters in awe.

"Yes, it is… surprising," Ethan nods. "At least now we can try and find Kelsy."

"Any clues where Ryan might be?" Kimberly asks.

"No. The Pyramid is the only thing we have to go off of right now. It might do us some good if we looked around there as well."

Electro shifts on the sofa, appearing to get ready to stand. "If Kel is on Frostfall, then I–"

"Um, actually," Kimberly interrupts him quickly, making the Electromancer pause, "it might be better if we go and get her… without you."

"Why?" Electro asks, astonished by her words.

"Something… happened. We don't know what specifically, but… it might be better if we explain what's going on to her first before she sees you again."

Electro sits still on the sofa, poised perfectly in the middle of his motion to rise, his muscles tense. His face is one of bewilderment, his gaze hollow. Ethan won't be surprised if he tries to pick a fight in protest. This is one of his old school friends they're talking about, after all.

The moment passes. The Electromancer sits back on the sofa once more, defeated. "Maybe you're right…" He just shakes his head and leans to his left, propping his elbow on the arm rest and placing his hand on his forehead.

"There's still time before classes," Kimberly says, breaking the silence. "Me and Jake can go to Frostfall and see if we can find her this cycle."

Ethan folds his arms and nods. "Sounds perfect to me. Would you mind if I came along?"

"Why?" Kimberly asks. "Weren't you going to look into the Pyramid?"

Ethan presses his lips together. He *was*, initially. That was his plan. Although, the more he thought about it…

"I don't really know much about what happened there,"

Electro had told him earlier. "I know he went there with a Serperas, and I know that she had to open this special room and was the one that brought the Shard to him, but that's about it."

"Do you know who this Serperas was?" he had inquired.

"I… know they had a fling. I think she was the… princess at the time? Although I might be wrong. I know he talked about *a* princess for a long while."

That princess Electro mentioned, which he's sure he's correct about, might be the current queen of Mirage. So if Ryan needed her when he went to Solari then they'll surely need the help of the crowned prince, Lukri, once again.

Maybe Amber would like to see him. It's been a while since those two have talked to each other, after all. And maybe, *just maybe*, he can convince Blaze to join them. It'd do him some good to get out of his dorm for a little while. Maybe it will help to ease his animosity with… well, *every being*.

Besides, if Electro's Shadow shows up on Gardall at all, then he'll have a second chance to put things right again, and he'd not want to miss such an opportunity. If they can stop it in its tracks, then there'd be no need to go searching for Ryan.

"If Electro's Shadow shows up, then I can try again to return it to his body," he finally speaks. "If you two run out of time, then I can stay and finish the search."

"But the Pyramid–"

"I was thinking about asking Amber and Lukri if they could look there for us," Ethan replies with a slight smile. "After all, the Pyramid used to belong to the Serperas, and it'd make Amber happy. It'll be safe. I hope."

A flash of worry crosses Kimberly's face, though it quickly disappears in favor of a small grin and an understanding nod.

"So we're going now, then?" Jake asks.

"Well, maybe when first term classes end," Ethan replies. "I can't necessarily ask her anything right now. Although, I do have something to do real quick, so meet me by the ASM

Archway when the bell rings."

"Will do," Kimberly nods.

Ethan flashes them one final smile, then takes his leave by stepping through one of the room's shadows. The coldness of the dark brushes against his skin momentarily as he wills himself to the boys dorm rooms. On his second step, the darkness recedes, and he appears in the hallway of where he wants to be.

He counts the doors as he goes. Though he doesn't need to do it, it provides him a small distraction from the impending encounter. When he reaches Blaze's dorm, he pauses.

He stands facing the door, contemplating. While he still cares about the Naturist, is this really such a good idea? He probably dislikes Amber as much as he dislikes Ethan right now. There's a good chance he'll just outright refuse without letting Ethan even speak a word of the situation.

He inhales, closes his eyes, and knocks.

Knock, knock, knock.

He opens his eyes again to silence.

As he waits for a response, his cape weighs heavier on his shoulders as he wonders if Blaze is even in there to begin with, or knows that it's him at the door somehow and is refusing to answer.

He taps his fingers against the sides of his legs anxiously. Then he decides to knock again.

Knock, kn–

"GO AWAY!" Blaze's muffled shout sounds from the other side of the door.

"C'mon, Blaze, I–"

"GO. *AWAY.*" Blaze repeats, his tone much more curt.

"It's important!" Ethan tries. His words echo up and down the hallway, but this time Blaze doesn't reply to him.

"I can't talk about it in the hallway," he adds with a heavy sigh. "Please, just hear me out." Still, there's nothing but silence.

"Blaze?"

Nothing.

"Answer me!"

Nothing.

Ethan shakes his head. He doesn't want to have to do this, but Blaze isn't leaving him with much of a choice. He rolls back his shoulders and stands a little straighter before stepping forward. With ease, he passes through the wooden door, the darkness warping around him as he does so, and emerges on the other side into Blaze's dorm.

Blaze, who sits at his desk, turns his head as if sensing his presence, then lets out a yelp of surprise and promptly falls out of his chair.

"STARS!" is the first thing he says, followed by, "You stars forsaken Shadow! How on Astria did you–"

Ethan shakes his head back at him in disappointment, the motion making the Naturist pause as he finally tries to process the scene before him. To him, in every sense, Ethan should not have been able to enter his dorm. He's tried not to do it, either, out of respect for his privacy. But not now.

"I'm not going to play nice with you this time, Blaze," he says, "so listen closely. Amber will be leaving Asandra shortly, going to Mirage and then Solari. Whether or not you decide to accompany her, if she returns with anything as small as a scratch on her, I will rip out your Shadow and leave your body here until I am done with it because at least *it* is nicer than *you*. Do you understand?"

Blaze remains on the floor, stunned. His eyes are wide in shock, probably at Ethan's dark and demanding tone. Though, to be frank, he'd most likely not listen to anything less than a threat, and he knows that Ethan can very well follow through on just about any threat he makes.

His friend's face twitches, wanting to turn into a scowl but daring not to show his distaste for his situation all the same.

"*Well*?" Ethan asks.

Finally, Blaze lets out a reluctant sigh. "Yes…"

"Wait for her by the school's Archway. And you *better* not give her any trouble. She can explain what's going on… if she's in a good mood."

With that, he turns on his heel and leaves the way he came in, right through the door.

***

Amber's heart flutters the moment she sees Ethan posted by the dorm building, his eyes staring at the door to her Hall intently. When he sees her, a smile spreads across his lips as he waves her over.

"Ethan," she says as she nears, her textbook hugged close to her chest as per usual. "You're… *here*."

He nods back at her. "Yes. I actually have something to ask of you. It involves a bit of Mirage and a bit of Solari–"

Amber's breath catches in her throat, and her heart skips a beat, excitement building in her chest.

"What is it?" she asks eagerly.

"You remember us talking about Ryan and Kelsy, right?"

"Yes."

"Well, we might have a lead as to where Kelsy might be, so Kim, Jake, and I are going to check it out. Finding Ryan, on the other hand, is proving to be a bit more difficult than we anticipated."

Amber nods, waiting for him to make his request. Her heart pounds and squeezes, almost as if it were going to burst if she's left waiting any longer.

"We know he went to the Great Pyramid with a Serperas of royal descent, and it's there where he found the first Shard. Could you get Lukri and try and retrace Ryan's footsteps for me?"

"Yes," Amber says without hesitation, her body already

pumped with energy and ready to go. For the longest time she wondered if leaving Asandra on another adventure would be what she needed to rediscover herself. Now, finally, she has that opportunity.

"Here," Ethan hands her two Keystones, one a light cream and the other a rich orange. "This one will take you to Mirage, and the other to Solari. I let the Shasks know you'll be coming. Just ask for Sir Taylor and you should be fine. Do you remember how to get to town?"

Town, referring to the town on Mirage the two of them were sheltered in, hosted by a kindly old Serperas called Anasi. She nods. Lukri told her which direction it was from the Archway before he left. Although, that was half a season ago now. She *hopes* she still remembers.

"There should be a being waiting for you by the campus Archway," Ethan tacks on at the end with an apologetic smile. "Don't... get mad. He needed to get out."

"Okay..." Amber breathes back, slightly confused.

"I should get going," Ethan tells her, turning to leave, "the other two are waiting on me. You should get going as soon as you can as well. We don't have a whole lot of time on our hands, you know."

"I know."

"Good luck, Amber. And... thank you. For everything."

"It's what friends are for."

"Right..."

With that, Ethan disappears into the shadows, leaving her standing all alone.

Still, she shakes with excitement. When's the last time she's felt this excited about anything? She can't remember, figuratively and literally. But it feels... *refreshing*.

Immediately, she makes her way to the campus Archway, ready to see Lukri and explore the Great Pyramid of Solari. The third terms get to go on class trips to the Pyramid, so she has yet to experience its majesty. Rumor has it, it's quite a sight to behold.

As the Archway comes into view, her spirits lower just a slight bit. The one and only Blaze, local shut-in and sour fruit, is posted near the Archway, his arms folded and his scowl radiating furious reluctance. *Now* Ethan's words make sense.

Sensing her stare as she approaches, Blaze looks up from the ground, and his face goes from dark to stony neutral in a snap. Amber pulls her best disinterested scowl and raises her chin into the air.

"Fancy seeing you here," she says.

"Likewise," he grumbles back.

"So, what got you out of your den again?"

"Ethan. Threatening me."

"Typical."

"Excuse me?"

"Well, you just seem the type to only respond to threats."

"Sassy, aren't we?"

Amber just rolls her eyes and turns to the Archway, the Keystones growing cold in her hands. "Can we just go?"

"Whenever you want."

Amber steps up to the Archway, holding up the Mirage Keystone high above her. The runes on the Archway glow in response, and a rip opens in its center, revealing a wall of orange dunes and letting through a blast of warm air.

"That's a lot of sand…" Blaze mutters under his breath.

"Oh, just wait," Amber tells him with a grin.

II

Discovery

Chapter 6

Kimberly has been to Gardall once before as part of a class trip. As soon as she, Jake, and Ethan step out of the other side of the Archway, she inhales the air. The cold swirls in her chest comfortably, making her feel right at home.

The group finds themselves standing at one end of a long wooded pathway lit with Firelight lanterns hanging from tree branches overhead, creating a dim yet warmly-lit entryway leading up to a distant wooden gate. The silence is strangely comforting as they approach the gate, their footsteps muffled by the dirt and their breaths that of awe and wonder. The leaves of the evergreens sway in the magical breeze only they can feel, creating a chorus of rustling.

The heavy wooden gate standing at the end of this path is guarded by two armored brown Yafiirs standing on either side. The gate stands partly open, revealing a bustling street beyond, the cobblestones lined with tightly packed wooden structures and a scattering of open-air forges, the distant ring of metal shaping accenting the murmur of the crowd. Off to their right, towering over the town is Frostfall Mountain, most of its rocky face covered in bright white snow, its imposing figure nearly incomprehensible to her eyes. If she squints, Kimberly can make out the snow-covered walls of the mining town near its peak.

"Leave the talking to me," Ethan says, holding up the navy blue Keystone in his hand. Without much choice, Kimberly and Jake both nod and follow the Husk to the guards.

"Sure is much colder than Asandra," Jake mutters beside her, his radiating heat lightly warming her right arm. He holds his sword loosely in his left hand, its tip scraping the ground as they walk. Kimberly shrugs back at him in reply.

"Welcome to Gardall, wizards," one of the Yafiirs says to them as they near. He holds out one of his paws towards the group expectantly. Ethan hands over his Keystone to the guard. The guard turns over the Keystone and inspects it closely, angling it to catch the light on its surface. After a long moment, he hands it back to the Husk.

"And the other two?" he asks.

"I'm taking responsibility for them."

"Swear on the Spirits that you will be held liable alongside them if ever they are punished in any way under the law of Gardall for as long as their visit lasts, even if they remain on the island without your presence."

Ethan pauses, a strange unease briefly flashing across his face. "By the Spirits of Light and Shadow, I swear to your terms."

The guard nods and cracks a toothy grin. "Enjoy your stay in Varenguard."

With that, the three make their way through the gate and into the walled town of Varenguard.

"It's best we find a guide if we want to venture around Frostfall," Ethan says to the other two. "Without Shadow, I don't feel comfortable going there with just the three of us."

"Where are we supposed to find one?" Jake inquires.

"They're usually in the inns. I think there's a couple this way…"

They turn into a narrow side street, pressing up against

the left side single file as other beings pass them on the right.

Kimberly had forgotten how tightly packed Varenguard is. With a large part of the forest around the town protected for historic reasons, the Yafiir have had to make do with the space they've designated for themselves. Thus, many of their side streets are only slightly more narrow than those on Asandra. However, the benefit of the streets being so small is that some of the heat lingers from the fires from within the buildings and the warmth of all the beings constantly passing through.

"There's one," Ethan announces, pointing to a hanging wooden sign up ahead, its face painted with a steaming bowl and silver mug.

Upon entering the inn, they're instantly hit with the strong smell of warm meat soup and the fruity tang of wine. Every table squeezed into the space is full, and the bar only has a few scattered seats remaining. The walls are decorated with all sorts of metal masterworks, from the likes of axes and hammers to large carving-covered sheets bedazzled with gemstones depicting the might of Yafiir smiths in their forges. The pillars that hold the roof in place above them are also expertly carved, each one unique in its own way as they flow from top to bottom with sculpted shapes and figures.

Without a word to the other two, Ethan steps up to the bar and flags down the Yafiir tending to it.

"Busy place," Jake comments, looking around the packed room.

"I don't remember there being this many beings here in Varenguard last year," Kimberly says.

"It's not a holiday, is it?"

"No, I don't think so..."

At the bar, the Yafiir Ethan had been talking to steps away, hurrying towards the tables by the back wall. Ethan folds his arms and leans up against the bar, eyeing the two still near the front door.

Kimberly laces her fingers together, feeling uneasy. Frostfall Mountain is so *big*, it's hard to say where they should even start looking. And they don't have a whole lot of time to search, either. Jake doesn't have much time before he has to go back to Asandra for class, and when he has to leave Kimberly might as well head back with him to prepare for her own.

As much as she doesn't like skipping school, she hopes they can find Kelsy this cycle at the very least. She can't wait to finally meet her mother. What does she look like? What does she sound like? Will they get along? What has she been doing this entire time? Does she even remember Kimberly in the first place? Just thinking about their impending meeting makes her chest flutter eagerly.

The barkeeper returns with a girl in tow. Her hair is bright orange, tied in a low ponytail that pokes out from under a light blue hat, with lively amber eyes and rosy cheeks. She wears a faded red jacket over a navy shirt, with pants made of brown leather and white snow shoes. Her shoulders are covered with a light gray cowl trimmed with enchantments in golden thread, and a pair of mittens hang out of one of her pockets. At first, the girl appears confused and mildly annoyed, her lips pressed firmly together. However, when the Yafiir waves a paw to Ethan, she freezes mid-step, her eyes widening as far as they'll go. Ethan's eyebrows shoot up in an instant, taken aback by her presence as well.

"Ethan?" the girl asks in disbelief. Ethan's mouth opens in response, his lips shaping into unspoken words as his eyes flicker up and down the girl, still trying to make sense of her presence. Before he can even manage to speak, the girl's mouth curves into a beaming smile and jumps forward, throwing her arms around his chest and burrowing her face into his shoulder. Ethan takes a surprised step backwards to prevent himself from stumbling, his arms out at his sides, unwilling to reciprocate her embrace.

"Oh, Ethan," the girl says happily into his shoulder, "I knew you hadn't Faded yet!"

"O-Opal," the Husk finally manages to stutter, "y-you… ah–"

Opal instantly straightens, still keeping him trapped in her arms as she stares into his eyes. "You remember me!"

"O-Of course I do! But you… Why…?"

"How long has it been?" Opal muses, leaning in close to his face. "I missed you, Eth…"

Finally, it seems like Ethan regains some sense of himself, and he leans away from Opal gently, turning his head away from her. Opal pauses, appearing taken aback by his action, then slowly lets him go with a worried frown.

"Eth?" she asks quietly.

Ethan shakes his head. "Not… *here*, Opal. Please." Her shoulders sag upon hearing his response.

What a surprise that they have run into a being that Ethan knows. He never struck Kimberly as the type to have a girlfriend, although the two of them being a former couple is the only thing that can explain the strange scene. It also makes her wonder how they even met in the first place, let alone grow that close.

She takes it upon herself to step forward, which draws Opal's attention, and holds out her hand in greeting. "Hi there. I'm Kimberly, one of Ethan's friends."

Opal smiles back at her and shakes her hand, although Kimberly notices that the curve of her mouth seems slightly strained.

"And this is my boyfriend, Jake," Kimberly quickly adds, nodding to Jake behind her. He briefly waves to Opal with his free hand from where he stands. That makes her relax, her grin shifting into something more genuine and friendly.

"I didn't realize you were with him," Opal replies. "I'm Opal, Ethan's girlfriend."

Out of the corner of Kimberly's eye, she sees Ethan do his

best not to wince, although his face still scrunches up uncomfortably. Opal doesn't notice.

"He never mentioned having a girlfriend before," Kimberly hums aloud, turning to him with a questioning eyebrow raised.

"Oh?" Opal mutters, also turning to look at Ethan with a disappointed frown.

"It's been five centuries, Opal," he finally defends himself, "I don't think we're still… like *that* anymore."

Opal blinks once, then smiles and shakes her head, turning back to Kimberly. "We've been apart for a while, but I'm sure we can get back together." Once again, Ethan appears troubled by this statement. Opal doesn't notice this, either.

"Jovan said you were looking for a mountain guide?" Opal asks, steering the conversation away from Ethan for the moment.

"Yes, we are," Kimberly nods. "We're looking for a wizard by the name of Kelsy Skyshield and we think she's on–"

"Frostfall," Opal finishes in an instant. "I know her." Kimberly's heart leaps in her chest. She knows her mother! "She lives up in the mining town. But… why are you looking for her?"

"Ah–"

"Not here," Ethan interrupts Kimberly, nodding towards the packed seating area. While he has gone back to his usual flat scowl, it feels a little darker in tone than normal. "Can we take this somewhere more private?"

"Sure," Opal agrees in an instant.

***

Opal guides the group out of Varenguard and into the thick forest of Gardall. She walks with a small spring in her step, almost as if she were about to break into a merry skip at any moment, though she does her best not to get too ahead of Ethan. The Husk, however, tries not to stride by her side as much as possible.

"So," Opal asks over her shoulder, "why are you all looking for Kelsy Skyshield?"

"She's my mother," Kimberly replies honestly.

Opal looks at Kimberly with wide eyes full of surprise. "Oh! She never mentioned she had a daughter."

The remark stabs at Kimberly's heart, her hope wavering. Kelsy never brought up the fact she has a daughter? She isn't expecting her mother to even recognizer her after all these years, but if she doesn't remember her at all then the reunion will either be extremely awkward or completely nonexistent.

"How do you know her?" she asks Opal, wanting to move past those dim thoughts as fast as possible.

"I used to visit the miners all the time. I talked with her occasionally, though I wouldn't say we're friends. She's... kind of cold. No pun intended."

"Do you not visit them anymore?" Jake asks.

Opal shrugs. "It's more like I can't."

"Why?"

"It's a long story," she sighs. Suddenly, she sharply angles to the right and steps off the dirt path and into the trees. "My cabin is this way."

The three wizards share a glance between themselves before following behind. Opal lives pretty deep into the forest.

"If we're going up Frostfall, we'll need a few things," Opal says as they weave between the tall pines. "Do any of you have snow clothes?"

"No," Jake mutters. Kimberly shakes her head. Being a Pyromancer and Cryomancer respectively, neither of them should have to worry about getting too cold.

Ethan, too, shakes his head in response to Opal's question. "Don't need it."

Once Ethan finishes speaking, Opal promptly turns on her heel to face the three, a dark scowl plastered across her face.

"No. You'll need it. All of you."

"Why?" Kimberly asks her.

"Blizzards," is Opal's reply before turning back around.

Eventually, there's a break in the trees, and the group of wizards step into a small clearing, a log cabin sitting in its center. It's dark in the windows, and no smoke billows from the chimney. Opal, however, rushes towards the front door, retrieving a key from her jacket pocket. She fiddles with the lock as the others make their approach and disappears inside without waiting for them to catch up with her.

"Come on in!" she calls from within. "Let me grab the snow gear from the back."

One by one, the three enter the cabin. Although unlit by candle or fire, the light of the cycle that streams in through the windows is enough to let them see the front room clearly. A small kitchen area lines the back wall as a sofa sits in front of the empty fireplace to their left. The far leftmost wall has been reserved for a long bookcase, which is completely filled with all sorts of colored leather spines of different sizes.

But that's not to say that the room is tidy. Strewn about the floor are various pieces of paper covered in black ink. Dirty dishes are stacked high in the old wooden wash bin in the kitchen; it doesn't seem like the cabin has indoor plumbing like the homes of Asandra. Even though the fireplace is empty of logs, it's covered in a thick layer of ash, and one side of the sofa has been taken up by a rather large rucksack.

Ethan lets out a sigh of disappointment. "Five centuries and she still can't clean..."

"Girlfriend...?" Kimberly inquires, remembering what Opal had said in the inn earlier.

"She *used* to be my girlfriend," Ethan admits, "but we haven't seen each other for a long time. I thought she would have Faded already."

"When'd you two meet?" Jake asks.

"Ah…" Ethan shifts his weight and eyes the far side of the main room, where a dark doorway stands. If she listens closely, Kimberly can hear Opal rummaging around back there. Ethan turns to the other two and lowers his voice to a whisper, saying, "We met last time I attended ASM. The last time before… I met you guys."

"So… she doesn't know?" Kimberly asks him.

Ethan shakes his head. "I didn't want to put her in danger. But… I'd appreciate it if you don't tell her anyway."

"Why?"

"If she doesn't already know by now then it's none of her business."

Kimberly nods back at him slowly. Makes sense that he'd not want to tell Opal about Shadow. If she knows, she knows. After all, it's a little hard to avoid all of the buzz about the new resident Fragment Shadow back on Asandra. But it doesn't seem like she does, and so it's better to save the headache of explaining everything to her and simply let her continue believing Ethan is a regular wizard like the rest of them.

Ethan lets slip a thankful grin and readjusts his hat, standing as straight as he can. "Right. Blizzards. It might be from… *that thing* she has."

"She could be Blessed," Kimberly poses. She doesn't actually know if her mother might be Blessed like she is, but she'd not be surprised if she can also use Snow.

"Blessed or not, *it* could always be amplifying her magic as well," Ethan replies.

"Between me and Kim-Star, we shouldn't have much trouble navigating it," Jake says confidently. Ethan, however, doesn't seem convinced.

Opal then appears from the back of the cabin, her arms full of various objects. Coats and mittens, rucksacks, and ropes, to name a few. She carries them over to the sofa and tosses the pile down with a loud grunt. She pulls free the coats and mittens and holds them up to the others with a grin. "If you want me to take you three up Frostfall, you're going to need to wear these."

The coats and mittens are all white. Slowly, the three wizards step up to Opal and claim their set of snow gear. As Kimberly holds Opal's loaned coat in her hands, the white fabric shimmers before her very eyes and turns a light shade of icy blue. Her eyes widen, mildly impressed.

She slips on the coat and fumbles with the copper buttons. She usually doesn't like wearing coats. She doesn't even own a coat. Not having her arms exposed feels a little weird, but it's a necessary sacrifice to make if she wants to see her mother.

As she slips on the mittens, which go from white to navy blue as she holds them, she looks over at the boys. Jake's coat is a bright red – that will certainly make him hard to miss in the middle of a blizzard – which he has tied around his waist for the moment as he fumbles with the leather strap that holds his gold shoulder pads in place. Knowing him, he's going to strap them back on again over the coat once he puts it on. Ethan, on the other hand, is currently in the middle of buttoning his own coat, which had turned void black. It's hard to tell if the color is supposed to be a reflection of his Shadow magic or his Death magic.

"I would offer snowshoes," Opal says to Kimberly as she stares at the Cryomancer's heels, "but I don't have any spares."

"I'll be okay," Kimberly tries to assure her with a small smile. Opal, however, shakes her head.

"These aren't normal blizzards. But… you'll still have to make do with what you have, I guess." She turns to Ethan in an instant. "Do you need help with that, Eth?"

"No," he grumbles back from under his hat. Opal disregards his reply and steps up to him anyway, her hands outstretched at the ready.

"Here, let me–"

Ethan turns away from her sharply. “I said *no*.” He returns to his buttoning without another word. Opal stands frozen before him before lowering her hands and stepping away, appearing reluctant to leave him by himself.

“Hey Opal,” Kimberly speaks up, drawing her attention. She turns to face Kimberly, her expression crestfallen. Kimberly, however, nods to the rest of the equipment on the sofa. “Will we need to carry that stuff, too?”

Opal takes one look at the pile of equipment, then lets out a heavy sigh and nods, finally stepping away from Ethan. “Yes. Each rucksack has some basic survival gear in it in case… well, in case something goes wrong. I don’t expect anything to go wrong, but you never know. It’s happened before.

“There’s some dried fruit and water containers, extra rope and some fire packets for non-Pyromancers.” Opal opens up one of the rucksacks and retrieves what Kimberly suspects to be a fire packet, which, in her hands, appears to be nothing but a simple orange square. Opal holds up the fire packet for Kimberly and Jake to see. “Do you know how to use one of these?”

“No,” Kimberly replies, shaking her head. “I’ve never heard of a fire packet before.”

Opal musters a small smile of sympathy. “Fair. Fire packets don’t really have much of a use outside of survival kits, so usually you only find them here on Gardall, but I know they're around other places, too. It’s simple, really. You just take the packet and clap your hands together,” Opal places the packet in the center of her palm, then mimics clapping her hands together lightly so as to not unnecessarily trigger the packet, “and it should light a small fire. It doesn’t produce any heat so it won’t burn you, and it lasts a good long while if you shield it from water and snow. If you ever get separated or lost, just light one of these and hold it up as high as you can.

“And the rope…” Opal puts the fire packet back into the rucksack she got it from and grabs one of the ropes that she had carried out. She holds it up in front of her like she did the fire packet, a bright yellow-green twist. "When we get to Frostfall, we're going to tie ourselves together using these ropes, so when the blizzard hits, and I know it will, we'll be able to stay together." With that, Opal hands out the rucksacks and ropes. When she offers a set to Ethan, he takes them and steps away as fast as he can. She stands there staring at him, hurt, before busying herself with the rucksack that was on the sofa from when they first entered the cabin.

Jake nudges Kimberly's shoulder and whispers in her ear, "Stars, they're so awkward."

Kimberly lets out a small sigh in agreement. It sure is odd to see these two act so… *childish* around each other for their age.

"Be glad *we're* not like them," Kimberly says, mustering a small smile. Jake only chuckles and nods back.

***

The moment they see snow in the grass, Opal stops the hike and beams at her followers, "Ropes, every being!"

Ethan scowls as he twists to reach the rope that he tied to his rucksack, Kimberly and Jake doing the same. On one hand, he's glad to see Opal doing well. On the other… she just can't seem to take a hint.

"You should go in front of me," Jake says to Kimberly as the two help each other tie their bright yellow-green ropes around each other's waists. Kimberly just nods back at him wordlessly.

A small airy breath escapes Ethan's lips as he sets to work wrapping his own rope around himself. If not for this stars-forsaken coat adding to his layers he'd not feel so *bloated.* Moving his arms around is a chore.

{*Hehehe,*} Shadow chuckles lightly in his ear.

[*I thought I told you to keep quiet,*] Ethan chides through gritted teeth.

{*Electro is training. I don't want to disturb him.*}

Ethan rolls his eyes as he fumbles with his knot.

{*Have you really gotten over Opal?*} Shadow inquires. It knows much of Opal. For about a decade she was all he would ever talk about, though sometimes it was through no fault of his own. Shadow loved the drama. Judging from its inquisitive tone, it probably still does.

Ethan steals a glance at the Enchanter, who stands awkwardly off to the side, her rope already around her waist. She watches the others with folded arms, her eyes trying desperately hard not to glance in Ethan's direction. When her gaze does eventually meet Ethan's, her cheeks flare and she instantly turns back to the other two behind him.

Part of him feels like he was a little too hard towards her back at the cabin. Yet, at the same time, he doesn't feel like she deserves any apology.

[*I… don't know…*] he admits. [*I think I have?*] He waits for Shadow to speak, but the silence only grows louder. *Has* he gotten over Opal? He had no idea she was even still alive up until now. But seeing her here and talking to her again…

He blows a puff of air through his gritted teeth, a storm of emotion swirling in his hollow chest. Sometimes he hates his own feelings.

"Who should I tie myself to?" Kimberly asks Opal as Jake is wrapping the other end of his rope to his girlfriend's waist.

Looking to Opal for instruction as well, Ethan sees her blush for a mere moment as she replies, "Ethan. And then he should tie himself to me, since I'm the guide so I'll be going first."

While he's not surprised by her answer, it makes him feel awkward all the same as he approaches Kimberly so she can tie herself to him. As she works on her knot, Opal walks up to him and points to the rope around her waist.

“Make sure it’s tight,” she tells him, her mouth twitching furiously as she tries her best to keep back a wild smile. Ethan keeps his mouth pressed firmly closed as he does what she told him to do: tie a knot and make it tight.

When he finishes, the four wizards now stand in a chain.

“Ready?” Opal asks.

“Yep,” Jake calls from the back.

“Yes,” Kimberly chimes.

“Just go, Opie,” Ethan sighs. It takes him a moment to realize that he just said her old pet name aloud. As soon as he does, he slaps a hand over his mouth, tilting his head downwards to hide beneath the brim of his hat, feeling the heat of his face flaring in an instant.

{*Ahahaha!*} Shadow’s laughter rings in his ears.

Opal says nothing. Instead, she puts one foot forward, tugging on Ethan’s rope, indicating that it’s time to walk. He, too, steps forward, taking in a deep breath to try and bury his embarrassment. He didn’t mean to say it in front of Kimberly and Jake! Stars above, he must have sounded so stupid.

{*Opie…*} Shadow echoes, making Ethan wince, {*I forgot you called her that.*}

[*Stop,*] Ethan grumbles.

It doesn’t take them long to leave the green grass and forest behind as they finally enter the mountain proper. The snow sparkles all around them as they find themselves staring up a rather steep incline sparsely decorated with Evergreens and large boulders. The top of the mountain seems so far away from down here.

{*Almost like a painting,*} Shadow breathes in awe.

Ethan holds back his urge to nod, conscious of the others around him noticing the strange behavior. He’s only ever seen Frostfall a handful of times himself. The sight never ceases to impress him.

[*Maybe we can come stargazing one of these nights,*] he

suggests. The view must be spectacular from its peak, much better than the one from the castle back on Korodon or from the dunes of Mirage. Shadow lets out a happy gasp that makes his head buzz.

[*Electro's training, you said?*]

{*He didn't want to stay in and wait around all cycle.*} Shadow admits.

Ethan purses his lips as he stares at the snow under his feet. [*He shouldn't be overexerting himself just yet.*]

{*But Eth–*}

[*Calm down, it's not like I'm going to tell Azna. But* you *have to keep an eye on him to make sure he doesn't hurt himself.*]

A cold burst of irritation blossoms in Ethan's chest. {*He's doing fine.*}

[*Shadow–*]

{*I want to explore with you, too!*} Shadow complains. {*I didn't ask to go from being cooped up in that castle to being cooped up inside a being I don't belong to!*}

[*We can explore when we get this mess sorted out,*] Ethan promises gently. Shadow doesn't reply, its frustration still swirling within him.

***

The suddenness of the emotion makes Electro pause. "Is… something wrong?" he asks under his breath.

He feels Shadow swirl inside him, disturbed by his voice. {*Why?*}

Electro straightens his posture and wipes the sweat off his brow. "All of a sudden you got so… annoyed."

{*Ah…*} Shadow breathes back, {*I didn't think you'd…*} Discomfort rises in his gut, one that isn't his own. This feeling is much more cold in nature, detached from his actual body.

Electro brushes his hands together to wipe away the dirt that clings to his palms. He was done with his push-ups anyway.

It makes him glad to see that the training grounds haven't changed much while he was in his coma. Targets and cloth-stuffed dummies are set up around the square room, the iceglass ceiling letting in the natural light of the cycle. The gray stone walls box him in, with a doorway leading back outside on one end and another doorway leading to a battle arena on the other. There are other wizards around as well, some taking breaks on the benches set up at the edges of the room while others stand around playing with their magic. All in all, though, it's mostly quiet, just as it was in the past.

Electro made sure to pick a spot away from the other wizards if ever the need to converse with Shadow arose, much like now.

{*They made it to Frostfall,*} Shadow reports glumly.

"You don't make that sound like a good thing," Electro replies, taking a seat on the bench behind him. The frustration is replaced with an aching longing.

{*I want to be there, too,*} Shadow says with a sigh.

"So do I."

{*But Ethan said I have to watch you,*} it grumbles.

"Were you not?"

{*I was… watching him while you were doing your push-ups.*}

Electro withdraws a stick of arcane gold from his pocket and pops it into his mouth to appear more like he's taking a short break from exercising. Its sweet taste tingles his tongue as his teeth bite into the soft metal stick.

{*He doesn't want you to overexert yourself,*} Shadow adds.

Electro rolls his eyes. He knows he hasn't really supposed to be doing his regular regime right now, either. If it weren't for Shadow, he might have only been able to handle one or two push-ups at the most rather than his usual fifty. But, at the same time, he didn't want to sit around in Kimberly's home doing nothing whatsoever, and he's not gotten a whole lot of time to explore Asandra again until now, just to see what might be different from what he remembers.

He wants to be hiking up Frostfall right now, too, but he's not in that sort of physical condition. Not to mention that whatever happened all those years ago to have made Kelsy leave Asandra behind entirely... he doesn't want to cause her any needless distress, either.

"I hate to agree with him, but he's right," Electro replies. "I don't know how much I'll be able to do when I get my Shadow back."

{*You'll be okay,*} Shadow says.

"Not physically. Not for a long time."

{*What do you mean?*}

Electro looks down at his thin frame, disappointment and shame swelling in his heart. "I wouldn't say my body is in peak condition right now." He used to be so proud with how well he kept himself fit. Now the sight of himself is demoralizing. All that hard work gone to waste. How long will it take for him to regain all the physical strength he lost? Years? Decades? Centuries?

{*I don't get it,*} Shadow mutters.

"Look at all those wizards over there," he says, turning his attention to the others in the large room. It's pretty much all guys, mostly Pyromancers. Half of them have large biceps that glisten with sweat as their veins bulge from their physical workouts. Those that are practicing with their magic stand strong, immovable as they slowly wave their hands and arms through the air, directing their magic with ease and precision. "They've been coming here for years, training their hardest to strengthen their bodies and connect with their magic. Then look at me."

Shadow is silent, though Electro can sense its stare through his eyes, a small pinching sensation just behind his pupils. Then his left arm goes numb and he watches it rise before his face without his command, placed next to one of the toned Pyromancers nearby. Compared to the stranger, Electro's arm is thin with barely any muscle on it, let alone fat. The chill of Asandra's air is cold enough to make him shiver if he were to stand outside for any length of time, whereas eighteen years ago he was warm enough on his own to where he didn't mind the atmosphere.

{*You're very thin,*} Shadow finally speaks.

Electro lets out a huff and tries his best to play it off as a joke, even as his heart aches with regret. "I used to be like them. Toned. Physically strong. It'll take a long time to build back my old body."

{*Why?*}

"Muscle isn't something that you gain overnight. You have to work for it, putting your body through pain and soreness constantly as you teach it to strengthen itself."

{*But can't you just use… What do you call it, again? The magic that changes your hair color.*}

"Glamour?" Electro hums, twisting the stick of arcane in his mouth. "I *could*, but that's cheating. If I were ever asked to lift something heavy, the use of glamour would be quite apparent." He stands from the bench and turns to leave the training grounds. "I'm feeling up for a run."

He walks out of the training grounds, passing through the small front lobby as he goes, where a sleepy receptionist snoozed behind their desk. Before them is a small board with a sign-in sheet and quill. It must be nice to work at the training grounds, with what little traffic it usually sees and a roof over one's head to hide away from the bright light of the cycle outside.

He steps outside and breaks into a light jog, trotting down the cobblestone roads of Asandra. The buildings pass him by one by one as he weaves around other beings that travel alone or in small groups of threes or fours. The din of conversation hangs over the rooftops, a constant buzzing that never leaves the city, no matter the time.

It's comforting to know not much has changed over the last eighteen years. The streets are how he remembers, and so are most of the shops scattered about. The Straightway is just as chaotic as it had been with the constant churn of businesses and rotating store fronts.

But once again his thoughts stray to his two old friends. Despite his feelings, he can't help but wonder what they're both doing now. Did they ever try to save him back then? Have they forgotten about him by now? Will he get to see them again?

{*You think about them a lot,*} Shadow idly comments. Though it realizes its mistake as Electro's brow furrows, sending a ripple of unease through Electro's gut. Its cold presence lifts from his mind once more. He didn't even realize it was there.

"I do…" Electro just sighs back quietly.

{*Were you all close?*}

"Of course we were," Electro replies, trying to mask his words with his breaths. "Me and Ryan sparred and Kelsy helped me with my midterm projects. Ryan and Kel liked to talk about books since both of them were history nuts, too."

Indeed, they made a great trio, despite Ryan's reputation. Electro personally never cared what Ryan did at school. At least, he didn't care about it all back *then*. But he's come to regret ignoring the warning signs and rumors, and he took them seriously way too late.

It felt like there was something new about Ryan every cycle. Time spent after school in the training grounds waiting for Ryan's arrival, he would hear it *all*. Blackmail, manipulation, cheating – on both tests *and* girls – and even outright bullying. Ryan made a better Illusionist than he did a Pyromancer, a comment he heard too many times to count. But Electro never saw any of it first hand, so he hadn't believed a word. He even stood up for Ryan more often than not, getting into fights on his behalf. That was, right up until Ryan crossed the line. *Hard*.

He could forgive the crazy antics when they were all in school. It's not like Electro was very well behaved back then, either. He was always looking for fights and Ryan practically delivered them to him. For four years, two immature guys were feeding each other's bad habits. If it weren't for Kelsy, Electro believes that it would have been a struggle to bring himself under control.

He thought cutting ties with Ryan was going to be easy. Threaten him to stay away and never see that Voidterror ever again. But oh how wrong he was. One cannot simply be rid of Ryan like that, he soon found out. And look at what's happened since then! At the very least, even though she also possesses a Shard, he hopes that Kelsy has been able to protect herself from him...

Chapter 7

The four wizards continue their trek up the mountain in relative silence, the only noise to keep them company being the crunch of the snow underneath their feet.

Jake almost feels bad for Kimberly and Ethan, who trudge through the snow in her heels and his plain shoes, while Jake and Opal wear boots of their own. Yet Kimberly continues on as if nothing is wrong and Ethan stares up at the sky aimlessly, seemingly bothered by a million other things.

He holds his sword tight in his hand but keeps it pointed at the ground, letting the tip leave a thin line in the pristine whiteness next to their bootprints.

The farther up the slope they go, the colder it grows, colder than Jake's magic can keep him warm. Opal was right to force them all to wear these puffy jackets. Then again, she's been going up and down this mountain for stars know how long; she might know more about this mountain than even Ethan!

"Boulder!" Opal calls from the front, the first word spoken in a long, long time. Sure enough, right in their path ahead sits a snowed over boulder, a large bulge of gray rock sticking out of the mountain slope. All around it, snow has piled up, creating a steep incline all around its sides. Looking a little farther up reveals even more large, semi-buried boulders.

"Stay close to the boulders," Opal advises. "We can use these as shields from the blizzard."

The other three wizards nod back at their guide. Right, the blizzard. Jake almost forgot about that, with how clear and uneventful the path up until now has been. How much farther will they get before the blizzard appears?

The group continues forward carefully, staying as close to the first boulder as they can without needing to crawl up the snow on their hands and knees. Jake uses his sword for extra support, plunging it into the snow and pushing himself up off of it every couple of steps. The snow is certainly *deep* here, enough to nearly reach his hilt if he presses with too much force.

They wind their way up the slope, one long step after the other. One might think that this sort of exercise would keep them somewhat warm in the middle of all this cold, but not this time. Every time Jake raises his leg, he feels his balance pitch, causing him to wobble. Each new step, the cold only sinks into his bones even more, trying to ice them over.

Still, he grits his teeth and presses onward.

When they pass their third boulder, from the clear sky above falls a flurry of snowflakes that sparkle in the light of the cycle. Jake looks up at the little flakes with wide eyes of awe. His heart flutters warmly as he turns to Kimberly and asks, "Kim, are you doing this?"

Kimberly turns her head to look at him, her expression that of mild distress. "No…"

The warmth quickly fades after that.

"Looks like it's starting," Opal says to the group. "Stay as close to each other as you can, and *don't* untie your ropes."

Once more, the three of them nod back at her in confirmation.

Perfect.

Jake shuffles up to Kimberly as best he can, placing his

free hand firmly on her shoulder. She might see it as a comforting gesture. He, however, uses her as his anchor to keep himself upright.

At the next boulder, the snowflakes seem to pick up in frequency, starting to stick to Jake's hair and make his head bristle with their icy cold pinpricks. Not even the internal heat of his magic is enough to melt them as they land. Could it be that these snowflakes are being sustained by magic? Or maybe it's so cold that nothing he can do can affect the falling snow?

The sky slowly darkens above them as they trudge onward, the glittering flakes of ice dimming into a blanket of white mist as the wind slowly but surely picks up speed. Jake grits his teeth even more as he pushes himself forward, his grip tightening on Kimberly with each step he takes. Kimberly's head turns each time as she casts him worried glances, but she remains quiet. For now, anyway.

The falling flakes of magical glitter quickly turn into a gale of thick, white chunks of snow hurtling themselves at the travelers' faces. They use the new boulders they come upon as windbreaks, providing mild shelter from the intense wind and tiny, whirling snowballs. But the cold still lingers in the air, a deathly chill that makes Jake's cheeks and nose sting. He can hardly see anything as his vision slowly blurs, and simply holding onto Kimberly's shoulder isn't helping his balance anymore.

He draws himself even closer to Kimberly, wrapping his free arm around her in an awkward half-hug, still using his sword like a makeshift cane.

"Jake, are you alright?" Kimberly asks him, her voice muffled in his ear.

"Yeah, just… a little unsteady," Jake replies.

"Well, I can't walk if you're wrapped around me like this…"

"Sorry."

Jake reluctantly lets her go, returning to walking by himself with his sword as his only assistance.

Opal eventually leads them to a pair of boulders with a small pathway leading between them, a good spot to get a brief moment of rest in this cold and dreary mess. One by one, they all squeeze into the tight space between the large gray stones.

"How are we all doing?" Opal calls over the wind.

Ethan is silent but holds up a thumbs-up, his face masked by the brim of his hat. Kimberly, too, gives a thumbs-up, before turning to Jake with a troubled frown.

"One…" Jake mutters, holding up a single finger. He kneels in the snow, his breathing heavy and vision swimming. Kimberly puts a hand on his shoulder to steady him as his upper body sways uncontrollably.

"Jake?" she says.

He shakes his head sharply and tries to put on a brave face. "Just… out of breath…"

Never has he felt this light-headed before as the cold continues to nip his body. He closes his eyes to try and collect himself, and he's instead hit with a wave of tired relief. The cold becomes a numb blanket as his muscles unwind in an instant, preparing for rest. The snow underneath his heavy body feels so soft. Will the others mind if he laid down for a quick spell…?

Heavy hands are placed on his back and shake him back and forth, doing little to break him from his stupor.

"*Jake*?!"

The call sounds so far away, muddled to the point he doesn't know who said it. All he can hear is the soft whistle of the wind as his mind slowly drifts from reality.

Then, out of nowhere, a sharp sting bites his cheek, and his head is snapped to the left. Finally, he manages to open his eyes once again, although the blizzard rages on in a blurry mess. Turning back to his friends, he finds Kimberly kneeling at his side, her mouth agape with horror. Ethan's dark figure looms over them with intense determination.

"Get yourself together!" Ethan barks. "We're halfway

there!"

"Maybe we should go back..." Opal suggests behind him, her voice masked by the howling gale.

Ethan shakes his head. "We need to keep going, Opal. This is too important to give up on!" He bends down and yanks Jake to his feet, throwing one of Jake's arms over his shoulders. Jake stumbles on unsteady feet but manages to raise his head just enough to see the path in front of him. Kimberly also stands, brushing the snow off her clothes and taking Jake's other arm, offering additional support.

Opal gives the three wizards a look of confusion and worry, but she doesn't voice any objection. Instead, she turns back around and starts off once more, the other three trudging along as fast as they can.

Each step Jake takes makes his legs wobble, and he is only able to remain upright with the help of his friend and his girlfriend. The snow batters his face, some of it landing on his sore cheek and making it flare in pain before melting away. Deep down, he hopes never to experience this level of cold again in his life.

"Kim, can you redirect some of this snow?" Ethan asks.

"I can try," Kimberly replies. She raises her free hand in a protective motion, her fingers glowing with a soft silver light. Slowly, the snow that attacks the group shoots around them instead, being redirected by unseen wind. It's not a very large bubble of calmness, but it works for now.

But even with the snow being redirected around the three of them, the same benefit isn't given to Opal. She continues to trudge on only a few feet beyond them, with only the faintest flash of orange from her snow clothes being visible through the white storm. Every now and then Ethan's rope goes taut, tugging him forward sharply, causing him to pull back on it to get her to slow down. Sometimes her face appears in the snow, one that's quietly frustrated whenever Jake's vision decides to clear, an eerie sight to behold. It's obvious that she wants to move faster, but if Jake were to try he'd probably fall face-first into the snow and never want to get up again.

His mind wanders in and out of lucidity.

He doesn't know how or why, if he hallucinated or if he somehow passed out in the middle of walking, but at some point during this last leg of their hike he thinks he hears the warm laughter of young children and smells something warm and dusty. Phantom energy pulses through his body, the type of a young boy let loose on the world, running freely wherever he wishes, and his fingers tingle as if they're dipped into something comfortingly warm. He wants to look around but can't, finding his head too heavy to carry out his commands. But when he finally manages to break from the spell, when he can bring himself to look up once more, the sensations quickly fade back into the coldness of the blizzard.

"H-How much f-f-farther," Kimberly asks, her voice quivering with cold. As she turns to look at Ethan, Jake can see that her nose and cheeks are as bright red as they can possibly get, and her lips are shivering. Even a Cryomancer like her has limits.

"I don't know…" Ethan replies, his voice deep and small so as not to let the cold wind enter his body.

But their worries are dispelled when Opal's voice manages to break through the chaos with an excited, "Just a little farther! We're close now!"

Jake sucks a cold breath through his teeth, making them tingle uncomfortably and his lungs hurt, but he doesn't care. With all his willpower, he forces his body upright and his legs to stiffen, propelling himself and his friends forward. If their destination is just up ahead, it's worth using the last of his strength to get themselves out of this storm faster.

Finally, like magic, the three step out of the raging blizzard and into a strange, snowless calm, where the light of the cycle once more shines down upon them and the only wind that howls is that of the blizzard behind them, a massive wall of thick, gray, swirling snow.

Kimberly's hand drops tiredly as she lets out a thankful sigh, no longer needing to hold the snow at bay. Ethan, too, lets a small smile of relief slip across his face.

Not too far away from the edge of the blizzard is a tall snow-covered gate, flanked on either side by a sturdy wooden wall. Thin gray wisps of smoke rise from beyond the gate, a sign of life and warmth, and the rest of their path is lined with small stacks of stones set up as markers, each one waving at them with little lengths of tattered red fabric. With Jake's swimming vision, sometimes these markers appear as little gray lumps in the snow with bright red tongues.

The four reach the gate. Kimberly is shivering from head to toe now, a shudder that she sends through Jake and into Ethan on the other side. Ethan is silent, his lips pressed together and his eyes downcast, lost in his own thoughts.

Opal bangs on the gate with both her fists.

"Who goes there?" a booming voice asks from the wall above them, although from this angle they cannot see what being may be up there.

"Espin, is that you?" Opal calls back. "It's Opal! Remember me? I know it's been a while since I've visited–"

"Opal!" the voice replies suddenly, sounding surprised. "Friend of Ulka and Sister Skyshield."

"Yup, that's me! I see you're still a little slow."

The being Opal called Espin lets out a snort of irritation. "One cannot be too cautious. I hope your trek wasn't hindered too much by the snow. What beings have you brought with you this time?"

"These are friends looking for Sister Skyshield. Although they're a little cold right now. Can you ask Ulka if she can let them warm up at her cabin?"

“I may be slow to recall a face, but not Ulka’s rage. Did she not throw you out last time?”

Opal smiles sheepishly up at the sky. “That was a decade ago! Surely she’d have forgiven me by now. Or maybe the Sister is free for them to use her cabin instead?”

“Sister Skyshield is down in the mines right now, so her cabin is empty,” Espin replies. “I will talk to Ulka, and if Ulka refuses then I will have to turn you and your friends away for this cycle.”

Heavy footsteps follow the voice’s final verdict as Espin descends from the wall. Opal turns to the other three behind her with an apologetic expression.

“Sorry, I kind of forgot about that,” she admits.

“W-What’s going on?” Kimberly asks through her chattering teeth.

“In order to get into the village, one of the villagers has to sponsor you,” Opal explains. “And last time I *might* have gotten my sponsor a little angry with me. But I’m sure she’ll have forgiven me by now.”

“And if she hasn’t?” Ethan inquires.

“Then you three might not be seeing Kelsy this cycle. Or… ever, for that matter.”

“Can’t we ask another being to sponsor us?”

Opal shakes her head. “If it were only that simple, Eth. The Yafiir are stubborn with their traditions.”

“I-I-I can’t walk b-back down l-l-like th-this,” Kimberly stutters. Jake wants to nod in agreement, but moving his head even slightly results in a wave of dizziness overtaking him. He doubts he’ll be able to make it back down the mountain in this state. Not by foot, and probably not conscious, either.

A long moment passes as the group, cold and tired, stand huddled together in front of the gate. Then, suddenly, a low groan emanates from the mass of wood as it’s pulled slowly backwards, revealing the inside of the walled town. As the crack grows, the group sees two Yafiir staring back at them, one with brown fur covered in glistening white snow and silver armor and the other wrapped in a long woven cloth of purple and gold.

"Stars above, Opal," the clothed Yafiir cries, throwing her paws up in the air, "why must you always show up with beings in need?"

"Sorry, Ulka," Opal replies, though her grin doesn't convey her apology very well.

Ulka shakes her head with a heavy sigh and shuffles forward, staring up at the wizards with a hard scowl as she inspects each one. She gives Opal and Ethan a quick glance, though with the two of them showing no obvious signs of distress she moves swiftly on to Kimberly and Jake. Her beady black eyes flicker once over Kimberly's shivering form and gives her a single nod. When she turns to Jake, pity gleams in her gaze.

"My poor boy," Ulka mutters, reaching out for him. She touches his chest with one of her paws and a bloom of warmth seeps its way through his puffy jacket and shirt, kissing his cold skin. Jake is able to collect himself, his exhaustion lightening the longer she presses.

"Ah…" he manages to sigh thankfully.

"Come," Ulka finally says, lifting her paw and turning away from the group, gesturing for them to follow her. "I have a spare bed and some soup."

"T-T-Thank you," Kimberly stutters.

"Are you sure this is a good idea, Ulka?" Espin inquires. "After last time–"

"I'm aware, Espin. I will be cautious."

Stepping through the gate, Opal gives Espin a small wave but keeps her mouth pressed shut, nervousness in her eyes, with Jake, Kimberly, and Ethan staggering after her. The buildings of the mining town are not nearly as tightly packed together as Varenguard. A handful of Yafiir are out strolling around, and as the strange group pass them by they pause to stare. Jake, being half-conscious already, doesn't mind the staring, for all he sees are blurry figures and bright colors in the distance.

As they are led to Ulka's home, Jake's attention slips once more, and again, like before in the blizzard, he can hear youthful laughter and phantom warmth spread across his body. His legs begin to ache as if he had been running. A distant voice calls out to him, the noise echoing in his ears. The white-gray of the snow-covered cobblestone street takes on an orange hue as his head hangs and vision swims, becoming grainy. His legs beg for rest as he heaves in and out, trying to catch his breath. He didn't even realize he was breathless to begin with, or maybe it's all in his head. At this point it's hard for him to tell. Something dry and scratchy tickles his nose. He feels pressure on his body pushing him downward, and he finds himself lying on top of an orange mound.

It's okay, a childlike voice whispers. *You can rest now.*

With a heavy sigh of relief, his eyes finally close, bringing Jake into a world of darkness…

***

Kimberly huddles next to the hearth, holding the bowl of soup as close to her as possible, letting the steam paint her face as she breathes in its delicious aroma. Never has she felt this cold before, and part of her hopes never to feel this way again. Whatever magic they encountered on their hike, she's lucky that she wasn't as severely affected as Jake.

She lifts her head to look across the large room to where her boyfriend lies. His shoulder pads, jacket, rope, and boots have been removed, his body now wrapped in a large blanket with only his head remaining visible as he rests atop a leather cot. His lips were starting to turn blue by the time they got to Ulka's home. Ethan stands over Jake, one hand to the

Pyromancer's forehead and his face full of concentration. Behind Kimberly, in a small cooking area, Ulka is preparing more bowls of soup to be passed out to the wizards who are still awake.

The roof is held up by four massive wooden pillars, where the smoke of the central hearth escapes somewhere above, with each space separated by rugs, fabrics, or carved wooden dividers. The wooden floor is covered in hand-woven carpet, with most of the remaining decor and furniture made from painted wood and sculpted metal. Each item is its own masterpiece, no two things alike in any way besides their usage.

"Do you want a bowl, Ethan?" Opal calls as she holds one in her hands.

"No," he replies flatly, his gaze fixed on the slumbering Jake.

"But Eth–" Opal starts, only to be interrupted by Ulka shaking her head back at the mountain guide.

"Go warm yourself, Opal," the Yafiir hums, nudging Opal towards the hearth. With a reluctant sigh, the Enchanter plops down on one of the cushions next to Kimberly.

"How is he?" Kimberly asks.

"Resting," is the reply from the distant Spiritist. "He got… extremely cold."

Kimberly takes a sip of soup, which tastes mostly of warm water with just a hint of spice to it. Mysterious food bits stir in the broth, but Kimberly isn't in the sort of mood to ask what it all might be. Poor Jake. He's been through so much already…

Her gaze darts to Opal next to her and notes that it doesn't seem like she's touched her soup at all since sitting down, her gaze to her lap and her lips pressed tightly together. Tension hangs in the air, somewhat distant but still present.

Ulka wanders over to the hearth as well and folds her furry arms, her eyes reflecting the red flames before her. After a tense moment, she finally turns to Opal.

"Well, now," the Yafiir says, "I never thought to see you

here again."

"Yeah," Opal replies nonchalantly.

"Why have you returned?"

The mountain guide nods towards Kimberly. "Apparently she's the daughter of Sister Skyshield, and they asked me to bring them here to meet her."

Ulka's lips part just enough to flash her fangs. "Them I'm willing to let stay. However, unless you have something to say for yourself, *Shard Hunter*, I'd rather you leave once your meal is over."

"I know."

Kimberly frowns, despite feeling rocked to her core by Ulka's sharp demand. Shard Hunter? *Opal*? No... Is *this* why Ulka is so frustrated by her mere presence? Does she know that the Shard is in Kelsy's possession?

And here the Enchanter sits, completely unconcerned by the beings around her. *Indifferent*.

Ulka inhales, turning her gaze to Kimberly. "Sister Skyshield is in the mines this cycle, and she won't be back until nightfall. I'm willing to allow you three to stay until then."

"We don't have that sort of time," Kimberly replies in a heartbeat. "Can we go see her in the mines?"

"The mines are strictly off-limits to guests," Ulka responds.

"But–"

But Ulka raises her paw to silence the Cryomancer. "I don't write the rules, child. You're better off waiting for her to return."

"What if I went with her?" Ethan pipes up.

"It applies to you as well," the Yafiir sighs. But Ethan isn't unfazed by the answer. He steps away from Jake's cot and approaches Ulka, motioning to her that he wished to whisper something in her ear. It doesn't take long for Ethan to change Ulka's entire demeanor. Her fur bristles as her eyes widen with shock.

No doubt Ethan played his ace. It's one thing for him to break the rules as any ordinary being foreign to the island. It's another thing if he were a Fragment Shadow. The news of Ethan's existence must be much more slow-spreading beyond Asandra, contrary to Kimberly's first assumptions.

"Impossible," Ulka breathes at last as he pulls away from her.

"I'll even swear to Kimberly's safety," Ethan adds. "She's already here under my name."

Ulka stares at the Husk in silence, her eyes now drinking in his presence before her as he gazes back with determination etched onto his face. If him being a Fragment Shadow doesn't get them into the mines, then their trip here might as well have been for naught.

Finally, the Yafiir nods. "I can bring you two to the entrance, but it's up to the guards to grant you entry. But *only* you two." She shoots a glare in Opal's direction, who continues to eat her soup silently. "Don't worry about your friend over there. I've cared for beings in much worse conditions before. He should be ready to travel back down Frostfall by the time you return."

Quickly setting her soup bowl to one side, Kimberly springs to her feet, her heart fluttering with renewed hope. "Thank you!"

The Yafiir casts Kimberly a slightly skeptical glance. "Are you sure you want to leave right now?"

"Yes!" Kimberly nods back. "Yes, please!"

Her eagerness puts a rare smile onto Ethan's face as he only nods in agreement with her sentiments. "The sooner we can speak with Kelsy, the better."

Chapter 8

It's odd traversing the vast Mirage desert on a swirling mass of vines, but since Amber's not a Creationist she can't make a sandboard, and if she can't make a sandboard then the vines are a lot better than walking.

Even though the sun isn't at its peak yet, Blaze's brow is red and covered with sweat despite the rush of cool air battering their bodies as he stands and directs the mass of plant matter. Maybe it's because of his magic use. Amber doesn't really know.

She *also* doesn't know why Ethan had to ask him to come along with her. Why would a Naturist need a reason to "get out"? Why *him* of all beings?

From where she sits, she looks out at the ocean of sand all around her. Everything looks the same; it makes her scared that they're going the wrong way. At this speed, they can afford to get a little lost, but if they don't find town soon, they could be stranded on Mirage for longer than either of them would like to be here for.

"So, what's going on?" Blaze asks over the rush of the wind and the rumble of the vines.

"Ethan didn't tell you?" Amber replies somewhat brashly.

"No," Blaze answers.

Amber lets out a long sigh. “All you need to know is that we’re looking for a being called Ryan Ashblade.”

“Alright…” She can feel a heated stare land on the back of her head. As far as she’s concerned, he doesn’t need the full story. He wasn’t there this time. Besides him accompanying her on this short journey, he’s not involved in this situation at all.

Then again, neither is she if she really thinks about it.

The two continue in tense silence a little longer before the the vines start to slow.

“There’s something ahead,” Blaze announces. Bit by bit, the two of them are slowly lowered to the ground, the green vines retreating back into the desert sand. The Naturist lets out a thankful sigh as he wipes his brow with his arm and the Healer gets to her feet. The grains of sand begin to seep into her shoes as they sink into the dune. She rubs them between her toes, both a comforting and irritating sensation.

Out of the corner of her eye, she sees Blaze begin to scale the dune. Not wanting to be left behind, she follows after him. When they reach its crest, she finally sees what he was talking about.

Below them is the flat plane of sand that rings the little town of the Serperas, from which they never venture. Or, at least, that’s the rule. But there’s no guarantee that Lukri will be in the town; being the crown prince of Mirage, he’d most likely be at the palace, wherever that may be, and they'll need to figure out how to get there if that's the case.

But it appears like something else is going on this cycle, and that mysterious something is what makes her hesitant to start the trek to the collection of small sandstone buildings. There’s a scattering of Serperas across the flat plane, waving their arms in the air to create and maintain strange patterns with the sand. Two stand near a collection of smaller dunes, little bumps in the sand that rise and fall as if the land itself were breathing. Six raise the orange-yellow grains in a grand ‘U’ shape. Another three farther down have cleared space for a pit, with the only way to pass the pit, aside from simply going around it, being a thin pathway cutting through its center. On and on, these strange constructions stretch.

"This is the town, right?" Blaze asks.

"It is…" Amber replies in an amazed mutter.

"Well, then, let's get going." He starts to stand up, but Amber is quick to grab his wrist and pull him back down. "H-Hey!"

"*Shh*!" she replies. "We *technically* shouldn't be here. Stars only know what's going to happen to us if we're seen!"

"And you tell me this *now*?" he hisses.

"Well, I wasn't expecting *this*," Amber replies, gesturing to the stationed Serperas below.

"What are they even doing?"

"I don't know!"

"Didn't you stay on Mirage for a couple cycles?"

"That doesn't make me an expert on the Serperas," Amber replies with a very exaggerated eye roll. Blaze lets out an incoherent grumble in response.

The atmosphere is silent yet electrified with excitement and anticipation. But *what* are they anticipating? *What* are they supposed to be excited for? How long will she and Blaze be stuck hiding on this dune for until the Serperas return to their homes?

Then, without warning, a large cloud of sand rises up over the town on its far side, almost directly opposite where the wizards lay in the warm dune, along with distant cheers.

Emerging from behind the town is a collection of sandboard-riding Serperas, all of them appearing to be about the same age, if not slightly older, than Amber herself. As the group come upon the different sandy constructions that ring the town, it finally dawns on her what's going on: it's a race!

The racers reach the breathing bumps. Some struggle to

follow the flow of the sand, being flung high into the air as the hills rise beneath them or stall out as the hills sink into deep ditches. But even those keeping up with the rises and falls are having difficulty maintaining their speed with each shift in the terrain. How any of them are able to remain upright on their boards is a complete mystery.

One Serperas stands out from the rest, however. Emerald eyes wide with eagerness and energy, Lukri weaves in and out of his fellow racers with exceptional skill, coming out the other side of the rather interesting obstacle among the top five racers. Though Amber notes the absence of his white sash, the one he had been wearing when they first met. If he hadn't been wearing similar, if not the same, clothes, she might have mistook him for just another Serperas having fun.

The racers come around the bend, passing the dune where Amber and Blaze are perched, heading to the next obstacle in their way. Acting on impulse, Amber begins to shimmy back down the dune.

"Wha– Hey! Where are you going?" Blaze exclaims.

"I'm going to follow them," Amber replies, already bouncing on her toes. If Lukri's racing, she wants to try and find the finish line. Granted, she'll probably make it there long after the race is over, but she doesn't care.

Running through the sand is insanely difficult as the grains attempt to suck Amber into their warm, rough embrace. Each lift of her leg takes considerably more effort with each step. Behind her, she hears Blaze release a heavy sigh, and in an instant she's swept off her feet by yet another mass of shifting vines. They wrap around her waist and arms, shifting in and out of the weave as she's lifted into the air and across the desert once more.

"You could have just asked," Blaze grumbles next to her, sweat returning to his brow. But his attention is trained on the racecourse as he guides the two of them around the plain of sand.

Craning her neck, Amber can make out the heads of the racing Serperas lagging behind as they duck and weave through a forest of orange pillars, then make their way around tight bends. But they quickly leave these Serperas behind as they come upon the middle group of racers as they try all they can to catch up to those far, far ahead of them. Much to her joy, Lukri isn't part of this crowd.

"Can't you make us go any faster?" Amber inquires. At the rate they're going, they won't make it to the other end of the plain before the race is over. If they don't catch Lukri now, stars only know how much longer it'll take for them to get to him. That, and she *really* wants to see who will win.

Blaze scowls at her question, though more out of concern than thoughtfulness. He doesn't seem to like the idea of going faster very much.

"Fine," he eventually growls, and with that single utterance Amber feels a lurch in her stomach as the wind's howl in her ears increases. The Naturist turns back to the race once more, but not before Amber is able to catch a hint of strain flash across his face.

Her worry lingers for but a brief moment. How could it not? Despite her disdain towards him, she's still a Healer, and she doesn't want to cause any being more pain than they need. But this is also Blaze she's talking about. He can take care of himself.

Finally, they reach the leading group of racers, each one vying for first place with determination and aggressiveness. Their eyes are locked on the racecourse and whatever opponent is ahead of them. Though, out of all of them, only Lukri is beaming from ear to ear.

She suppresses the urge to call out to him. As much as she wants to cheer him on, she doesn't want to distract him from the race. Honestly, the surprise of her even being here might as well be enough to make him fall off his board if she makes so much as a peep. So she bites her tongue and lets her enthusiasm boil in her gut.

This is exactly what she wanted to feel again. Not necessarily the enthusiasm, but the *thrill*. With Riona, the thrill didn't come until the very end of the adventure, when she and Lukri burst from the bowels of the castle. Her heart leaps as she thinks back to that moment. How exciting it all finally felt, how her body shook with adrenaline as she fended off the darkness, how her magic flowed as Lukri drew upon it for the last hurrah. It had been so tense; if he had missed, or somehow his magic didn't pierce Riona's dark veil, then it all would have been over. Right now she can feel that very same tenseness, albeit to a smaller degree from life-or-death, as she merely spectates such a tight race between Lukri and the other four competitors alongside him.

They jump and swerve in a delicate passing game, each racer having their brief taste of being in the lead. These five are certainly in their element as they pass each new obstacle with so much grace that Amber can't even tell if there *are* any obstacles in their way. Their heads each bounce up and down over the dunes that separate them from the two wizards on the other side as they leap into the air. Each time, Amber's heart jumps into her throat. When it's Lukri, she wonders – *hopes* – that he'll notice them. When it's the other racers, she worries about being seen.

Cheers in the distance slowly grow the farther they travel. They must be nearing the finish line.

The closer they draw, the lower the vines start to hang. Amber's shoes skim the sands as her speed slows, and she comes to a stumbling halt as the vines eventually release her from their grasp.

"Go on…" Blaze grunts. Amber turns to see him staggering forward unsteadily, his face bright red and shimmering. His chest puffs in and out with his heavy breaths. One hand is shoved into the nearby dune in an effort to support himself, the other across his chest and glowing with green energy.

He's injured? How? Amber can't help but wonder.

Her eyes and thoughts don't linger on Blaze for very long, though, as her excitement wells up once more, distracting her. She works her way across the sand as fast as she can, getting ever closer to the dull chatter of the crowd.

It's hard to tell how close she is to the gathering of Serperas with how little they converse. With a small sigh, she picks a dune to climb and crawls her way up its side. Poking her head over its crest, she sees the Serperas surround the young racers. Even though they're all beaming as wide as can be, it's almost unnerving how their mouths hardly ever move as they celebrate.

The winner of the race has been lifted up into the air by a mass of hands, being taken away from the finish line and deeper into the town in celebration. But she still spots Lukri nearby, surrounded by a small gathering of his own, being patted on his back as he converses with the adults and some of his fellow racers.

She was expecting him to look a little more frustrated. He was in the leading group the entire race; no doubt he must have been close to coming in first, right? Maybe he came in second or third instead? She can't wait to ask him.

So entranced by the Serperas and especially Lukri, it doesn't register to her that she could still be seen from where she observes. That is, until she notices one of the Serperas raise a hand, gesturing quite clearly in her direction, their eyes wide with surprise.

Heads quickly turn as Amber's heart squeezes with fear, and she promptly dips below the dune once more. They must have noticed her bright pink hair. On the other side of the dune, a small commotion begins to rise from the gathering of townsfolk.

She looks around for Blaze, but he's nowhere to be seen.

How far away is he? How much longer will it take him to recover from… whatever he's recovering from? If a fight were to break out, she doesn't have the magic to defend herself! That is, if things escalate to that point.

"*Amber*?"

The sound of her name makes her jump with a panicked shriek, falling from the dune's slope and landing in the trough below. Lukri is staring at her from the dune's peak, both bewilderment and relief clearly written across his face. The two stare at each other in silence.

"Hi," Amber manages to breath through her shock, her heart still beating as fast as it possibly can. Lukri's mouth hangs open, his lips forming soundless shapes as he struggles to find his words.

"Well?" a shout from below calls.

In an instant, Lukri spins around and assures the crowd with clear annunciation, "It's okay! It's just a friend."

Amber picks herself up from the sand as Lukri crosses the dune's crest and dashes down to her with a wide smile.

"Sorry," she says with a thin smile. "Some race that was, huh?"

"You saw?" Lukri breathes.

"A little. What place did you finish in?"

The young prince beams with pride as he announces to her, "Fourth!"

"Fourth?" she echoes in disbelief. How on Astria did he come in fourth place? He deserves to be in the top three!

Lukri nods. "Fourth is really good for me. I was expecting to be sixth."

"But you practice, don't you?"

"Not like them," he replies, shaking his head disappointingly. "This is my first race."

"Oh." Amber still smiles and claps her hands together, golden sparkles bursting from her fingers with joy. If he's happy with how he finished, then she's happy for him, too. "Well, congratulations!"

"Thank you!" Lukri beams, but his smile quickly turns to a confused frown. "Why are you here?"

"We need your help with something," Amber replies. "I can explain everything on the–"

"I can't," Lukri interrupts her. As much as he appears excited for another adventure with his wizard friend, he shakes his head with reluctance. "I'm–"

"Lukri! Get away from that wizard this *instant*!" a sharp demand rings out from the dune above. The gold circlet sitting atop this Serperas' head makes Amber's breath catch in her throat, though the lavish white dress, long green fabric draped over her chest and arms, and the water pellet embroidered belt strongly confirms this Serperas' identity. She didn't notice that the *queen of Mirage* was present at the race as well!

Flanking the queen are eight guards, four on each side. Four have bows drawn with the others brandishing long silver spears.

"Sorry," Lukri mutters as he slowly steps away from Amber, though he keeps his back to his mother as he walks halfway up the dune.

"I won't let you steal my son away for a second time," the queen says to Amber, her eyes ablaze with anger.

Amber is completely at a loss for words. Ethan dealt with the queen the last time she appeared, though they also benefited from facing her from behind a sturdy metal gate. Amber, however, doesn't have the sort of courage Ethan does. With nothing standing between her and the angry queen's guards, she switches into survival mode.

Behind the guards, other Serperas peer over the dune to see what's going on, their curiosities piqued. The pressure is mounting for some being to do *something*.

Slowly, Amber raises her hands and takes a cautious step

backwards. "I-I'm not here to cause any harm–"

"*Liar*," the queen hisses. She raises a hand and orders, "Arrest her."

Two of the spear-holding guards start forward, and in her panic Amber summons her own spear in a flurry of golden glitter, pointing it right back at them. It's nice to have a weapon of her own for situations such as this, even though she has hardly ever swung a sword in her life, let alone learned how to properly handle a spear. It's the same one she took to Korodon; Lukri let her keep it. The only advice she can currently recall him giving to her is that spears stab.

The sudden appearance of her weapon makes the approaching guards hesitate momentarily, but upon sensing that she only summoned it out of fear, they continue their advance.

"Mom, she's not–" Lukri tries to argue, but he's quickly shut down by the queen saying, "This is the last race I will ever agree to take you to, Lukri. Not even our town is safe from their presence."

"*Mom*!" Lukri exclaims to no avail.

"Escort him back to the palace," the queen orders one of the archers. They nod and start towards the prince as Amber continues to back away, waving her spear in a poor attempt to ward off her oncoming adversaries.

Where are you, Blaze? she thinks in desperation. No wonder Ethan wanted him to come along with her. That Husk knows more than any being on Astria that she can't fight. She survived Korodon entirely on her apparent harmlessness and reliance on the others there with her for protection.

Suddenly, the sand beneath Amber's feet begins to tremble and shift. The roar of the quaking desert fills her ears as she falls backwards onto the dune behind her. Bright green tentacles burst from below, wrapping themselves around the two guards near Amber and the one archer charged with escorting Lukri away from the scene, lifting them up into the air and trapping their weapons by their sides. The other Serperas spectating the scene, Lukri, and even the queen herself stare at the vines in utter disbelief as the guards struggle against their bindings.

"Can't leave you alone, now, can I?" Blaze sighs, approaching the chaos he just created. Amber can only stare back at him with a wide-eyed stare, still rattled by all that's going on. She's relieved that he's finally here.

The Naturist takes one look around at the gathered beings and says to the queen, "We need to borrow your son."

"N... *No*!" the queen sputters, still in shock. She lifts her hand, and in a gust of sand a long jade staff appears in her grip. Anger returns to her eyes as she asserts, "You wizards are not welcome here on Mirage or anywhere near my son! Release my guards and remove yourselves from this island at once."

"Look," Blaze says, his voice calm and level with only a hint of mild irritation to it, "I think we got off on the wrong foot here. We're not leaving without Luke–"

"Lukri," Amber quietly corrects him.

"Whatever," Blaze sighs. "I don't know what we need him *for*, but it'll only be for a little while and then you can have him right back. We're not 'stealing' him. We just need his help." He waves his hand, and the three entrapped guards are lowered back down to the desert sand and released. Stunned, they look to the queen for further orders.

"Contrary to what you might think, I'm not one for violence," Blaze adds. "But if my hand is forced, I will not hesitate to defend myself and Amber here."

The queen remains stiff atop the dune, though the fire in her eyes dulls ever so slightly. In a cold voice, she says, "You wizards think you can do as you please. Lukri is forbidden from leaving this island just like every other Serperas here."

"But Mirage is still part of Astria," Amber speaks up. She picks herself up from the sand and cautiously stands beside

Blaze, holding her spear close to her chest. Taking a deep breath, she continues, "Lukri helped us save Astria last time. If he wasn't there, we probably wouldn't have succeeded. Those dark clouds are gone, right? And the attacks on the palace have stopped, too. That was all because of him." Well, it was *mostly* because of him. He landed the final blow on Riona. Whether or not her death caused those clouds to disappear or if it had been Shadow reclaiming its magic, she can't say for sure.

"We *need* his help again," she adds, "or else Mirage will be facing a force that none of you will be able to stop."

"That bad?" Lukri asks.

"What sort of force?" the queen inquires sternly. Blaze's gaze shifts to Amber as well, that very same question glowing in his eyes.

"Um…" Amber isn't sure if she should say it in front of all the other Serperas that are spectating from behind the queen, their curious faces having grown in number while they have been conversing. Are they even understanding what they're saying in the first place? Will she be putting them all in danger if she announces their intentions aloud?

They're all waiting for her to speak. Maybe she should just say it.

"A… force that's trying to find the Shards to the Font of Magic," she reveals.

"*WHAT*?!" Blaze is the first one to react with a cry of outrage, blowing out Amber's left ear with his shout. "Stars above, Amber! The Font of Magic is *much* more important for me to know than whatever being this Ryan guy is! You–" Lacking the words to convey the rest of his thoughts, the ground trembles beneath her as his eyes blaze with rage; he looks about ready to tear Amber apart with his own two hands.

Above, the queen issues another order to her guards, "Disperse these Serperas."

They set to work in an instant as the queen makes her

way down the dune, gesturing to her son to join her. Hesitantly, Lukri staggers back over to the wizards and his mother.

The air has grown dreadfully serious as Amber now stands face-to-face with the stern queen of Mirage. Blaze folds his arms and silently seethes, not helping to ease the tense atmosphere. Lukri stands awkwardly off to one side, still taken aback by the speed that everything is moving at. Amber doesn't blame him. She, too, is struggling to think straight under the queen's sharp gaze.

"You mentioned a being called Ryan," the queen states, her eyes briefly shifting to Blaze. "What is his last name?"

"Ashblade," Amber answers honestly.

The queen lets out a sad yet frustrated sigh. "I thought I'd never hear that being's name again."

"You know him?" Blaze inquires. His voice is still stiff with anger, but he does his best not to sound like it's directed at the royal.

"Mom?" Lukri only breathes in confusion.

"Why are you looking for Ryan?" the queen asks Amber, leaning forward with intense interest. "Leave out no detail."

Amber nods timidly. "Well, we're not really looking for him to reunite the Shards, but there is a being that *is*. And if that being is successful, then… the Spirits only know what will happen next. So we're trying to find him. Warn him. Protect him? And keep his Shard safe.

"But we don't know where Ryan is right now. We know where he found his Shard, so the hope is that if we retrace his footsteps, we'll figure out where on Astria he's hiding. And in order to do that… we need Lukri."

"You speak of the Pyramid of Solari," the queen says. Her gaze grows distant as she takes herself back in time. "Ryan… brought me there many years ago. Yes, the Shard was housed within it, in a place only royals are allowed to enter. If you are indeed looking for his current location, you will find your answer there.

“I was a fool to give it to him. If you do find him and are able to, I request you return the Shard to its rightful place within the Pyramid. That thief does not deserve to have it, let alone protect it.”

Lukri looks at his mother with surprise. “You... knew a wizard?”

The queen doesn't regard him, her stiff frown contorting into the look of deep shame. “My son, I know you already feel betrayed by the knowledge of kings; I am as well. I never knew, either. But I have every reason to hate the wizards as strongly as I do. My parents warned me just like I have tried warn you.” The queen finally turns and places a hand on her son's shoulder. “Ryan Ashblade is nothing but a liar and a cheat. A stranger that will use you for his own ends. Do not be surprised if these wizards turn out to be just as evil as him.”

“You’re letting me… go?” Lukri breathes.

“I am,” the queen nods reluctantly. “You’ve gone with this one before, and you came back safely. But beware the others. Serperas and wizards…” Her thought trails off as she shakes her head.

“I... know,” Lukri replies. Still, he gives her a hug and a smile. “I’ll be back soon.”

“Ancestors guard you,” the queen replies, awkwardly returning his embrace with a single stiff arm. Her gaze once more strays to Amber, her eyes full of skepticism. She doesn’t blame the queen. Yes, Lukri ran away with Amber once, and he returned to Mirage in full health. The queen entrusting her son to Amber once more is a big risk, but knowing full well what’s at stake if she refused to let him go – the safety of her island and Astria at large – Amber should be grateful that the queen is at least somewhat willing to let Lukri leave this time.

The queen lets Lukri go and warns the two wizards, “I will not hesitate to go to war if anything happens to my son.”

“He’s in good hands,” Blaze attempts to reassure the royal, but he’s only answered with a cold glare. Still, he looks up at the sky and hums, “We’ve wasted enough time. Let’s get going.”

Chapter 9

Kimberly is quietly bundled up in her new snow jacket at Ethan's side as the two follow Ulka through the town. He opted to leave his jacket behind, and thank the stars! He rolls his shoulders, happy to be free of that puffy nuisance. However, it only brings his attention to the weight of his new cape, one that hangs from his body just as heavily.

Also, he's feeling much better now that he's away from Opal once more. He thought that five centuries would have done *something* to help her change her old habits, but this entire trip has only disproved that assumption.

There's clearly a lot of history between Opal and Ulka, but he doesn't want to inquire. Her business is her own now. He's not here to solve any of *her* problems. Not this time.

Even so, somewhere in his cold, hollow shell, he still feels a strange warmth whenever he catches her fleeting stares. He doesn't quite know what to think about it. It's a pleasant feeling, one he doesn't want to let go of, but it's smothered by this weight of... *dread.* That he shouldn't be feeling it at all. At least, not when she's around.

He places a hand on his chest, trying to make sense of himself. He never remembered his emotions being so complicated before.

“Are you okay?” Kimberly asks suddenly, catching Ethan off guard. He turns his head just enough to glance at her. He should probably be the one asking her that question; he's never seen her look so pale.

“When you and Jake are together,” Ethan speaks, tilting his head to hide his face from her, “what is it that you feel?”

Kimberly is quiet, her eyes turning away from the Husk as she contemplates his question. Now added to this dreadful warmth is the knotted swirl of anticipation. It's not helping him feel any better.

“Contentment,” she finally replies, “and love.”

“What do those feel like?”

A small puff of air leaves Kimberly's mouth. He... doesn't really know what to make of that sort of response.

“What... do you mean?” she finally inquires.

“Physically. What do they *feel* like?” Ethan repeats.

“Why are you asking?”

Another glow of warmth blooms inside him, but it's different this time. A tiny ember that flickers with fleeting bursts of warmth. It's... comforting. For a brief moment.

“It's Opal,” he replies, speaking her name with a heavy voice, devoid of emotion. The ember within him peters out once more, chased away by her presence on his mind.

“What about her?” Kimberly presses.

Ethan lets out a heavy sigh, his breath dripping with magic. He lets it buzz against his lips as he gathers himself.

So much comes to mind all at once. So many cycles spent shopping, partying, staying out until first light. He didn't mind skipping class just to be out and about with her. Being with her, he felt that warmth he had been so desperate for ever since Riona put him in chains. But...

“Well...” he begins, finally raising his head. Thoughts and memories swirl within him, but he doesn't have the time to get lost in them now. They're nearing the entrance to the mines, a guarded tunnel cut into the snowy rock of the mountain. He shakes his head. “Maybe later. We're almost there.”

He catches Kimberly pulling a mildly disappointed yet concerned frown before she, too, turns to the task at hand.

“Halt!” one of the Yafiir demands as they near, holding up a paw. From under their helmet, their beady eyes regard Ulka coldly. “Ulka, why do you bring guests here? You know the rules.”

“I know,” Ulka replies, gesturing to Ethan, “but they are here at the request of a Fragment Shadow. Who am I to deny the divine?”

The two guards turn to Ethan in an instant. He can feel their skepticism in the tense silence. He doesn't blame them. He still doesn't quite like being addressed as a Fragment Shadow, either. But this is the only way they're going to be able to see Kelsy.

He steps forward. “My apologies for all of this chaos, but my business is urgent. I have a message to pass on to Kelsy Skyshield.”

“What is it, then?” the second guard asks gruffly. It's clear they don't want to be dealing with some being claiming to be a Fragment Shadow. Surely that sort of thing isn't a common occurrence here, is it? “I'll deliver it for you.”

Ethan shakes his head firmly. “I must deliver it myself.”

“No entry,” the second guard promptly states, slamming the butt of their pike on the ground. The first guard nods in agreement.

Ethan can't keep back a dark glower. Even without Shadow's presence, the long figures of the houses darken and tremble, elongating across the snowy ground. Perhaps he should rip out their Shadows and–

Kimberly steps forward, hands on her hips. “We're not Shard Hunters, if that's what you're so concerned about.”

The guards waver at her assertion.

"Sandshard has brought nothing but trouble to our town," the first guard finally admits, narrowing their eyes. "How are we to believe you'll be no different?"

Ethan stiffens. He had heard Ulka mention the Shard Hunters earlier, but he hadn't made the connection until now. Stars above, has Opal been *using* them this entire time? No wonder the Yafiir are so cautious around her!

"How about I introduce myself, then?" Kimberly says. She puts on a grin and starts her spiel, "I'm Kimberly Starshield, Blessed Cryomancer and owner of *The Magic Cone* on Asandra. And this is Ethan, the Fragment Shadow that saved Korodon."

The guards stare back at the wizards in silence, their eyes darting from one to the other in amazement. If they haven't heard of Kimberly before, *surely* they'll know of Korodon's restoration.

But Kimberly isn't done just yet.

"Kelsy's the one in danger here, with or without her Shard," she continues. "If we took it, we'd only be putting ourselves into her position. But if we told you two what's going on, how can we trust that you'll pass on our warning to her in time? If we explained to you everything that's going on, it might be too late for her. Please let us see her, just this once."

The guards huddle close and grumble to each other as Kimberly rolls her shoulders back. As they wait, a dense pit of shame forms in Ethan's hollow chest. He can't help but shake his head, trying to clear it of the darkness that had briefly overtaken him.

To even *think* of doing any more Tearings as a way to get what he wants sickens him. Yet it was his first idea. If Shadow were with him... would he have actually done it?

"Ethan?" Kimberly speaks, drawing his attention. Her brow is furrowed with concern as she turns to meet his downcast gaze. "Are you alright?"

Ethan tilts his head to hide his face under the brim of his

hat. He can't bear to see her staring at him like that. She must have sensed it, too.

"Maybe," he answers in a quiet mutter. He doesn't quite know himself.

Eventually, the guards shift, and the wizards refocus their attention to the situation at hand. The guards return to their posts on either side of the mine's entrance, standing as straight as they did when the two wizards first arrived.

The first guard clears their throat. "Go on. Make it quick." They gesture to the open tunnel with their spear.

Kimberly almost jumps as she starts forward. Speechless, Ethan can only drift after her like a shadow, not even giving the guards another look.

The tunnel slopes almost immediately, and it's quite a steep drop at that. White marks from Yafiir claws digging into the ice and rock paint the ground. Kimberly takes a few uneasy steps down before she starts to slip.

A sigh escapes Ethan's mouth, the buzz of magic tickling his lips, as he lets his feet leave the ground behind. He offers Kimberly a hand as he says, "I can fly us down."

"Thanks," Kimberly nods back, taking hold of his arms. She wraps him in a hug as she plants her toes on top of his shoes, using him as a platform. He'd appreciate it more if he wasn't in such a... *state*.

Slowly, smoothly, he brings the two of them down the entrance shaft. The crisp wintry air of the mountain turns stale and stuffy the farther they descend, and the distant ringing of swinging pickaxes fill the air with their melody. The tunnel itself crackles with burning wood, torches illuminating the mountain's bowels with ease.

As they go, Ethan can feel a soft beating against his chest. It's a warm, rhythmic drumming he can't quite place. Though it's weak and distant right now, its intensity is slowly growing the farther into the tunnel they float.

Kimberly's arms tighten around his neck as she hangs on.

"I'm worried, Eth," she states in his ear. "What if we get there, and..." She trails off, her grip tightening even more. Her frosty breath leaves behind cold vapor that batters the side of his face, making it prickle uncomfortably.

He raises a hand to give her a reassuring pat on her back but hesitates. He can feel her Shadow waver beneath his fingers, even without touching her.

"It's too late to turn back now," he says, lowering his hand.

"I know," she replies. She leans back, her face popping into view, pale as can be with a worry-stricken gaze staring back at him. "You didn't finish your thought earlier. About Opal."

Ethan's lips stiffen, bubbles of anger rising inside him. "That doesn't matter anymore. She hasn't changed."

His harsh reply takes Kimberly aback, her eyes widening with shock.

"She used us," he adds, a hint of disbelief in his voice. Somehow he thought that, maybe, after all this time, she would have changed. She remembered him, held on to their relationship, spent all this time hoping he'd return. It even got him wondering...

Was that all just an act?

He shakes his head, mindful of how close the brim of his hat is to Kimberly's face, and furrows his brow. "Why did I think she would be different? Why did I feel...?" His lips move silently, trying to find the word to fit the emotion always just out of his reach.

He sighs in defeat, shoulders sagging. Nothing comes to mind.

But all his doubts are gone now. The thing he was so conflicted over, solved in a few words. Opal is not a being they can trust anymore. She probably doesn't even care about getting back with him at this point. He's just her latest ticket to Kelsy and the Shard.

So why should he still care about her?

Finally, they reach the bottom of the shaft's entrance. Cautiously, Kimberly steps down from Ethan and onto the small rocky ledge that overlooks the famous mine of Gardall. She shuffles as close to the precarious edge as she is willing to go, staring down into its depths with wide eyes of amazement. Ethan remains close by her side, prepared to catch her if she slips and falls.

The two now overlook a deep pit that glitters with minerals of all types and colors, some of them reflecting the light of torches scattered about. Bridges made of stiff planks of wood cross the pit over and over and over, as far as the eye can see downwards to where they disappear into impenetrable darkness, the melodic ring of pickaxes so grand and echoing that it's nigh impossible to tell where the miners even are, let alone how many there might even be. Some Yafiir haul around sacks full to the brim of mined resources back and forth, disappearing into one tunnel only to appear out of another at random, the sharp claws on their furry feet clacking and scraping across the stone and wood. While Ethan isn't too concerned about falling, the lack of guardrails still worries him. How the Yafiir are able to work safely in these conditions, how any wizard looking to help them isn't constantly scared for their life…

"Wow..." Kimberly breathes in awe, her eyes slowly scanning the pit, absorbing as much as she possibly can. Ethan nods in agreement; this is his first time seeing the inside of Frostfall for himself, too.

He tries not to get too lost in the grandeur, his gaze turning from the glittering gems to the wooden structures. There doesn't seem to be a direct way up and down, though he is reluctant to use the maze of bridges and tunnels. Going the normal way will take too long.

He extends a foot over the side of the ledge. The moment his shoe passes beyond the ledge's threshold, the hands of gravity grab hold to drag it down into the dark depths below.

A pit so deep it touches the center of Astria, he recalls reading once. It's a myth that many beings believe in, including the Shard Hunters. Though, unlike the Font of Magic, Frostfall is nowhere close to being that deep. Many are quick to forget that this pit is the result of innumerable years of mining. There will always be a point where no normal being can descend any further.

But it's deep enough that Ethan can't feel the bottom. He has no idea when he would and he's not here to test that thought right now.

Once more, he holds out a hand to Kimberly. "I'll carry you."

"Are you sure?" she asks.

"It's the fastest way," he replies.

Her hesitation is much more apparent as she stares back down into the darkness below them. The tunnel was one thing; at least there was ground beneath them if anything were to happen. But here there are only the bridges to keep them aloft. Ethan can't fly if there's nothing beneath him.

"You can wait for me up here if you–"

"No," Kimberly interrupts, reaching out. "I'm coming with you."

Ethan helps her climb onto his back, her arms wrapped around his neck to where she hangs from him like a second cape. He has to tilt forward to prevent her from accidentally choking him.

"Ready?" he asks.

"As I'll ever be..." Kimberly replies, a slight waver of uncertainly to her voice. Her grip tightens anyway, determined to see this adventure through. Ethan wraps his own hands around her wrists, careful not to accidentally snap her bones as he holds her in place. With his friend secure on his back, he takes off.

Through the air, he glides from bridge to bridge as the two

descend into the pit, passing Yafiir and wizards alike on their way. Shouts of alarm and confusion echo above their heads as they leave these beings quickly behind. It's not long before the rush of the air fills Ethan's ears completely.

The farther they spiral, the dimmer it becomes. The small mounted torches become braziers cut deep into the rock, their low flames still burning bright enough to illuminate the space. The minerals embedded into the pits' walls change colors and clusters and frequencies, turning duller and smaller the farther they go. There's no life to be seen around them anymore. Besides them and the wind, it's eerily quiet.

Ethan is trying his best to find a balance between speed and comfort, but the farther they spiral the harder it is for him to push back the blooming warmth in his chest. It feels as though a being is trying to hammer their way out of him, beating against his shell in a rhythmic pattern. Its pace has been quickening steadily, an eagerness that's trying with all its might to make him go faster.

But the weight on his back tells him otherwise. Kimberly's struggling to breathe, with short inhales and long exhales that stick to the back of his head. She doesn't speak, but her grip has certainly weakened. If he goes any faster, he may only make her sick, or worse.

He knows they're getting closer to Kelsy, bit by bit. He *feels* it.

Eventually, he kicks his feet out under him and brings the two to a gradual stop, landing on an old bridge being eaten away by ice. He releases Kimberly from his grip, who collapses behind him with heavy breathing. It's rather dark down here, the braziers few and far between. One would certainly need a personal light source to be able to see anything properly. Minerals appear quite scarce this deep, the walls of the pit hardly glimmering at all. The tunnel ahead of him is bathed in shadow, with a small orange glow deep within it. The quiet echo of ringing pickaxes manages to reach his ears. Apart from whatever beings are working down *there*, the two of them are utterly alone.

Ethan places a hand on his chest to feel the pounding within him, fast and forceful, filling him with a magical strength so overwhelming that he has to focus hard on his breathing to have it not be lost in the storm within.

There's no doubt in his mind that they're in the right place.

"She's down there," he announces, his words filling the void of the pit around them.

"Really?" Kimberly asks between her breaths. Ethan nods back.

"*Thank you for the confirmation*," an ethereal voice cackles. A deep chill runs through Ethan as the darkness of the tunnel warps, and two glowing red eyes stare back at him. Electro's Shadow grins gleefully at the two wizards as it stands between them and Kelsy. Lightning sparks from its figure, burning the aging bridge wherever it lands. "*I knew following you would be a good idea.*"

What?! It had been following them this entire time?

Before Ethan can do anything, it raises a hand, then swings it down towards the bridge. The rope where the structure is tied into the dark rocky pit is assaulted by a beam of bright, burning light. In an instant, the far end of the bridge goes limp and starts to fall.

Ethan whirls around, grabbing Kimberly's arm and propelling the two of them into the dark tunnel behind. Out in the pit, a resounding *woomph* fills the air as the wood sharply collides with the rock wall, masking most of the Twisted Shadow's malicious cackle. It turns and shoots down the tunnel, leaving behind bright bolts in its wake.

"Ah..." Kimberly breathes shakily, drawing Ethan's attention. She slowly brings herself to her hands and knees before rolling to the side to sit against the tunnel's cold wall. Her arms and legs are badly scraped.

“I'm sorry,” Ethan says, kneeling down before her. Thankfully, none of them are that deep despite their looks. He closes his eyes and mutters under his breath, “Spirit of Life.”

The warm thrum in his chest expands, filling his entire shell. The smell of soil wafts up to his nose as he attempts not to squirm uncomfortably. As he cracks his eyes open once more, he sees soft green light glowing around Kimberly's injuries.

Ethan can't help but sigh in defeat. “I should have been paying more attention.” He should have been more cautious. He should have kept a better eye on the darkness around them. He should have expected it to be watching them and he didn't.

“Don't worry about that now,” Kimberly assures him. “What about Kelsy?”

The drum in his chest beats more heavily now, filling him with urgency as the last of Kimberly's wounds close. He stands, turning his gaze to the pit. The echo of the collapsed bridge still lingers in the air. The orange light at the other end has been dulled. White flares dance in the distant darkness.

He looks down, searching the darkness for another bridge he could use to fly to the other side of the pit. To his dismay, none of them are aligned the way he needs them to be.

“Can you make us a bridge?” he asks.

“I've never done that before,” Kimberly replies as she, too, rises from the ground. She steps to the tunnel's opening, rubbing her hands together anxiously as she stares down at the endless void below. She takes a deep breath and extends her arms sharply, palms pointed towards the opposite opening in the rock.

The air cools rapidly as a bright blue streak shoots through the dim darkness, crackling as ice meets air. It starts wide enough where they stand, but it only thins the farther out it stretches. By the time the ice implants itself on the other side, it's smaller than the size of a sewing needle. The ice is hardly thick enough to support the weight of even a single being anyway, though that's only if they were to cross it on foot.

"Stay here," Ethan instructs as he lifts off the ground.

"What–?" Kimberly starts, but by that point the Husk is already off. He shoots through the air across her blue bridge with determination. He must deal with this Shadow. He won't let another one of his friends fall to it.

The air of the tunnel is electric, making his shell buzz with its energy as the thumping within him grows ever louder. His magic is practically itching to be used.

"*...Kelsy? I thought you would be happy to see me!*" Electro's Shadow taunts, followed by a blast of cold air, then the sound of ice shattering in full force.

He can see the battle now. The Twisted Shadow dances in and out of the darkness, its form appearing more liquid than solid, granting him glimpses of the chaos it's causing. A little farther down is a wall of ice, behind which is a small group of Yafiir cowering in both awe and terror at the scene, their faces lit by burning torches. And standing in front of the ice wall is a wizard that can only be Kelsy Skyshield.

A wild and unwinding braid of white hair tumbles down from beneath a faded purple hat. A cape lined with fur is pressed against the back of her warm clothes – a thick sweater and long pants – which are dipped in an array of blue and white dyes characteristic of Cryomancers. A glowing wand is gripped in her right hand, a shaft akin to a spike of ice headed by a jagged diamond, and her cold blue eyes are wide with shock.

Fire... With a roar, Ethan extends his hands, and from them red flames fill the space. The Shadow's dancing ceases the instant the darkness surrounding it fades, and it turns around in surprise to be greeted by the burning light barreling towards it.

[*Shadow!*] he calls as the flames sputter out. Electro's face is gradually revealed, its crimson eyes staring back at him in annoyance. Its forearms have turned to mist from the damage it took.

Shadow's presence swirls in the back of Ethan's mind,

alerted to the situation at hand. {*I'm–*}

[*Stay with Electro!*] Ethan demands harshly. [*Just give me something!*]

The warm pounding within his chest is quickly overrun by the dense and uncaring chill of Shadow's magic flooding his hollow figure. As darkness returns to the tunnel, he presses his hands together. On either side of the Twisted Shadow, black walls rush out from the rock, seeking to crush it where it stands. Predictably, the Shadow reaches out to try and stop it, only for it to hold back the oncoming force by its upper arms instead of its hands.

Now it faces a predicament. If it holds the walls for too long, its forearms will reform inside them, essentially trapping it where it stands. If it were to release the walls, however, it'll be crushed and returned to its body. If it moves backwards, it'll run into Kelsy and her Shard. If it moves forwards, it'll run into Ethan and likely return to its body anyway, so long as Ethan can grab hold of it. If it stays, it runs the risk of being killed anyway by Kelsy from behind.

"*Interesting,*" the Shadow chuckles beneath the strain.

"Kelsy!" Ethan calls to the Cryomancer. Her form stiffens as she looks up at the Husk, a deep-seated horror glowing in her eyes. Still, she grips her wand as tight as she can, leveling it with the monster before her.

Her wand flares with blue light as the wall of ice behind her trembles. Long icy needles shoot from around her figure, each one racing to be the first to stab at the Twisted Shadow. Each one shimmers with the golden light of the torches burning behind Kelsy, light that Ethan hadn't taken into account.

The Shadow snickers as the dark walls that hold it in place lose form, the light chasing away the darkness Ethan had been using. It leaps forward towards Ethan, the needles right behind it. Ethan braces himself for an attack, only for the Twisted Shadow's evil grin to melt into what little darkness remains.

Ice... Ethan's body reacts before he even has the time to think, raising a wall of his own to block Kelsy's oncoming attack. The needles come to a halt as they embed themselves into his defense.

He didn't think he'd need to worry about the torches. If Shadow were here, maybe that would have been the case...

"*I just wanted to have a chat with my wife,*" the Shadow's taunt echoes from the dark. Ethan whirls around to watch it reform farther down the tunnel away from the wizards and Yafiir. Its forearms are fully reformed as it grins in the shadows; despite how unconvincingly disappointed it sounded, it's savoring the moment of chaos to the fullest. "*I see that is too much to ask for.*"

Ethan's ready stance wavers as what it said registers in his mind. *Wife?*

The Shadow springs forward, taking advantage of Ethan's confusion. Its fist drives itself into his gut, sending him crashing into the ice wall right beside where Kelsy stands.

"I didn't marry a monster!" the Cryomancer bites back. The tunnel crackles as a layer of frost shoots itself forward, surrounding the Twisted Shadow and extending into the dark behind it. Once more, needles rise from the walls and ground around the Shadow. However, just as they come near its body, bright bolts of hot lightning leap forward to shatter their forms with ease. Electro's Shadow remains still, smiling back at the distressed wizard with glee.

"*Come now, Kel,*" the Shadow hums, extending a hand towards her, "*there is no need to fight like this. Just hand it over and–*"

"Never," she growls back.

Lying dazed next to her, Ethan's chest flares with indescribable heat. Its intensity makes him ache as he slowly rights himself on the ground. The thumping returns in full force, jumping into his head and filling his ears. He grits his teeth in frustration. Why must this strange sensation be so distracting?

The Shadow chuckles out of amusement. "*How much more convincing do I need to get?*"

Just as it finishes speaking, it sparks once more, and out of the dim tunnel emerge ice spikes hurtling themselves into the fray. The lightning catches each one and drives them down into the ground. They burst into a flurry of sharp ice and clumps of snow, some of which batter Ethan and Kelsy.

"*There you are!*" the Shadow cries with delight. It turns in an instant, lightning licking the walls of the tunnel with enthusiasm. More ice flashes in the dark and more crashes follow as they are caught by the Shadow's magic. Until, eventually, it twists its body into a battle stance. It drives its knee into the assailant's gut before grabbing and flinging a body out into the faint light that manages to reach the two.

It takes no time at all for Kimberly to fall to her knees, one of her arms being held behind her back by the cold hand of the Twisted Shadow. She lets out a cry of surprise as her legs scrape against the hard, rough ground of the tunnel.

"*A family reunion!*" it announces eagerly. "*What a surprise!*"

"Kim!" Ethan can't help but cry out, finally finding the strength to rise to his feet. What part of his order did she not understand?! Kelsy can only stand helplessly at his side, staring down the tunnel in abject horror.

"*Look at you,*" Electro's Shadow hums in disappointment. It gives Kimberly's arm a bit more twist and Kimberly tries to twist along with it, her face morphing into pain. "*So much power with hardly any training. What a shame.*" It applies more pressure, making the young wizard gasp through gritted teeth.

"Ely–" Kelsy breathes.

"*Your parents hardly raised you at all,*" the Shadow continues, continuing to twist ever harder with each word. "*Oh, wait. Your mother ran away, and your 'father' was a failure. No wonder you turned out this way!*"

"Ely!" Kelsy cries out once more. The Shard glows in her hand, mirroring her distress. "Stop it!"

"*If you want me to stop,*" it says, its bloodthirsty eyes flickering up to meet Kelsy's horrified face, "*you know what you have to do.*" It raises its boot slowly into the air, aiming it at the young wizard's outstretched arm.

"Don't," Ethan warns. His mind races to try and find a solution. There has to be a way to save Kimberly without giving up the Shard–

"Stop."

The Shadow's head rises, boot poised and ready to strike. Kelsy steps forward and tosses the Shard towards the Shadow, and Ethan watches in horror as it clatters to the ground. The Twisted Shadow's smile widens as it stares at its prize triumphantly. It starts towards the Shard, keeping Kimberly tightly in its grasp as a shield.

No! Ethan starts forward, rage swirling in his chest, only for Kelsy to extend an arm to block him.

"What are you–" he starts, meeting her forlorn gaze.

"He honors his word," she says.

It almost physically hurts to stand by and watch as the Twisted Shadow approaches the wand softly glowing between the two parties. The drum inside his shell pounds, fighting for release, trying with all its might to make him rescue the Shard before it falls into the wrong hands. But if he did, what would it do to Kimberly? This is the second time he's been unable to protect his friends from this monster. With the Shard in his possession, what guarantees he'll be able to turn the tide?

Kelsy didn't even seem like she took any time to try and unlock the Shard's true power, either. All he saw her use was her Ice magic. At the very least, shouldn't that bode well for them? The knowledge that Kelsy, who's held onto the Shard for eighteen years, can't use it to even a fraction of its full potential?

The Twisted Shadow finally bends down and plucks the

wand from the ground. The moment its hand closes around the shaft, it flares with brilliant light that forces all in the tunnel to avert their eyes. As the glow gradually dies, Ethan turns back to find its crimson eyes wide with glee as it holds its prize high in the air. A tiny star rests in its black hand, winking back at him with the warmth of overwhelming magic. The whole tunnel rocks in its presence; even though it's only a third of the Font, it still demands respect.

With a yelp, Kimberly is thrown forward, landing at Ethan's feet.

"Kim!" he manages to breathe beneath the Shard's light, bending down to aid his friend.

"*See how easy that was?*" the Twisted Shadow says coolly. Its wicked grin is the only thing that rivals that of the Shard's glow as it stares back at the three wizards. Its fingers curl around the Shard, snuffing out its light in an instant. *"It was nice to see you again, Kel,"* it adds, though it doesn't sound sincere about it. It leaves them in the darkness, its triumphant laugh echoing through the derelict tunnel.

Kimberly in his cold arms, the beating within Ethan dies with the Shadow's exit. The Shard is gone.

"I-I'm okay," Kimberly stammers. Ethan's grip on her arms to tightens in frustration.

"I told you to stay *there*!" he rages, though careful not to shout too loudly and injure her ears. "Why didn't you?" Kimberly grits her teeth, turning her head away to hide her face. With a wordless growl, he releases her and stands, redirecting his rage to Kelsy. "Why did you give it the Shard?!"

Kelsy's dark expression avoids the Husk's gaze as well. She turns to her ice wall, where the Yafiir miners huddle together in confusion and fear.

"Surface without me," she instructs them. "We're done for the cycle." There's a collection of shell shocked nods as the miners set about gathering their things and themselves.

Tense silence envelops the wizards as the miners slowly take their leave. Ethan steps away to attempt to untangle his racing thoughts. So many things didn't go his way. He wasn't vigilant enough, or else he would have known they were being stalked. He thought that Kimberly wouldn't have been a factor he would have had to consider. She must have found another way to cross the pit. Of course, Kelsy just *stood* there, hardly giving it her all!

"Who are you?" Kelsy's voice cuts through the air, echoing through the tunnel sharply. He turns to give her a glare as she stares back at him from the darkness with dull eyes. A single torch illuminates her, left behind by the miners for them to use. "To have come all this way with that *monster*."

"We came to *warn* you about it," Ethan replies through gritted teeth.

Kimberly picks herself up off the ground, holding her arm as steady as she can manage. She looks Kelsy in the eyes and states, "My name is Kimberly Starshield, daughter of Jay Starsong."

Kelsy's icy stare softens. The cold air around the two Cryomancers swirl. There is no recognition in the woman's eyes as she gazes at her daughter. Only a deep sadness.

"How is he?" she finally asks.

Kimberly doesn't reply immediately. Her body trembles as her face struggles to keep back her brewing emotions. Even though she is cast in heavy darkness, the glimmer of building tears winks at Ethan.

"'How is he?'" she repeats, her voice on the verge of cracking. "*That's* your first question?" Kelsy remains still as the temperature of the tunnel sharply drops. "Why did you *leave*? Where have you *been*? You never wrote, you never visited–"

"It was *because* of you," Kelsy replies coolly. "I couldn't fathom putting my child in the path of that *monster*. If I had stayed–"

"You didn't *have* to stay," Kimberly bites back. Kelsy just shakes her head back at her. Her lips stiffen the longer she stares at her child. That same hesitation she had facing Electro's Shadow glimmers once more.

"*Don't* get involved in this," Kelsy says at last. "You shouldn't be fighting my ghosts."

"Sorry, but I'm *already* involved," Kimberly replies with a small spit, even as her eyes begin to sparkle with frustrated tears. "Electro's at my house! *We're* trying to *help* him! And he wants to help *you*."

Kelsy sucks in a breath of air at the sound of Electro's name. Alarm flashes across her face briefly before it's swallowed by her hollow sorrow. She holds her chin high, trying to appear more composed than she actually is. Her fingers begin to curl at her sides. An air of hostility fills the tunnel rather quickly.

"Excuse me?" she asks cautiously. "He's... *where*?"

"He wanted to come see you himself," Kimberly explains, her voice starting to become tight with hot emotion. Little wet streaks begin to appear on her cheeks as the tears begin to fall. "He's been–"

"Split in two," Ethan cuts in, stepping forward with a tense glare. "But we don't have the time to stand here and tell you everything. The Shard is gone so we have to go, too." He gives Kimberly a slight nudge. She sucks in a shaky breath in response, promptly turning away from Kelsy as her expression breaks.

"Don't worry about the Shadow," he adds rather curtly. "*We'll* deal with it this time." He extends a hand to Kimberly and gently presses on her back as he starts to stride off. Kelsy doesn't stop them, her alertness gradually easing the farther they get. He hates to cut things short, but they have other, more pressing matters to tend to. They were here for the Shard first and foremost, after all. And... Kimberly needs some time to calm down.

"Don't fight my ghosts…" she mumbles at last once she feels they're far enough away from her mother, wiping her face in an ill attempt to dry it, even as the tears still fall from her eyes. She blows through her teeth, a puff of angry mist dancing through the air before them. The sadness slowly morphs itself into mocking rage. "*Right*. How can we *not*? She didn't even *bother* to do it the first time! *Sure*! Go lock your ghosts away and then *run* from *everything*..." Her next breath is softer. A lot more broken. "...This was a bad idea," she whispers finally.

Ethan folds his arms and remains silent, biting back the snide remarks that rest just on the tip of his tongue. Everything about this excursion became one big *bad idea*.

Their hopes now rest on Ryan and the third Shard, wherever that may be. With any luck, Amber and Blaze will uncover something useful. What little time they might have started out with has now been cut considerably shorter, though he doesn't expect for Electro's Shadow to bother following them around anymore. Now that it has a Shard in its possession, it can use that to find the remaining pieces.

They reach the pit. The ice bridge has been swallowed by sparkling white snow with threads of blue winding their way throughout, reinforcing its powdery form that turns the fragile needle into a sturdy, walkable pathway above the darkness. He turns to Kimberly, wanting to comment on the structure, but hesitates. He's not sure if he should commend her in her current... state. So he holds out his hand instead, wordlessly asking if she's ready to go. She takes it with a tense squeeze.

Chapter 10

The door opens once again, causing Jake to turn away from his bowl of warm soup. He's wrapped in thick blankets, huddled by the hearth of Ulka's home, though he casts everything aside once Ethan steps in with a distressed Kimberly by his side.

"Kim!" he cries, rising to his feet and dashing over to the two. Despite the chill that continues to permeate his bones and the frosty mist his girlfriend radiates, he promptly wraps his arms around her in a tight hug. Kimberly buries her face into his shoulder, her face wet with tears.

Stars above, what happened down there? he can't help but wonder. He was already upset he was unable to descend into Frostfall with them, but seeing her in this state... Why did he have to succumb to the cold? If only he were there with her...

"You're back!" Ulka says as she lumbers over. Her beady eyes glance briefly at Kimberly before asking the Husk, "How is she?"

"Unharmed," Ethan replies, his voice stiff. "She'll be surfacing soon." His dark eyes scan the great room. "Where's Opal?"

The question makes Jake's blood run cold. Though

Ethan's face gives nothing away, malice radiates from his figure. Out of the corner of his eye, Jake can see Ulka's fur bristle beneath the weight of the Husk's stare.

"She left just now," the Yafiir responds.

The Husk is quiet. The light of the hearth dims and the dark corners of the room tremble.

Eventually, he turns back to the door. "I'll meet you two at the gate." His cape swishes as he makes his exit. A blast of cold Gardall air washes over Jake as the door slams shut, making him shiver.

Jake finally leans away from Kimberly, though he leaves his hands on her shoulders to keep her steady. "What happened?"

She stares at the floor, her lips quivering. She takes in a breath as if she were to start speaking, only to exhale and deflate even more. Jake continues to hold her, waiting patiently for her to find her words.

"We lost the Shard," she mutters. "His Shadow took it."

No wonder the two of them came back so defeated. The loss of a Shard is troubling indeed. Electro's Shadow was difficult to fight before, but now? He doesn't know how they're ever going to be able to fight back.

But that doesn't seem to be the worst of it. Frustration over failure is one thing. But Kimberly *cried*. That's not normal.

"What about your mom?" he asks her.

Her breath quivers as she inhales, shaking her head. "Not now," she whispers.

Jake can only stare back at her helplessly. It pains him to see her so upset like this, but he's at a loss for what he should do. Embers sputter within him, unable to answer his question.

"WHAT KIND OF FOOL DO YOU TAKE ME FOR?"

The question echoes across the mountain top, making the house shake beneath its sheer rage. Jake's stomach drops with dread as Kimberly is shaken from her sullen stupor. The two lift their heads to the ceiling above.

"FIVE CENTURIES LATER, AND YOU EXPECT ME TO COME CRAWLING BACK TO YOU?" Ethan's roar continues. "AFTER EVERYTHING I'VE BEEN THROUGH, WHY SHOULD I?"

In a panic, the two wizards rush outside, stepping out into the bitter cold air. Jake bites down on his tongue as the chill hits him. He tightens his hold on Kimberly for his own sake, just in case he collapses.

From where they stand, they can see that the front gate to the Yafiir town have been thrown open with so much force that the ground beneath it has been wiped clean of snow, revealing flat gray rock below it. Ethan floats in the air just beyond the opening, his black silhouette somehow feeling larger than life. Anger permeates the air, seeping into Jake's heart and making it blaze with inexplicable fury.

"DID YOU REALLY EXPECT ME TO FORGIVE AND FORGET EVERYTHING THAT YOU'VE DONE? YOU HAVEN'T CHANGED AT *ALL*! *YOU* ARE THE *LAST BEING* DESERVING OF EVEN A SMALL *FRACTION* OF A SHARD!"

There's no sign of Opal anywhere as the Husk yells at the sky. Can the whole island hear him? Could he have always been this loud before?

There's a pause to the shouting, the hot air fading as quickly as it had been created. But ease and relief doesn't fill the void in Jake's heart. Only a hopeless hollowness, along with a kind of sorrow that can only be birthed in the absence of emotion. Is this a change in Ethan's emotions, or how Jake actually feels?

"We should... probably get going," Kimberly says in a low, exhausted voice. She turns to Ulka, who has been stood staring along with them in the doorway to her home, and tells her, "Thank you."

The Yafiir nods back slowly. "Safe travels."

Kimberly takes Jake's hand, pulling him along as they walk down the quiet street. The mountain has become strangely still. The silence of the town is almost eerie. Even the chill of the air has lost its biting edge. It's not just the beings affected by the overwhelming emotion. The mountain itself is absorbing it, too.

He squeezes her hand. She squeezes back. A small ember jumps for joy within him, bursting into a tiny flame and a thin smile.

As they approach the gate, he can see clearer now the scene that just unfolded. Opal is pressed deep into the snow, her eyes wide and fearful as she's held in place by Ethan's stare. She hardly even breathes, thin puffs of air the only thing that indicate life. Nearby are the rucksacks and some of the spare clothes she had lent them, stacked in one big, messy heap.

"Ethan!" Kimberly calls.

The Husk twists around in the air to face them. His dark eyes hold no lively spark as he regards them. Beneath his gaze, Jake feels something inside him shift and stiffen, braced for the worst and hoping for the best.

"Are you two ready?" he asks, his lips barely parting. Together, the couple nods back. Kimberly then lets Jake's hand go and steps towards the Enchanter. She takes off her loaned snow coat and tosses it towards her.

"Thanks," she says simply. A blast of annoyance radiates from Ethan, but his face remains stiff and unreadable.

***

{*They're back,*} Shadow announces in a dull voice.

"Is Kelsy with them?" Electro asks.

{*No.*}

The Electromancer lets out a sigh as he slumps back into the sofa. His body aches from his exercising. It's a dull throb that's calmed only by Shadow's cold presence, holding his wiry frame together through his exhaustion.

He was hoping against all hope that she'd come back with them. Now he can't help but wonder if he'll ever get to see her again. Even though he knows where she lives now, would that kind of trip be worth it? He had been told to stay behind for a reason...

"Was Ryan there with her?" he inquires.

{*No...*} Shadow cautiously replies, though it casts doubt onto his mind as it starts to squirm within him, suddenly unable to settle itself. It's been suspiciously quiet since he went for his run.

"What happened?" he demands.

Shadow takes its time answering. When it finally does, it mutters quietly, {*Just... wait.*} Its agitation grows stronger.

He closes his eyes, settling in to the silence. He is having a hard time recalling her face, a swirl of colors and abstract shapes trying to fit themselves into her image. But her voice, her laugh, her smile, all of that is gone. He can't help but feel bad for letting her fade away from his memory. His heart aches, begging for her presence. Yet this oppressive haze continues to linger, no matter how much effort he puts into his thoughts, both in and out of his coma. He has been helpless all these years, only able to watch her slip away.

It makes him angry. Angry at Ryan. He must have done this to Electro, too.

The little bell below chimes, and he opens his eyes to the blaring lights of the room. He hears two sets of footsteps climb the stairs, the newcomers not speaking a word. Jake steps into the room first, casting Electro an annoyed glance, one hand on his hip. Ethan files in behind him, though he lingers near the doorway with his head bowed.

Electro leans forward on the sofa, bracing for the worst, as he asks, "It got her Shard, didn't it?"

Ethan's face darkens as he lowers his head, hiding his

eyes beneath its wide brim. He clenches his hands into tight fists partly visible beneath his heavy-hanging cape. "Yes."

"So what now?" Jake asks.

"We wait," Ethan answers plainly. His head turns towards Electro. "We need to talk."

With a small grumble, Electro rises to his feet and drifts after the Husk as he leads the way into the shop below.

The two stand alone with the large mixers and coolers. Despite him wanting to talk, Ethan keeps his back to the wizard as he asks, "Were you and Kelsy married?"

Electro's hand strays immediately to where his wedding ring should be on his finger. He brushes against his own cold skin, almost fooling himself into the believing that it's still there. It pains him to even think of his answer.

"Once," he confirms.

Ethan's arms shift as he falls into an uneasy silence. Shadow's presence shrinks within, condensing itself as much as it can. It doesn't take long for Electro to grit his teeth angrily. There's more going on here that these two aren't telling him. Not yet.

"What does our marriage have to do with anything?" he asks harshly.

"Everything," Ethan replies. He finally turns to face the wizard, his dark eyes aglow with realization. His shoulders sag as an invisible weight presses down on him. He takes a deep breath in an attempt to collect himself.

"Don't tell me Ryan was *there*," Electro says, his tone dark and threatening.

"No, he wasn't," Ethan assures him. A rush of relief expels itself through his mouth as a constriction in his heart that he wasn't even aware of eases in an instant. Thank the stars! At the very least, she's safe from *him*.

"I recall," Ethan says slowly, drawing his attention once more, "you mentioning you had a daughter once."

Sparks start to dance across Electro's clothes, dread seizing at his chest where his tense anticipation once occupied. He's not bringing this up out of nowhere... "Don't tell me she's not with her," he breathes.

"I had only presented it as a possibility, not a definitive," Ethan corrects.

"Where else would she *be*?" Electro asks, trying to keep himself from yelling. All this time, holding onto hope – that *Ethan* gave him! – that Kelsy would be watching over their child. But if Kelsy doesn't have their daughter... then *what*?

"She's been *here*, on Asandra, this entire time," Ethan answers calmly. He makes a sweeping gesture to the room around them. "You've met her already. Kimberly Starshield."

The world feels to fall away from underneath him as he stares back at the Husk. Everything is numb, his mind blank except for her name.

Kimberly Starshield... Starshield... Star...

His hands turn to fists that tremble. He can feel his veins bulge as the hue of hot anger creeps across his vision. His magic flares, lightning dancing around the room unfettered, sparking off metal and searing the tiled floor. Shadow's presence is consumed by the storm, leaving behind an all-consuming hatred.

STARSONG!

It's all so clear now. He almost wants to laugh.

"Electro...?" Ethan asks, his voice tight with caution. At once, the electrical storm ceases, though Electro remains tense.

"Where is he?" he asks, his glare razor sharp. "Where's Jay?"

"Jay?" the Husk echoes. He's lost in confusion though it doesn't take him long to reply, "I don't know. You'll have to ask Kim–"

Electro shakes his head. He doesn't want her to see him in this state. But it shouldn't matter. He's only asking to see if his suspicions are correct. It's been eighteen years, after all. Plenty of time for Jay to have packed up and moved... if he were smart.

"Forget it," he growls, finally turning away. "I'll be back."

Chapter 11

Every single fiber of Blaze's body is on fire, in a constant state of being ripped to shreds by millions of tiny needles. It's hard to describe what it's like forcing a single vine up through the sand. The sensation of pushing away the grains both weighs him down and uplifts him at once, making standing on the moving mass of plant matter feel very strange. The breeze is hot and sticky against his face. He can't wait to be gone from Mirage.

Amber and Luke – Luki, Luri, however his name is pronounced – sits on the mass of vines behind him, chatting about something he can't quite hear. Through the pain and heat and concentration on his magic, he can barely make out the sound of his own breathing right now. He was able to recover from some of the damage done to him already, but not completely. He hates to admit it, but he's extremely out of practice, even with all his education. Asandra is hardly a place where he can rip up the ground with minimal complaints or property damage. He's more used to causing tremors with his vines, feeling the cool dirt shift and slide against his skin. Dirt is a far cry from sand.

It has certainly been nice to feel the light of the cycle shine down on him. He hadn't been expecting the air of the desert to be so clear. It's not as crisp as Asandra, though it doesn't carry that claustrophobic mustiness that always hangs around the tightly packed buildings. Or maybe it's just him. Open green spaces are extremely hard to come by on Astria.

Since he's out and about, maybe when he's not needed anymore he can spend some time sitting under the willow tree. He's hardly been there as of late and he feels bad about that. It's always so peaceful there, a place where he can truly relax. The last time he went, he had to deal with a distraught Amber. Well, actually, he didn't *have* to. It just… felt right, to do for her what Ethan once did for him. Maybe this time he'll have no hassle to sour his already dreary mood.

The dunes that hide the Archway appear in the distance, their peaks rising high above the orange ocean around them. As much as Mirage enchants him, relief still floods his being. Solari is their next stop, if he remembers correctly. It'll still be somewhat sandy, but at least he'll not need to transport them very far.

As he brings the three of them to a rolling stop, his senses start to return. He still feels hot and sweaty, and that's because he is. The rumble of the vines in his ears dies out, and finally he can make out the end of the conversation between his two companions.

"…why?" Luke asks, sounding mildly upset.

"They're just trying to preserve it the best they can," Amber replies simply. Blaze casts a glance over his shoulder. The Serperas is frowning, even as an adventurous glimmer glows in his emerald eyes.

"But it's ours," he states, emphasizing each word he speaks. "They have no right–"

"Have you *seen* how far away the Archway is?" Amber cuts in, gesturing the way they just came. Blaze's vines have carved out a large ditch, a scar that cuts through the dunes without care. The Serperas' town is nowhere to be seen, having left their sight ages ago. “Besides, how would you stop them if they just did it anyway?”

Luke folds his arms and scowls down at the sand, thinking, though it’s not for very long. He shakes his head, lost for words yet still upset.

“It’s not that bad, really,” she promises him, though she looks to Blaze for confirmation.

“What’s not bad?” he asks.

“The Pyramid.”

Luke also turns his head, waiting for Blaze to answer the question. No wonder he sounded upset. With the Pyramid belonging to the ancient Serperas, hearing that some foreign beings have simply wandered inside with sticks and paint to fix up the *Serperas’* art must not be the most pleasant thing for the prince to hear. Amber hasn’t even gone on her class trip yet; she wouldn't even see the remnants of Solari officially until her third term at the earliest as of right now, maybe even her second if the rules end up changing.

Blaze folds his arms and turns to the tall dunes behind him. “You’ll see when we get there.”

The three shimmy their way up and over the dunes that hide the Archway, sand filling his shoes and rubbing against his skin irritably. As Amber searches for her Keystone – Ethan must have given one to her, for how else would a first term be able to access the restricted island? – Blaze sits down to clean out his shoes.

Out of the corner of his eye, he sees Luke points a finger at him. “*Bla-say*?”

“Blaze,” he mutters back, “like a fire.”

The Serperas blinks. His eyes flicker up and down, staring at his bright green outfit. “But you're a... a Healer? Like Amber.”

He stares down at the sand beneath him in silence. *Not this again...* he almost huffs aloud. “Yeah. Yeah, I'm a Healer,” he glances up at the back of Amber's head as he adds, “but I'm nothing like her."

She finally raises a hand, presenting the Archway with a new Keystone. The tilted structure glows and rumbles as the rip opens, revealing the excavation camp and the base of the Great Pyramid. She turns to the two boys behind her and asks, "Ready?"

With a small grunt, Blaze refits his second shoe and stands up, trudging over to her, Luke trotting along after him.

His class took a field trip to the Pyramid towards the beginning of the school year, back when they were still setting up the lights inside. The Pyramid was dark and drafty, full of dust and ancient rooms shrouded in enchantments and shadows. He didn't get to see much of the place due to how unsafe it was back then. He'd be lying if he said he weren't at least a little excited to get a second, albeit unofficial, tour.

Blaze leads the way through the rip. As he steps from the soft orange dunes to hard-packed and sandstone, he braces for a change in atmosphere, but the change never comes. Each island's environment is completely different, all except for Mirage and Solari. Moving through the Archway, going from the vast desert to a fragment of land still bathed in the Mirage sun makes the hairs on his arms bristle uncomfortably.

"Woah…" Amber breathes, staring up at the Great Pyramid in utter awe. Sparkles shine in her silver eyes. Blaze lets a small grin slip briefly. There's just something about seeing her like this that makes him feel… content.

He shakes his head sharply to release the emotion's hold over him. Now isn't the time to be enjoying the sights. They have more important things to worry about right now.

"Alright, we're here," he says to Amber, snapping her from her spell. "What now?"

"Oh, uh…" she mutters, "Ethan said to ask for Sir Taylor. But… um…" She takes one look at the tents before them and tenses up. All of her earlier confidence and gusto is gone, just like that. Then again, she wasn't really as confident as she was sassy. He still had to step in and save her from those Serperas. For whatever reason, she's trying to put on a facade and is failing at holding it.

Blaze rolls his eyes, the first of the three to take a step forward. "Fine, then. *I'll* ask."

He takes the lead, striding over the packed sand and heading towards the collection of colorful tents, his two quiet companions in tow.

A wizard rushes from one of the tents, his arms full of papers. His eyes dart this way and that, making sure he doesn't run into any other being, but he falters when he sees Blaze and his two quiet companions approaching the makeshift camp.

"Students?" the wizard speaks in disbelief. "You three shouldn't be–"

"We're here to see Sir Taylor," Blaze interrupts. "Where is he?"

The wizard's eyes immediately light up with recognition. "Oh, you're the ones that Fragment said were coming. He's inside the Pyramid right now supervising the clean-up crew. Wait right here; I'll drop these off and I can take you inside."

The wizard rushes off, disappearing into a tent directly on their left. Blaze takes this opportunity to turn to Amber and say, "See? All you need to do is ask."

But he finds only anxiety in her gaze as she shrinks further into herself, her eyes darting to her feet. She looks like she wants to make a retort but lacks the will to even speak. *What is wrong with her?* he can't help but wonder.

"What is this?" Luke asks, drawing Blaze's attention. He's standing next to the tent on their right, tugging at its fabric gently and rubbing it between his fingers to feel its texture.

"It's a tent," Blaze replies.

"*Ten-tuh…*" the Serperas slowly repeats, looking the structure up and down. Then he looks to Blaze and inquires,

"What does it do?"

At first, Blaze can only frown. *What do you mean? It's a tent,* he almost speaks, but he holds his tongue. He doesn't want to upset the royal with something so brash. Besides, Luke looks genuinely lost. Saying such a thing would only make him seem like a jerk.

It takes a moment for him to realize that the Serperas has probably never seen a tent before.

"It's a... temporary house," he answers. "You can take it down, move it around, and put it back up again whenever you need it to be."

"Wow." The Serperas turns back to the tent, continuing to fiddle with the small piece of fabric in his hand. Funny how he's more amazed by something as simple as a tent while Amber could only gawk at the sandstone structure many times her own size.

The wizard from earlier emerges from his tent at last, wiping his sweat-ridden brow and smiles at the two students and Serperas. He appears to be in better spirits now that he has been able to free himself from his previous duty. "This way. Try not to fall behind."

"Lukri, come on," Amber says softly to the Serperas, taking his free hand and gently pulling him away from the tent. Luke frowns back at her silently with mild disappointment.

The air inside the Pyramid is musty and still warm, a displeasing combination for Blaze to breathe. He raises a hand to his mouth and stifles some coughs as they leave the Mirage sun behind them.

The massive main hall is in complete disarray. Most of the beings work carefully with the sandstone, attempting to clean off small black marks clearly not part of any of the paintings or stonework. Wizards shepherd around large buckets of water and various brushes and rags as the Shasks do what they can to save the ancient walls.

Lukri stares at the walls with his mouth agape as they are led down the hallway of chaos. He radiates both awe and horror at the state of the Pyramid, his people's pride and joy. Amber keeps a firm hold on the Serperas' arm to keep him close by. She can't help but glance at the walls herself, but she seems more distracted with the prince and making sure he doesn't cause any problems.

Eventually, the wizard the three were following stops and gestures to a grand doorway splitting off from the main hall. There's a short pathway that leads to a grand chamber beyond that's been left in shambles.

Any flat surface is carved with deep runes of various sizes and shapes. The sandstone is heavily scorched, too. The ground is covered with chunks of rubble large and small, all organized into different piles arranged by size. Some of the workers simply stand around scratching their heads, most likely wondering where they're going to put all this mess and how they're going to transport it all there, wherever "there" winds up being. In the middle of the mess stands a Shask dressed in a fancy yet stiff-looking red outfit. Their wizard guide points to this Shask.

"That's Sir Taylor right there," he says.

"Thanks," Blaze mutters automatically as the wizard briskly takes his leave, returning to whatever work he was doing before. Blaze turns to his two companions and asks, "Either of you want to go introduce us?"

Amber doesn't exactly shake her head, but it certainly twitches from left to right, anxiety returning to her gaze. Why is she here again? Because Ethan asked her to be?

Luke appears more willing to go speak to the Shask, but he, too, is struck by fear of his own. He points to the Shask's legs and attempts to put his thoughts into words, "What...? Why...?"

Blaze just lets out a huff and shakes his head disappointingly. What is he supposed to be? The muscle or the negotiator? Doesn't matter. Looks like it's all up to him again.

He takes off into the chamber, his head held high and chest puffed out with purpose. As he nears the Shask, he clears his throat to grab his attention.

Sir Taylor turns his head, a single mechanical blue dot for an eye widening with a series of clicks. A chill ripples through Blaze's body as he stares back at the Shask. He tries not to mind their augments, but that doesn't mean he agrees with what they decide to do to themselves. It's unnatural.

"My, a student!" he says with surprise.

"Ethan sent me," Blaze speaks before the Shask has time to shoo him away. He jabs a thumb over his shoulder to Amber and Luke behind him. "They're with me, too. We need some help."

The Shask fully turns to Blaze and nods.

"Ah, yes, the Fragment told me to expect you," he chuckles. He extends a mechanical hand towards Blaze, his joints clicking as they adjust themselves. "Sir Dalton Taylor."

Not wanting to be rude, he shakes the Shask's hand. "Blaze."

Sir Taylor moves to Amber and Lukri, offering each of them a welcoming smile and a handshake. Amber shyly reciprocates as she brings herself to meet the Shask's mismatched eyes.

"Amber," she mutters.

Luke completely disregards the Shask's hand, fully entranced by his mechanized legs. Amber gives him a nudge on the arm and whispers, "Hey, he wants to shake your hand."

"O-Oh..." he stammers, finally looking up. He rolls his shoulders back as he, too, gives the Shask a firm handshake. "Lukri, prince of Mirage."

"The *prince* of Mirage?" Sir Taylor asks back with a polite laugh. Though the Shask might not believe him right away, Luke nods back with a smile. The Serperas knock his heels together, and in an instant his legs fuse into that of a long emerald tail that curls around him to form a supportive base to keep him held up as high as he can. Even so, he's gone from slightly standing over Amber down to just below her chin. A series of loud clicks come from the Shask as he radiates an air of surprise and disbelief. Blaze quietly slips his hands into his pockets, staring at Luke's tail as well. Granted, he was *just* on Mirage, faced with both tailed and legged Serperas alike, but it hadn't crossed his mind that they could switch between the two. He just assumed that they were more like the Feni, where some are born with bushy tails and some are not.

"Well," Sir Taylor says, "it's quite the honor to have an esteemed Serperas such as yourself visit the Pyramid!"

Luke blinks, processing the Shask's compliment. "Thank... you." His tail fades away as quickly as it had appeared, and Luke once again stands on his own two feet. He clears his throat, wanting to get down to business. "I need to access the center of the Pyramid. Where is it?"

"It would be this way," Sir Taylor says, gesturing with his hand the direction in which he wants the three of them to follow him as he starts off.

They make their way back to the main hallway and turn left, heading further away from the Pyramid's entrance.

It's a lot calmer this direction, with the damage being age and not burns. The Shasks take great care with the pictures, redefining their forms and revitalizing their colors. Passing these beings by, Lukri appears to be much less tense than he was before, quietly studying the pictures for himself.

It doesn't take them too long to get to the hallway's distant end. It narrows into a small doorway, which promptly widens once more into that of a sunken chamber. It's shaped into a semicircle with tiered platforms curving around a small dais at the very bottom. Behind the dais appears to be an entrance to a tunnel, leading off into the darkness. The room is lit only by a few bulbs running along the wall near the hallway opening. Did this place used to be a theater or gathering center? Blaze can only guess.

"This is the center?" Luke asks.

Sir Taylor shakes his head. "No. It's through that tunnel there, but... well... Oh, how do I explain this?" The Shask scans the chamber briefly, searching for his words. "Not just any being can waltz right in."

"What does that mean?" Blaze says.

"We had an... *incident* not too long ago," Sir Taylor explains. "A small group of workers tried to explore the tunnel below, but the moment one of them reached that dais, they went mad and attacked any being who got close to them *and* the tunnel."

Mad, the Shask says? What a clever way to keep unwanted beings out, by turning them against one another.

"Do you know why?" Blaze continues to interrogate Sir Taylor.

"No, sadly," the Shask replies. "None of the Enchanters want to approach the dais. But we suspect that it's a type of security measure left in place by the ancient Serperas. Do you know what's down that tunnel?"

"No," Blaze answers.

The Shask smiles eagerly, the ear of the uninitiated lent to the expert. "It's the Grand Prophecy, boy. It is a room that is said to be able to tap into the power of the Fabric of Fate to answer any question. Though with power like that, only the Mirage royals were allowed to use its power to its fullest extent."

Blaze lets out a thoughtful hum. Such a room wouldn't be without heavy protection, then. Even if the expedition was able to get past this strange spell of madness, no doubt there would be even more obstacles for them to overcome within that dark tunnel.

"Guardian spirit," Luke finally speaks up. He points down

to the dais below them. "A thief cursed to protect the heart of the Pyramid. It will guide the royals of Mirage. That's... what I learned, anyway. One person steps on the dais, and the spirit will take the royal to the center." He immediately looks at Amber.

"M-Me?" she stammers back. "You want me to–"

"I'll do it," Blaze interrupts, stepping forward.

"But–"

But he's already making his way down the center steps, his mind made up. He doesn't want Amber to get hurt because of this supposed guardian spirit. Sure, Ethan will have his head if *that* happens. But offering himself to go first just feels... like the right thing to do. His left shoulder feels stiff, but in a good kind of way.

He makes it to the bottom of the chamber, and is now standing face-to-face with the tunnel's mouth. He was expecting it to be longer than it actually is. Bathed in darkness, he can barely make out its other end. It looks solid enough – a door, perhaps? – with carvings flashing in and out of the black murk. But in order to really know what it is, he'd have to go down there and touch it.

He takes a deep breath and steps onto the dais, bracing himself for what's to come. He's still just a student, after all. There's only so much he can do. But he's also the best being to be the test subject. The prince is too important and Amber is too… *fragile*.

Standing there all alone, nothing happens. He feels completely fine. With a small frown of disappointment, he continues to move towards the tunnel.

But as he plants his first foot forward, he freezes. A sharp chill rushes over him as a surge of magic bursts from the core of his very being. The magic doesn't belong to him; it's foreign, its icy touch spreading across his limbs like a malicious infection. It wraps itself around his bones and heart, collecting his power and draining it into his chest. Numbness is slowly starting to set in, and with it comes fear and panic. It's not the same as when Shadow first appeared to him, how it held him in place with force, but the loss of control over himself is as real as it had been then. Only instead of his essence being held down to be ripped from him, something else has invaded his being and aims to manipulate his essence from within.

And he's powerless to stop it from happening.

For better or for worse, he, at least, still has his mind. He can see and experience but not act. That control is now in the grasp of whatever darkness has planted itself inside him. But even the luxury of clear thought becomes tainted by ghostly whispers and urges that seek to override his remaining senses. The entity makes their goal extremely clear to him: *Protect this sanctum from all outsiders.*

His fingers twitch. His magic begins to be pushed around by this foreign force, molding in ways it does not wish to be shaped, stretching and compressing to its limits. It's methodical; this is not the first time this entity has possessed a living being, nor will it likely be its last. It knows magic. It knows how to use it. But every time it tries to exert its control, every slight movement made from Blaze's body, there is an unruly lurch of staunch protest in response.

Pinpricks of pain start to dance across his skin, starting from his left shoulder and radiating outwards. Warmth is slowly returning to his body, but it's not the kind that restores his dormant senses. No, a new power has been awakened, a dense force of energy residing just beneath his skin. The warmth is *anger*.

His magic lashes back out, swirling against its constraints as the spirit tries to regain control. Beneath the sandstone, he can feel the coarseness of sand rubbing against his vines as they sprout up from the depths of the island and rush their way upward to its surface. The ground begins to rumble and shake, a gentle hum that grows ever louder.

With the physical pain added to the spiritual war, his body falls to its knees. Oddly enough, *that* is painless, the impact but a very distant pressure he hardly feels at all.

His left shoulder feels like it's on fire, a small star burning its way through his skin, as he tries desperately to hold himself together. The tremors grow more intense the harder he resists.

"Blaze!" he hears Amber cry out in alarm. She starts down the stairs; he senses her approach… somehow. A body of energy moving through mist. The closer she gets, the stronger his shoulder burns and the urge for violence grows.

"*Stop*!" he manages to shout back, his voice sounding like it has been magnified tenfold. It fills the room so sharply that Amber stops dead in her tracks. He can hardly see straight through the conflicting energies within him. The most he can bring himself to do is remain knelt in place, suppressing his vines as much as he can. He won't let them tear through the ancient structure. He doesn't want to be the cause of a disaster. He doesn't want these beings to hate him even more than they already do.

{*I cannot harm her.*}

But she is a threat.

{*Those are my orders.*}

And I have mine.

He doesn't recognize either of these voices, even if the first one sounds like him. Neither feel as if they belong, completely untethered from his thoughts and feelings. One comes from that being living beneath his skin – his Shadow – and the other from the spirit that now haunts him.

He is not the one fighting for control. His Shadow feels so detached yet so anchored, and the mysterious spirit so foreign yet so commanding. And his mind floats in the ether, trapped helplessly between these two forces. He doesn't know what to do.

{*There are beings here I must protect,*} his Shadow says.

And I must protect this place. So, we are at an impasse, the spirit huffs. *Tell me, is there a royal of Mirage among you?*

{*Yes. The prince.*}

The spirit hums skeptically, making his head buzz. *I saw no prince.*

{*Believe me or not, he is here,*} his Shadow insists.

Then I must conduct my test. So long as none pose a threat, I will not force you to do harm.

His Shadow doesn't reply, its presence instead quietly receding to the background, granting the spirit free reign over his body. But it still stirs unhappily as his shoulder throbs, alert and prepared to step in once more if the spirit decides to cross his body's boundaries.

His body stands, the spirit in complete control. He turns to face the three beings at the top of the chamber. Amber's posted midway on the stairs. Luke and Sir Taylor haven't moved, though their bodies are tense with anticipation regardless.

"Only members of the royal family of Mirage are permitted entrance to this sacred place," he speaks. Though the words are spoken in his voice, he is not the one behind them. His eyes dance from the pink-haired girl to the living metal monster and finally to the plainly clothed being standing awkwardly off to the side, giving each of them a special sneer of disgust. "I was told that one of you was a prince."

"I-I am," Luke speaks up, stepping forward. Despite his tenseness, he holds his head high, authority radiating from his lean figure. "I am Lukri, the current crowned prince of Mirage."

But Blaze's body frowns back skeptically. "Where is your sash? Your circlet?"

The Serperas' eyes widen with surprise and alarm, his hands straying to his chest in an instant. "It's…" he mutters, "at home. I was racing–"

"Blood does not make a Mirage royal," he interrupts harshly. "If you have no proof of your 'princehood' then *leave*."

So this entire trip was for nothing? All this way just to find out that Luke left all the things they'd have needed behind.

"But–" Luke starts, only for the spirit to swiftly shut him down, "I am a guard. I am not here for conversation. I did not write the rules to this place. I only enforce them. Do you wish to try my patience further? This boy says that there are beings here he cannot harm, but that will not stop me from fulfilling my duties."

Blaze wants to roll his eyes. *He* wasn't the one who said that. It was his Shadow that did, and he doesn't know why, nor does he really care. The sooner this spirit releases him from its hold, the happier he'll be.

"You said yourself, that blood doesn't make a royal," Luke states. "Neither do the symbols. Any Serperas can present *a* circlet or *a* sash and lay claim to the title of 'royal'! What makes a royal is leadership and wisdom and the people's approval."

The spirit is quiet, absorbing his words. Eventually, Blaze's face contorts into a snarky grin. "A test, then." His arms rise and his magic shifts within him as the room flares with green light. It's harsh as it is brilliant, born from the spirit's own power. Pictures flash upon the walls with ghostly green flames, images of Serperas adorning regal attire and either silver or gold circlets.

"Prove yourself to the court of your ancestors, and I will acknowledge your status as a royal," the spirit announces. "Show them that you are worthy of leading their descendants. Inspire them with your wisdom. If more than half of these lights fizzle out, all of you will *leave*."

Luke stares back from the top of the room, startled by the blast of magic but determined all the same. He nods, accepting the spirit's challenge.

Almost immediately, pictures start to disappear, their flames winking away into darkness unceremoniously. Mouths drop open in surprise. Blaze's jaw would probably drop, too, if he could. Luke hasn't said or done anything yet and they're already leaving? Is this even fair?

"You judge already?!" the Serperas yells out in frustration. The pictures don't respond, only that they continue to disappear, one by one.

His bares his fangs but doesn't make any further comments despite his displeasure being quite apparent. Instead, he takes some time to think, closing his eyes and lowering his head to concentrate.

Still, the spirit quietly molds and shifts Blaze's magic within. Hot and cold spots dance across his numb skin, soft and tingly yet present all the same. Its fingers poke around at random, and wherever its fingers touch, another flame flickers out. Are Luke's ancestors *truly* in the room with them right now, or is this spirit pulling some elaborate trick? He can't say, figuratively *and* literally.

Finally, Luke takes a deep breath and opens his eyes. He rights his posture as he opens his mouth, prepared to speak.

"I am not here to prove or disprove who I am," he says, slowly and methodically, making sure each word is heard. "I know that I am the crown prince of Mirage, as does every person I know. The Serperas accept it, and the wizards acknowledge it. I... *be-seech* you, ancestors, to grant me access to the Pyramid's heart for Astria's sake." Some of the pictures flicker, dimming but not quite disappearing.

"I know the Shard has been taken," Luke continues, "and that it was a wizard who tricked my mother to obtain it. But, as you see, there are other wizards trying to find this thief, too. They want to protect Astria, including Mirage. Why should we be different from them? We should not forget what they've done to us, but we should not be quick to forgo the safety of the world because of them.

"I have heard the stories of this chamber, and I know what I will be getting myself into. I will never be ready to bear the burden of knowledge, but I am the only one able to do so. It is a sacrifice I am willing to make to prevent disaster."

The silence is eerie as the flames flicker and wave in mysterious patterns, but no more pictures snuff themselves out. Blaze's head tilts. Is the spirit listening for something? Is it considering the Serperas' words?

"It is decided," he speaks at last. With the wave of a hand, the pictures disappear all at once, and the soft glow of the light bulbs returns. Then he gestures to Luke grandly. "Approach, my prince."

Slowly, the prince makes his way down the center staircase, stopping briefly by Amber's side as he passes her. The two have a quiet exchange, Amber shrugging as Luke stares at her with a lost look. She mutters something and gives him a reassuring pat on his shoulder and a smile as he finally nods back.

As the Serperas steps up to the dais, one of Blaze's hands rises, fingers spread, and from his palm ignites a small green flame that hardly flickers as his arm moves around, gesturing for the Serperas to follow him. The green tinge must be from the spirit using his magic as its primary source of power; he's never studied Fire magic before.

Together, the two make their way into the dark tunnel.

The walls and curved ceiling are just as engraved as the rest of the Pyramid, though this time the images are much more regal and symbolic than a simple prophecy. The way they each curve and flow into one another makes it hard for him to find where one symbol ends and another begins.

The green light from the ghostly flame doesn't make anything feel real, either. Where shadows should reside in the deep grooves of the carvings, there are none to be seen, making the tunnel feel rather flat. Not even the dark figures of their bodies are cast along the sandstone.

"I apologize for my harshness," the spirit says, its low voice still echoing up and down the enclosed space. "I was simply following the rules."

"It's okay..." Luke replies quietly. He much more interested in the symbols than he is with talking to Blaze's possessed body.

"And forgive me," the spirit adds, "for not stopping that thief when I could. If I had known his intentions, I would never have released him from my grasp." Shame and anger boil inside Blaze's gut at the spirit's request. "As such, I cannot vouch for the accuracy of the Grand Prophecy anymore with the Pyramid's heart gone."

Luke finally turns to Blaze's body, his eyes sparkling with determination. "It's still worth trying."

It doesn't take them much longer to reach the end of the tunnel. If Blaze weren't inhabited by this spirit, he'd think that this would have simply been a trek to nowhere. But with this spirit, he can see what he would have overlooked otherwise. It's a circular door that protects the Pyramid's center from outside forces. Its surface glows with the same green energy as the fire in his hand, special runes that only the guardian spirit can see.

He raises his free hand and waves it over the door, his fingers brushing against the runes as he does so. With each one the spirit selects, it flashes a brilliant white before dulling to a dark jade color.

"I cannot accompany you inside, my prince," the spirit says, "but once you step through this door, place your hand upon a wall and ask it what you wish to know. But I warn you, search only for what you *need* to know. Knowledge brings wisdom, but in return it takes ignorance. And that ignorance, most often, is better to keep."

With the runes dealt with, the tunnel begins to rumble as the door slowly starts to roll.

The spirit turns back just in time to catch Luke nodding along, though whether or not he understood the spirit's warning is hard to tell. Slowly, he enters through the circular doorway, disappearing into the chamber beyond. The spirit turns its gaze back down the hall, waiting patiently for the prince's return.

{*You were a thief, too?*} Blaze's Shadow asks, wanting to spark some conversation.

The spirit frowns. *Formerly, yes.*

{*You were after the Shard, weren't you?*}

What else would there be worth stealing here? the spirit huffs. Blaze's eyes close as the spirit reminisces. *I was also a Pyromancer, and a Shard Seeker.*

While the specific term is new to Blaze, he naturally assumes that the spirit was simply another Shard Hunter of their time. So it must have been bound here to set an example for future Hunters, then.

I should have known better, the spirit continues on, its frustration growing within him, *but I allowed myself to be convinced otherwise. How could I have forgotten the oldest tricks so easily?*

His eyes open again just in time for Luke to stagger back out into the dim hall. His shadowless face is flat, his gaze far away. He gives Blaze's body the briefest glance, then wordlessly starts off back the way the two had come.

The spirit once more sighs, rattling Blaze's body as it quietly trails the prince. *I warned him.*

They make it back to the main chamber. Amber sits where she stopped on the stairs, staring at the tunnel blankly. Once Luke emerges, she springs to her feet, her face regaining some of its liveliness. Sir Taylor remains near the chamber's entrance, observing the scene from his perch.

"Lukri!" the Healer exclaims, rushing down to his side. As she approaches, the spirit doesn't react like it had done before. Does it no longer see her as a threat? Or is it because its current mission is at an end? "Are you okay?" she asks. Luke nods slowly, giving her a pat on the arm before turning to Blaze expectantly.

The spirit steps back onto the dais. Once both feet are planted firm on its surface, the spirit's power rushes out of Blaze in an instant, a cold wind finally blowing itself away. His body unwinds as his Shadow falls back asleep, its dominating presence fading to a dull throb along his left shoulder. He can't help but let out a sigh of relief as he steps down. It feels as though he's just awoken from one of his long naps.

"Are you kids alright?" Sir Taylor calls from above.

Blaze gives him a thumbs-up. "Yep."

"Let's... go," Luke says, reaching for Amber's hand and pulling her along back towards the stairs. His eyes are having trouble staying raised, frequently dropping to the floor. Something heavy weighs on his mind, no doubt.

"Thank you," he says to Sir Taylor, slowly and methodically as to not trip up. "We are, uh, going now."

"So soon?" the Shask asks, mild disappointment befalling his mechanical face. "I hope you learned all that you needed, young Serperas." He gestures back down the hallway, its exit from here but a small blotch of light against the yellow sandstone and shifting amalgam of beings.

Even though they're on their way out, the three of them are still shadowed by some being or another. Sir Taylor stopped half way back, needing to return to his work. From there, eyes gaze upon their journey cautiously, making sure that the children don't wander off to places that they shouldn't be. Luke drags Amber along behind him at a quick pace, his urgent stride bordering on a light jog. Blaze does his best to keep up.

Things don't start to unwind until they make it back to the Archway. Amber fumbles around for yet another Keystone as Luke stares off into the Void, lost in thought. Blaze almost wants to ask him what's going on, but a blast of cold air beats him to it.

Amber holds a white Keystone in her hand, and beyond the Archway he sees the familiar sight of the ASM campus. A weight lifts itself off of his shoulders as he gazes upon, well, *home*.

Stepping through the rip, it feels nice to have the cold air against his body once again. If he spent any more time beneath that hot sun, he would have started overheating in his sweater.

Amber takes over as the guide this time, walking Luke through the school's campus quietly. The Serperas, however, keeps his eyes down on the ground rather on that of his surroundings.

Blaze can only roll his eyes as he drags his feet behind the two. He eyes the fanciful Halls, but he sees fourth terms slipping in and out of the doors. He looks to the dorms but feels no draw to them. He *is* tired, but not for a bed.

When they get to the lake and the long stretch of vivid green grass, he stops. He glances over at the willow tree in the near distance, its leaves gently brushing the surface of the water.

"Blaze?" Amber asks. He steals a glance in her direction; she's stopped walking, probably sensing his hesitation.

"Go on," he assures her.

Amber's brow furrows, confused by his statement. "Aren't you coming with us?"

Blaze just shakes his head. His body hurts, his magic is agitated, his temper has worn thin, and frankly none of this is even his problem to begin with. Sure, if not for him, Amber would have struggled to get things done, but as for the rest of it, it seems like the others have it all under control. He only helped because Ethan… *asked*. Involving himself further feels like he'd only complicate things even more. He's not looking to be branded as a Shard Hunter. Best to stay away.

"It'd be better if I didn't," he answers. He turns towards the willow tree and adds, "You know where to find me."

He feels Amber and Luke's gazes linger on him as he strides across the grass, heading towards his favorite resting spot. With each step he takes, the heavier the world weighs on his battered body. The soft rustle of the grass beneath his feet makes him smile. He had only been away for half of the cycle, yet the sight of the greenery makes him feel as if it has been many years instead.

He brushes aside the curtain cast by the willow, its leaves soft to the touch. Inside, the cool shade curls itself around his figure welcomingly. He takes his seat at the base of the tree, its trunk his backrest and its swaying leaves his calming melody.

Third term classes are over for another cycle. This fact doesn't worry him. Not anymore. He does feel bad, but it's also not the end of the world. Besides receiving a very strong reaming from his teacher next cycle, he's far from being punished for skipping. Maybe he'd care more if he wasn't so exhausted. If anything, he learned a lot more from his little adventure than he would have from all of his classes combined.

His fingers run through the grass on either side of him, brushing against the rough bark of the willow's roots, feeling the moistness from the lake in the dirt. The lake's waterline has dipped below its rim; Asandra is certainly due for more rainfall soon.

Taking a long, deep breath, Blaze closes his eyes and settles into nature, letting the tranquility connect his body to the vast ocean of energy that all of Asandra sits upon as his consciousness drifts away into darkness…

Chapter 12

Lukri walks close to Amber's side, careful not to let her out of his sight. As magical as Asandra still is to him, with its high buildings of bright stone and a mass of beings all in one place unlike anything he's seen before in his life, he just can't bring himself back into focus.

They make it to the big road, and he has to force himself to look down at the ground to avoid the bombardment of all the lights and colors. The last time, they were enthralling. Now, if he sees one of them, he might get sick instead.

"Lukri?" Amber asks, her voice full of concern. He reaches out and holds her hand, squeezing it tight. He doesn't want to speak yet. He doesn't want to be forced to repeat what he saw. He'll say it once, and then he'll try and forget it.

If only she had been there with him. It was all so stunning. He could hardly believe that his ancestors made all of that by themselves. It's amazing and heartbreaking all at the same time. His people have fallen so far from their glory days. He read so many stories about the Great Pyramid and its importance to his kind, about the ancient city of Solari and its sudden disappearance into the Void. But actually *being* there makes it all feel real and not just a distant memory preserved in tiny fragments inside of books destined to turn to dust.

Amber guides him down the road, the noise of other wizards filling his ears and making his heart leap. Deep down, he's happy to be back in Asandra. There's still so much of the place he hasn't seen yet. But that happiness only goes so far.

"Amber! Lukri!" a distant being calls their names, causing Lukri to raise his gaze. Through the crowd, he sees Ethan rushing towards them, his cape billowing behind him as he pushes the brim of his hat upwards to reveal his face. The Husk beams at the sight of them, relief glowing in his eyes. Lukri forces a smile across his own lips. It's nice to see him again, too.

"How did it go?" he asks Amber first, jumping right to business. "Where's Blaze?"

"He's… resting," Amber replies slowly. Her face twitches awkwardly, not seeming to know what emotion it wants to display. "Where are the others?"

"Kim's at class, Jake's resting, and Electro's... out," Ethan answers. "We're still free to use the shop, though."

"Alright."

He turns to Lukri and his smile falters. He clearly wants to say something, but he doesn't know what or how. Lukri feels the same way; as much as he's happy to see Ethan again, he can't think of a good greeting.

The moment passes. Ethan turns away and gestures for the two to follow him. Through the crowd they push, eventually coming upon a building painted blue and white. Its interior is dark, no being in sight. Hanging on the other side of the clear door is a sign that reads "Closed" in bold letters, but it doesn't deter the two wizards. Ethan steps up to the door, walks *through* the door, turns around, and opens it for Amber and Lukri. Amber steps forward, nodding at the Husk in thanks. The Serperas, however, has to stand still to process. Last he checked, Ethan couldn't walk through doors! Is this a special door that anyone can walk through? It can't be, since Amber didn't follow him. Or maybe she didn't want to leave Lukri standing in the street all alone.

He touches the door. It's cold, and when he pulls his hand away, he leaves behind a white smudge wherever he made contact. It's also unnaturally smooth. Whatever the door is made out of, it's not wood or metal or sand. Beyond the door, the two wizards stare at the prince with bewildered expressions.

"You..." he starts, addressing Ethan, though he still can't quite put his question into words. So he pokes at the door again to see if that helps him. "Y-You..."

"Oh," Ethan mutters, realizing what Lukri might be trying to say. He shifts his weight uncomfortably and folds his arms, his smile appearing sad and detached. "Yes, I can... walk through things now that I have Shadow back."

"Hm."

Lukri walks inside, and the door swings shut behind him, a little bell ringing merrily in his wake.

The room is cold, something sweet hanging in the air. He smells a collection of fruits, but he can't quite name them. They all smell so familiar, reminding him of the fruits grown on the palace grounds at home, and yet he gets the feeling that none of them are any that come from Mirage. How could they be? Mirage hasn't traded anything with any other island in a long time.

Ethan raises his hand, and in an instant the windows to the outside turn black, blocking out all light and sound. Panic grips Lukri's heart and squeezes it tight as he sucks in an anxious breath. Then, suddenly, light beams down from the ceiling. Lukri blinks a few times to regain his bearings.

"How's Jake doing by the way?" Amber inquires as she steps away from the wall and a little white switch mounted on it.

"I wouldn't be surprised if he caught a cold," Ethan replies somewhat dismissively. "You can check on him later." He turns to Lukri expectantly. "What did you learn?"

Lukri closes his eyes and takes a deep breath, readying

himself to recount what he saw.

In his mind's eye, he can see the room clearly, a small box that stretched upwards so far he could hardly see its ceiling. Each wall was completely blank at first, apart from evenly-spaced lines that divided each wall into a series of stacked rectangles. In the room's center was a small stone podium; empty, though the curved indent in its center suggested that it used to hold something, most likely the Shard.

He followed the spirit's instruction, placing his hand onto one of the walls and, through his body heat, asked his question: *Where is Ryan Ashblade hiding the Shard?* And before his very eyes, he watched the walls burst to life with pictures and colors that spiraled up into the darkness, each small scene a story from history. Starting from the left wall and moving to the right, he read the following:

~

The followers of Day and Night were locked in fierce battle for many months. The nation of magic remained strong, safe within their borders, but with limited resources and dwindling numbers.

~

The Night first Blessed His followers with magic beyond comprehension. But with the Day's command over Her mortal army growing, the Night saw no other option but to intervene directly.

~

He turned to His youngest child and commanded for the conflict to be brought to an end. He gave His child the strength needed to control the Divine's greatest creation of all: The Font of Magic.

~

The child of Night descended onto Astria and sought the council of the Night's seven most loyal followers. Together, they decided what was to happen to the followers of the Day.

~

Using the Font, the child of Night sacrificed itself to spawn a golden wall of stars. With it, the ocean disappeared, and so did the followers of the Day.

That night, the stars danced with the victors.

~

The Night did not rejoice in His followers safety. The sky thereafter became lightless as He mourned the loss of His child. He took the Font and shattered it, hiding it away to prevent further harm.

~

One was given to the Serperas, guardians of past and future.
One was thrown deep into the ground, beneath tree and stone.
One the Night kept for Himself.

~

But the Shards will be found and united:
One of Fire, surrounded by metal.
One of Ice, friend of the mountain.
One of Shadow, with a heart full of Light.

~

He opens his eyes again to find Ethan lost in thought, Amber standing quietly at his side.

"Hiding the third Shard inside of a Fragment Shadow," he hums. "It's smart, but…" The Husk frowns with deep concern. It appears there's part of the story that he's having a hard time wrapping his mind around.

Ethan pinches the bridge of his nose, squeezing his eyes shut. He tilts his head down to have the brim of his hat hide his face from the other two.

"No," the Husk states harshly. He raises his hat just enough to where he can give Lukri a deathly glare and continues, "No, it *has* to be a lie."

Lukri can't help but shrug back. He doesn't know what he's talking about, but his assertion isn't *wrong*. "Without the

Shard, it could be inaccurate..."

"That must be it," Ethan nods quickly. "That must be..." Still, his eyes continue to search for... *something*. "But which one would have agreed...?" he mutters to himself. He begins to pace back and forth, completely lost in frantic thought.

Lukri looks to Amber, confused. She catches his gaze and shrugs back, shaking her head. She's probably wondering the same things Lukri is. What's going on with him all of a sudden? Is he alright? Is there something wrong with what Lukri said?

Without warning, Ethan steps up to Lukri, his hands clamping down on his shoulders and drawing him close. The brim of his hat brushes the top of Lukri's head as he leans in close. His dark eyes bore into Lukri as if trying to extract an answer from him for himself.

"Did you learn *anything* else?" he desperately asks, giving him a rough shake.

"No," he lies, wishing it were true.

The Husk releases him with a small shove, grumbling something terse and angry beneath his breath. Eventually, he shakes his head hopelessly. "'Surrounded by metal'," he can hear Ethan say aloud, though his voice grows distant with each word he speaks. "Kendon, perhaps?" "Maybe," Amber tentatively agrees, who he can barely even hear, "but where?" Ethan lets out a growl, but now Lukri's thoughts have fully absorbed him.

He's not sure how he should feel. Relieved, or angry? Both? Neither? Something else entirely?

But those images will forever be burned into his mind, and he blames no one except himself... and Ryan, whoever he is.

A hand lands on Lukri's shoulder and gives him a firm shake, bringing him back to reality. Ethan's fingers are as cold as ever as the wizards stare at him with concern.

"Is there... something you want to talk about?" Amber asks softly, approaching his side.

His eyes sting. He raises a hand to rub them and finds a

thin layer of tears waiting to fall.

He can't help but be brought back to that dark night in the ruined palace, having his whole world crashing down around him as his new friends comforted him. With Ethan and Amber by his side once more, he almost spills his thoughts once more. But he bites his tongue instead. This isn't something he's ready to share with anyone just yet. He only knows the story, but not the *truth*.

"No," he answers.

***

Electro strides through the streets of Asandra gracefully. Even though it has only been eighteen years, he still expected for some of the old pathways to have shifted, so it's a pleasant surprise to be able to retrace his old footsteps.

{*Where are we going?*} Shadow asks. It swirls around anxiously the more his anticipation grows.

"Can't you figure it out yourself?" he replies.

{*Would you... want me to do that?*}

He doesn't think he'll ever get used to not only having his body be inhabited by some other entity, but also having said entity be able to read his thoughts. Though after their first conversation in the infirmary, it has mostly withdrawn itself.

"We're going to see an old *friend* of mine," he finally answers with a great big sneer of disgust. He jabs a thumb at his chest, right where he feels the concentration of Shadow's power. "*You* stay out of my way, okay?"

Shadow frowns, its cold face etching itself into his skin. {*...Okay.*}

He comes to a crossroad, one that he's quite familiar with. He almost laughs when he sees the front door, adorned with its old snowflake crest. The Voidterror didn't even change *that*!

He raps on the door hard and fast. A Cryomancer he has never seen before answers.

"Yes?" he asks.

"Is Jay home?" Electro inquires. No sooner does he speak, the wizard in question appears in the hallway. How fun it is to see his face fill with dread! "Ah, there he is!"

The Cryomancer that answered the door turns around. "For you."

"Electro?!" Jay only breathes back in disbelief.

"Yep, it's me alright!" Electro chirps, inviting himself into the house. No being stops him. He smiles ear to ear, arms out wide to trap the man in as big of a hug as he can. Jay squirms in his grasp. "How's my dearest *brother-in-law* doing?"

"*You're* Electro?" the other wizard hums in amazement. He steps forward as Electro releases poor Jay, hand outstretched. "I'm Ian, Jay's husband."

"Husband, eh?" Electro hums back as they shake. He casts Jay the smuggest look he can muster. "*All* that whining and complaining! Good on you!"

"What are you doing here, Electro?" Jay asks sharply. He glares in an attempt to look intimidating but he has hardly ever been the type. If Electro wasn't so scrawny-looking, Jay would certainly be scared witless.

"Why, I'm just here to have a chat about my *daughter*," Electro replies. His clothes begin to spark with delight as he gestures to the living room. "Why don't we sit down?"

Reluctantly, Jay leads the way into the living room, taking his favorite rocking chair. Even though Electro was the one that suggested sitting down, he stands before the sofa with his hands in his pockets. Ian trails in behind the two, looking to Jay with confusion written all over his face.

"Jay, what's going on here?" he demands. "*His* daughter? Isn't Kimberly yours? Is he related to Kel? Do you have a sibling I don't know about?"

Jay lets out a sigh of defeat, head bowed and hands clasped in his lap. It gives Electro the space to pile onto his troubles.

"Keeping secrets from your family, now?" he hums gleefully. He watches Jay intently as he continues. "Never bothered to mention that Kelsy's your *sister*?" He can practically feel the aura of surprise radiating from Ian. Still, the traitorous Cryomancer's lips remain pressed tightly shut, his glare becoming sharper with each word spoken.

"Younger sister, actually," Electro corrects, continuing on his little rant. He turns to Ian and flashes him the widest smile he can. "She was in the same term as me and Ryan. You remember Ryan, don't you? The little Voidterror of ASM." Wordlessly, Ian nods along, even as his face is lost in a sea of confusion and questions.

"I should have known," Electro sneers back at Jay. "Your *darling* little sister was being led astray by some *wild* Electromancer. Wouldn't their child be better off in some other being's hands? Just to make sure that everything's kept *in line*." A full bolt of energy leaps from his looming figure, striking the wall just behind Jay's seat. The mark it leaves behind steams black as the wallpaper curls, its edges glowing red with scorch.

"Whose idea was it to send me to die?" he asks.

"I wanted what was *best* for Kelsy," Jay speaks at last, his voice heavy with anger.

"I did, too, you know," Electro retorts.

Jay stands sharply, jabbing an accusatory finger in his direction. "You didn't deserve her!"

"It's nice to see you haven't changed much," Electro hums, a sadistic smile creeping its way across his mouth once more. "But to kill me and steal my child? Stars above, I never expected you'd go *that* far!"

"It's not theft," Jay defends. "Kelsy asked me to–"

"Of course she did!" Electro laughs. "Who else would she have turned to? Not Ryan, obviously."

"Keep *that* name out your mouth," Jay growls back

sharply.

"Or *what*? Scared he'll come knocking if I say it too much?" He waves a hand at Jay, an old point proven true. "See? I *tried* to warn you about him, Jay, but *you* didn't listen, and now he's backstabbed you, too!"

"He said you weren't going to come back. H-He said that the seals would hold!"

"Yeah, well, look at where trusting his word got you," Electro replies gleefully. "Wasn't it nice living in fear all that time? Bracing yourselves for my inevitable return?"

Ice springs up from below, jagged spikes that cut through his clothes and dig into his skin with their chilled touch. Jay's feet sparkle with frost as he glares murderously back at the Electromancer.

"We should have just killed you ourselves," he states.

"Mm, murder wouldn't have made Kel very happy," Electro replies. Jay's magic twists itself into him even more. Wherever their tips touch begins to ache with pain.

"Jay, what on *Astria* are you doing?!" Ian exclaims.

"Kel never took our bloodline seriously," Jay says, ignoring his partner. "I've worked so hard to preserve it–"

Electro chuckles. "You *really* let that stupid family legacy of yours get to your head." No sooner are his words spoken than one of the spikes sinks deeper into his ribs. No doubt it has cut skin, but it's so cold he's numb to the pain. Shadow swirls within him, curling around the spike as it stems his wounds.

"You think you'll be able to explain this to Kimberly?" he asks. Jay doesn't react at the mention of her name. No feeling flashes across his face other than the murderous glare that already paints it. The man must already be resigned to whatever fallout may occur. He doesn't fear his family anymore. He has already had his way with her life.

"Callous. *Ngh*–" The icy knives twist themselves further into his body. He wants to flinch, but Jay's magic holds him in place. If he were to move, he'd only add to his pain. He can feel Shadow's rising anger within, a dense ball of fire that thrashes against the ice. It's getting impatient.

"Jay, stop!" Ian cries, stepping forward. His hand is outstretched, but Jay gets to him first. He waves in Ian's direction, creating a drift that pushes his husband back.

"I'm sorry this is how you had to find out," he speaks, little remorse in his voice. The ice presses ever further into Electro's body as he smiles through the pain and frostbite. Jay is being purposefully slow, wanting him to feel every little moment as his life ebbs away. If it weren't for Shadow, he might have passed out by now. He's in no danger here. *Go on, Voidterror,* he quietly urges. *Just a little more...*

Ian grits his teeth and holds out his hands before him. Ice of his own springs from the floor, weaving its way between his fingers before eventually blossoming into the head of a giant hammer. He lifts the sparkling blue weapon high over his head and brings it crashing down on Jay's ice drift, shattering it in a single blow.

Jay's attention immediately shifts as his husband surges forward, intent on stopping Jay and his murderous plan. He leaps backwards, narrowly missing Ian's wide swing. Wherever he steps, the floor around him freezes.

"Stay out of this, Ian," he says, his hands raised, ready for combat.

Ian shakes his head. "I'm not going to be an accomplice to murder, Jay!"

Jay's gaze meets Electro's once more, his hatred burning bright. Then he clenches one of his hands into a tight fist.

He can feel the spikes surge their way forward in an instant, piercing through his body entirely. They emerge from his sides and around his shoulders, snaps and pops rebounding off the walls of the living room. Ian spins around, eyes wide with horror.

His body grows cold, dropping away into nothingness. He only gets the briefest flare of anger as Shadow finally surges forward. Its essence expands, filling his body with its might, pressing itself against his consciousness. Raw and untamed power crushes the ice within him, freeing Electro from his icy prison, its stare trained solely on Jay.

Beneath Shadow's gaze, the murderous Cryomancer appears to stiffen. All of his gusto dies as he stares back at the awakened horror.

I won't stand by, Shadow speaks, *and let you kill this wizard.*

If Electro could smile, he would. Thank the stars Shadow isn't as heartless as it used to be. Now Jay *really* has it coming!

Ian turns back to Jay in an instant and makes his strike, thrusting his hammer forward. It catches the stunned murderer off guard and he finds himself pinned to the living room wall. He lets out a pained yell as he claws at the ice, trying to push it away. Ian, however, holds firm.

At the same time, Shadow raises a hand, the flow of its power shifting. It calls forth the darkness of the room to wrap itself around Jay, tearing his arms away from the hammer's head and pining him to the wall. Slowly, step by step, it makes its way across the room. Though he's numb, he can still feel his innards shift around inside of him, punctured and frozen, kept together only by the Fragment's power.

It reaches out to Jay, its dark hand stretching beyond his own, making his fingers fall limp against the Cryomancer's chest as its essence sinks beneath his clothes and skin. His squirming is brought to an immediate halt, his eyes widening and his breath becoming shallow.

I'll make sure this is as painful as possible, it promises in a quiet hiss. Its fingers twitch, and so too does Jay's body. His jaw drops open, but no sound emits from it. He has no idea what it's doing to Jay, but so far the man doesn't look very comfortable in his own skin.

This is what he gets for provoking the divine unaware. Electro just came for a nice chat, not to torture the guy like this. Taunt him, sure. Maybe a small scuffle. He's not done with his conversation with Jay, though he doubts Shadow will just hand back his body right now, injuries and all. Just a few more words.

Can it hear his thoughts now? Will it even listen?

Hey! Let me talk to him! he tries, willing it out into the cold, dense darkness that encases him.

Shadow's looming presence turns, a goliath that stands firmly in control. {*NO.*}

C'mon, I'm not done with–

{*NO,*} it interrupts forcefully.

At least ask him about Ryan for me, he says. *We still have to find that Voidterror.*

Shadow audibly sighs, heaving the chest a bit too much. *Where's Ryan?* it growls to its captive. Jay makes a strange choking noise, attempting to keep down his words. Shadow's fingers twist, and the man blurts out the answer.

"I-I-I don't know! H-He cut contact years ago. I haven't heard from him since the Pyramid!"

That's not entirely surprising to hear, but still disappointing. He figured that the two of them would have kept in contact somehow, what with his Shadow having been locked up all this time. Guess that hoping your enemy never returns is better than preparing for doomsday.

Shadow retracts its hand from Jay, leaning away from the man. He takes a shuddery breath as his head hangs limp, finally released from the Fragment's power. Its angry stirring is gone now as it announces, {*I'm done with him.*}

Hang on. I still want to tell him something.

{*If you insist,*} it relents. He feels his mouth warm. Just to test, he parts his lips and sucks in a gulp of air. He can feel it run down his throat and expel itself into his chest; he can keep sucking forever and never fill his lungs. Stars above, Jay *really* did a number on him.

Staring at him now, Electro's unsure if these words will resonate with the wizard. He doesn't know how much of a heart this murderer has left inside of him.

“I'm sorry, Ian,” he says. “And... thank you.” Shadow turns his body to face Jay's husband – for how much longer? – who stares at the wall with a forlorn scowl, still holding his hammer cautiously.

His eyes shift to him, and he asks, “You're Kimberly's birth father?”

“I am,” he confirms.

The Cryomancer looks him up and down quietly. His eyes reflect only parts of the horrific sight: Electro is riddles with holes that ooze with dark mist, the edges of his clothes stained with blood. He must be wondering how the wizard before him is even still alive.

“And Jay knew this entire time?” he eventually speaks, his gaze returning to Electro's face.

“He did.”

Ian turns away from the scene, one hand rising to his forehead. “Stars above, what am I supposed to say to her...?”

“She doesn't know yet,” he says. “I can't promise it'll stay that way for long, but I didn't come here to reclaim her. I came to get back at Jay for what he did, nothing more.” Ian gives him a confused look as he begins to lay out his thoughts, “She might be my child, but I didn't raise her. If she ever asks me I won't lie to her. But she's still *your* daughter. It's up to you if you want to tell her in full or not.”

Ian nods. He turns back to Jay, still strung up on the wall. “Alright.”

“I'm going to have Shadow let him down now,” he warns.

“Do it.”

Shadow lifts a hand, gesturing to Jay, and the darkness

that surrounds him recedes. The man drops unceremoniously to the floor, falling limp. Ian stares down at him, quietly absorbing the scene and sifting through his own thoughts. Electro, however, is done here.

"Well," he hums, "take care, Ian."

"Yeah... You too," he mutters back in a daze. Just as Shadow turns away from the scene, he sees ice encircle Jay, rising to securely cover his body in a thick dome. Then Shadow steps out onto the street, shutting the door to the house behind it.

{*Get some rest,*} it says.

Yeah, yeah, he sighs. He doesn't need to be told twice. He's already letting his consciousness drift off, now that he's away from that maniac. He has quite the injuries to heal from, so he might as well let Shadow do its work in peace. *Thanks for the back-up.*

Shadow doesn't answer. Its presence recedes once more as it's drawn away from his body, distracted...

Chapter 13

"Azna–"

The old Feni looks up from himself, his fingers mid-fidget with a golden button. His navy blue Council cape is draped over his shoulder, freed from the shadows of his robe for the time being. His tired frown deepens as he gives Ethan a once-over.

Ethan's hands stray to his cape in an instant. "Sorry, I–"

Anza shakes his head. "Don't apologize. Just make it quick."

Still, Ethan draws his cape close to his body, trying to hide himself inside it. His eyes turn away from the Feni, choosing instead to fixate on the papers on his desk.

"Electro's Shadow has one of the Shards now," he says. "We're still trying to find Ryan. And the third…" He pauses to lick his lips. "The third is in my Father's possession."

Out of the corner of his eye, he notices that Azna barely reacts to the news. He closes his eyes and releases a long breath.

"If the Spirit is in possession of a Shard then the Font shouldn't be a problem anymore, correct? All there is left to do is stop–"

"No, the Font is still a problem," Ethan interrupts. "I just..."

He closes his eyes and lets out a conflicted huff. "I feel like I should ask Him about the Shard, but... I don't want to see Him, either."

Azna's eyebrows rise. "Why not?"

Ethan shakes his head. He doesn't know what he should say. His emotions swirl in his chest in a massive storm of confusion he has yet to sort out.

"I can't help you if you don't tell me what's wrong," Azna adds.

"I know."

The Feni turns to his desk and sits down patiently, waiting for Ethan to find his words. As much as he appreciates Azna being here for him, he's also keeping the Council member from his meeting, whenever it's supposed to start.

He lowers his head, his hat hiding his face from the Feni's watchful gaze.

"I... think He lied to me."

He has been trying not to believe it, but deep down he knows that it's true.

What Lukri told him earlier, about what he saw in the Pyramid, is accurate. He has been trying his best to fool himself into believing otherwise but he can't. Not with all the history that he has read. Reality is now staring him squarely in his face and he can't deny it any longer.

It was an event well documented by many close to the Generals. They all spoke of the arrival of a Fragment Shadow, the first one seen since the children of the Spirits left Astria. It planned to use the Font of Magic to bring the Great War to an end, but it wanted to hear the wizard's thoughts on what it should do. Thus, the Border Barrier was agreed upon and that is what Astria got. Once the Fragment Shadow left the castle, however, it was never seen again, and shortly after the wizard's victory, the starry night sky fell dark for six long cycles. The event was commonly described as "the Spirit of Shadow in mourning".

Ethan – *Shadow* – always wondered which Fragment used the Font but that question never got an answer. Father always skirted it and none of the written records could say for certain, either.

But the Pyramid said "His youngest child" very specifically. At the time of the Great War, Nonavem was the youngest Fragment, but he doesn't think it would have even cared about the War, let alone have listened to Father's request to stop it.

Though now he can't even ignore what he has been dismissing this entire time. Two very important stories that have been written into history by all of Astria. For according to the ancient Astrians, the Spirit of Shadow has always had a hundred children. The youngest of this pantheon was Centi, the Shadow of the Knight, founder of what became the Guardians of Light and who fought the heartbroken Dragon and sent it into a slumber that it remains in to this very cycle. But despite Father telling him that *he* was Centi, Ethan could not lay claim to those accomplishments; they happened well before he was made.

The Knight protected the world once from its own sibling and left behind an organization of knights meant to guard the beings of Astria in its absence. It would *never* have turned a blind eye to the suffering of the wizards, especially not at the hands of the Guardians.

He could never wrap his mind around how there could have been a Knight before *him*. But now it feels like everything is starting to make sense and the truth only makes him feel dizzy and sick.

"Lied to you?" Azna hums back.

He should nod but instead shakes his head, trying to rid himself of his thoughts. "I don't know *why* He did. It's... It's so... It doesn't make sense why He would."

He lifts his head to get a glimpse of Azna's face. The old Feni stares back with a troubled frown, his fingers laced together a bit *too* tightly to simply be contemplating.

"Perhaps it wasn't His intention to lie to you," he offers. His ears twitch uncomfortably as he adds, "Perhaps... you weren't yet ready to know the truth."

"The truth of *what*?!" Ethan yells back in a fit of anger. "The truth about what I *am*? What I'm supposed to *be*? Why tell me that I'm the Knight when the Knight already exists? Why fool me into believing I represent something that I don't?"

He pauses to take a breather, pinching his nose hard as it tingles and the soft drum in his chest pounds faster.

What are *they*, then – him and Shadow – to Father? A replacement? A stand-in? A fantasy? Why force the mantle of the Knight onto another Fragment? Why keep this secret all this time? Did He *want* them to find out on their own? Or was He... selfish?

He both does and doesn't want to see Father. He wants to confront Him on everything that He has ever said – ever *lied* – about. But just the thought of seeing Him again makes Ethan seethe; he wants nothing to do with Him.

Azna shifts, leaning forward in his chair. His emerald eyes are dull yet firm. "Then you *should* speak with Him. Speculation alone can create... unnecessary wedges between beings. I'm sure that the Spirit meant well."

"What kind of being is able to look at their child and knowingly lie to them?" Ethan asks through gritted teeth. The Feni shifts in his chair and looks away, his ears finally drooping. "Is that what families do?"

"No," Azna answers. He reaches across his desk for a single piece of paper and stares down at it momentarily. "No being is perfect. It could be that they are prideful, or scared, or even ignorant. But *we* have an excuse. The Spirit, however, does not act without purpose." He folds the paper in his fingers and quietly slips it into his robe. "Just like any other being, He has His reasons. But unlike any other being, He is privy to knowledge that we all must find ourselves."

Ethan narrows his eyes. The Feni's platitudes don't make him feel any better, only more confused. One would think that a child of the Great Spirit would understand Him better than any being *ever*. At least, he *thought* he understood. Now... he doesn't know.

Azna stands from his desk. "I must go now. The Council is waiting on me."

"Of course," Ethan mutters. He steps aside, clearing Azna's way to the door to his office. As the Feni passes, he gives the Husk a stiff pat on his shoulder.

"Talk to Him," he gently advises once more before disappearing into the maze of the infirmary.

***

Alone, Amber walks back to her dorm, the stars already in sharp view overhead as the light of the cycle clings to the edges of the sky for as long as it can. Windows and lamps burn with small Firelights, illuminating the city of Asandra with their soft glows. She might have walked with Ethan if not for the fact that he had left with Lukri much earlier before the sky began to even change, offering to house the Sepreras at his dorm for the time being while they continue to sort out this whole... *mess*. So of course they had to beat the onset of the nighttime cold.

Her head is empty of thought as she stares at the path ahead of her. She's not looking forward to class next cycle. She has a sinking feeling that the others will start their planning without her.

The buildings give way to the open green of the small lake. The Library stands tall at the other end, bathed in shadow. No light winks in its windows since it's closed for the night, all students and staff already shooed out its doors long ago. The still water shimmers with starlight as it reflects the sky above.

Her eyes, however, are drawn to the willow. Tiny rays of yellow-green light emit from the tree's long branches that sweep the grassy ground. Odd. Most beings are already home or in the dorms by now.

Curious, she decides to approach the tree.

The grass masks her footsteps as she strides across the open space, her breathing the only noise she can hear. As she nears the tree, the feeling of magic grows against her skin, wrapping around her arms and legs with its mist in a strange sort of hug. It welcomes her presence, drawing her closer.

She pulls back the curtain of leaves to reveal the source of the strange light. Flowers of all shapes and colors bloom around the tree's base, their petals alight with magic. The air swirls with tiny specks of yellow, dancing through the darkness without a care. Along the tree's bark climb thin strands of ivy pulsing with energy. The aroma is sweet like sugar yet earthy and somewhat damp but not in a bad way.

At the origin point of all this wondrous nature is Blaze, his eyes closed and body stretched out as he slumbers in the shade. The flowers crowd the sides of his figure as small vines wrap themselves around his arms and feet.

The aroma beckons her forward. She hesitates at first, her eyes cautiously trained on the Naturist. Is he sleeping? Would he mind her inspecting some of the flowers?

She lets the willow's leaves she has been holding up fall, the curtain closing behind her. As they brush against the grass, the Naturist doesn't stir or shift. A good sign. Perhaps she *will* get a little closer…

She takes her first step forward, carefully lowering it down onto the grass before her. She still watches Blaze tensely, worried that he'll wake at any moment and reprimand her for even being here.

Second step forward. Still, he rests quietly. His goggles reflect the orange lights hovering above his head, making it look like dancing stars floating across a painted sky.

Third step forward. The flowers seem to brighten, as if they sense her approach and want to try and impress her by outshining all the other flowers around the Naturist. As much as she finds it cute… how are they able to do that on their own?

Fourth step forward. Blaze's body tenses in an instant, causing her to freeze where she stands. She watches with dread as the scene unfolds rapidly before her.

The floating lights fizzle out. The flowers snap shut and retreat into the dirt, taking with them their sweet smells. The ivy shrivels and shrinks. The vines release their hold over his body. By the time Blaze opens his eyes, the magical scene is gone, replaced by the darkness of night and the chill of the cold Asandra air.

He takes a moment to blink, bringing himself back into the waking world. Amber just stands off to the side, her hands clasped over her mouth, regret making her gut churn. Did she just ruined something special? She didn't mean to! She just wanted to admire the flowers…

Blaze sits up and turns to her, though in the tree's darkness she can't make out his face. "Amber?"

Her breath catches in her throat. He doesn't sound upset with her. Not yet, anyway. She shifts one of her feet backwards a half-step, bracing herself.

In the silence, the Naturist looks at his surroundings. "Nightfall already?" he asks with a long sigh. He leans forward, draping his arms over his knees, turning his attention to the ground, and rubs his hands on the sides of his face.

He's still absorbed by the world around him. How long will it be before he turns his attention to *her*?

Amber wants to move, but she doesn't have the courage to do so. Should she run away? Should she continue her approach? Should she wander down to the lake's edge, even?

"Do you need something?" Blaze finally asks her. His

voice is flat and tired. Her skin crawls under his gaze. Is he judging her? Is he upset with her?

Will he hit me?

"Um…" she replies in a small chirp. "I… just wanted to see the flowers…"

The silhouette's head tilts to one side, processing the statement. It's not long she feels the coolness of his gaze turn away from her face, letting the heat of embarrassment flare in her cheeks.

Blaze bends over, extending his hands down towards the dirt below. Between where his hands hover, a little light sprouts from the grass, shooting upwards before spinning and unfurling its petals into that of a shimmering flower. Its glow illuminates Blaze's hands, gently cupped around the flower as it blooms, and his face, furrowed in concentration. The petals pulse with magic, a soft vibration breaking the stillness of the air. Still, Amber remains rooted in place, unwilling to approach the Naturist.

Once more, his gaze turns to her expectantly. He nods to the flower, inviting her over. The flower's glow dances in the reflection of his goggles, hiding his eyes behind it. He waits patiently for Amber to work up her courage to approach, a slow and reluctant trudge across the grass to where he sits.

She strides around his hands, looking down at the tiny, delicate flower. It's not the petals themselves that glow, but the veins that run through them, each one filled with flowing starlight. As she stares, she lowers herself to her knees to get a better look.

Blaze draws back his hands, his fingers twitching as he gives Amber more room to gaze upon the little plant. It sparkles and winks back at her, its light bringing her robe and face into clear color in its presence. The flower itself isn't exactly white, but more of a light purple. Its center houses tiny yellow-orange orbs that appear to hardly give off much glow.

She doesn't realize she's reaching out to touch the magical plant until she sees her own hands slip into view. Her outstretched fingers curl inwards sharply as she stops herself. She shouldn't–

"You can pick it up," Blaze reassures her, gesturing to the flower.

She hesitates, biting her bottom lip. Gradually, her fingers begin to stretch towards the delicate light before her, brushing the bright petals against the sides of her palms. It's warm against her skin, vibrating with the magic that pulses through it.

She lifts it from the ground with ease; though it sprouted from the dirt, it has no stem to speak of, letting the plant float atop the grass as its support instead. She brings it to her face and, closing her eyes, takes a deep sniff, almost burrowing her nose into the plant's center.

Once again, she is hit with that sweet planty smell from earlier. It tickles her nose and swirls in her lungs. As she exhales, she opens her eyes again and finds that some of the orange orbs are starting to rise from the flower, whirling into the air to chase away some of the darker shadows. She follows them quietly, watching them dance.

Her mouth opens, stiff and somewhat dry. "I didn't know you could do this."

Blaze is silent, shifting in the grass. Amber tears her eyes away from the orange orbs to find him leaning back against the willow's trunk, his head turned to *her*. The glowing reflections continue to shield his eyes in the night's shadows. His expression remains unchanged.

"Do you like it?" he speaks slowly, almost as if he were scared to even ask her such a question.

Amber nods back. "It's beautiful."

The Naturist hardly reacts to her answer. She was expecting a smile at least, a twitch of his lips, or maybe even a proud huff. But no, nothing about his face changes. It remains in a strange half-disappointed, half-sympathetic scowl. To whom these emotions are directed, she can't tell.

He raises a hand, his fingers closed around something invisible, and begins to turn his wrist as if he were twisting a dial. Amber's eyes are drawn down towards the flower once more as its whitish-purple glow slowly fades into a rich blue, then gradually turning a light green, and onward into soft yellow. Her eyes widen with astonishment.

When the flower turns hot pink, Blaze lets out a chuckle. "You're cute when you're in awe."

Amber looks up in an instant, her cheeks flaring once more. She doesn't know whether to take his statement as a compliment or a twisted insult.

So she presses her lips together and says nothing at all.

The moment of levity passes, and in its place Blaze frowns once more. His lips part briefly, something on his mind that he's debating on sharing with her.

Eventually, he asks her, "Do you hate me?"

Amber bites her tongue to stop herself from blurting anything back at him. On that level, right then and there, she does, yes. But when she actually thinks about the question more, her emotions become confused and unclear. There's a reason why the phrase "actions speak louder than words" rings true, for despite all he's said to her face and all his attitude, he has been more selfless this cycle than any wizard she's been with so far. His Shadow was helpful and caring, and now he has become... *nice*.

Does she hate him?

"I don't know," she replies, even as she gently leans away from him. Once again, she feels split. With all she remembers, she'd never want to be caught dead hanging out with *Blaze* of all beings! So why is the void within her oozing with recognition? Despite never knowing him personally, it still feels as though the two of them have been... *friends* all this time.

Maybe he reminds her of some other being she used to know. A being she hasn't remembered yet.

Her head starts to ache, so she shifts the magic flower to one hand to free her other to rub her temples. *Not now... Please not now...*

"Are you alright?" Blaze asks, leaning forward, his body tensing.

"...Yeah," she answers quietly. The Naturist lets out a slight breath of relief, though he remains alert regardless.

It takes what's left of her willpower to push the void back down and wipe her eyes dry as tears sit ready to fall. She's been doing so well, keeping herself together. She wishes she was of more help this cycle than she was. She tried to put on a tougher exterior, but it failed miserably, leaving her almost unable to talk to any being other than those she already knew.

She stops massaging her head and simply holds it, bending forward to rest her elbow on the dirt in front of her. Her other hand sits on her knee, the flower's glow pulsing with a tiny amount of carefree warmth.

"You're trying too hard," Blaze says. Amber sits up, her eyes watery. He sits with a slouch, arms crossed and hands draped lazily over his knees. Having gotten her attention, he raises a finger and points at her. "Whatever you're trying to do with yourself isn't working, and if you keep pushing it, there's a good chance you'll only do more harm than good."

"But–" she breathes back, though her hopes for a retort fall through when nothing comes to mind. She looks down at the flower she still holds as her throat constricts.

Blaze shifts in the grass. "I've seen many beings at ASM try and reinvent themselves. And most of the time, it doesn't work. It's not as simple as donning a new personality. You have to convince yourself and every being around you that *that* is who you are. And *now* is not the time to do things like that."

Amber bites her tongue. Like he'd know anything about

wanting to become a different being. She just wants to understand who she was. She wants to be whole again. But she doesn't think he'll take her seriously if she were to try and explain all of that to him.

What is he insinuating, then? That she should give up trying to change? That she's incapable *of* change? That no being will ever believe in her change or support her trying to change? That she's destined to be stuck as some shy, emotional Healer unable to offer a helping hand beyond the infirmary?

It's a very swift and thoughtless action. Her fingers curl around the flower, squeezing it in her tight grip, unleashing her boiling frustration on the tiny plant.

"*Gah!*" his cry rings out sharply, filling her ears. The ground begins to rumble and shake as she lifts her head in alarm. Blaze is bent forward, one hand clawing at his chest as the other trembles, trying to keep his body upright. He sputters for breath, something dark dripping down from his face. From where, she can't tell.

Before she can do anything, the grass below splits open, and up into the dark night rise long, pointed tentacles. They bend towards her first, stretching over Blaze protectively. Amber's breath catches in her throat as her heart begins to pound in her head, frozen in place as they rush towards her.

Then... they stop. Quivering only inches away from her head, the vines halt their advance. A giant claw towers over her, prepared to strike her through her sides with its vicious might.

Deep in the shadows, Blaze's hand glows with his magic as he continues to wheeze. The rest of him, however, she can't even make out.

Slowly, she looks back down at her hand. Her fingers uncurl from the glowing pink flower, its light weakly flickering back at her. Its petals are crushed, trying hopelessly to fall back into place as she gives it room to spread out. The filaments inside are all bent and broken.

Yet it continues to shine.

She drops it and scrambles back, out of the clutches of the dark green claw. The flower floats down to the grass and rests just in front of where she sat. Once she's moved away, the vines surge forward, clamping down and sealing the Naturist within its clutches.

She takes the opportunity to catch her breath and calm down. She rests her hands on the edge of the lake, the very tips of her fingers dipping themselves into the cold water. It all makes sense now. His pained expressions were real. Does that mean he could feel whatever his vines were feeling, too? Was moving through the sand *that* difficult for him?

What that spirit said – that there were beings that he couldn't harm – springs to mind as well. Especially since... well, those vines were definitely intent on harming her, yet they didn't. Is it possible that his Shadow's Branding is still in effect?

She closes her eyes, a dour blanket gradually being cast upon her. No wonder she's been feeling so strangely about Blaze. It's because he's not really *Blaze* anymore. He's not the wizard she first met. Altered to protect her against his own will. Did Ethan have Blaze venture with her because he knew she'd need the extra help, or because he knew that Blaze would do anything to shield her from harm?

Eventually, the vines shift once more, and she opens her eyes again. She watched them peel themselves back as they retreat back into the ground. The Naturist is standing already, his hand dropping from his chest down to his stomach as his other is shoved into his pocket. His head turns to her, and her blood runs cold.

"I-I..." Amber stammers.

"I'm alright," he interrupts. Amber's mouth only hangs open, lost for words. She doesn't believe him. How could she? All cycle, she's been causing him so much pain. How can he be "alright" so fast?

"It's late," he adds calmly. He steps up to her and offers his free hand. "Let's get back to the dorms."

She starts to lift her arm but stops herself. She doesn't feel like she deserves this gesture. She doesn't even know if he's doing it out of kindness or obligation. She just can't understand *why*.

She twists and picks herself up off the ground instead, brushing her skirt off and avoiding his silent gaze. Now that she's standing, she can see his simple lie; there's a soft green glow emanating from his pocket. He's still healing.

"I'm sorry," she mutters.

"It's not like you knew what would happen," Blaze replies dismissively. "Only a few beings know about–"

"Not just that," she interrupts. She finally looks up at his darkened face, though now she can barely see past his goggles' reflections. There's no crimson sheen to his eyes as he regards her. "I didn't treat you fairly and I leaned on you too much. You... shouldn't be forced to do things you don't want to do, either." She clasps her hands together, a weak flurry of golden sparkles falling from her fingers. "Do you know what happened on Korodon?"

"No, and I don't *want* to know," Blaze snaps suddenly. He scowls with frustration as he adds, "I don't care *what* you say, I'm *not* a hero."

Amber blinks, absorbing his outburst. That's... not what she was expecting to hear. Maybe she should have made her question a little clearer. "No," she replies, shaking her head. "Do you know what happened to your *Shadow*?"

"Stars above..." he breathes through gritted teeth, growing more irritated than she intended. He's the first one to turn away, starting to head towards the willow's hanging leaves. "Like I told Eth: I. Don't. Want. To talk about this!"

So he knows *nothing*? Ethan never told– No. Blaze never let *any being* tell him what happened to his Shadow? He's not even aware of the Brand on his shoulder?

Amber takes a deep breath. As strong as his insistence to ignorance is, this isn't something he can turn a blind eye too. Has he not questioned once why he's been doing the things he's done this cycle? Has he come to accept this change in his personality without so much of a second thought? He should at least be aware that he *isn't* the same as he used to be anymore. That this isn't his fault at all.

"Your Shadow was marked with an order to protect me and Lukri!" she states. Blaze freezes, the leaves draped over the back of his hand to reveal the quiet night beyond the tranquil tree. "It was so you couldn't hurt us while we were on Korodon, but... I guess it's still in effect. Maybe you should ask Eth to remove it for you, just so that... you're not forced to act like a being you're not."

Blaze is still, hardly even twitching as her words fade into the night.

"I've always wanted to protect other beings," he says. "I was willing to put my life on the line to save an entire island. Brands and Shadows and threats aside, I wouldn't have done this cycle any differently, either. But thank you for letting me know." His head turns, though he keeps his face hidden. "Now, are you coming or what?"

That's right. It's almost too easy to forget that he was supposed to have gone to Korodon with Ethan, before Blaze's Shadow was taken and she wound up in Ethan's care instead. They had been planning for *years*. She knew that going to Korodon at that time was practically a death sentence, but never crossed her mind that he was doing it for good reason. He *knew* it was likely going to be a one-way trip. Yet he made his preparations anyway. *She* was just a burden.

Heart heavy and body weary, she starts forward herself. Hearing her approach, Blaze steps through the curtain of leaves, Amber only a few steps behind. Her eyes sink to the ground, unable to raise themselves.

Maybe Kimberly was right. Maybe she should just focus on her studies from now on and let the others handle this mess. Maybe she's more helpful to them by staying out of the way. Then she wouldn't be hurting any being or becoming a burden. No being would need to worry about her.

Out of the corner of her eye, she sees Blaze drop back to stride by her side.

“I'm worried about them, too, you know,” he tells her. “Chasing after the Shards isn't easy. Just... have a little faith in them. I'm sure things will work out.”

She wrings her hands. “I just wanted to help.”

“And you did, didn't you?”

“I don't really know.”

“I'd say you did. Stars only know what would have happened if you *hadn't* offered to help.”

Amber can't help but let out a reluctant sigh. “I guess...”

“You *did*,” he insists. “And now it's up to *them* to see things through.”

It still doesn't shake the dark cloud hanging over her. She can't help but feel defeated, like she still did things wrong. Ethan could have done everything they did in half the time no doubt. If it weren't for her, Blaze wouldn't have missed his class or hurt himself or gotten possessed.

“You just have to take your mind off of it for a little while,” Blaze adds, giving her a light elbowing, “and spend some time outside of your head.”

“That's a little hard,” she comments.

“Yeah, well, you're not the only one dealing with memory loss.”

She finally raises her head. Sure, she isn't the *only* being on Astria struggling with missing time. Electro is, too. But their issues are far from being the same. Though... does Blaze know any of that?

"I rather not agonize over what I don't know," he clarifies. "Whatever happened on Korodon *stays* on Korodon. I'm fine with that."

"Wait," she says, promptly stopping in her tracks. Blaze pauses a few steps away, caught off guard by her sudden halt. "How did you know I have memory loss?"

Blaze turns to her, retrieving something from his pocket. It's small enough to be mostly shrouded by his fingers, but she can still make out a flash of dark red and shadowed white. Something small rattles around as his hand moves.

He holds up the thing to her, his fingers parting to let her see. It's a small red box with an image printed on its surface. He has one of his fingers pressed against its bottom, which is white, as if he were holding it in place.

Her heart jumps into her throat, her head starting to pound once again. She can't stop her face from contorting into an expression she doesn't know. Impossibly, she recognizes the box, even though she can't put a name to it. It's wrong. It shouldn't be there in his hand. But it is.

Blaze shifts his weight. "Do you know what this is?"

"I-I... Yes," she mutters.

"What's it called?" he asks.

But she shakes her head, raising a hand to her temples once more. It feels like its name is on the tip of her tongue, but the harder she tries to recall it, the more the void hammers her skull. She can't even muster her voice to speak.

"It's a matchbox," he answers for her. All at once, the pressure releases. Relief leaves her lips in an airy breath. The ache still remains, though, as the question shifts.

"Where did you... *get* that?" she manages to inquire, her voice small and stiff with pain.

He turns the box away from her and begins to tumble it in his hand, flipping it over and over with his fingers expertly. The little white tray occasionally starts to slide out, only for him to promptly push it back with little thought. "Truthfully, I don't know myself. But trying to figure it out is more pain than it's worth." He looks down at the matchbox like it's a key to some ancient mystery. "You're the first being that knew what this was."

"*Really*?" Amber breathes back. Blaze nods back, regarding her with a new light in his eyes as he slips the matchbox back into his pocket. They sparkle with curiosity and what Amber feels to be a soft kinship. Over what, neither of them know. But there is something special here. Something they can't quite put their fingers on.

His soft expression hardens into something a little more typical of his attitude, tired with a hint of annoyance. "But it's a bit late to be digging into this now." He holds out a hand, gesturing for Amber to join him once again. She nods in agreement. It's certainly a lot for her to absorb and think about right now, especially since she needs to be up early for class next cycle. But... maybe they can continue this conversation later.

Together in heavy silence, they make the rest of the trek back to the dorms.

III

Reconcile

Chapter 14

Each of the Great Spirits has Their own connections to Astria, and through them the wider universe. The beings believe that these items are sacred, and that if one is to be destroyed then the entire universe would be thrown into complete disarray.

Like many of their ancient myths and legends, it's not entirely inaccurate. Yes, the destruction of the Spirits' "anchors" would greatly limit Their ability to commune with the beings of Astria, but it'd take much more than that to completely cut either Spirit off from the universe at large. As much as the Spirits seem to resent each other, They made the universe together. No doubt They have other anchors elsewhere among the stars, and that They would seek to rectify any and all imbalances. At least, that's what Ethan believes.

But at least the fear of complete universal upheaval has protected Their anchors thus far. Ethan makes his way down a dark, forgotten hallway, carved into the stone various ancient runes of protection. When the castle of Korodon was still used by the Generals, and before them the royal family descended from the first Storm wizard, this hallway was used by them when they wished to commune with the Spirit of Shadow. But after the disappearance of the Generals and the takeover of the island of

Asandra, the existence of this hallway gradually faded from the memory of all but the Spirit of Shadow and His children.

He reaches the ancient door at the hallway's end and opens it, listening to the metal hinges squeak and squeal as their joints grind together. Beyond the door is a sunken circular room, its curved walls etched with a mural of the pantheon of Fragment Shadows. It's both stunning and strange every time he sees it. To think that his siblings once walked among the beings of Astria as freely as he does now, worshiped by the masses as they did the Spirit of Shadow Himself. Now most of them rest in obscurity, many lumped into others for the sake of convenience. Sadly, even *he* doesn't recognize most of his siblings, though that's mostly because they were never interested in getting to know him, either.

No, he thinks, shaking his head, *they weren't interested in Shadow. This will be my first time even seeing the Shadow Realm.*

It's so easy to conflate Shadow's memories and experiences with his own. There was a time when he *was* Shadow, a crafted shell being pulled around by the entity who wore him. But after waking as… well, *himself*, an entity that could exist completely separate from Shadow, he doesn't want to co-opt its life. At least, he's been trying not to.

Right in the mural's center, directly opposite the door and small set of stairs, are the five eldest Fragments. Uno, the Dragon, wraps its wings around them protectively, the menacing yet kindly glare of its eyes expertly carved into the rock. To its left is Duo, the Prophet, its arms wrapped in what Ethan can only guess is the Tapestry of Fate, its length weaving in and out of each of the Fragments in the mural. To its right is Tria, the Raven, the bringer of wisdom. Beneath them are the Twins, Quadri and Quin, opposites in every sense of the word. They all bore witness to the makings of Astria, with Uno as ancient as the concept of time itself, second in age only to their Father. Ethan can only wonder what the universe looked like back then.

There are some others he vaguely recognizes, mostly due to all the legends that he has read about his siblings. The Puppeteer, the Judge, the Thief, the King, the Healer, the Crafter, and the Malign stand out the most. Others he has to infer. One Fragment is a nightmarish and twisted creature, a mass of arms and legs and eyes thrown haphazardly together. Another is a figure separated into individual joints, cut into perfect pieces by what he can only assume to be a blade. What they possibly do or represent, he has no idea. But they're there.

He turns to the right, passing over the long line of his siblings in favor of finding the last Fragment he knows. Standing at attention next to the doorway is the Knight, its hands folded over its longsword at the ready to strike down any and all threats. Its helmet conceals its emotions, though being part-judge, part-executioner, it doesn't need to feel much beyond its sense of noble justice. It would do anything to protect the weak and innocent, even if it meant going against its own family…

At least, that's how it has been characterized in the legends. He thought it was simply all a fabrication by the ancient Astrians, a selfless figure that Shadow, and by proxy himself, would eventually become at some point in the future.

He turns away from the mural, anger towards Father bubbling in his chest.

At the bottom of a short set of stairs is a stone dais carved with runes unlike anything any being has most likely ever seen. The language of the Great Spirits, unreadable even to Their children. If he were to close his eyes, it would almost feel like Shadow just emerged from this very same dais for the first time, eager to see the wonders of Astria.

He steps onto its surface, a storm of emotion swirling inside his shell. He's curious and excited, but also anxious and upset. But he knows that he doesn't want to live in this state of confusion, constantly wondering about the truth. The answers will be difficult to hear. There's no preparing for that.

[*Don't get into any trouble,*] he warns Shadow.

There's a slight buzz as it sighs, mildly unhappy that it had to be warned in the first place. {*I–*}

Then its presence disappears entirely. A cold and empty chasm is left in the wake of its incomplete reply... and his incomplete self.

Panic shoots through his body as he turns his attention back to his surroundings in an instant. The room around him has already quietly melted away into darkness, with only himself and the dais beneath his feet remaining. It's cold here, a cold that can only be felt in the very depths of one's essence. Somewhere in the distance, strange whispery voices drift their way into his ears, filling his head with their incoherent noises.

He didn't even think that their connection would have been cut off once he was in the Shadow Realm, though it makes sense that it would. He and Shadow now exist on two entirely different planes of the universe; despite their close bond, there's only so far it can realistically stretch. Still, he can't help but raise his guard now that he's all alone.

To his right, there is nothing but void for as far as he can see, however far that might be. To his left, however, there is light and color beaming down on his small figure. A long ribbon stretches from one distant point to another, its surface swimming with colors of all shades. It has wrapped itself into a dome, its entrance only outlined by a thin black rim and the subtle shift of something residing within it.

Centi? a booming voice asks from within, calm and gentle. He vaguely recalls this voice, though it's been a while since even Shadow has heard it. Still, the name stabs at his chest, making it ache with anger waiting to be unleashed. *Is that you?*

Seeing no other option besides wandering off into the endless darkness of the Shadow Realm with no clue as to where Father might be, Ethan makes his way into the rainbow dome.

The glow of the dome is a welcoming respite from the Realm outside of it, not just because of the color it adds to the black world but also the sense of orientation. Directly opposite the dome's entrance is a mass of… *something*, wrapped within the endless stretch of ribbon, shifting around as if it were trying to find a comfortable sitting position. The Fragment's face is so high that he has to crane his neck just to catch a glimpse of its chin.

Upon sensing his stare, the Fragment casts its gaze downwards and flashes a curved stretch of white, a smile. Its eyes are a light pink instead of crimson red; it feels as if the Fragment is not actually looking *at* him, but rather *through* him.

"Hello… Duo," Ethan says stiffly.

The Prophet shudders within its wrappings and shrinks so fast one could have blinked and missed its transition. It still sits towering over Ethan, though now it's much easier to meet its glassy gaze. Its floats just above whatever constitutes the ground in the Realm, its slender legs folded and arms floating out at its sides, the ribbon of light wrapped weaving its way in and out of its body.

A sort of sad joy radiates from Duo as it says, *Ah… it has been so long since I have heard your voice.*

"I've… been away," Ethan answers. He folds his arms and shifts his weight uncomfortably, looking around the dome. "Do you know where Father is? I'm looking for Him."

Oh. The smile on Duo's face disappears, falling back into the darkness of its formless face. *He is probably busy. But…* It lowers its legs and strides over to Ethan, its smooth hands outstretched cautiously. Its cold fingers brush against his cheek and neck, lightly at first, making sure it's truly him that it's feeling. *You have a shell now,* Duo remarks with restrained awe. It starts to move its hands cross his face, but Ethan is quick to shake the Fragment off and step away.

"Stars, don't do that!" he says.

Duo stands frozen for a long, silent moment, its hand still poised before it. The Tapestry that clothes it pulses with light, brightening in a flare of color before ebbing away just as quickly. Its head turns first, glancing off at the Tapestry that surrounds them. Then its posture resets, kicking its feet up into the air and having its arms glide back to its sides. Once finished staring at whatever demanded its attention, its gaze returns to Ethan.

A strange chuckle then escapes its figure and its body ripples and distorts uncomfortably. The air of its emotions is hard to read; the weight of sorrow presses down on his shoulders, yet at the same time he feels the hollowness of indifference.

Father brought you here for a reason, Duo says slowly. It's much more composed now, much more confident now with when in time it currently exists. *You come seeking answers. To challenge His words. But you are not ready for that conversation, which is why you are here with me... Ethan.*

His name rolls from its mouth stiffly as the air of the dome shifts. It knows.

"Father's not coming." The disappointing fact slips from his mouth with surprising ease. He feels somewhat relieved by it.

Not right now, Duo lightly corrects. It waves a hand, and from the darkness rises a cushioned chair and a red rug. It doesn't speak its invite to him, but he gets what Duo wants for him to do. He takes a seat before the Prophet. For as comfortable as the chair feels, Ethan sits on its very edge, unwilling to relax.

Both beings are quiet. Ethan waits for Duo to speak, expecting it to start answering all his burning questions. As the Prophet, it must already know everything he's come here to ask. Yet searching the Fragment's pale eyes, he doesn't feel like Duo is present anymore. It has gone stiff again, staring off into space, as the Tapestry wrapped around its body pulses with incomprehensible power.

"Duo?" he asks. The Fragment doesn't respond or react.

Shadow didn't spend any time with Duo, so he's not sure if this sort of behavior is common for it. One moment, being aware of all past, present, and future, all the while still being anchored to a single point in time, able to feel and speak as any being can. The next, being removed from reality so suddenly and completely with no warning at all.

Eventually, it draws breath, a burst of fear filling the bright dome, though it quickly disappears as fast as it emanated. Its fingers bend cautiously as it brings itself back into its body once more.

Ask, it commands.

Ethan looks down at the black ground. He has so many questions, each one equally as hard to vocalize. So he starts with the easiest one: "Do I have a Shard to the Font of Magic?"

Yes.

Ethan has to sit back as his chest starts to thump loudly in his ears, filling his hollow shell with the light of warmth. He closes his eyes and places a hand on his chest, feeling the Shard beating inside him. The answer is strangely comforting to hear, like a weight he didn't even know was bearing down on him has finally been lifted off his shoulders. There is no doubt now that this is how he has been able to defy all the rules of life.

The Knight is gone now, Duo adds, *no matter what Korodon has said.*

"So it *did* die."

It... Duo looks up at the dome around them once more, searching for its answer. It sounds like it wants to correct him, but it doesn't seem too sure of itself. *It... It did.*

The confirmation forces its way from Duo's figure, and with it the Fragment grows anxious. The Tapestry curls itself around its form tighter, as if trying to protect the Fragment from external harm. The thought of a Fragment Shadow dying doesn't appear to sit right with it. Or, perhaps, it is having a hard time coming to terms with the fact that one of its siblings has already died.

"Didn't you know it was going to happen?" he asks.

I did, Duo nods. *But... just because I know the order of every event to ever happen does not mean I know what has already passed.* It pauses, turning its head back to Ethan. *Tell me, are you still in chains?*

Ethan's hands stray to his gauntlets automatically, his wrists turning deathly cold. He's been able to forget about Riona's spectral chains due to being so busy. He doesn't like to be reminded of them.

"I am," he confirms with a flat voice.

Duo nods, a smile returning to its face. Its dull gaze appears to become much more lively and present, drinking in Ethan's presence before it, studying every detail there is to him. *Ah, there you are. Thank you. I was having a hard time finding this moment.*

"Why?"

Because the distance between the Knight's death and... now *is not even enough time to be filled with anything noteworthy.* It pauses, the Tapestry's glow brightening once more, though this time its silence is much shorter. *Riona will be forgotten soon enough, although it might still seem many years away. Your concept of time is much different right now, but the more you grow, the more you will stop caring.*

"Or maybe that's just *you*," Ethan blurts, his hands gripping his knees tight. Even if Duo can see all of time, that doesn't mean it understands what he and Shadow have been through.

Duo frowns, then nods slowly. *Indeed. We are different.*

Still, Ethan turns away from Duo, unable to look at it anymore, disgust swirling in his chest. It doesn't know the half of it.

"So Centi is dead," he states. "What does that make Shadow and me?"

That, Duo replies calmly, *is an answer for you to find yourself.*

He leans forward in his chair in an instant, his voice raised with frustration as he starts, "You mean Father–"

Ethan, Duo's annoyed voice rumbles, filling the dome with its might. He is pressed back into the chair as anger radiates from the Fragment before him. The lengths of the Tapestry that float from its body shudder, their swimming colors gradually forming shapes and shadows he can barely recognize. Old and forgotten power stirs just below Duo's surface, only restrained by an incomprehensible amount of lifetimes of learned discipline. *You are still young and naive, and your anger is justified, but I will not stand for you coming here just to tarnish the name of our Father.*

The eldest, yes, we were given a purpose, but the Knight was not told to be how it became. The Astrians had order and law, judges and executioners, but no enforcement. That *was how the Knight came to be. Even in the Knight's absence, the Astrians of the present still look up to it in their own ways, as they do the rest of us. The Fragments are not just real entities, but ideas and legends that we have forged for ourselves.*

You are no Knight, despite our Father wanting you to be. There is no need for one anymore. If you are not the Knight, then what are you? It is not an answer that can merely be given.

The colors of the Tapestry finally find their meaning, and before him a scene is shown on its surface. On Duo's left, the Knight is wrapped in golden sparkles, its dark figure broken up by seams of white light. Despite the cracks of light most likely being extremely painful, the Fragment appears to be in pure bliss, completely unaware of its body crumbling before its very eyes. In its hands is a sphere as bright as the stars in the night sky. That must be the Font of Magic.

On Duo's right, there is himself, his body entangled in hundreds of thousands of strands of colorful lights. Around each of his wrists are white disks etched with incomprehensible runes of magical power, pulsing with the same energy as the sphere in Centi's hands. But the scene doesn't give him the comfort that it probably should. His hat and cape are gone. His head is turned away, gaze cast to the lights around him. His hair hides his eyes. His mouth is curved upwards into a distant, careless smile.

Discomfort swirls inside his chest as the Shard beats heavier with dread.

Duo's voice rises to fill the space with its grand declaration: *The Font will be reunited, one way or another.*

Chapter 15

"Well, you *did* have a fever coming on..." Amber hums as she lifts her hand from Jake's arm. He can't help but release a thankful sigh as he sinks further into the sofa. He still *feels* cold, but not quite as bogged down as he had been feeling since their return to Asandra.

His gaze remains fixed on the table before him, his body heavy and his eyes dry. He can't find it in himself to even mutter a thanks to the Healer right beside him.

A small shimmer of gold still rains from her fingers as she hovers close to him, her face painted with silent concern. Her lips are parted, ready to speak. He wouldn't be surprised if she asks him about Gardall, but he doesn't know if he'll be able to answer.

"You should... probably get some rest now," she advises gently. She drifts away from his side, her gaze not once leaving him until she disappears back into the hallway. It doesn't take long for a muffled conversation to start up again downstairs.

Jake shifts, lying down on his side and kicking his feet up. His heavy pauldrons rest on the living room table, though he kept his boots on. Dirt and grime is by far *much* easier for him to remedy than gaping holes. Sleep doesn't sound too bad right about now. He never realized just how cold the place truly was until now, without his inner fire to keep him warm.

His eyes droop, the world turning blurry. He's disappointed with himself. He wasn't able to be there for Kimberly on Gardall, just like he wasn't there *that* night. Her soulless stare rises from the recesses of his mind, a cold body bent and twisted before him, likely wondering why he let *this* happen.

He vowed to never let it happen again. He thought he changed all he could to protect her from whatever may cross their path. Yet he let the *cold* of all things keep him from being by her side! If he can't even be there for her, then what kind of protector is he really?

His thoughts are broken up briefly by a strong draft that jolts him back awake. He glances up, expecting to see Kimberly trudging into the room, only to find Electro staring back at him instead. Well, his body, anyway. He's covered in a thick layer of black smoke, obscuring his clothes and skin yet still retaining his shape. Brief flashes shine through as his body shifts, though it's never long enough to get a clear enough glimpse.

Shadow's crimson gaze lingers on the Pyromancer before it opts to sit down on the lone mattress, leaning back against the wall. Its presence feels more like an absence, a dense hole in reality. It, too, appears just as exhausted as Jake feels.

“Uhhey,” he mutters, though those two basic words manage to slur themselves together as they leave his mouth.

I didn't mean to wake you, it says. Jake rolls his eyes, his brief burst of energy leaving in a gust. He was only dozing, probably not for very long. Though he can't keep his gaze off of the Fragment and Electromancer for very long. Why are the two of them like... *that* all of a sudden?

Shadow's eyes seem to flicker in and out of reality, entirely ignoring Jake's staring. It sits perfectly still, appearing more like a steaming black statue than a living entity. The magic it exudes rests itself on top of Jake's body, gently pressing him into the sofa's cushions.

The bell below rings out as the door swings open. Jake sucks in an expectant breath and finally musters as much energy as he can to sit up at the very least. Kimberly *should* be home by now. If it isn't her... His eyes shift, albeit somewhat reluctantly, to his sword, propped up against the sofa nearby.

"I'm back," Kimberly yells. Her heavy footsteps climb the stairs slowly, one after another.

"Hi," he mumbles as she trudges into view. Icy air rolls from her body, flooding the room with its sharp bite. She, too, has a drifting gaze just like him and Shadow. Defeated from a long cycle of heartache and fighting. Though as she surveys the room, she straightens, taking a deep breath as she readjusts her grip on her textbook.

"How are you feeling?" she asks Jake.

He can't help but shake his head. "Cold. Tired."

"Aren't we all?" she passively jokes, even releasing a halfheartedly amused huff. Jake finds himself smiling along with her. Inside his chest, there's a brief flurry of warm embers that dance about, easing some of the mounting exhaustion out of his system.

"Well *I'm* not supposed to be," he bounces back, his voice starting to warm up. "What good is a cold Pyromancer?"

Kimberly smirks, rolling her eyes. She sets her textbook down on the living room table and answers, "He certainly can't cook."

"I..." he starts, though he pauses before he makes any more comments. Amber said he *had* a fever coming on, so he probably shouldn't put himself in the kitchen. The smile on his face fades as he leans back into the sofa's cushions. "If you're okay with it."

"What's wrong?"

"Well, Amber said–"

Kimberly's mood shifts immediately before he's even done

speaking. “How bad was it? Do you need a blanket?”

Jake musters a weak grin. “I'm just tired, Kim. But if I came back with something from Gardall, then...” She nods in agreement, knowing what he's implying. “But I'd *like* a blanket.”

She rushes off, gesturing to him that she'll be back in a moment. She does return eventually, carrying in a white comforter she must have pulled off of her bed. She dumps the unwieldy mass into his lap. Instantly, his body starts to warm further wherever it touches him.

“Get comfortable,” she says with a smile, turning to leave once more. “Dinner will be ready soon.” She casts her gaze to Shadow still sitting silently, staring off into the ether. “Would you like... something to eat?” she asks it. Or maybe she's trying to address Electro.

Shadow's crimson gaze flickers up to her face briefly before it stares down at the dark hands draped over its knees. *I probably should,* it eventually replies.

“Is Electro okay?”

It looks back up at her, frowning as irritation floats throughout the room. *He's resting.*

With a sigh, Kimberly leaves it alone, making her way to the kitchen to start cooking. Shadow shifts on the mattress, returning to its listless staring. All the while Jake wrestles with the comforter.

He manages to wrap it around his back, drawing its edges close together to entrap his body in its thick warmth. It's nice to finally be free of the chill of Astria in all its forms for once this cycle. Some amount of liveliness finds its way back to him as his magic manages to ignite itself into a tiny flame. It feels like it's been many years since he's felt the contentment of comfort.

He closes his eyes, his attention being drawn to the flame within. Beneath the embrace of the comforter, his magic finally draws itself out of his bones and rushes towards the flame, a soft red flicker born anew. It takes little coaxing for it to gradually grow, feeding off of the flow of dormant power and thawing it out. Reinvigorated, a warm air blooms above the flame, expanding and filling his body with its glow.

He must admit, that banter is just what he needed. Fuel for his fire.

"Dinner," Kimberly's voice suddenly cuts through the silence. He opens his eyes and takes a sniff of the air. The sweet scent of fruit dances about, its aroma quite pungent. Kimberly holds a steaming plate in each hand, smiling somewhat wistfully to herself. She sets the steaming fruit before him, handing the other to Shadow. Its hands stretch out and accept the meal from her and pops one of the caramel slices into its mouth without consideration for its heat. Using its *fingers*. It doesn't seem bothered at all, but what about Electro? If it's not bothering him, either, then Shadow wouldn't have just done *that*, right?

"That was fast," he mutters in a daze. He tries to ignore Shadow throwing further sticky and steaming slices into its mouth with *bare hands* as he reaches for his own plate. It doesn't even wipe or at least lick its fingers afterwards!

Jake brings his plate into the folds of his comforter, resting it on his crossed legs. He lifts one of the fruits to his mouth and gives it a blow before consuming it. Once more, the fire within him flickers as a smile can't help but spread across his lips. As delicious as ever.

Catching a flash of blue out of the corner of his eye, he lifts his head as Kimberly returns with a plate of her own, snuggling up to Jake on the sofa. She leans over, pressing herself up against the white wall of the comforter. He can feel her Ice magic worming its way through the blanket to kiss his warm skin.

"It's very sweet," Jake comments, giving her a light nudge, "just like you."

A smile works its way across her lips, even though it's clear her mind is occupied with other thoughts.

"Thank you," her soft voice answers. Still, it's enough to make his fire leap and curl.

She holds her fork loose between her fingers as she stares down at her food. She pokes at it gently, rubbing the tines in the caramel juices. Weariness befalls her face as she leans further against Jake, resting her head on his covered shoulder. Her eyes open and shut, inhaling like she wants to speak, but exhales her words in a single heavy breath.

"Want to talk about it?" he prompts her.

"I don't know, Jake..." she mutters back. She lifts her fork, and he thinks she's going to stab one of the fruits on her plate. Instead, she licks the tines, her eyes distant and glossy.

"...Sucks we lost one of the Shards," he comments, slipping another bite into his mouth.

A strangled laugh escapes Kimberly, empty of any of the usual emotions that elicit such a response.

"Is it strange to say I don't really care about that?" she asks.

"A little," he admits, even as he shakes his head. The Shards feel like such a large issue that's out of their control. It doesn't feel real, them chasing after the pieces to Astria's heart and soul. Besides, they have no idea what Electro's Shadow is going to do with the Font once all three are reunited. Probably nothing good... but it's not like they know for sure.

He can't help but glance over at Shadow still sitting quietly on the mattress. It's done with its dinner, its plate set aside on the ground between its feet. It's strange to see Electro's face covered in darkness and *not* feel the need to jump up with his sword ablaze.

Kimberly heaves a deep breath, her shoulders rising and falling, rubbing against his own.

"It was a mistake. Seeing her." Tears start to fall from her eyes, even as her voice remains eerily calm. "The way she looked at me... She didn't seem to even care I was there. The first thing she asked about was... Jay." She tries to wipe her face dry, or perhaps at least clean herself up a bit, but the tears keep flowing. She slumps forward, staring down at her untouched dinner, the wisps of steam fading into the air as it cools.

There's something he wants to say to her. It rests on the very tip of his tongue. But bringing up his own personal matters right now feels like the *wrong* thing for him to do.

He knows how she feels. He's seen that look for most of his life. The look of a being who doesn't see you how they *should*, who doesn't treat you how you wish they did.

He frees an arm from the comforter and wraps it around Kimberly's shoulders, drawing her in closer. He does his best to provide her support as he tries to hide his gritted teeth.

Kimberly doesn't say anything else as she closes her eyes and sniffles, letting her boyfriend hold her. Her hand drops her fork entirely, shoving it onto her plate.

"Maybe you should turn in early," he gently suggests.

"Maybe..." she mutters back, her voice on the verge of cracking. She sets her plate down on the table before her and rises to her feet. She sways as she stares off into the distance, her hands straying to the folds of her skirt in a hopeless effort to smooth it out.

"Good night," she says eventually. She's gone before he can even reply, her footsteps drowning out any call he could make back to her. She even left behind her comforter. She might come back for it... or she might not. She might just be happy to finally get some rest and move on from such a chaotic cycle.

With a reluctant sigh, Jake sets his empty plate next to hers and stands from the sofa at long last, sliding the comforter off of his shoulders. The building doesn't feel as cold as it did before as his fire does its best to chase away the chill. He peers out into the hallway, looking for signs of Kimberly returning and finding nothing. His hand strays to the light switch. In one little motion, the living room plunges into darkness.

Jake takes his time returning to the sofa as his eyes adjust to his new environment. He hears Shadow shift on the mattress off to the side as the comforter gradually fades back into view. He takes the blanket and shoves it aside, giving himself some room to get situated.

As he plops back down, he can't help but stare at Kimberly's uneaten dinner. Seeing as she hardly touched it, he doesn't think she'll care if he finishes it for her. If it's left out overnight, it'll simply spoil.

She won't mind, he finally concludes as he leans forward. His mouth waters as he holds the dish in his hands, still warm despite the steam having long faded away.

Azna's at the Council this cycle.

The sudden yet true thought catches him off-guard as he begins to dig into his seconds. It *is* that time for their regular meeting, though it would have started *ages* ago. He might be back at the infirmary by now.

Or he might not be.

He squeezes his eyes shut and shakes his head, trying to rid himself of this annoying voice. Even if Azna's away, that doesn't change anything. There are still the same problems he will have to overcome. He couldn't in the past, so what's so different about trying again now?

Why not ask Shadow to help? It can–

He shoves another bite into his mouth forcefully, his teeth cutting right through the fruit slice with the full force of his frustration. Now is not the time to be thinking about this!

Yet... he can't really help himself. It feels as though the stars have granted him his one chance to finally act. Shadow is more or less available to him, and he knows that Azna is away and will be for quite some time. He no longer has to question if he can do it all by himself. He doesn't have to worry too much about any other being getting caught in the crossfire.

But *should* he?

The easy answer is no, *obviously*. It's been a few years and he's done his best to stay away from the infirmary. He hasn't been so hung up as of late, probably because he's much more focused on getting through school and supporting Kimberly as best he can. In the grand scheme of things, it's really not that important.

But with all of Kimberly's family troubles cropping up now, he doesn't think it'll be long before his do, too. His hasn't been resolved yet, after all, only put aside for the time being in the face of larger issues.

Kimberly doesn't have to know. Not right away. Granted, there never seems to be a good time to tell her anything, but she'll find out eventually. By then, this will all have blown over, and maybe things will be better. But he can't keep waiting around.

Should he? No. But he's going to anyway.

Carefully, he sets the plate down again, picked clean of even the caramelized juices. He looks over to where the mattress rests, his fire burning with determination.

"Shadow?"

Two crimson lights flicker into existence, piercing through the dim night, staring at him quietly.

"You want to help me with something?" he whispers.

What is it? it asks. Its voice makes the darkness grow thicker and vibrate, making it carry throughout the room with ease.

"I... remembered I have to pick something up from the infirmary," he lies. "But I'll need some help."

What about Electro?

"You could just leave him here." He'd rather *not* involve this random Electromancer in his business. If he were to wake up at any point, he'd likely only cause complications.

A blast of unease washes over him. *I don't think I should...*

"It's not like he's awake right now, right? You can leave him for *one* night."

Shadow doesn't respond. Not verbally, anyway. Its gaze turns away from Jake, contemplating his words. Then its soft crimson glow disappears. In its absence, something icy cold wraps itself around Jake's wrist, sending a chill down his spine in surprise. Though as he looks down to inspect it, he doesn't find anything there, despite the hairs on his skin bristling like mad.

A strong magical buzz rocks his body, causing him to look up once more. Shadow's form now floats above the Electromancer, its body darker than the lightless room itself. Its bright eyes shift, giving him a ready nod.

Jake takes up his sword, his fire swirling merrily within.

"Let's go," he announces.

Chapter 16

Clare is sitting at the front desk, like always, working diligently away. Her sandy hair hangs in a long braid laced with silver ribbons. It's one of his favorite hairstyles to see her with. He thinks it suits her quite well.

"The keys are in a drawer hidden in the wall behind her," Jake mutters. "I can't keep her distracted for long, so try and be quick."

Shadow is silent, but Jake doesn't wait for it to respond before striding forward. The Enchanter lifts her head to see who it is that's approaching and gives Jake a wide smile.

"Jake!" she greets him. "It's so nice to see you! Well... when you're not back *there*."

His flame licks at his aching heart as he smiles back. "Yeah. How's it going?"

"Oh, you know, the same old," she sighs, gesturing to the mess of papers before her. Though as she turns back to face Jake again, the shadow she casts behind her darkens and quivers, a pair of red eyes appearing flat on the ground where her head is. A pang of surprise rips through Jake's body, along with nervousness. He can only hope this will work.

A dark hand stretches out from her shadow, reaching for

the wall, as Clare draws his attention back to her, "How about you? How's your girlfriend doing?"

"Business is booming," he replies. "She couldn't be happier."

"That's nice," Clare hums, nodding along.

An air of awkward silence passes between the two. Clare's enthusiasm to see him again is quickly fading into an expression he's much more accustomed to seeing her wear. It's partly his fault for it, too, but she *is* the infirmary's current receptionist...

"Azna's at a Council meeting, if you were here to see him," Clare states.

"Oh," Jake hums, doing his best to sound disappointed by the news.

"So what's changed?"

"What do you mean?"

"Well," she hums, her head tilting as she thinks, "the senior Healers all say you swore never to come back."

"That fight happened *years* ago," Jake replies. He doesn't really want to be reminded of it, let alone talk about it. He said some stuff he's come to regret. Now he's just being petty.

"You're here to make amends, then?" Clare attempts to guess.

Jake shakes his head. "Not... exactly. I can't really talk about it. You'd probably not believe me, anyway." His eyes can't help but dart to the darkness behind her again. Shadow's hand has gradually crept its way up the side of the wall, fingers outstretched and searching for the drawer. Can it not see the little gold handle poking out of the white wall? A nub so small that any being would glance over it in an instant, but to him, it's all he can see. *Just a little longer...*

Clare chuckles. "After what Amber's been through, I don't think I'd be so quick to dismiss any amount of insanity now."

"Heh, yeah..." he mutters back.

"*So*...?" she hums. She scoots her chair forward, leaning towards Jake with interested eyes. With her, Shadow jolts as well, its hand being dragged away from its target. He almost lets out a frustrated hiss, but he clamps down on his tongue to keep it in. *Stars forsaken!*

"What?" he asks stiffly, trying not to glare at her. Behind her, Shadow is doing its best to correct itself.

"Why are you suddenly looking for Azna?" Clare clarifies. "If it's not to apologize, then...?"

"He's... helping us out with... *something*," Jake vaguely replies.

Her curiosity dies in an instant.

"This is about your birth records again, isn't it?" she asks.

Jake sighs in defeat. "Sort of."

"Well, you know his answer."

"The situation has changed," Jake replies firmly. "He can't keep it from me anymore."

Shadow's hand *finally* finds the nub of the drawer, and it slips its fingers inside, not even bothering to pull it out first. The longer it lingers, the more anxious Jake grows.

"Thought I'd just stop and say 'hi' first," he adds.

Clare gives him another smile, her hands pressing firmly on the edge of the desk. She's going to push herself away, changing positions yet again, as Shadow's arm is still stuck inside the wall. It *has* to find those keys right now!

"The infirmary is always open to you, you know," Clare replies, repelling herself back down the desk. The long shadow behind her shifts once more, the black stain retreating from the wall. The eyes disappear into the darkness. "The other Healers miss having you around."

"I know," Jake nods. He's still not coming back. He steps away from the desk himself, turning to leave. "I'll wait for him in his office, then. Thanks." Clare gives him a parting nod.

He walks past the desk and through the entrance to the

infirmary beyond, but instead of turning right to head to the offices, he takes a left instead. Healers bustle about as usual, escorting patients or wheeling around medical supplies. But the crowd parts around Jake as his boots stomp down on the tiled floor, smiling faces beaming back at him.

"Hi, Jake! How're you doing?"

"Jake? You're back?"

"'Sup, Jake?"

The more senior-looking Healers chatter excitedly upon seeing him. Two of them even give him a pat on the back as he passes by. The younger Healers, however, stare and whisper in confusion, ultimately staying out of his way. But the friendly faces far outnumber the unfamiliar ones.

However, his gaze skips over every being as he searches the darkness for his accomplice. Shadow is the one with the keys, after all, assuming it managed to find them.

After many twists and turns, Jake finally makes it to his destination. The walls turn from white tile to metallic silver. The doors here are thick and heavy, each with bulky locks and large handles. The records wing.

He stops at one of the doors, the letter "J" embedded deep into its metal. This entire place is made of white iron, the same type of iron that Astria's coins are minted from. A metal that no wizard's magic is able to alter, perfect for protecting precious items. This is the only reason why he's been unable to simply break into the record room himself.

"Shadow?" he asks the empty hall, the hustle and bustle of the rest of the infirmary a distant echo. There's no response at first, aside from a brief flicker from the glaring light above him. But then a cold, foreboding presence makes itself known, and Jake can't help but spin around.

Shadow stands quietly, its red eyes dim as it holds up a thick ring of keys for Jake to see, each one engraved with the same letters as the doors. Hope blazes within him as he takes the ring from the Fragment, flicking through each key as fast as he can, though careful not to skip over the one he needs.

Ah! He holds the key up for Shadow to see, a smile across his face. "Finally..." he breathes. Shadow doesn't react much, other than tilting its head.

He turns to the door and unlocks it, the click unexpectedly loud but pleasant to hear. He spent *years* trying to open this door. Now...

He gives it a hefty push. Slowly but surely, the bulky thing slides open under his weight. He slips through the crack once it's wide enough to fit him, where he finds that the walls are as thick as the door itself. A lot of white iron must have gone into making this place over the years.

He's hit with the musty smell of dust first as his eyes adjust to the room. It's dark inside, the only light illuminating the space being whatever manages to stream through the crack in the door. Rows upon rows of bookshelves stretch on into the darkness, making the room seem almost endless from where he stands, and packed onto each shelf are papers of all colors, sizes, and ages. Each row is labeled with more letters.

Shadow steps through the door like a ghost. Though its dark body blends in with the heavy shadows, its crimson eyes emit the faintest glow. Jake holds out his hand, and in a fiery blaze his sword appears. With it, his magic flows freely. Three little Firelights dance around his head, providing him the light he needs to see.

What are we looking for? Shadow inquires, its question filling the space effortlessly. It's not an echo that carries its words, but the darkness itself speaking along with it, making its voice exist everywhere at once.

"My birth records," Jake answers, turning his attention to the shelf labels. They're currently at 'LAB U'. To his right is–

This way, the darkness speaks. The glow of Shadow's eyes appears farther down to his left. Cold pinpricks dance across Jake's body as he shifts to face it, startled. Did it find the row they need already?

He wobbles forward beneath Shadow's eerie gaze. It feels almost as if he's walking through a dream, being pulled along by a will other than his own. The Fragment Shadow follows along beside him, its presence known only by the dense chill of magic pressing itself against Jake's warm arm and, of course, the traveling pair of eyes. Not even his Firelights are able to illuminate it.

Finally, Jake is brought to a halt, the world coming back into focus. He looks up at the shelf, pressed all the way at the far end of this large room. 'BIRTH A' is painted in big black block lettering.

His breath catches in his throat. Room J, birth records A, section K. This is it.

He dashes down the stretch of shelves, keeping an eye out for section K. The longer he runs, the more he can't help but wonder how large this room even *is*. By the time he catches a flash of the letter 'K', he's already out of breath and starting to sweat.

It's etched deep into the wooden shelves, and sitting within them likely hundreds of thousands of colored papers of various ages and sizes. There's no way he'll be able to sort through all of *this* in even a single night!

“Shadow–”

He doesn't even finish his sentence before Shadow rushes forward, becoming a blur of black that streaks through the papers. Up and down the Fragment flies, scanning the files as fast as it possibly can. Seeing no other option, Jake folds his arms and waits for it to finish its sifting, holding his breath.

Will it know which of these documents are his? Will he even be able to verify that it's *his*, either? He doesn't even know the names of his parents, where they came from, or even what magics they both practiced. As much as he hoped for hints, they never came. Now, on this one night where he needs literally *anything* to go off of, he just has to hope that, somehow, against all odds, the Spirits smile upon him and grant him what he seeks.

Shadow emerges from the darkness yet again, waving its hand at the papers on the shelf. About a tenth of them fly forward, hovering before him, which is still way too much for him to start manually combing through.

He'll just have to try and narrow the scope with whatever knowledge he has on hand.

"Jake – J-A-K-E – no last name," he says. A bulk of the papers return themselves to the shelves, but it's still not enough. "One or both parents are Pyromancers with natural affinity." Another good chunk of the papers retire to their resting places. He bites his lip, racking his brain for other possible ways to eliminate more of these records. "Was born... roughly eighteen or nineteen years ago." This leaves him with probably twenty records left. Quite the leap, but a welcome one nonetheless.

He hasn't met many other Jakes at ASM, but he knows that there are a few of them scattered across the other terms and magic branches. If only he could narrow these records here down to those that are attending ASM, he'd have significantly less to look at. Alas, in that case, he'd probably have been better off breaking into the ASM records instead. This is at least a much more manageable selection of records for him to start sorting through.

So he starts, plucking one set of documents out of the air at a time. As his fingers close around each one, he feels the weightlessness fade away, dropping into his awaiting grasp. It's a set of three: a certificate and a form for the child, and a form for the child's parents. But each one he looks at fills him with... apathy. None of the names strike him as beings he might have known once. None of the details seem to indicate that the child would have likely wound up like him. Deep inside his gut, he *knows* that none of these are his.

As he tosses each one aside, Shadow resumes control, sending the papers flying back to the spaces they once occupied, as if they were never moved to begin with. By the time Jake gets through the last set of papers, he lets out a frustrated growl and throws the papers down at the ground. They never land; Shadow catches them like it has all the others. The fire inside his chest is hot with emotion.

"How are they not *here*?" he asks aloud to no being in particular, glaring at the shelves as if they were going to come alive and answer. Did Azna take them somewhere else, knowing that he'd manage to break his way into the record room one cycle? Or did he possibly overlook it, thinking that it wasn't his own? Did he accidentally have Shadow eliminate his early, his assumptions false information? Is there another place for parentless children that he doesn't know about? He'd think he'd *know* about something like that, seeing as–

The air shifts. He pauses. Golden sparkles begin to light up the darkness, twinkling like stars. He doesn't hear the approaching being, but he knows that he's out of time.

He turns around, just as Azna strides into view. He wants to be angry, but the fire within him cools to a low flicker and refuses to heed him.

"I know you're angry, Jake–" the Feni speaks first.

"Turn. It. Off," Jake demands forcefully.

Azna's bottom lip stiffens, but the golden glitter eventually fades away. The cold, stagnant air fills with Jake's warmth as he tightens his grip on his sword's hilt. Now he's able to give the Feni the sharp glare he's always wanted to.

"Where are they?" he growls. "What did you do with my records?"

The Feni takes his time answering. He takes a deep breath and closes his eyes, appearing to be preparing himself. There's no excuse for him to ignore this issue anymore. If Kimberly gets to meet her long lost mother after all this time, why can't he finally learn about his true family?

Azna's eyes open once more. Meeting Jake's intense stare, he states plainly, "Your birth records don't exist."

The world tilts beneath Jake's feet as the Healer's words ring up and down the tight corridor of wood and paper. He shifts his foot backwards to steady himself.

"What?" he breathes. There's no possible way he'd not have any birth records! Is Azna lying to him? Is this a bluff?

Azna just lets out a tired hum and bows his head. "I was asked to take you in, but not by your parents. A student found you lying beside the Asandra School of Magic's private Archway." He looks up again, his emerald eyes filled with an unreadable emotion. "Not even I know who your parents are. But... I had a test done." He pulls a piece of paper from his robe and unfolds it. His stare lingers on the sheet for a long, tense moment. His eyes flicker back to Jake every now and then, most likely contemplating whether he should show him whatever has been written. Finally, he steps forward, his navy blue Council cape fluttering gently behind him as he offers the paper to Jake. "Would you like to read it?"

Jake snatches the paper from Azna's hand instantly, spinning it around for him to read. There's no need for him to be asked. Of course he wants to read it! Anything is progress.

As he scans the paper, his brow furrows. Words and numbers are written in black ink neatly on the page, uniform in size, shape, and spacing. It must have taken ages to pen this report. If only he could actually read the stars forsaken thing!

Naturally, his eyes shift to what he can read. Handwriting fills the margins, thin letters barely visible in the low lighting. Various arrows and circles have been drawn around the incomprehensible in an attempt to make the chart easier to follow. Some of the words feel old as he scans them over and over and over again, but he can still understand what most of them say.

> Sample – Male // Pyromancer (dominant; [unreadable]) // Brown (hair) // Green (eyes)

> 1 – Male // Pyromancer ([unreadable]) // Brown (hair) // Brown (eyes)

> 2 – Female // Serperas ([unreadable]) // Red (hair / red – yellow) // Green (eyes)

Translation to Astrian might not be conclusive

"What is this?" Jake stiffly asks, looking up.

"It's a new technology," Azna says, bending over to see the paper's writing as well. "A test that uses blood to reveal certain traits about yourself and your birth parents."

Jake stares back down at the paper. "I can't read any of it."

Azna positions himself at Jake's side and places a hand on his shoulder, pointing to the legible writing. "That's all you need to know."

Jake shakes his head, shoving the paper back into Azna's hand. If that's all there is to it then he's done looking at it. He doesn't want to see it anymore. He doesn't want to be *here* anymore.

His head feels like it's spinning. He tries to steady himself by holding his forehead, but the motion only feels to make it worse.

"Jake–" Azna tries. The boy jerks himself away from the concerned Healer, keeping his head lowered. He doesn't even want to catch a *glimpse* of that Feni.

A string of ice tightens around his wrist, and with it a rush of cold wind overtakes him. Wordlessly, Shadow embraces him with its magic. The bookshelves, along with Azna's presence, disappear in an instant, leaving him standing alone in the dark, his Firelights continuing to dance around his head lazily.

He raises a hand to his mouth and presses his finger

against his teeth. As sharp as they all are, none of them poke him any more than the rest.

That final note at the bottom did say that the results might not even be conclusive. It could all be wrong. He could have even *read* it wrong!

The darkness recedes when he looks up. He's outside now, the cool breeze of Asandra rolling over his body. The stars dance in the sky above as he's backlit by the light of the infirmary. Shadow stands off to the side in the darker shade of a nearby building, its crimson eyes beacons begging to be noticed.

“Thank you,” he mumbles. He hadn't even asked it to remove him from the record room. It's hard to make out its form but his tired eyes believe that they saw it bow.

“Did you return the keys?” he asks.

I did, Shadow confirms.

Jake can't help but cast a glance over his shoulder. He can see Clare standing behind the reception desk, that bulky key ring held in her hand. She exudes an air of panic and confusion that manages to drift all the way to him.

He waves back.

“Let's go home, Shadow.”

The two quietly disappear into the darkness of the night. Jake's boots feel much heavier than normal as his troubled mind tries to make sense of itself. Once again, his hand can't help but stray to his mouth... just to double check.

Not even his own parents wanted him...

He always knew his parents abandoned him, but not like *that*. He thought one of them asked Azna to watch over him. That was always the impression he got. It never even crossed his mind they left him to *die* at the same school he now attends. And here he is thinking that flunking his third term is the worst ASM can get for him...

He has to stop and catch his breath. The hot fire of his anger has died, giving way to a dense smoke that fills his lungs and stifles his calming breaths. He drops his hand from his mouth and brings it to his chest instead. He holds it there as he struggles to keep himself collected.

He feels Shadow's gaze fall on him. The air it exudes is empty, humming with nothing but the power of magic.

If it is any solace, Shadow speaks, drawing Jake's attention, *our Father lied to us, too.* The glow of its crimson eyes is rather faint as it hides in the darkness. It's hard to see its face. Sometimes a Firelight catches it just right, and he gets a fleeting glimpse of its nose or the corner of its mouth.

Jake's brow furrows. "The Spirit?"

Shadow nods as its aura grows even colder. The little red lights drop slowly to the ground as it floats in the darkness beside him.

Our identity is constructed around falsehoods. Would you say... yours is, too?

Jake shifts his weight from one foot to the other, his eyes searching the night for an answer to give. "Which parts of it?"

This gets a small glimmer of emotion to fill the air. Anger and heartache. Shadow's eyes snap back to Jake in an instant, their glow intensifying. *Everything! Our names, our purposes. Even our appearances! Everything we are has been built on* nothing*! Everything... Everything* I *am...* Its voice cracks, taking Jake aback. The darkness cast by the buildings wavers beneath its might. The air shifts, becoming cold once again but not lacking in emotion. It is a void, a piece of the world missing from its place, crying out for answers as to what it should be.

Jake takes another breath, slow and steady. "I... can't say I don't relate completely." He turns his attention away from the hole in the world next to him, casting it up to the stars high above him instead. They dance and sparkle, forever out of reach, holding secrets back from the beings far below them. They make him feel small, adrift among them, forever searching for answers. But not about who he is. He knows who *he* is.

“All I ever wanted to know was where I came from,” he speaks. “Who my real parents were. Why I wound up where I did with the beings that I knew. And I hung on to what I could. My affinity for Fire. My interest in weapons. My sense of humor.”

You were never told what to be?

“I was told what I *wasn't*,” Jake replies stiffly, “and what I was *supposed* to be.” He lets out a hopeless sigh, letting his shoulders sag and his eyes close. “Though I can hardly call myself a 'Pyromancer' in the first place...”

He can feel Shadow's presence shift with agitation. It takes a while for it to finally ask him, *What do you think I am?*

Jake returns to the distressed Fragment and the two share rather muted expressions. Neither of them know what they want to show the other. Jake's eyes droop against his will, betraying his growing exhaustion within him. He doesn't know what to say. He doesn't even really know what Shadow is asking him to answer with. It is having a hard time speaking its mind openly.

After a long moment without answer, Shadow eventually clarifies, *I am not the Knight. I am not Ethan. I am not Electro's Shadow. I... do not even feel like a Fragment Shadow. All I have ever been is a slave, but I am not even that either. So... what am I?* It stares at him intensely, searching for an answer.

Jake once more takes a long, deep breath, suddenly feeling a lot more uneasy. It's looking to him for direction. Saying anything remotely close to an answer that it's looking for feels wrong, but he doesn't want to say nothing at all.

“I don't think *any* being telling you what to be is right,” he replies.

But Father told the others what they were, Shadow adds quietly.

Jake shakes his head. “Just because you're *told* you are something doesn't instantly make you that *thing*.” He can't keep back the bitterness from leaking into his voice. “All my life I've been told I'm a Pyromancer. But there's more to being a Pyromancer than being called one. Fire magic is only a part of it, not *all* of it. There's standards. There's expectations. There's a whole... *thing* around it." He gestures to Shadow. "Just like there's more to being a Fragment Shadow than being a child of the Spirit. There's... ah... certain level of... authority? Respect? I... I don't really know. But it's not just a title. It's... *you*. But you're *also* not going to be it right away. Does that make any sense?"

Shadow is quiet, its presence still and its stare steady and sharp. It doesn't answer. It's hard to tell if Jake's explanation got through to it or not.

So he gives another example. Another *personal* example. "I don't have a father, for instance, because the being who I would have called my 'father' did not uphold anything that a 'father' is meant to be. Caring. Loving. Present. P-Proud. A 'father' makes time for his kid. A 'father' should help his kid learn. A 'father' does not *shut down* any efforts made by his kid to even *talk* to him. He can call himself a 'father' but he is *not*. So that is not what he is."

Jake breathes heavily, keeping down his desire to shout out his frustrations for the whole island to hear. However, he doesn't want to wake any being. He'd only get in trouble.

But it's not like Azna would care if he were in any amount of trouble anyway.

He turns away from Shadow, continuing in a quieter voice, "They can call me a Serperas too if they want, but I'm not that. I'm not one of *them*. I know nothing about their culture or their habits or... *anything*. I've lived here as long as I can remember. I've been a wizard all my life. And that's not about to change..." But he can't help but doubt. Things have *already* changed. His diet, for instance. He can still eat meat but it's a struggle now. He might not have fangs or even a tail he doesn't think, but... Kimberly fell in love with a wizard. A *Pyromancer*.

He's failing school. He might not even graduate. Because

he *isn't* a Pyromancer. That alone might be enough to have her break up with him.

When you graduate, Kimberly's eager words echo within him. It's always been when *he* graduates. That's always been the idea. He can hide being a “Serperas” but he can't hide his failings forever. Even if he somehow is miraculously given the opportunity to repeat his third term... Kimberly will know he isn't doing well. When she finds out, what will his future look like then?

I... think I understand, Shadow speaks up once again, its words slow and methodical as it processes its thoughts aloud. *But... what if I'm not 'the Knight'? If no being calls me that... If I'm not, why would they even call me that in the first place? I can't be what I'm not. So... I would find something* else *then? To call myself. And what would it even* be*?*

Jake doesn't reply. Instead, he puts a foot forward again, heading off deeper into the night. Shadow is too lost in its own musings to notice he's moved on, but once it eventually realizes it is being left behind it rushes forward through the darkness, rejoining Jake's side. The void it exudes has dulled, replaced with a glimmer of hope. It has been given some semblance of direction, yet still feels to be somewhat lost among the new concepts.

Are you a Pyromancer, then? Or just a wizard? it asks him eventually. It sounds curious, somewhat innocent. But it still pokes at the ashes settled at the bottom of his gut, making his stomach churn.

“I will be a Pyromancer if I graduate,” Jake answers with a flat voice.

You speak like it won't happen.

“Because... it might not.” He raises a hand to rub the back of his neck, finally admitting his deepest worry aloud, “I'm failing my third term.”

A small burst of surprise washes over him. *You* are*?*

"Well, no being has ever cared about my grades," he replies, a hint of his anger and frustration returning to his tongue. "Yeah, I'm failing. I have been for a while now. I just... never said anything about it."

Why?

"Azna doesn't care. I don't want Kim to break up with me. And my teacher has *tried* but thanks to *this thing* it's been a nightmare!" He holds up his sword in front of him, a small flash of disgust making his lips twitch. But he lowers the weapon again with a defeated sigh. "Electro's right. Weapons aren't aids."

Have you tried using an actual aid before?

"I did," he confirms, "but they didn't feel... *right*. Though maybe it's less about what *feels* right and what *is* right." As much as his sword makes him feel comfortable with his magic and himself, it has been the source of all his struggles, unable to properly pair it with his magic. As much as Ethan has complimented him on his "style," in his current state he is merely a boy waving around a sharp stick of flaming metal. He was able to improvise his way through his first and second terms, but his third term demands much more than that now. Demands that he just can't seem to meet. And there's no other being he knows that might be able to help him. But if he just used a staff or a wand – things that *every being* knows in some capacity – then perhaps a lot of his headaches and worries wouldn't have ever gotten to this point in the first place.

But he feels a nudge against his blade, making him pause. Looking down, emerging from the dark is a black needle, its point glinting in the starlight as it gently pushes his arm back. Shadow's crimson stare is soft with sympathy yet firm with determination.

You don't know how to use it, it states.

"N-Not... Not really, no," Jake answers, not entirely sure as to what it's eluding to. "Wizards don't use weapons anymore–"

Shadow steps forward at last, melting from the darkness it

hid within all this time. It's still strange to see Ethan's form wrapped in blacks and grays – it's not like Jake has seen much of Shadow at *all* since it was first introduced to him – making him suck in a startled breath. It grips its sword in one hand casually, gently pressing its blade against Jake's even harder as it emerges.

I may not be the Knight, it says, its crimson gaze full of intent, *but I know how to wield a sword. How about we spar?*

Jake blinks, his head whipping around to stare at their surroundings. "What? *Here*? But–"

Shadow flashes its brilliant white mouth back at Jake as the air around them chills. The dark of night responds to its unspoken call, pooling around their feet and rising up around them, forming massive, shapeless black walls that block out the starlight and the rest of Asandra from their view. Shadow takes a few steps back, raising its sword in front of it and it presses its other arm behind its back. Despite the black backdrop, Shadow's figure stands out bold and proud. Jake, however, is still taken aback by the suddenness of... well, *everything* that's happening. But it's not like he can really back out now, right? Shadow has already prepared their arena; where is there for him to go?

The temperature isn't helping with his weariness, sinking into his bones like the snowy slope of Frostfall and urging him to rest. Yet the dense air of magic exuded by the dark holds him upright.

"Are you *sure*?" Jake feels the need to ask.

Don't hold yourself back, Shadow nods.

Jake takes a deep breath and finally turns to face the entity beside him, raising his own weapon out in front as he squares his hips. His ready stance makes Shadow's face contort as it observes him but makes no comment.

Jake takes the initiative to lunge forward first, his magic surging. He wills his fire to ignite itself, chasing away the smoke of shame and hurt so he can show Shadow what he is. The last time they fought each other, he and Shadow were roughly an even match. Though that was under very specific circumstances, too. Now that it is no longer hindered by anything or any being other than itself, he wonders just how skilled it actually is. If he had only gotten lucky with their first encounter.

He takes a swipe, flames leaping from his ruby blade as Shadow shifts out of the way, its gaze calm and collected as its crimson eyes reflect the orange and red glow of Jake's magic. The second swipe Jake takes, Shadow actually raises its arm to block it, and he is met with what feels to be an immovable wall. His arm shakes as he applies more pressure, turning up the heat bit by bit, but he feels no give on his opponent's side. Jake grits his teeth as he lifts his blade and shuffles back, looking for a different angle to attack from. He tries a low thrust, turning the tip of his sword into a burning arrow as he drives it forward. But the Fragment bats him away with ease, sending a sharp jolt of force up his arm and into his shoulder. It twists to the side, pressing Jake's blade out of the way with its own, causing him to miss. Then it turns, bringing its blade away and around to his back, where he feels its icy essence lightly tap against his neck. All the while Jake is still stuck in his extended thrusting position, not even given time to retaliate.

You seem to have gotten the bare basics, Shadow hums as it lifts its blade, allowing Jake to stand properly. It presses the tip of its sword between its fingers, staring at its weapon with a thoughtful gaze. *The problem isn't your magic. It's your swordsmanship, and it is reflected in your magic as a result.*

"How?"

You don't know what you're doing.

Jake lets his head hang. "I don't..." he admits aloud. He never has, really. He was just sort of going with what *felt* right to do, and, again, there was *no being* that could teach him what he needed to learn. At least, no being until *now*.

Shadow presses its sword beneath Jake's chin and slowly

lifts his face back up again. He doesn't know what to make of its stare as it quietly studies him. It reminds him of his teacher giving him an evaluation, cold and stern yet trying to find the best way to put the criticism.

You also lacked a drive to kill, it adds. Jake's blood runs cold with its assertion. *Or, maybe that kind of thing is easier to evoke when under serious threat?*

"Why would I want to kill you? Or any being?" Jake asks with disbelief.

Shadow lets out a small huff. Jake reads it as annoyance. But the emotion that he feels it exude is a little more on the side of disappointment. But disappointment at *who*? Him?

You had no problem fighting me the first time we met, it points out. *You would have taken my head.*

"That's because I didn't know what was going on!" Jake exclaims. "Kim was in the infirmary, and *me* being a target? Yeah, of *course* I was going to try and kill you then! But you're not–"

An opponent is still an enemy, Shadow smoothly interrupts. It raises its sword across its chest once more, pinching its tip. *And weapons are meant to kill enemies of any kind. That is what makes them different from a simple wand or staff. It is not just a channel for magic, but a tool that, by itself, is an instrument of destruction and death. It is a responsibility. Even if it is simply sparring, every time you wield it, you hold in your hands power over life and death. Not just that of your enemy, but of your own as well. To win is to live and to lose is to die. That is how it should be.*

The longer it lectures, the heavier Jake feels his sword become in his hand. It feels as if its true nature has been awakened, something dark and twisted he has been blissfully ignorant of all this time, and his fire flickers nervously in response. On some level, he already knew that weapons were meant to kill. Though he found comfort in the fact that he never had to wield it against any being, that it was merely an aid for his magic, that his fire manifested with how he swung and nothing more beyond it.

But now it feels like the weight of the world is bearing down on his shoulders. He had thought wrong this entire time. A sword is a weapon, forever and always. Its true nature is to kill, no matter what else it is intended to be used for.

Shadow gestures with its blade out into the dark recesses of their formless environment, and Jake lets his wide-eyed gaze follow its point. From the dark rises a figure holding a sword very much like Jake's. The only difference between the two is that the figure holds their weapon with a lot more conviction than Jake does. They lift their arm, their body moving fluidly with it as they strike at the empty air. Each swing of the blade splits the air around its sharp edge, and in its wake bursts a mass of swirling gray flame, gigantic walls Jake can only dream of one cycle being able to produce himself. He can feel the intense heat batter the front of his body, along with a sharp chill running down his spine as he thinks, *That could kill me.*

This is what I mean, Shadow speaks as the figure continues their dance before them. *Find your form and your conviction and your magic will follow naturally. Do you understand?*

"I... think so," Jake nods back slowly. With his words, the figure melts back into the puddle of black sludge from which it came from, leaving the two beings alone again. Shadow turns its attention back to Jake, shifting into a ready stance.

I promise I won't win so quick this time, it says with another smile. Jake frowns back, even though he knows that it's trying to be lighthearted. Once more he raises his weapon as well and starts.

It's hard getting into the "killing" mindset when he knows now who and what he is facing. That, and having his opponent always prepared to block or sidestep his every strike. It's like he's trying to cut down a wall that's always moving farther and farther away. Shadow bends like water, curving around Jake's sword with ease as he attempts his thrusts over and over again. Yet it also stands firm like rock, hardly ever wavering as Jake tries to press through its parries and blocks. Every stumble it allows him to stand from. Every trip it catches and chastises. It taps at his body where he leaves himself exposed. Though, honestly, it feels like Jake is being led around in circles rather than being *taught.*

Time in here is meaningless as he endlessly chases after Shadow. He is very quickly exhausting himself from the weight he is putting into each of his swings as he tries and fails to imitate the sheer power of the dark figure Shadow had shown him earlier. Shadow's energy, however, feels limitless. Though even it senses the Pyromancer's fading strength. His magic flickers weakly and his face is layered with sweat.

That's enough, Shadow eventually announces as Jake huffs and puffs. It gives him a rather apologetic stare as he falls to his knees, his stomach feeling about ready to drop out of his body. *I'm sorry. I forget... Ah...* Its shaky voice falls silent, and Jake watches the darkness recede from beneath him, giving way to the cobblestone street and the light of the stars above once again. *It's too late. We should go.*

"Yeah..." Jake breathes back in agreement, slowly staggering to his feet. He wipes his brow with an arm and releases a heavy sigh. He'd like nothing more now than to sleep. To process all that he's learned this cycle, and to prepare for whatever will be coming next cycle.

They reach the Straightway at long last, the bright lights of the Illusionboards streaming down onto the sparsely populated street. The air is tinged with not just buzz of magic but the faint scent of wine and the distant sound of music. It's not hard to spot the drunkards from the late night travelers. He can't help but eye the staggering beings cautiously and pick up his pace, Shadow drifting along not far behind.

The lights within The Magic Cone are off, as expected, and the front of the store is absent of revelers and stragglers. Exhaustion weighs on him harder with each step he takes closer to the storefront. He can't wait for the bliss of sleep to carry him off, setting his worries aside for the next cycle.

“Thanks,” he says to Shadow.

The Fragment nods back, and with it a weight unties itself from Jake's forearm. He's not quite sure if it was his tired imagination playing a trick on him or not, but as he glances down once again, he swears a violet chain flickered into being, untangling itself from him.

He turns back to the store and in an instant his heart drops. He can see the little protection rune plastered high above the serving counter, though the fact that he can make it out at all is not a good sign.

It's *extremely* faint but enough to have panic shock his entire body. The rune is glowing!

He rushes up to the door, reaching for its handle. He tries to twist it but it doesn't budge. He hadn't left out the front door. Did the intruder get in through the back then?

Is something wrong? Shadow asks behind him nonchalantly.

He whirls around and exclaims in as low of a voice he can manage, “There's some being inside the shop! Kim is–” His words catch in his throat as Shadow promptly bursts into a cloud of smoke, evaporating into the night. Its presence scatters and fades, the suffocating pressure of its magic easing off his weary body. Did it just... *abandon* him?!

Stars forsaken! He returns to the lock, raising his sword without hesitation. Fire curls around the ruby blade as it glows in his hands, his magic surging forward in a flurry of flames. There's no time for him to get to an alley to reach the back of the shop, and with Shadow having disappeared on him, this is his only option.

He puts the rest of his lingering strength into his downward swing, his blade slicing through the metal frame that rings the glass. It comes to a halt once it reaches the lock. Teeth gritted, he leans forward and presses down with everything he has, and the flames of the blade grow in response. The fire slowly begins to melt the glass, but there's no sign of it cutting through the lock until he feels the block of metal give way, and he stumbles forward as his blade falls.

He bursts in with his shoulder, using the door's inward swing and his passing speed to yank his sword free from the melted door. The little bell that normally greets the customers chimes violently in alarm.

As he steps past the store's threshold, the protection rune flares with brilliant blue light, only this time it's not to warn him. Bathed in its glow, Jake's bright fire is snuffed out in an instant, his magic falling silent. If he were here when the intruder broke in, it would be the other way around. Sadly, the protection rune can't tell the difference between a regular resident returning from an evening stroll and a bad actor by itself.

He vaults himself over the counter, careful not to hit the till as he swings his legs up and over. At the very least, he still has his sword, and despite not being the greatest at wielding it, he's grateful that he's not at a complete disadvantage.

Above his head, loud thumps rap against the ceiling, a scuffle already breaking out on the second floor. Is Kimberly awake and dealing with the intruder already? As he reaches the stairs, he's blasted by a wave of static. Yells of panic ring out as the fight continues, filling his ears as he focuses on his climb.

“Kim–!” he yells, finally coming up to the doorway to the living room. He slides, planting his feet to brace himself for a fight, only for the tip of a black sword to rise to his neck.

Jake lets out a shaky breath. Electro is standing, bolts of lightning leaping from his clothes. But his eyes are crimson and his body mostly wrapped in darkness, the makings of a helmet faintly visible around his head. There's a nasty gash across his neck that has been filled with what looks to be black ink.

Oh, Shadow hums, retracting its sword, *it's just you.*

"You stars forsaken Fragment!" Jake can't help but yell, barging into the room. It steps out of his way quietly. His sword is still raised high as Jake surveys the situation.

It's not just one intruder but three. All are dressed in dark clothes but it's very clear that they're not wizards. The soft clacking of gears and shifting of pistons fills the room as they groan and regain their bearings.

One of them landed on the sofa, sprawled out across its back and armrest. The white pile of comforter is stained with small black burns. The other two lay in the dining room, one tangled in the chairs and the other slammed against the back wall upside down.

"Jake? Jake!" Kimberly's distant cry sounds, and the hurried pounding of feet make their way down from the third floor.

"Kim!" he calls back to her. He turns around just as she dashes into view, her nightgown flowing behind her as the air glitters with flakes of snow. She looks at Jake, then Electro and Shadow, and finally at the three intruders, taking it all in.

"Are you alright?" she asks, stepping forward. Her hands stray to his shoulders as he nods back. Without his magic, he can feel the cold air that she radiates in full force. He does his best not to show it, but her biting chill makes him feel even more exhausted than he was before.

"Who are these beings?" she wonders next, turning back to the room.

"I don't know," Jake replies.

Shadow steps up to the being on the sofa with determination, one arm outstretched. Electro's pale hand rests against the Shask's body, but from it, Shadow's arm sinks beneath the intruder's clothes, reaching for their essence. In one smooth motion, it draws from the Shask their dark double, its single organic eye glowing bright red. It stands before Shadow with an air of surprise radiating from its figure. Then it looks up at Electro's intense stare and stiffens in an instant.

Why are you here and who sent you? it demands.

The Shask's jaw quivers, though it eventually starts to stammer, "W-W-We were sent by Ryan A-Ashblade to kill a-an Electromancer called E-E-Electro."

Shadow draws a sharp breath as the name strikes a chord within the wizards. Ryan Ashblade – the very same being they're looking for next – wants Electro dead? Jake stares at Electro's misty form, wondering why on Astria that would be? Weren't they friends once?

Where is he? Shadow asks next.

"A-Ashblade Smelting and Smithing," the Shask answers.

Shadow speaks no more. It flicks its fingers against the risen one's forehead, and its form bursts into mist, rushing back towards its body. Before they can even begin to recollect themselves as their essence resettles, Shadow takes them by their collar and tosses them into the dining room with their two other friends. With a wave of its hand, the shadows rise around the three, shoving them all together within their new dark bindings. They all grunt and wiggle against their restraints and gags to no avail.

"Thank the stars you stopped them," Kimberly sighs with relief.

I... didn't, Shadow plainly admits.

Kimberly blinks back at it, her brow knit with confusion. A nervous pit drops in Jake's stomach, bracing himself. It's not like he was expecting assassins to show up, though now she's likely going to find out that the two of them were away...

"But if you didn't stop them," Kimberly hums quietly, "then who did?"

Shadow's eyes shift, staring off into the distance. It's hard to tell what it might be thinking as the void of its power grows even denser than before. It eventually returns to Kimberly's worried gaze and answers, *Electro's Shadow.*

"Seriously?!" Jake exclaims. If it knows where they live, aren't they all in astronomical danger? It could come back at any time and–

It has a vested interest in the survival of its Husk, Shadow replies calmly. *Seeing as these beings were here to kill Electro, it only makes sense that his Shadow would protect him from them.*

"But what if it comes *back*? How are we supposed to deal with it *then*?!" He can't fight Electro's Shadow again just yet! He's hardly improved his combat abilities since his field trip! And what about Kimberly?

Shadow shakes its head. *It won't. Not unless we have a Shard it thinks it can take from us. Or,* it takes a quick glance over at the would-be assassins, *unless it feels that its Husk is in danger.*

"How do you know *that*?"

There's a very visible shift in Shadow's demeanor as it shifts its weight from one foot to the other. The flood of magic ceases in an instant, replaced by powerful static. Electro's clothes sparkle with brief snaps of electricity as Jake finds himself locked eye-to-eye with the wizard's amethyst gaze.

"Gee, I wonder how it knows so much about *myself*," he growls back with a great amount of irritation. "Now, would *you* like to explain where on *Astria* you and Shadow were during all of this?" He gestures sharply at their hostages.

"Ah..." Jake feel's Kimberly's cold stare land on him curiously.

"Jake? You weren't even *here*?" she breathes in surprise. Out of the corner of his eye, he sees Electro fold his arms and begins to tap his foot impatiently, his glare sharp and imposing.

“W-Well, I...” Jake stammers, “I was having a hard time sleeping, so I went for a walk. But, um... I kind of melted the front door's lock...” His voice is barely a whisper by the time he finishes with his weak excuse. Kimberly is silent, staring at him with a blank face and stiff jaw. He can't help but turn away from her, unwilling to meet her gaze any longer.

“Well, it was due for an upgrade anyway,” she mutters at last. “I... think I'll go... report this.”

“Good idea,” Electro agrees.

Kimberly strides around Jake, her blue figure a blur that passes across his vision. She takes her icy air with her as she makes her exit from the chaos, first to her room to put on some more appropriate outside clothing before she starts her trek to the nearest authority outpost. The other two stand in silence, waiting for her to depart. It's not until the icy air begins to warm when either of them opens their mouths.

“How did you know Shadow wasn't–?”

“The moment it left I went right back into limbo,” Electro spits back. “I've been awake ever since. Heard every word those Voidterrors were saying but couldn't lift a finger. You as well, and your loud feet.”

Jake can't help but let out a defeated sigh. “I didn't realize... I'm sorry.”

Electro lets out a grumpy huff and throws himself back down onto his mattress. “Just let me sleep, alright? No more sneaking out. You, too, Shadow.”

***

“No, you do *not* get to cut me off!” an angry voice disturbs the dark. Jake stirs, his eyes heavy and yet they slowly open anyway. The colors blur before him, the world a swimming abstraction. If it weren't for the rage permeating the air, he'd probably have fallen right back to sleep.

"*Why* did you listen to him?" Ethan's voice demands, keeping his yelling back. "*Why* did you leave Electro? If *this* is what you're going to do when I'm not around... Stars forsaken!"

Jake lifts his head. He fell asleep sitting upright after such a busy night entertaining a swarm of authorities, so naturally his back and neck ache profusely. Ethan's looming figure slowly melts into view, his cold and intense glare bearing down on him without remorse.

"And *you*," he growls at his waking friend. "I never thought you'd be one to *break into the infirmary's records*!"

"Eth..." he mumbles, barely lucid. The Husk's cold hands clamp down on his shirt and he yanks Jake close to his face with one powerful tug. Shock and surprise jolt Jake fully awake as he gets a face full of Ethan's merciless glare.

"I can't *believe* you!" he spits. "Taking advantage of *my* Shadow like that!"

"I was just asking for some help!" Jake tries to defend himself.

"*Calm down*," Electro sighs. The wizard rises from the mattress and brushes his pants as Ethan spins around to face him. A jolt of electricity bounces towards the two as he points a finger at Jake. "He's well aware what he's done. And his well-deserved punishment will be accompanying me to Kendon this cycle."

There's a moment of silence as the two stare back at him with surprise. Jake's mouth drops open in an instant. *He's* going to *Kendon*? With *Electro*? After last cycle, he thought he'd have some time to rest up!

Jake is forcefully pushed back into the sofa's cushions as Ethan turns his full attention to the Electromancer. "You're *not* going to Kendon," he firmly asserts.

Electro promptly shakes his head, planting his hands firmly on his hips. "Me and Ryan are old buddies. It should be handled as such, like the… *adults* we are." His stare is sharp; he knows what he wants to do and he won't allow himself to be held back this time.

Ethan lets out a hopeless huff, pinching the bridge of his nose and bowing his head in frustration.

“This ain't negotiable,” Electro adds, his gaze darting to Jake. “I'm going. He's going. All we need is a Keystone.”

“How soon do you want to leave?” Ethan asks, each word drawn out and airy, laced with thick frustration.

“Now.”

The Husk emits a hollow growl, though he capitulates regardless of his unspoken thoughts. “I'll meet you at the public Archway as soon as I can.” He gives Jake one last glare – a warning – before he trudges off into the hallway, the thick shadows enveloping his figure.

Electro claps his hands to capture Jake's attention, smiling eagerly.

“Chop, chop!” he orders. “Let Kimberly know and let's get going!”

Chapter 17

Thanks to the early wake up call, Electro was able to push the two of them out of the door rather quickly. And thanks to it being first light, the public Archway is barely in use, despite the decent number of beings bustling about. Small trinket stalls and cozy cafes dot the circular space surrounding the Archway, their vendors arriving and setting up their spaces, preparing for another steady stream of visitors to Asandra. The stones that pave the ground are brightly painted, proudly displaying the six magic branches that the wizards study, practice, and master. It's a reminder to all just how important they are to the survival of Astria.

Jake stands off to the side, slipping on his sparkling gold pauldrons since he hadn't been given permission to do that earlier, his jaw unhinging to release a large yawn. Shadow tugs at Electro's gut. It has been since Ethan came to yell at it. It's hard to tell what it's feeling, though he guess it's somewhere between remorse and annoyance. But it hasn't said a word at all. Not to him, anyway.

Thankfully, they're not left waiting *too* long. Ethan melts from the crowd, his cape flowing behind him as his glower lands on Electro. In his wake, another being follows, bright-eyed and ready to take on the cycle. His clothes aren't that of a normal wizard, not even an Enchanter.

Ethan gestures to his companion. "You two haven't been introduced yet. Electro, this is Lukri, the Serperan prince of Mirage." Lukri gives him a firm nod, his lips twitching as he suppresses a smile. "He wants to come with you, too."

Electro frowns as he regards the boy, shifting his weight from one foot to the other and tilting his head to get a better look at the newcomer. Lukri certainly has an air of importance hanging around him as he holds his head high. He never thought he'd come face-to-face with an actual Serperas while he lived. Of course, he's surprised Lukri has legs instead of a tail. Guess they evolved out of them, sort of like most modern Feni with theirs.

"Why?" he asks.

"Business," Lukri plainly answers.

"With *Ryan*?" he huffs in amusement. Ethan folds his arms as he quietly observes Lukri with his own curiosity. "What's he to you?"

Lukri's eyes dart around the small gathering, considering his situation. His hands come together with the clear intent to fidget nervously.

"Look," Electro says to him, "this isn't going to be a very *amicable* meeting, and I rather not need to be concerned with looking after more beings than necessary. If it's a good reason to go beat Ryan up, I'm all for hearing it. Otherwise, you're not coming."

Lukri lets out a reluctant sigh, his head bowing as he weighs his words.

"He tricked my mother to steal the Shard inside the Pyramid of Prophecy," he finally answers. "He must be punished."

Electro grins in an instant. Another crime to throw atop Ryan's mounting list of dastardly deeds. He gives Lukri a thumbs-up. “I don't know if you'll get the Shard back, but teaching a thief a lesson I can promise!”

“I... can come?” Lukri asks.

“Sure, why not?”

Jake lets out a small disapproving grumble behind him, but he doesn't protest. The prince lights up with excitement.

With that settled, Ethan holds up a Keystone to Electro, smooth and red with a silver-painted gear chipped into its surface. He offers it up without much hassle right up until Electro tries to take it from him. The Husk's grip tightens as his fingers wrap around the Keystone.

“Are you *sure*?” he asks, though judging by his gaze, he's addressing Shadow more than Electro. “I can come with–”

“Yes,” Electro cuts him off forcefully. He yanks the Keystone in an effort to get the Husk to release his hold on it.

“Not *you*,” Ethan growls back with a frown.

“I know,” Electro replies. “It will be *fine*.”

Ethan's jaw stiffens, his glare not once easing. “*Don't* cut me off.”

“I'm sure it won't.”

Ethan finally lets go of the Keystone. He still doesn't look happy. He'll just have to get over it.

He turns to the two boys and holds it up to them triumphantly.

“Ready to get going?” Lukri nods, determination burning in his eyes. Jake shifts his weight as he rests his hand on the hilt of his sword, shaken from his thoughts.

He gives Jake a quick pat on the shoulder as he steps up to the Archway, speaking in a voice only the student can hear, “Keep your hand off your hilt. Don't want any being thinking you're looking for a fight.”

Jake's eyes widen as his hand immediately shifts to his hip.

The smell of warm metal fills the air as the Archway rips

open, making Electro's nose curl. The three travelers emerge from the other side of the rip in a grand room, its high ceiling held aloft by big pillars of white stone and filled with a soft air of warmth. The walls are made of brick, lined with metal pipes, gears, pistons, wires, and other various mechanical parts that rumble and click, filling the space with an ever-present background drone of hollow humming. Hanging down from the ceiling is a fancy crystal chandelier that produces a blinding white glow, lighting the room with a harshness that makes Electro's eyes ache with confusion. The gray metal floor is carpeted by lush rugs of all different colors and styles.

Despite the clash of engineering and opulence, the room still retains a natural flow to it. The wires spring up from various brassy machines fixed to the walls, where beings of all kinds huddle around anxiously. Shasks in suits wander around, offering aid to those that appear to be struggling with the technology and guiding others through the process of arriving on the island. The wires then travel up with the piping to the top of the room, where they exit through the wall above the doorway.

"Well, kids," Electro announces grandly, gesturing to the room, "welcome to Kendon."

Lukri stares at the walls with amazement, his mouth slightly parted an attempt to remain composed without letting his jaw drop *too* much. Jake, on the other hand, turns to the machines scattered about.

"What now?" he asks.

"We check in," Electro answers with a smile.

He waltzes right up to one of the unoccupied machines with cool confidence. He's been to Kendon a number of times with Ryan in the past, so he knows the system well enough. The technology is quite intimidating when encountering it for the first time – it *is* state-of-the-art stuff, after all – but since it needs to be navigated by even the most technologically illiterate beings on all of Astria, it's quite simple in practice.

The screen of the machine flickers to life as it senses his approach. He's bathed in green light as the mechanical box hums and shudders softly as it types up a short welcome message. Each character starts out as some alien symbol Electro doesn't recognize, which then begins to flash between more equally confusing characters at a rapid pace before finally morphing into actual letters that he can read.

WELCOME TO KENDON

PLEASE PLACE YOUR KEYSTONE IN THE
RECEPTACLE BELOW TO BEGIN

Electro lets out a long sigh as he sticks the Keystone into the aforementioned receptacle below the screen. Once his hand withdraws from the machine, it whirls to life in an instant. A blue light flares around the Keystone as the box gently vibrates. As the light works its mysterious magic, the screen flickers and prints a new string of text.

WELCOME TO KENDON

PLEASE USE THE KEYPAD ON YOUR RIGHT

KEYSTONE IS REGISTERED FOR
[[Ethan Nightshade]]

INSERT NUMBERED CODE GIVEN BY
KEYSTONE VENDOR

"Number?" Electro mutters in confusion.

{*Number?*} Shadow asks as well. There's a brief period of silence before its voice hums, {*He said to try 94-26-10.*}

"*Try*?" Electro echoes in annoyance. Ethan isn't even sure

about his own Keystone? Still, with few options, his hand strays to the small gray keypad painted with white numbers and letters. Each button makes a small *beep!* as he jams his thumb into them. The “6” key is slightly sticky.

{*If it doesn't work, he'll have to go ask for the number again,*} Shadow explains as he works.

“How long would *that* take?” he breathes.

There's a long pause, though just as he presses the last key on the pad, it answers, {*Too long.*}

He stands a little straighter, trying not to look too troubled as he watches the screen with bated breath. It flickers as the machine begins to rattle. Is it supposed to be doing this, or did he just so happen to pick the most defective model there is in this blasted room?

WELCOME TO KENDON

PLEASE USE THE KEYPAD ON YOUR RIGHT

CODE CONFIRMED

ARE YOU TRAVELING WITH GUESTS?
1 – NO || 9 – YES

A sigh of relief escapes Electro’s mouth as he presses the “9” key.

WELCOME TO KENDON

PLEASE USE THE KEYPAD ON YOUR RIGHT

ENTER THE NUMBER OF GUESTS YOU ARE BRINGING INTO KENDON

[[2]]

USING THE KEYPAD, ENTER THE FULL NAME OF GUEST #1

NAME WILL BE ENTERED WITHOUT SPACES
SUBMIT BY PRESSING AND HOLDING KEY 9

His fingers dance across the keypad, turning his attention to the tiny letters printed under each number. Bit by bit, he slowly enters Jake's name.

"Last name?" he asks, turning to Jake.

Jake shakes his head. "Nope."

WELCOME TO KENDON

PLEASE USE THE KEYPAD ON YOUR RIGHT

GUEST #1: [[JAKE]]

USING THE KEYPAD, ENTER THE FULL NAME OF GUEST #2

NAME WILL BE ENTERED WITHOUT SPACES
SUBMIT BY PRESSING AND HOLDING KEY 9

"Lukri... how do I spell that?" he asks the Serperas.

"Ah..." Lukri breathes with surprise, taken off guard by the question. His eyes desperately search the room for his answer, a single finger pressed to his chin. There's no way on Astria that he doesn't know how to spell his own name, right?

"You know what, just put it in yourself," Electro eventually suggests.

"Alright," Lukri nods, stepping up to the keypad. His finger hovers in the air before the nine marked squares hesitantly. His face scrunches into a confused frown as he stares at the numbers and letters.

"Well," Electro hums, leaning in and gesturing to the buttons, "this one right here is for the letters J, K, *and* L. And if you press it, it will put them on the screen." He taps a single finger against the green display.

"*All* of them?" the Serperas breathes in surprise.

Electro can't keep back an amused snort. "No, just the one letter out of the three that you need!"

"Okay."

Of course, Electro soon realizes his greatest and most hilarious mistake assuming that Lukri knew what to do from his basic instructions. Electro's eyes flicker up to the screen as Lukri hunts across the keypad for the letters that he needs. Right now, there's a J and a T on the screen. *Odd*, crosses his mind in mild confusion. He didn't realize Lukri's name started with a J. Is it a Serperas thing to pronounce a J like a L, then? The T, however, makes his stomach churn with a pang of dread.

Then *another* J flares onto the screen. Now he sees what has gone wrong.

"Hang on, hang on, hang on!" he exclaims, stepping in once more, right as Lukri's finger presses down onto the key "7". The Serperas looks up at him in confusion, which make sense because he has *no idea what he's just done*.

Electro points to the screen. J-T-J-P is already written. Well, it's a bit too late to change that second J, but at least he can salvage the rest of it. "I... don't think that's how you spell it, right?"

Lukri blinks at the jumble of letters, processing whatever he's reading. Then he shakes his head in confirmation, his face going pale with panic.

"Hey, it's okay," the wizard attempts to console. He points back to the keypad and demonstrates the key piece of information he accidentally left out. "Right, so, you have to press the same key *repeatedly* to change the letters. Pressing it once give you P, and pressing it a second time changes the P to a Q, because they're on the same button."

Hesitant, Lukri presses the "7" once more, then looks to the screen. Just as Electro said, the P has now become a Q. A third jab of his finger transforms the round Q into an R. The Serperas turns back to Electro, eyes wide and completely lost.

"Is that the letter you want?" he asks.

"Yes," Lukri nods. "And then one more letter, but... will I change it? It's..." He points back to the keypad, to the "4" key – G, H, and I.

Electro shakes his head. "Nope! If you press a new key now, it'll add another letter, but then you can't change the previous letter."

"O-Oh..." Lukri stares at the screen sadly as he works through his last step with his new knowledge. He's *very* careful to make sure he gets this last letter right. Then, at long last, he steps away from the keypad. Electro finishes the process by jabbing the "9" key.

WELCOME TO KENDON

PLEASE USE THE KEYPAD ON YOUR RIGHT

GUEST #1: [[JAKE]]
GUEST #2: [[JTJRI]]

PROCESSING...
PLEASE WAIT...

The two wizards and the prince stare at the screen in awkward silence as the machine works away.

"*Jtjri*?" Jake is the first one to attempt to pronounce the gibberish, but ends up lost in laughter instead. Lukri glares at him with his cheeks bright red with embarrassment.

"Hey, it's okay," Electro tries to assure the Serperas. "It's your first time. Mistakes are bound to happen."

The blue light around the Keystone fades away, and dispensing down onto the Keystone are two small ticket-shaped pieces of paper. Once more, the text on the screen changes.

WELCOME TO KENDON

TAKE YOUR IDENTIFYING TICKET(S) – { I.T. } – AND KEYSTONE FROM THE RECEPTACLE.

GUESTS MUST CARRY THEIR { I.T. } AT ALL TIMES WHILE VISITING KENDON. FAILURE TO DO SO WILL RESULT IN A FINE OF 1,000 IRON FOR BOTH THE GUEST AND KEYSTONE OWNER.

IF A GUEST'S { I.T. } IS LOST OR DESTROYED, RETURN TO THE ARCHWAY CHECK-IN IMMEDIATELY AND RE-REGISTER ALL GUESTS.

WOULD YOU LIKE TO RATE YOUR CHECK-IN EXPERIENCE AND TAKE A QUICK FEEDBACK SURVEY BEFORE YOU LEAVE?
1 – NO || 9 – YES

Electro can't help but roll his eyes as he punches the "1" key.

WELCOME TO KENDON

ENJOY YOUR VISIT!

"*Finally*," he mutters as he takes the Keystone and the tickets from the machine's open cavity. Printed on each of the small slips of paper are the names that were put into the machine, along with part of the numerical code for Ethan's Keystone, one ticket for Jake and one for… *Jtjri*. A small snicker escapes Electro's mouth as he hands the tickets to his companions. Lukri scowls down at his horribly misspelled name.

"Just put it in your pocket and forget about it," Electro advises. "You can get rid of it when we leave."

The three move away from the machine, its purpose fulfilled, and start to move with the flow of the crowd towards the large open doorway. On either side of the doorway are suited-up Shasks, each one drawing the attention of those passing by, gesturing to Keystones and tickets.

"Welcome to Kendon!" one of the Shasks says brightly to the three beings. He holds out a mechanical hand to Electro expectantly. "Please show me your Keystone and guest I.T.'s."

Electro shoves the Keystone into the Shask's hand as Jake and Lukri step forward with their tickets. Lukri appears nervous, and rightfully so, as he gives the Shask his misspelled ticket.

The Shask glances at the items in his hand, flipping the Keystone over as he does so. It doesn't take very long for him to return the items, a smile crossing his... mouth?

"Everything's in order. Please enjoy your visit!" he announces, gesturing to the doorway to invite them deeper into the city.

Kendon, the indoor island. A mess of hallways and atriums, with pipes pumping water and air and wires bringing power to every inch of the massive enclosed city. Such a controlled environment is perfect for the Shasks to thrive in, needing not to worry about the natural elements interfering with their carefully constructed machinery. The place is a mess of brass and brick, the clashing chaos somehow organized into works of engineering marvels.

Still, Electro shifts his weight uncomfortably as he begins to search for a way out of the place. The warmth of the air was nice at first, but now it's starting to bug him in a way he can't exactly describe. The lighting is too harsh for his liking, and the air tastes stale. His magic jolts and shifts inside his chest, and so does Shadow, as it tries to find its connection to the Void beyond the walls. Everything about this place is antithetical to magic – artificial, manufactured, and uniform. He doesn't understand how some wizards can stand to come to Kendon on vacation, let alone settle down and *live* here.

{*I don't like it here*,} Shadow mutters weakly.

"Me either," Electro confirms. "Let's find Ryan quickly."

The hallway they wander down is quite large and thick with foot traffic, mostly of beings foreign to Kendon. Right now, he wants to find a place not quite as crowded for him to gain some bearing of the place. All he knows is the name of Ryan's business, but not *where* it is or how to even *get* there.

As they walk, they pass by many other open doorways on their right, each with large metal signs nailed above them. They're mostly souvenir and snack shops, selling little mechanical knickknacks and local treats to visiting beings. On their left, the wall is one long window broken up by the occasional brick pillar helping to hold the iceglass in place. Beyond it is one of the city's many atriums, this one filled with potted plants arranged into vibrant patterns and stone-tiled pathways. Nestled between the greenery are a handful of benches, some of which are already occupied by families and couples. However, the three are currently two levels *above* the atrium, granting them a decent view of the space but not access.

Electro doesn't suspect that Ryan would be located near the surface of the city anyway. If he really does "smelting and smithing" as the name of his business implies, then it's more likely that he'd be closer to the lower levels.

They reach an intersection. The hallway continues on ahead, a sea of beings moving in and out of doorways, pushing and shoving one another to have some personal space of their own. It also bends to the left, continuing to run alongside the atrium. However, to the right is a large stairwell, and near its entrance is yet another boxy brass machine that beings huddle around, each of them waiting for a turn to stare at its screen.

"This way," he announces to the two boys following him, leading the way through the shifting crowd. This machine is a bit too crowded, and he doesn't have the time to wait his turn. So, hopefully, somewhere near these stairs is one that's more readily available and *quiet*.

Lightning sparking eagerly off his clothes, he takes the stairs two or three at a time, bounding downwards to the lower levels of Kendon. Round and round he turns each corner, the crowd gradually thinning the farther he descends.

He quickly loses count of the levels he passes by, and he has no idea how well the other two are keeping up with him. They'll probably keep going until they find him somewhere.

He eventually comes to a halt... *somewhere* deep within the city's bowels. He's left the stars high above him, as well as the dense crowd of beings, as he leans against the machine he's been looking for, breathless and dizzy. He thinks it has grown warmer, too; he wipes the sweat from his brow as the rest of his body starts to feel sticky.

Sensing his presence, the box hums to life, bathing him in the green glow of its screen. KENDON DIRECTORY prints itself in big bold letters, along with a prompt to FIND DESTINATION. There's no sticky keypad here, but a full-sized board with dedicated buttons for each letter and symbol, along with four arrows for moving around the screen. It even has the ability to delete typed letters!

His fingers fly across the keys with lightning speed and accuracy, inputting Ryan's business into the search bar. The machine hums as it thinks, the input prompt disappearing for a moment before turning into a list of written directions. It's... quite long. At least it comes complete with a proper address: AS&S, F26H, 7311-12.

There's a pair of huffing and puffing beings making their way towards his level, and he leans over to greet the two boys with a wide smile. Lukri stumbles forward first, leaning against the wall to catch his breath as Jake passes him by, doing his best to appear not quite as winded as his eyes betray.

"Good news!" Electro announces. "I know where we're going now!"

"You mean... you didn't before?" Jake breathes back.

"We got to keep going down," Electro replies simply, gesturing to the next set of stairs.

Above, Lukri releases a heavy sigh. His legs take on a jade hue as they fuse themselves together, elongating into a shimmering tail. *So he* does *have one!* He keeps one hand on the wall beside him as he smoothly glides down the last length of stairs to join the two wizards. "Slowly this time," he requests between breaths.

Electro can't help but laugh. His hand strays to his pocket and casually withdraws a stick of arcane gold. "I'm not in *that bad* of a rush." If his Shadow gets to beat up Ryan before he does, it still counts. He'd just be mildly disappointed.

Though, there *is* the Shard to worry about, too. It can't stay with Ryan, but they shouldn't let it be taken away like the last one. The possibility of reuniting the pieces of the Font of Magic and returning it to its rightful home has never been more feasible in all the time since the Great War. It's an honor that will only ever come once in all of history, it feels like. Too bad part of the credit has to go to a selfish Voidterror who stopped two-thirds of the way through, all because of some personal hang-up.

He still takes the steps two at a time as they continue further into the sprawling depths of Kendon, his eyes fixed to his boots as he bites down on the gold in his mouth and reminisces. Ryan was a Voidterror who got lucky. He doesn't know *why* the Spirits rewarded *him* of all beings with the honor of discovering the locations of the Shards, but he was.

In hindsight, he can't quite say if Ryan had a crush on Kelsy or if Ryan wanted to keep Electro close to him and Kelsy was pulling him away. A bit of both, perhaps? Or neither and he wanted to drive a wedge between the two of them because he felt like it. Whatever the case, his ambitions got himself forcefully kicked from their lives. And being the sore loser that he was, he went looking for the Font of Magic for quite *obvious* reasons, all the while, somewhere along the way, colluding with Jay to break up his sister's happy marriage alongside using and abusing yet *another* woman – a royal at that! – to get what he wanted.

Well, joke's on him, then. In the end, his efforts got him no girl, no best friend, no status, and not an *ounce* of goodwill left in any being that knows about him. He has systematically destroyed his own future prospects of happiness. Unless, of course, his heart has become so black now that he's happy being hated by the universe instead.

There comes a point where the stairs end and the three are forced into the winding tunnels lined with pipes and lighting that makes their eyes sting inexplicably. Electro releases a soft puff of air through his nose. Somewhere on this level is the entrance to the "industrial zone" as the directory put it. From there, it should just be a straight shot down to floor 26. First, they need to go... straight?

He leads the way down the hallway, keeping his head held high. It's going to be hard not to get turned around here, though he figures he can always knock on one of these doors and ask for directions if they do wind up getting lost.

Behind him, Jake lets out an exasperated breath. "Could you stop doing that?"

"Doing what?" Lukri asks innocently, completely clueless

as to what the wizard is requesting him to stop doing.

"*That*!" Jake replies with somewhat restrained irritation. "Whatever *that* is! It's distracting."

"My... body?"

"All those shifting colors are giving me a headache."

Lukri is quiet, possibly taken aback by the wizard's words. "But I am... *re-gu-la-ting* my, ah... heat," he answers somewhat awkwardly. It doesn't take long for him to add, "You can see my body heat?"

"Is that it?" Jake hums back. "I guess so."

Electro steals a glance over his shoulder. Lukri's eyes are wide with surprise and wonder, something about Jake suddenly fascinating him. All the while, Jake's shoulders are tense as his head is turned away from the Serperas, his expression sour and his stare to the wall beside him, conflicted. He's doing his best to walk as far away from Lukri as he can.

Electro turns back around and mutters beneath his breath, "What happened last night?"

Shadow drops like a pit to his gut, a hollowness overtaking him. The sudden void of absent emotion catches him off guard to the point where his foot kicks against the ground off-sync and makes him stumble. He tries to mask it as best he can, leaning into it as if it were a normal thing for him to do.

{*He found out he might be a Serperas,*} Shadow answers honestly. A small pang of what he thinks is regret flashes into existence briefly before becoming swallowed by the endless dark. He can't help but be unnerved by its mannerism. It feels as if it's suppressing not just its emotions, but its own will entirely.

"Rough," he only comments. That certainly explains why he's so irked by Lukri's presence.

They do eventually manage to find the next set of stairs that they're looking for, helpfully labeled by a metal sign plastered on either side of its opening that reads INDUSTRIAL DISTRICT bright and bold. Waves of intense heat waft up from its depths, more than anywhere else in this massive city so far.

They are swallowed whole. The staircase rings with metal chains and hammers. Distant yells direct important operations. The walls feel like they rumble from all the activity.

They finish their lengthy trek downwards as they spot the sign that they're looking for, floor 26. The walking space here is triple that of the cramped hallways far above them, likely meant for moving large machines and quantities of product around with ease. Before them is a flat wall that extends to their left and right, and bolted to its surface are signs directing beings on which way they should go. “Tunnel H” is to their left, so that is the way Electro leads.

They pass more hallways that branch from the one that they walk, each one plastered with a big block letter on brass plaques. It's not long before they stumble upon the tunnel that they're looking for, towards the far end of the space. From here, the subsequent doors are each labeled with different numbers, along with company brandings and slogans. Some are big and bright, expertly crafted with countless iron spent. Others are a little more tacky, either painted onto the wall or even some look to be hand-forged.

Soon enough, the three travelers find themselves standing outside of the door that they're looking for. It's a little strange seeing wood in this stony, metallic environment, but it's a welcome sight. Bolted to the wall above the door is a metal sign with a small picture of a pair of tongs lifting a molten bar of metal and letters that read “Ashblade Smelting & Smithing”.

A smile creeps across Electro’s face. Finally, he’ll be face-to-face with that Voidterror once more. This time he feels more than prepared to face whatever Ryan might throw at him.

“Alright, boys,” Electro says, turning to Jake and Lukri. “Ryan has a Shard at his disposal, so be prepared for anything. But I get the first punch.”

The two boys seem to can't help but frown back at him

with a mixture of worry and confusion between them.

Satisfied by their wordless response, Electro opens the door and steps into the shop. The front room is small, most likely because the business doesn't service many customers on a regular basis, but decorated as much as can be. The walls are covered with all sorts of metal tools and weapons, each one made at different times with different materials and techniques. No two items are the same in shape or color. The more aged pieces hang on the wall behind the front desk, darker in color and less polished, where the newer pieces gleam from their mounts much closer to the entryway. The light from the bulb in the center of the room casts strange shadows across the forged pieces, making them appear almost flat and untextured, as if they weren't even real to begin with. But Electro's hanging static buzzes as he stands surrounded by the items, his energy being drawn in every direction. They're all real alright, and pretty well made, too, to his untrained eye.

Still, he can't help but doubt their true legitimacy. There's no way Ryan would be running an honest business in his mind. Especially not with a Shard in his control.

From behind the counter pops up a Shask dressed in a black smithing apron, arms fully exposed and mechanized for all to see.

"Hello there! Welcome to Ashblade Smelting and Smithing!" the clerk chimes cheerfully. "How can I help you three this cycle?"

"Hi there," Electro replies merrily, stepping up to the counter in an effort to appear friendly to the poor, unassuming being. They're just doing their job. He takes the stick of arcane out of his mouth and holds it between his fingers as he suavely leans against the counter. "I'm looking for the owner."

"Mr. Ashblade?" the clerk asks with a slightly amused huff. "Do you have an appointment with him already?"

"Nope. I'm his friend."

The Shask's smile fades as they shake their head. "I'm sorry, but Mr. Ashblade doesn't have the time to see friends at a moment's notice. I can help you schedule a business appointment though–"

Electro slams his free hand down on the desk, interrupting the Shask sharply as he turns his body to fully face them. Their mechanical frame clacks as they shudder from the sudden shock.

"Nah, you don't understand," he says, tapping the tip of his gold against the countertop. "I ain't playing by his rules anymore. He tried to have my head last night." The eyes of the clerk widen, fear beginning to glow in their dark glossy eyes. "But that's not the worst he's done to me. I'm here to sort some things out with him. So you're going to let us through, or I'm going to fry your wires one by one until you do. Okay?"

Still, the Shask stands stiff. It's unclear whether they're petrified by his threat or is having a hard time processing Electro's demand.

Eventually, the Shask finally moves, walking to the far end of the counter and unlocking it, raising the flat wooden bar for the three wizards. They say nothing, but the air they exude and the glare they give Electro oozes with reluctance.

The wizards follow the clerk behind the counter and through a metal door which takes them into the back room of the shop. It's quite a sizable space, only made to feel small by how overcrowded it is. Shasks and wizards with small mechanical augmentations rush about, weaving expertly between workstations, piles of scrap metal, and crates of finished product. Along the back wall are various metal trays, each one filled and labeled with different ores brought over from Gardall. The nuggets range from a ball just big enough to fit into the palm of Electro's hand to the size of his head.

The room is also extremely hot from the open lava troughs that are scattered around the cramped space. Some have slatted grates over them, where ingots of metal sit and slowly melt down or at least soften up to be shaped. Others have no protections, and the workers with long tongs dump their products in and out in quick succession or hold them over the red-orange liquid as if they were standing near an open fire.

Some of the workers stall and stare at the visitors as the desk clerk guides the three wizards through the space, careful not to bring them anywhere near one of the lava troughs. Electro stares back at them with soft glares. He can't help but be skeptical about whether or not this is all up to code. He's not versed on Kendon law at all, but he wouldn't put it past Ryan to have cut some corners here and there. Or perhaps this is all above board. Really, he doesn't care.

The clerk gestures to a small rectangular hole at the very back of the workspace, closed off by a sliding gate. Beyond it appears to be a lift, its thick metal floor suspended by four strong cables, and activated by a control box inside.

"This will take you to the Magma Zone," the clerk says stiffly. "Mr. Ashblade is down there."

"Thank you," Electro replies, flashing the clerk a grin as he gestures to the other two to follow him onto the lift. Under the clerk's watchful gaze, he peels back the gate and steps onto the lift. The floor shifts under his weight, but it bounces back up and stabilizes quickly.

Lukri bounces onto the lift as well, his eyes wide as he stares at the cables. "What is this?"

"It's a lift," Electro answers. "It moves up and down."

"It *moves*?" the Serperas gasps.

Jake, on the other hand, doesn't appear too enthused. He stares at the lift, standing in the doorway. He's trying not to show it, but glimmers of anxiety slip through his tough facade.

"How far down is it?" he asks, turning to the clerk. The clerk just stares back at him and shrugs, unable to answer. The wizard turns back to the lift, his anxiousness much more apparent now.

"Oh, come *on*, it's perfectly safe!" Electro assures him. "Look!" As hard as he can, he stomps his foot against the floor of the lift. It makes a hollow thumping sound as the floor shifts and bounces up and down, though never enough to throw him off balance. The cables hold fast. Still, Jake sucks in a hesitant breath.

"We don't have all cycle to wait around for you," he tells the young wizard, folding his arms now.

Slowly, cautiously, Jake puts his foot out, leaning into the lift with his hands gripping the wall. He carefully puts his boot down, hardly making any sound as it comes into contact with the metal floor. The lift doesn't shift, at least not until he puts his weight on it. The breath escapes him as he freezes in place. Just like it did with Electro and Lukri, the floor does rebound, steadying to support his weight along with the other two. Only when it's even again does Jake take his second step, entering the lift completely, and quickly rushes towards the lift's center.

The clerk closes the gate behind him as Electro presses the "down" button on the lift's controls. Somewhere in the shadows above them, the lift's cable mechanism roars to life, gears whirling and wires humming. There's a slight jolt as the machine finally kicks on, a jolt that makes *some being* release a small yelp of surprise and panic, as they finally start their smooth decent into the bowels of the island of Kendon.

Jake, pale as can be, slowly takes a seat in the middle of the lift. There's a slight jitter to his movements. Lukri drifts to the edge of the lift, staring at the rock that passes them by. He raises a hand, holding close to the rough walls but not touching them.

"I wouldn't suggest touching the walls," Electro warns him, causing the prince to spin around. He reaches into his pocket and withdraws a stick of arcane gold, which he pops into his mouth. "It's a good way to tear off your skin."

Horror flashes cross Lukri's eyes. He lowers his hand.

In the dimness, it's hard to make out the small pipes and wires running down the sides of the shaft, though they glint at them whenever they pass by a small light. The white bulbs flash them with their unnatural lighting before fading back to a more natural light the farther they get from each of the light sources. Somewhere in the background is a distant buzzing that Electro can't unhear. It's starting to make his head pound. His magic swirls inside his chest, agitated.

He's more than ready to see Ryan. Each time the thought emerges from the back of his mind, that he's getting closer to his ex-best friend, his heart jumps. The anticipation bubbles in his gut. His hands twitch eagerly. *Won't he be surprised to see me*, he thinks, a wicked grin spreading across his lips.

The lower they go, the hotter the air becomes. Almost oppressively so, to the point where breathing feels like knives are tearing at one's chest. Sweat rolls off Electro's brow in waves. He has to wipe some of the drops away as best he can to avoid them getting into his eyes. He… didn't think this part through. Well, any part, really, but *especially* this. The only thing that keeps him even remotely cool is Shadow and its dense ball of icy power.

As if sensing his growing discomfort, the cold blooms, spreading across his body and chasing away the heat. It curls itself around his bones, not quite taking control away from him but more trying to share its power *with* him. The tight space still shimmers, but at least he doesn't feel like he's suffocating anymore.

The only downside to Shadow keeping him cool is that he finds moving his limbs now to be… *awkward* to say the very least. Each shift of his body is fought by an opposite force trying with all its might to bring him back to his original position. The urge to fit some invisible mold is overpowering. However Shadow stands, he must follow suit, for the Fragment has taken control. *Mostly*. He can still *feel* – the heat still presses itself against him, trying to force away the chill that keeps him from burning to ash before he can ever reach the bottom of the lift's shaft – and he can will his limbs to *move*. He might be cold but he isn't numb like before. Shadow knows that it doesn't *need* to direct him in this instance. But that doesn't mean he's free to move however he wishes.

His frustrations compound with Shadow's delayed response. If he tries to roll his head, it takes a moment for Shadow to move with him. By that time, his head has already gone back to where it was before – to where *Shadow's* head was before – and instead of the movement feeling natural, it's forceful and unwanted. Although, asking it to predict his spontaneity sounds like a bit much...

The rocky walls of the lift eventually open up into that of a metal cage, and beyond it is a sight that leaves them all stunned.

The massive lava lake is like a moving painting as it glows, bubbles, and shifts. Stretching down from the cavernous ceiling are small yet thick metal pipes aglow with large runes, extended deep into the sluggish liquid. Burrowed into the ceiling are even more circular shafts that allows the hot air to move up to the surface. The edges of the lava lake are divided by metal walls, each section belonging to different companies. Some have large signs that proudly overlook the lava, others don't. Ryan's place by the lake is pretty sizable but very small in comparison to some of the other sections. It's clear down here that he's just a hole-in-the-wall smithy lucky enough to even *have* space by the lake to call his own.

In Ryan's space, there aren't any workers around. Then again, there isn't much equipment here, either. There's a platform near the rock wall that overlooks the space, and atop it a small room with open windows, revealing a desk and mounds of paper inside. And Ryan himself.

The wizard sits forward in his chair, flipping through papers with a tired scowl. He's cut his hair short and made it orange, though his ruby red eyes remain the same. He wears a leather jacket over what looks to be gold plate armor. He looks to wear those eighteen long years without Electro quite visibly, with his face weathered and wrinkled from stress. Electro catches a glimpse of Ryan's greatsword resting off to the side. He doesn't seem to have noticed the descending lift yet even though it's in his full view. Electro's gaze remains locked on the unsuspecting wizard, not wanting to miss his reaction when he does finally take notice.

As the lift nears the bottom of the shaft, it starts to rumble and slow as the mechanisms brake. Jake sucks in a sharp breath and plants his hands on the floor, bracing himself, as Lukri jumps in surprise. Right before they're lowered out of sight, Ryan's head finally lifts to see what all the noise is about. For the briefest moment, he locks eyes with Electro.

It's not long enough to catch any of his following emotions, but Electro can't help but smile anyway. He hopes he's panicking.

He steps off the lift first, seeing as he's the closest to its exit. It's just a simple archway cut into the metal, no gate or safety bar in sight. Each footstep he takes is heavy, Shadow trailing in its reaction time. It takes it a few strides to finally find his rhythm, and as it learns its weight gradually lifts from him, granting his steps more fluidity and confidence. In this lockstep, its chilly presence gradually fades into the background as it begins to nestle itself between his bones and muscles.

Its comfort is easily disturbed, however, when he comes to an abrupt halt, disrupting the flow it has just found. Its presence roars back into focus, agitated and confused.

"Back off," he mutters under his breath. If he's going to tussle with Ryan, the *last* thing he wants is Shadow getting in his way. With a pang of reluctance, Shadow follows his command, its icy tendrils releasing their hold over his bones. The heat of the nearby lava presses against his skin eagerly, slowly chipping away at the lingering cold. He should have enough time to deal with Ryan before the heat starts to get to him again. At least, that's his hope.

He flicks his stick of arcane away. It bounces against the rock, each strike ringing out across the small space.

"Electro!" Ryan calls from overhead. He's on the walkway now, leaning over the railing to get a better look at the trio. He smiles at them, appearing to be pleased to at least see his old friend after all these years. "It's good to–"

A burst of energy propels Electro upwards, his eyes wide with anger and teeth grit with anticipation. He draws his fist back, bright bolts of energy leaping from his knuckles.

He clears the railing, kicking off the top bar and leading into his strike. With a yell, his fist surges forward, aimed right at Ryan's chest. Ryan, however, manages to leap away just in time, letting Electro's punch strike at hot air.

He quickly finds his footing on the metal platform and raises his head. Ryan now holds his greatsword at the ready, the blade materializing in a long streak of flame. There's a small red gem embedded in the sword's hilt that glows gently in Ryan's hands.

Though he holds the sword before him cautiously, it remains lowered. Ryan's grin is weak, his thin facade being forced together for just a little longer.

"Come on, Ely," Ryan says with a small breath trying to pass itself off as a chuckle, "this is hardly the place to spar."

Electro's eyes dart to Ryan's left arm. It's entirely made of metal now, the red-painted frame disappearing up into the Pyromancer's jacket. Its interior is packed with all sorts of pistons both large and small, with a forest of wires woven between them. *That thing will certainly help his swings pack more of a punch,* is his first thought. His second one is, *What a sellout*.

His gaze snaps right back to Ryan's oh-so-punchable face. "Drop the act, Ryan. You know why I'm here."

"No, I don't," Ryan replies, his head shaking so slightly it might have not even moved at all. "Come on, Ely, let's not make a scene. Just lower your fists and we can step into my office–"

The longer he talks, the lighter Electro's head starts to feel, and his will for justice quietly ebbs away. There's no doubt in his mind that he's trying to use the Shard's magic on him, just as he did all those years ago. So, with a roar, he rushes Ryan again. There's not much space behind him left for him to use. If he just keeps pressing him…

Ryan's foot shifts, turning his body to the right, and Electro's fist flies right past him. Ryan stares with a smug grin, pleased with himself for timing his dodge just right. Then it flashes to horror as Electro swings his arm outward, his elbow clocking Ryan right on the side of his lower jaw.

The Pyromancer staggers as Electro spins around, not letting up his pursuit. He brings his knee up to Ryan's gut, then continues with his boot striking Ryan's crotch. Out of surprise, Ryan topples over onto his back. As he lays dazed on the metal platform, Electro plants his boot onto Ryan's chest to keep him pinned down.

"I don't take kindly to beings that want me dead," Electro says. "And I *especially* don't like cowards who hire muscle to get it done."

"What are you… talking about?" Ryan grunts back.

"I've already has a chat with *Jay*," he continues, spitting down onto Ryan's face. "Play dumb all you want. It ain't going to change what you've already done!"

Ryan smiles back. It's a wicked smile, one that mocks Electro and his naivety. His eyes finally glow with life, basking in the moment. Why does he look so proud of himself? He's already been brought down–

Electro's static reaches out, striking something in front of where he stands, rushing at him fast. In blind panic he leaps backwards. He watches Ryan's blade appear out of thin air, its tip fading into reality right where Electro stood a mere moment before. Ryan's downed body disappears, turning into a smudge of color that blends itself into the environment.

The gem shimmers and distorts the air around it as Ryan appears standing before him once again. Unlike Jay, he doesn't look like he's going to play around. A dark shadow is cast across his face as he grins, relishing his murderous aura.

"When I'm done with you, no being will even remember you being alive," Ryan says. "My hands will remain clean of a crime I never committed."

Fire swirls around his greatsword as he raises it above his head. As the blade bears down upon Electro, he scrambles to the side, barely managing to slide himself past the mad Pyromancer. He spins around, given only enough time to raise his arm before he sees Ryan shift his body, twisting his downward swing under his arm, cutting through the metal floor of the walkway with ease, and up again into Electro's face. A sharp, hot cut rushes across his chest as Electro propels himself away at the last moment. Shadow swirls within him with alarm, already setting to work easing the pain and patching his wounds. He doesn't have much time to glance down at the damage, but he can feel a large chunk of his left side has been sliced through and seared.

Ryan leaps forward, a funnel of white flames curling around his body as he travels. Electro jumps, kicking his legs out to the side as Ryan swings his greatsword horizontally. The blade passes right under him, deadly heat slicing through where his torso once was.

Electro lands in a low crouch, his clothes and exposed injury passing through the lingering flames of Ryan's blade, sending a burning sting of pain across his body. He glances up, planning to spring forward and tackle Ryan to the ground again, but instead he finds the flaming goliath already preparing another downwards stroke. How did he manage to set that up so fast?

He rolls backwards as the blade once again melts through the walkway, giving him little room to collect himself. Ryan is once more in his face, magically prepared for a forward lunge. Electro does his best to sidestep, only for the sword's direction to change and follow close behind him as a sideways swing.

Teeth gritted, Electro flings himself over the railing, getting himself well away from that wild sword. That *must* be him using the Shard. How else could he keep up with Electro without needing any recovery time and completely change the swing of his sword like that?

He lands on the hard ground, finally able to find his footing once more. Ryan still lingers on the walkway above, his figure swirling with his magic. The intense heat of the lava lake bears down on Electro even harder now, drenching his body with sweat.

The fact that Ryan can use Illusion magic is a grave concern. Electro hasn't ever fought an Illusionist before, mostly because none of them are the fighting type. Even so, their magic usage is *obvious*. With Ryan, however, it's impossible to tell when he's going to use it and how. He thought he already had Ryan on the ropes once he pinned him down. But was that Ryan always an illusion? When did he make the switch? How was he able to do it without Electro knowing right up until he revealed himself?

Before his very eyes, he watches the metal walkway start to melt, the bars beneath Ryan's feet turning a bright red, almost white. The floor begins to dip, stretching itself down to the ground around him, liquid enough to drip yet solid enough to carry him down with it. As Ryan steps off onto the solid rocky ground that surrounds the lava lake, the metal rebounds back to how it was before, how it always has been, not a spot of damage to be seen. The air around him shimmers with heat and magic, small embers leaping from the ends of his hair.

"Electro!" a sharp yell suddenly rings out. The two boys Electro brought along with him unfreeze themselves from confused spells. Jake draws his sword with his face full of intent, a determined fire blazing in his eyes. Lukri, meanwhile, waves his hands through the air, commanding a small cloud of orange dust to gather before him and come together into the shape he needs.

But neither of them even makes it two steps before Ryan taps his blade on the ground with a mildly annoyed glare, and from it a long glowing crack rushes towards them. The sharp red line sections the two boys off from the rest of the plateau before suddenly bursting into a curtain of spewing lava that consumes the sight of the boys.

Electro's body grows cold, the Fragment within curling itself around his bones once more, as he raises his fists in preparation. He feels himself fall away to its endless power as it ripples out from his chest. His skull tingles as long fingers stretch themselves across, poking and prodding at the edges of his mind. Each tingle carries with it a pang of hesitation, along with a correction. The boundless ripples alter their flow, bending themselves to fit the jagged flow of his Storm magic. It wants to help but doesn't seem to know if it should.

He forces himself to leap back as Ryan flashes forward, just narrowly missing another strike from his blazing sword. Each small movement he makes jolts his system back awake momentarily, but he's not quite as agile as he was before. The heat of the flames, at the very least, doesn't feel as bad.

Each step he takes, each swing he attempts, he forces his way past Shadow's mold. It does its best to keep up with him; as he tenses his arms, it, too, prepares to swing, and as he crouches, it braces itself to jump.

Ryan finally manages to get in a strike. The blade digs itself into Electro's ribs. He can feel the burning metal slice through his bones like they were paper. He stumbles, taken aback by the blossom of pain in the midst of Shadow's aura.

What are you doing*?!* he wonders, though it doesn't seem like Shadow heard his angry thought. It remains wound around him, its icy gaze staring back at the Pyromancer from his forehead. Whatever it's thinking about doing, it either has to do it *now* or it needs to get *out of his way*!

Its glare drops from Ryan, its form shifting once more. A dense strand of darkness finally presses itself against his mind and suddenly everything clicks. The cold coils fade away into the background, only noticeable as the hot air rushes past his moving body. The flow of his magic has never felt smoother, the jolts of energy stimulating his movements rather than eagerly looking for escapes. The ache of his chest wound remains present, however, even as it chills with Shadow sealing it from within. Even though they're of two entirely different beings, neither of them have felt more at peace with this strange coexistence.

He takes a deep breath and feels his lips buzz with strange air. But it feels... *good*.

Ryan's following swing travels towards him impossibly slow. He can watch the developing trail of the lightning that leaps from his clothes and strikes at the metal blade closing the distance between itself and his waist. This is... new. But completely natural all the same.

It doesn't take much to propel himself away. In fact, it only feels like he gave the ground the slightest kick with his toes, and he finds himself having traveled nearly a whole five or six marks away from Ryan. His sword and fiery afterburst strike at empty air that still crackles with his afterimage. The Pyromancer blinks in surprise, but he doesn't process Electro's movements fast enough.

Electro flashes forward, the hot wind stinging his cheeks and arms as he reels back for a swing of his own. He gives Ryan just enough time to let shock paint his face before smothering it with his fist. He feels Ryan's nose bend beneath his knuckles as he's sent flying into the large metal divider with a resounding, hollow *clang*.

Able to finally breathe again, Electro flexes his fingers, and he feels his knuckles pop and tingle in a delightful way. This is how he is meant to be.

The world is brought back into focus as a blur of red once again fills his vision. Ryan has already closed the gap yet again, sword raised high. He grips his sword hard but has reeled it back far enough to inhibit his speed. That, and Electro is *much* faster now. He leaps out of the way with ease, allowing the fire to curl around his clothes this time without any issue. Though even as he thinks Ryan now needs to set up for his next attack, the Pyromancer is already midway through another arc from a completely different direction.

Ryan has had his Shard for a long time now. Having been given room to formulate more coherent thoughts, Electro is quite impressed with how well he can wield but a small portion of its magic. To any other being unaware of Ryan's skills and unfamiliar with how he likes to fight, this tactic is sure to overwhelm his opponent. He faces Electro, though, and they've sparred too many times to count.

Ryan has always been a heavy hitter. His speed comes down to his efficiency, though he's still slow regardless. His fire would still be a challenge for him to combat in a regular scuffle, but with Shadow fueling him now, all they do is tickle.

Electro's lightning sparks off of something behind him, and he jumps into the air once more. Two swords swipe from different angles, from both the front and behind. He takes a quick glance over his shoulder to find a second Ryan standing at his back.

Now he has two on his tail as he ducks and weaves around the swinging blades. Their roars of effort are disjointed and out of sync, almost like Ryan managed to split himself into two independent yet identical copies of himself. Now that there are two of them, it's easier to spot how they're able to charge and change their swings. When the arc fails to reach Electro, the blade shifts and distorts, along with his arms in a blink-and-you'll-miss-it moment. When their forms stabilize once again, he's already set himself up for another direct attack.

As he searches the pair for an opening to exploit, a third blade manages to sneak its way into the fray. Another Ryan has appeared to his left, complicating things once more. It's not long before a fourth and a fifth join in. Looks like the tactics have changed; if he can't keep up with Electro, he'll simply overwhelm him instead.

He's fast enough now to keep some breathing room between himself and the horde of Ryan's spiteful face. He doesn't even know where he should begin, which one he should target first over the rest. Is the real Ryan even part of this mass of red and silver? He can't tell.

Electro plants his feet, shifting his weight. There's only one thing to do in this case. He'll just have to knock them *all* out!

He throws himself into the fray at last. He socks one right in the face, then ducks under the swing of another. With a powerful leg sweep, he trips a third nearby, who crashes into a fourth. He jumps, planting his hands on a passing blade and driving his heels square into another Ryan's jaw before propelling himself into the air, crashing down onto another clone right below him. His lightning bursts from his body, the atmosphere around him supercharging with unbridled energy. Any metal nearby starts to vibrate and spark as it becomes supercharged. Every swing of a sharp blade sings loud and clear, a *vroomph* of disturbed electric air.

There's seemingly no end to the number of illusions that Ryan can throw at him; every time he turns away from an empty space, two or three more blades materialize out of thin air. Even with his newfound strength, Electro is struggling to keep up with it all. One or two cuts manage to shred his clothes, making his arms start to sting unpleasantly. The world has become a spinning blur of browns and reds, the sharp stench of his lightning and the suffocating heat of the lava mixing into an unpleasant smog that sits at the bottom of his lungs.

"*STOP*!"

The command stabs itself deep into Electro's preoccupied mind. In an instant, his legs turn to stone as his flow is brought to an abrupt halt. As much as he tries to push his way through it, his body refuses to heed him. The single word is stuck ringing in his ears, tying him down.

The only thing he *can* do is stand in place and stare back at Ryan. The real one. The copies stand nearby, their arms extended along with his own. But even though their swords all converge on Electro, there's a single cold spike that has been driven straight through his gut.

"It's a shame, really," Ryan says with a grin, his words buzzing in Electro's ears. "You were such a reliable wizard. I was grateful to have a being like you keeping all my detractors at bay. But then you just *had* to steal Kel away from me..." There's a firm shove as the cold shifts and slides. "Look at what you made me do, Ely. Now *no being* gets to have her. And *you*... just a loose end to tie up." There's no remorse to be found in his glare as he commands, "*Die*."

The edges of his vision begin to blur and darken as his thoughts shift of their own accord. Despair floods his slow, aching heart. All his fighting has been for naught. He can't keep defying the odds forever. He should really be dead, shouldn't he?

His body falls away as darkness descends on his mind in full force. But it's not death that has come to claim him. Shadow surges forward of its own accord, swallowing the haze that Ryan placed upon him in full. Its glare releases a blast of cold force that slams into Ryan and throws him into the air like he's nothing.

He lands hard next to one of the metallic corner supports for the raised room. It turns its attention downwards, to the greatsword shoved clean through Electro's stomach. He watches his hands rise, wrapping themselves around the sword and yanking it free with one swift motion. The deep wound is deathly cold, full of the Fragment's miracle magic.

Just another reminder that he would have died long before this point if Shadow wasn't here with him.

Even numbed by Shadow's presence, Electro can feel the vibration of the Shard in the greatsword, making the weapon shudder in his grip. The gemstone in its hilt glows with a hazy ring of light. A Shard finally rests in the palms of his hands...

As his fingers close around the gem, it flares with brilliant light, answering his unspoken call. The prismatic rays morph themselves into a mass of tendrils that float in the air around him. They feel the world around them before turning their attention to him.

His hand tingles and aches as the multicolored strings worm their way under his skin wherever they can. When his hand is no longer an option for entry, the strings rush their way up his arm to his shoulder, wrapping it in their collective embrace. They're neither hot nor cold, yet both at the same time. The sword is as heavy as all of Astria and as light as empty space. His shoulder aches from the nothing-weight of the strings sinking into his body.

The magic is raw and overwhelming, each string fighting the others for their place inside Electro's hollow body. They swirl and tangle, invading every single corner of his being. They push out the flow of his own magic, override it completely, and smother Shadow's presence with their might. If he didn't know any better, he would have thought that Shadow left his body. But, if that *did* happen, he'd no longer be standing.

The strings burrow into his wiry frame wherever they can and begin to pull. In what direction? *Every* direction. Forward, backward, inward, outward. They want him to jump into the air, burrow into the ground, run in circles, lie down, shout, laugh, kick, dance, *release*. They crave it. They *demand* it.

He holds the greatsword casually with only one hand and stares down at it with indifference. The worthless thing of shaped metal is nothing more than a conduit that constricts the Shard, pressing it into an unholy form concocted by a being with no respect for its magnificence. A jewel meaninglessly inlaid in metal? It could be *anything*! It could have even been the blade itself!

He pries the Shard from its prison with ease and casts the sword aside. The little red gem glows back at him, molding itself into that of a small star plucked from the night sky. It loses its color, returning to a blinding white. Out of the corners of his eyes, he sees all nearby beings reel away from the Shard's majesty, unable to lay their eyes upon its form. To Electro, however, he holds part of a sphere. Sharp lines cut in complete, incomprehensible perfection show where it was broken away from its other two pieces. Its outer shell curves so cleanly that it rests in Electro's palm without him even needing to close his hand around it to keep it in place. It simply sits there in its incomplete perfection.

{...tro!}

His body grows numb once again, and with it reality roars back into focus. The strings fade away into the background; although he cannot feel his limbs, he can sense the strings humming throughout his entire being.

His eyes ache and his head pounds as Shadow wrestles control away from the Shard, yanking Electro backwards. Just as his feet leave the ground, he quite nearly gets a face full of red and orange as Ryan's body is thrown right at the spot Electro was standing in mere moments ago. The Pyromancer lands with a heavy *thump* and a pained yell. But a different, much more *familiar* voice overpowers the moaning with ease.

"*YOU!*" his own Shadow cries out in a rage, its Twisted form rushing across the space like a long black streak. It plants a boot squarely on Ryan's face and kicks off of him as it quickly closes the gap between itself and Electro. Each fist it throws crackles sharply. Even Electro can feel the rush of air that it leaves in its wake. "*GET. OUT. OF. MY. BODY!*"

Shadow does its best to curve out of its way, though it can't dodge the lightning that leaps from its body. Each shock worms its way to Electro's consciousness, wanting him to feel it just as much as Shadow does. *Stars above*, is this truly what other beings feel when he zaps them?

Shadow is driven down the rocky plateau, the heat of the lava growing even more intense the closer it gets. Not even its magic is enough to keep back the heat. Small waves manage to break their way through its defenses, searing whatever its spectral fingers touch. Electro's mind tenses with each blast.

Weightlessness lifts his body into the air, the Shard still cradled tightly in his hand. His Shadow springs up after them, its fury blazing. Each new spark of lightning that strikes the lava below them propels it higher, creating tiny ripples that travel across its sluggish surface.

A fist manages to clip Shadow's side, which turns into a sharp jab of an elbow right to the hole Ryan carved into his body. Before Shadow can even reach back out in reaction, his essence flies away. The energy of the bolts shifts with its body as it leans back and forth, guiding itself through the air with ease. When it finally returns to him, will he be able to do that, too?

Wrapped around its left arm is a band of light, a series of glyphs that spins slowly, glowing with power. Kelsy's Shard.

"*I should have known,*" it spits. "*Abusing* my *body for your own twisted pleasure! No* wonder *I could not sense it.*"

Electro feels his mouth warm, an invitation for him to speak.

"If you've got such a problem with it, then why don't you

just come back?" he asks, yelling over the bubbling lava below. He can feel the strings of the Shard shifting inside him, pressing themselves to the back of his throat and turning his breaths for air into a syrupy essence of raw magic.

His Shadow smiles back, chuckling to itself. "*I am not ready for* that *just yet. Can I not enjoy my freedom while I have it?*"

He tightens his grip on the Shard, Shadow's presence weaker beneath its arcane power. "Cut that out. What are you trying to do?"

"*Is it not obvious?*" it mocks, its arms stretching out wide. "*Surely* you *would know!*"

It's not wrong; all he has to do is put himself in its position. Its wants and desires aren't going to be too far off from his own. It's seeking revenge.

It extends a hand towards Electro, gesturing to the piece of light in his hand. "*Hand it over.*"

Electro shakes his head, an eager smile tugging at his lips. "I don't think so."

His Shadow flings itself forward once more, wearing a wide grin that matches his own. The two forces collide, Electro catching its fist with his hand expertly, and a burst of chaotic streaks of light radiate from their joined hands. Its cold skin is so comfortingly familiar touching his. It's a shame that he has to fight it like this.

The two duck and weave around each other. Arms and legs fly, and each time the two touch, the hot air electrifies. The metal pipes buzz and spark as their clash no doubt draws the eyes of the Shasks from all around the lava lake. Shadow keeps Electro afloat as best it can as he tussles with himself.

For the most part, they're evenly matched. It helps that they're more or less the same being. He can see all of the tells and knows how to counter them exactly. A sharp jab is easily pushed to the side, negating the follow-up knee to the groin. A side-kick is easy to vault suspended in mid-air. It's the elbows that they *both* have to watch out for; being parallel to any kind of extended arm is a surefire way to have it come folding in their direction.

Though there is something else about his Shadow that he's noticed. It's not just static that it exudes, but a heavy, frosty air as well. There are sharp snaps of cold meeting hot in their connections, buried just beneath the lightshow. He can feel the sting of frost against his hands as he shoves his Shadow away from him time after time. It weighs down against his body, attempting to shackle his limbs. It must have started learning how to use the Shard's magic for itself. The question is, how much progress has it made? Is it holding back, waiting to unleash it at the most opportune moment?

Its arm flies past his head, narrowly missing his face. But just as he moves to retaliate, his arm grows numb, Shadow's essence surging forward from within him. Its dark hand outstretches, phasing through his skin and making his hand and wrist fall limp as it latches itself to the Twisted Shadow's wrist. It reels back, caught off guard, and yanks more of Shadow's arm out from Electro's body.

Return, it demands coldly.

Electro's Shadow glares back, its white teeth gritted in irritation. "*Not.* YET*!*" it roars. It twists its body around, ripping the Fragment from its hiding place. Shadow does its best to anchor itself, its essence digging deep into Electro's muscles to no avail. It was unprepared, and so it is flung through the air, sucked right out of his body. He feels himself go limp, but the darkness does not claim him. His eyes remain open as the Shard latched to his hand fills the empty space with its arcane warmth. He pulses with a calm, rhythmic pressure as the strings weave themselves along his skin.

The world shifts and spins as he is sent falling through the air. Shadow is out of his sight. But his is not. Its attention turns to him in an instant, eyes wide with panic as it realizes the danger it just put its own Husk into.

It grabs his wrist. That he *can* feel. But his head drops and he finds himself forced to stare into the bright depths of the lava below. It burns into his vision, the dull orange splitting into various shades that swirl together, as the bubbles burst into yellow rings.

His Shadow squeezes him. There is a yearning somewhere, a *want* to return. But there is also a deep rage gnawing away at it, leaving it in a constant state of restlessness. It wants to finish whatever it has in mind first. Stars only know how long it'll be before it wishes to return to him by its own accord.

The Shard is lifted from his hand. The strings that fill him are drawn out as it's pulled away, like a brush being gently run across his body, down his arm and up to his fingers, and leaving the void that is his essenceless existence in the sensation's wake.

"*You can have him back,*" his Shadow says. He's helplessly thrown through the air once more, the world around him but a streak of bright color, right up until he feels another pair of cold hands clamp down on his body. "*But if I* ever *see the two of you again...*" It unleashes a malicious laugh, amused by its own unspoken ideas. Then it leaves. Its presence within him disappears, a sensation only apparent when it's gone.

***

Jake grits his teeth, holding his stance firm. He entraps the Serperas prince in his arms as he thrashes and squirms against his powerful hug. He has even tried using his tail to get Jake to trip over to no avail.

"How *dare* you!" Lukri screams at Ryan. "Let me *go*!" he orders Jake.

The adult Pyromancer lies broken on the ground, blood pouring from his nose and mouth, his breathing ragged. His clothes sport a collection of small black lightning burns and sharp sword-made holes. Lukri's sword has been thrown to the ground nearby, the thin edge of the blade bright red.

Once the Shard was out of Ryan's hands, the curtain of lava holding the two back disappeared in an instant. While Electro and his Shadow fought in the air over the lava lake, Lukri rushed the dazed Ryan with murderous intent. It took all of Jake's strength to disarm the Serperas. He's smart enough not to have thrown him onto the ground like he did when he was a Twisted Shadow – Lukri used his tail to knock Jake off-balance then, too, to much greater effect – so he settled for a strange under-the-arm hug instead.

He gets that Lukri's angry, but *this* isn't it. And he'll keep holding on until the Serperas calms himself down.

"That's enough," a call comes from behind. It's not quite as demanding as it is weary, an airy breath betraying the speaker's lack of will over wanting to deal with the situation before them. Lukri's kicking dulls as Jake turns to glance behind him. Electro descends from the air above. His amethyst eyes regard the two boys with indifference. In fact, he seems much more distracted by the new adornment on his arm. Sparkling blue ice engulfs his left arm, from the tips of his fingers to the top of his shoulder and even digging into his armpit, though it's thickest around his wrist. He keeps shaking it sharply, trying to get the coating to crack and bend to no avail. It shows no signs of melting, which is odd, seeing as they're standing right next to a lake full of lava.

He takes one look at Jake holding Lukri, then down at Ryan who writhes on the ground before them.

"What happened?" he asks.

"He tried to kill him," Jake answers.

"*He* is a *thief*!" Lukri cries out, jumping against his

restraints. Jake has to stiffen up again or else he'd risk the prince escaping. "A thief of the highest order!"

Electro purses his lips, taking another good, long look at the injured Pyromancer. He steps up to his side and crouches down. He pokes at his left arm with his icy hand, making the wizard wince even harder.

"Where'd the augment go, Ashblade?" he hums. "Lying about that, too, eh?"

Ryan manages to turn his head and push a glare out through his pain. "Ely–!" he rasps, devolving into a yelp of pain as Electro presses the ice against a place that's a little more tender.

"Ah, it's okay," Electro says, standing once more. His gaze locks onto Jake, and he gives him a nod. "You can let him go now."

He raises an eyebrow back, but does as he's told, releasing the Serperas from his arms. Lukri stumbles a bit as he finds his footing again. But then he goes right for his abandoned blade.

"He–" the prince starts, anger lighting in his eyes once more.

"–is going to get thrown in jail for the rest of his life," Electro finishes his thought for him with a bright smile. "Once we tell some being about him skimping out on an augment, that is. You know what that means, Lukri?"

Lukri pauses, his sword already raised high. Slowly, he shakes his head.

"It *means*," Electro says as he plants a boot on Ryan's rolling head, "he'll be atoning for his misdeeds for the rest of his immortal life! The Shasks won't let him Fade away until his sentence is served. The Shasks take their augments *very* seriously." A being must have an augment to be considered a resident of Kendon. To somehow cheat oneself out of such a thing and still freely reap the rewards is the greatest sin to commit against the Shasks.

Lukri's arms drop, the blade thumping against the stone ground. His mouth hangs open, but his vengeful gaze sparkles. Electro lets out a merry laugh, completely at ease with the fact that he now lords power over the freedom of the being beneath his foot.

He does eventually step off, waving for the other two to join him in his waltz back to the lift. “Let's go. We're done here.”

Jake can't help but release a hopeless breath. Sure, he'll dread the sheer climb of the stairs once they're back up top, but he does *not* want to take that lift. It's just something about being suspended high in the air that makes him so... *uneasy*.

But he reluctantly steps back on with the other two, taking his position at the center. Electro steps up to the small console fixed to the side of the lift, searching for the button that will take them back up.

Beep! Ka-chunk...

The mechanism starts to rev, raising them up into the depths of the rocky shaft once again. It takes a while for it to pick up speed, but pretty soon Jake's stomach is left somewhere below in the large lava pit.

He closes his eyes and takes a deep breath as the metal platform shudders beneath his crossed legs. It will hold them. It will bring them back to the surface safely. Nothing will happen. They won't fall to their deaths, far, far below them...

CRACK! Sharp icy shards batter Jake's queasy body, causing Lukri to jump as well, making the platform sway ever so gently. But Electro doesn't seem to care much about the boys or their safety as he raises his arm for another go at striking the passing rocky wall beside him.

“Hey–!” Jake manages to yell before he needs to duck for cover, another spray of ice pelting his hunched figure.

“And one more time!” Electro announces. He sends more sharp rain down upon the Pyromancer. The shards make a light tinkling sound as they strike the metal and rattle along with the clacking of the gears.

The Electromancer lets out a relieved sigh as he inspects his arm. Most of the ice as been shaved off by the rock wall, though it appears more scraped and less shattered. Still, he smiles with satisfaction as he twists it, and with each bend glittering dust falls from the structure.

So his Shadow already knows how to use the Shard to make ice, then... It's only been a single cycle since it got a hold of it.

Jake shifts on the ground, settling himself back down into position. He couldn't have even helped, though it's not like there was a whole lot he could have done this time. He can't fight over lava like they did. So he did what he *could* do, which was keeping Lukri in check.

He turns to the Serperas. He doesn't want to, but he feels the need to check on him. His arms are folded tightly, his gaze transfixed on the walls of stone that pass them by in a blur. Sensing his stare, Lukri's eyes shift to him and his stiff frown quivers. Then he quickly bounces back to the moving wall.

"*So*," Electro hums, trying to spark some conversation, "tricked your mother, eh? How'd he do that?"

Lukri shifts his weight around uncomfortably. "She thought..." he trails off, his eyes scanning the wall for more words to use. The corners of his mouth twitch, wanting to frown but being unable to do so as he holds himself back. "She loved him."

Electro shoves his hands into his pockets. "Wow... Sorry."

Lukri shakes his head. "No. No sorry. Not you." He lets out a heavy breath. "Excuse me." His jade eyes stray to Jake again. Many thoughts stir behind them.

"It was more than the Shard, though," he says slowly, carefully, thinking each of his words through as he says them. "She... had... kids. Me. And... one other."

Jake's stare turns sharp in an instant, not liking where this

Serperas is taking this story. "*Stop*," he demands through barred teeth. "I don't have *parents*."

"But the Pyramid said–"

"I don't *care* where you heard that from!" Jake barges in. He rises to his feet and jabs a finger into his chest. "I don't have *parents*. I am not a *Serperas*. I am a *wizard*, born and raised! That test is wrong – *you* are wrong! – and I don't want to hear *any* of it!"

Lukri blinks, taken aback by his sudden outburst. Well, sudden to *him*. Jake huffs and puffs through the hot air, his body lurching along with his forceful breaths. He turns his back on Lukri. He can't stand to look at that copy of himself any more this cycle than he already has. Screw whatever he saw inside that stars forsaken Pyramid. It's probably wrong anyway. Just like how it's only a coincidence that Lukri is as close to a physical reflection as he'll get. His hair is slightly lighter than his and he has fangs. That's enough to make the two of them worlds apart in differences, right? Perhaps the queen of Mirage had children with a *different* Pyromancer.

He parts his dry lips, a question emerging from the depths of his mind. A sickening question. Ryan, a Pyromancer. And Lukri's mother, a Serperas.

Slowly, he turns to Electro, his intense stare making the Electromancer shift uncomfortably.

"Did Ryan have a natural affinity for Fire magic?" he asks.

The wizard lets out a thoughtful hum as his eyes scan the lift for a concrete answer to give, rubbing his chin with his fingers for some good luck. "I don't know. He might have? Even so, maybe the Shard... But could it...?" He shakes his head, meeting the Pyromancer's eyes at last. His answer is a short shrug. "Sorry."

Still, Jake has to breathe deep to calm himself, though it feels like it only makes his heart race even harder. His mind is blank; he doesn't want to think. He *refuses* to let any of it enter his head. This *has* to be a sick joke. It's not funny at all, but still a joke.

Yes, that's it... Just one big sick joke...

Chapter 18

The atmosphere is tense as the group of wizards occupy Kimberly's dining room. Lukri has taken a chair. The rest stand. Electro and Ethan situate themselves at one end of the table, with Kimberly opposite them at the other. The only one not present in the room is Jake. He opted for the sofa, sitting quietly with his head held in his hands. Kimberly can't help but worry about him as Electro gives a short briefing on the events that transpired on Kendon. She's never seen her boyfriend appear so... *defeated* before. She can only wonder about what is gnawing at his mind. Is it the loss of another Shard or something else entirely?

"Well, Electro?" Ethan inquires once the wizard's overview concludes. "What do you think it might do now?"

Sparks of static jump from his clothes as Electro stares down at the table. "Well, now that it knows that Shadow is using my body, I don't think it'll be eager to show its face any time soon. If anything, it'll know that we'll bring the final Shard right to it. It just has to be patient."

The Husk lets out a tired sigh, his head turning away.

"Do we even know where the final Shard is?" Kimberly asks the room.

Lukri shrugs, his head tilting from side to side. He might have an *idea*, but not *where*. Ethan, on the other hand, stiffens. The room shakes as the shadows grow longer.

His onyx eyes lock with hers as he places a hand on his chest. “I have it.”

A pang of surprise shoots through Kimberly. He means to say that he's been wandering around with a Shard to the Font of Magic inside him this *entire time*? How did she not know this? Did *he* even know?

He scowls to himself. He doesn't seem all that happy admitting that fact aloud, either. His fingers curl, tugging at his shirt as if he were trying to dig his way through his skin and rip the Shard from wherever it's being held within him.

“It learns fast,” Electro warns. “It's already figured out how to use Ice magic.”

Dread descends upon the room. That's not a good sign. If it's actively learning how to use the Shards it has already, then they can't just leave it alone and take their time gathering strength. No matter what, it will always outclass them if they leave it be.

An eager smile worms its way across Electro's face as he says what every being is thinking, “Looks like we'll just have to take the fight to *it* this time!”

“'We'?” Ethan echoes, folding his arms with a hard scowl. “Me and Shadow is one thing. *You* on the other hand–”

“This isn't just *your* problem,” Electro cuts him off rather forcefully, his mood souring in an instant. Bolts of lightning jump from his clothes and hair as he stares the Husk down. “I'm coming with you. This is still *my* Shadow we're dealing with here.”

Ethan gives Electro a strong, silent glare of unhappiness, though it eventually shifts to the rest of the group. “Well? What about the rest of you?”

Lukri's hand instantly shoots up into the air. “I will go!” he states, each word spoken sharp and clear. "This is important to the Serperas. I will not let it get away with taking our piece!"

"*Lukri*," Ethan grumbles, shaking his head. He looks like he wants to refute the prince, but he can't bring himself to turn him down. Kimberly wants to speak up, too. He might have survived Korodon. He might have managed to return from Kendon unscathed. But surely the only heir to Mirage would be a little more cautious about wanting to face even two parts of the Font of Magic!

"I don't think you going is a good idea, Lukri," she voices. Lukri twists around in his chair, his eyes wide with offense and determination and his fangs barred. "You should really care about your own safety. What if–"

"I fought before!" he retorts. "Do not treat me like–"

"What if you never return?" she proposes. "What do you think your mother will do?"

Her question shuts him down with ease. His face contorts, wrinkling in confusion as he tries to determine what emotion to express. That fighting fire blazing in his eyes whittles away, until he is left with nothing to do but stare listlessly at the wall behind her.

"You shouldn't make your family worry," she adds gently, "or your people."

"I will go," a new voice chimes in. Jake stands in the center of the archway, staring at the others with a dull gaze. Despite how tired he looks, he manages to hold his head up high with confidence. This proposal disturbs the young Serperas, making him jump out of his chair.

"But!" he exclaims.

Jake's eyes shift to Kimberly. She sucks in a deep breath. He's committed to going, and he knows that she is, too, despite having not announced her intention yet. His head tilts forward as he says, "I go where she goes."

"Kim?" Ethan prompts, his expectant stare befalling her.

Kimberly nods back, confirming his unspoken thought. "I would like to put this family matter to rest."

"Absolutely *not*!" Electro's voice suddenly fills the room. Full bolts of lightning arc from his hair and fingers as he slams a hand down onto the table with a thunderous *boom*. The very core of her being quivers before his cold gaze.

It takes her a moment to recover from her shock. His powerful response leaves her feeling extremely confused. What about her offering to help would elicit such a response like that?

She clears her throat and straightens her back, answering his intense stare with a cold look of her own. "I'm *going* with you."

"*Kch*," he blows through his gritted teeth, his head turning away from the group sharply. He heaves each breath in an effort to settle his emotions, though his body remains stiff. His fingers claw at the table, trying to tear the wood apart by his nails alone. He doesn't appear to like his own thoughts the longer he is silent for.

"I'm Blessed," Kimberly feels the need to add, tilting her body forward. "I can do a lot with Snow already!"

"*No*," Electro states again, meeting her gaze with an electric stare. "You're still a student. You *both* are." Though he hardly make an effort to include Jake in his statement. From all the way over here, her skin crawls and hairs bristle with his magical energy, as if he were standing right in front of her.

"I would like them to come, too," Ethan adds, jumping in to help. "The more, the better."

"Have either of you *sparred* before?" Electro asks, his eyes not once breaking away from Kimberly.

"In class," Kimberly promptly answers.

"...As a Shadow," Jake adds tentatively. "Both of us did."

"Jake..." Kimberly can't help but sigh. That's the *last thing* she wanted to be reminded of right now despite it being true.

Electro falls silent again, electricity arcing from his clothes in a furious storm. His glare only continues to intensify by the second, leaving Kimberly even more confused than before. There's something *deeply personal* about all this, she feels. But... what?

"*Fine*," he reluctantly growls at last, and at once his magic withdraws from the air around them. He turns to Ethan and demands, "I want to see how good she is first."

The Husk tilts his head. "Just Kim? Right now?"

"Shadow vouched for Jake. So if *she* can handle herself, I won't argue," he states. "If she can't, she stays here."

Kimberly sucks in an eager breath. A test of her magical skill to win him over? This will be her chance to prove herself in battle, not just to Electro but to herself as well. To show that her poor judgment on Gardall was just a fluke, a stroke of bad luck and poor timing. She's better than that. She *knows* it.

Kimberly nods, agreeing with the Electromancer. "Alright. I'll do it."

Ethan folds his arms. His lips purse as he thinks, his eyes searching the table.

"Whatever you want to do," he sighs at last. "I'll meet you by the lake next cycle." He looks at Lukri and adds, "Let's go before it gets too cold for you." The prince gives him a tense nod and stands from his seat. He takes one last look at Kimberly and Jake, sucking in his lips like he wants to say something. Instead, he gives them each a quiet nod as Ethan rests a hand on his shoulder, gently guiding him out of the room.

"Well," Kimberly says with a small, tense sigh, turning to Jake, "I guess I'll see you in a bit."

A frown works its way across Jake's tired face. "What? No, I'll come with–"

"You look tired," Kimberly interrupts him gently. "You should sleep as soon as you can."

"But–"

Kimberly shakes her head. "We won't be gone long. Don't

worry about me."

Jake presses his lips together, contemplating her words. He doesn't like the idea of staying behind just to sleep. But Kimberly will be with Electro *and* Shadow. She'll be more than safe even though they're sparring.

Finally, he hangs his head. "Alright. Just... be safe."

"I promise," Kimberly replies with a soft smile.

***

Electro leads the way to the training grounds. His stare is dark and distant. He doesn't appear all that pleased with the situation he's found himself in. Kimberly walks a few steps behind him, also silent, her hands clasped tightly in front of her. Part of her wishes Jake were here if only to keep her company in this awkward situation she's found herself in. But he's not here to keep her company this time.

The training grounds are quiet at this time of the cycle. The sharp scratch of the quill as Electro checks them in at the front counter breaks the stillness briefly. Inside, there's only a single Illusionist meditating in the far corner, the air shimmering around them. Their eye cracks open as the two stride past into the sparring area in the back.

It's a spacious circular room with the center fighting ring sunk below a cone of raised seats. Soft yellow light streams down from above, Firelights flickering in small iceglass orbs. There are windows at the top of the room, providing them with a cool draft as they walk down to the dirt ring below. With each step, the atmosphere grows heavier, pressing itself against her skin. Kimberly can't help but run her hands up and down her arms to try and alleviate some of the tension.

She'd be lying if she said she wasn't nervous. She's never really sparred properly before. Sure, she's had to forcefully remove some troublesome customers from her shop before, and

ASM does teach lessons on theoretical combat scenarios, but that's about all she knows. In practice... well, she's already seen her performance there.

She probably shouldn't compare herself to Electro too much. Just because he's been in a coma for eighteen years doesn't mean he doesn't know what he's doing. His Shadow can fight *scarily* well. She doesn't doubt that he, too, is around that same skill level, which means he must have sparred a lot in his younger years or was quite the Voidterror himself.

Electro stops and turns around, a dark shadow cast across his face as he regards the Cryomancer. Lightning crackles around him, electrifying the night with the buzz of its power.

"My Shadow won't hold back, so neither will I," he warns. Each crack of his knuckles snaps sharply. Despite his meek figure, his radiating magic does its best to make the pair feel intimidated. After all, Shadow is propping him up, too. "Hit me with your best shot."

Kimberly stiffens. This doesn't feel right. Granted, she *is* scared, but she's also not sure if Electro should be doing this in the first place. She doesn't want him to strain himself.

"Are you sure?" Kimberly asks.

Electro's cold stare meets her eyes. "If it were up to me, you'd stay. But since it's not, I want to be sure that I won't be going with a dead weight. So prove to me you can hold your own."

The air around Kimberly starts to sparkle with flakes of white snow. The air shifts, carrying the specks on its back, washing away any warmth around her. All she needs to do is envision it, and it appears. The snow clumps, and from its soft powdery base, ice begins to emerge, sharp and pointed.

"Alright..." she mutters beneath her breath. Even as she prepares her magic, Electro doesn't move. He bends his leg to tap the ground with the toe of his boot, his head tilted as he observes the two wizards across from him. It doesn't look like he's going to make the first move...

She raises her hand, her fingers spread and her will focused. The air sends her spikes flying forward, converging on a singular point. Though, as they near him, his magic spurs into action. Bright white fingers reach out to meet her spikes head-on. Some are caught and are redirected around Electro's body, being pushed down to the dirt or to the curved wall just over his shoulders. Others, however, are obliterated where they are, bursting into an explosion of cold glitter. He doesn't even move, let alone flinch.

Once the onslaught concludes, he rushes forward, his feet leaving the ground. She knew Electromancers could move fast if they wanted to, but not like *this*!

In reaction to the oncoming threat, she throws her arms to the ground. Ice shoots from her feet, rising up into a wall of sparkling blue. Though it's opaque, she can still see the shadow he casts steadily darkening as he nears the wall.

Crash!

He bursts through the whole thing in one strike! His arms shield his face and head as the wall rains down on top of him, though his momentum has been completely killed.

In the brief moment that he's frozen for, Kimberly raises her hands again, gathering her magic for another barrage, letting her spikes fly unfettered. Electro's gaze flickers upwards, a crimson sparkle flashing across his eyes, and in an instant a wall of dense darkness rises up to meet the oncoming fire. One by one in rapid succession, the projectiles burst against the misty barrier. She puts a foot forward, letting her ice race across the ground. Her hope is to trap him with only one way forward, that being through the shadowy barrier. However, a bright purple blur streaks away from its cover before she can even begin to think about raising thick walls.

She sucks in a breath and quickly twists to try and track

Electro as he skirts the edge of the ring. But her eyes can't focus on him at all as he begins to kick up dust.

Right... She grits her teeth and wills her ice across the ground in long sparkling arrows, curving up onto the wall that surrounds them. With the slightest thought, the walls grow five long pillars, appearing almost like spokes on a wheel. With a bright electrical burst, Electro leaps into the air, just narrowly missing one of the pillars as his dash is forcefully interrupted, though the storm of lightning he leaves in his wake already chips away at the pillar's edges, sending puffs of white glitter fluttering through the air.

She throws an arm out at him, throwing at him even more projectiles. Just like before, they either burst or are driven elsewhere by the Electromancer's lightning. He stares down at her with an expression she struggles to read. It's not condescending, which is her first gut feeling, but also not disinterested.

Then he lands with a mighty *thud*, twisting his body towards her. And he launches.

His arms are reeled back, ready to strike, his gaze that of deadly focus. Kimberly's stomach drops sharply. There's no doubt in her mind that he's looking to *actually* strike her. A shriek of surprise escapes Kimberly's lips as her arms shoot out at the ground. She manages to raise a glittering blue wall just in time to block the incoming Electromancer... only for it to shatter to pieces in one strike. Only now he's still coming at her, unlike last time. And *fast*.

She throws herself to the ground. The air left in Electro's wake jumps towards her, kissing her skin with its power. The wizard skids to a halt not far away, already turning his body around to face her again.

Kimberly pounds a fist on the small patch of ice she is surrounded by, redirecting her bright blue streaks. Three large pillars rise between her and Electro, giving her just enough time to scramble back to her feet. Parting the wild hair from her face, she sees Electro laughing in front of her as he descends from the sky, lightning striking the ground around him in a furious storm.

Stars above! her mind gasps as her body reacts. Her arms shoot forward, and a wall springs up between the two of them. Then she swings them out to her sides, and the ice stretches out into two curved drifts of jagged spikes, enclosing Kimberly in a circular ring.

She only manages to gulp down two breaths of icy air before Electro jumps back into view, soaring over her walls with ease. They weren't very tall to begin with, but she didn't think he would have been able to scale them in just one jump! He beams down at her from above, legs bent and arms extended, flashing with brilliant light.

But he's up in the air again. Right in front of her too. The perfect chance! Kimberly arcs her hand through the air, summoning the snow to her side once again.

Her spikes throw themselves at Electro's suspended figure in a massive wave. Each one fired has a second right behind it, and a third behind that. As expected, as each spike nears, the Electromancer's magic catches them, and the bolts make the air glitter with broken ice. How long can he withstand the barrage for, though? There should come a point where he won't be able to keep up, and there's nowhere else for him to go but down!

But that hope quickly dies as she watches her ice explode and veer, completely leaving the paths that she sets for them. Electro doesn't appear to be hindered by the onslaught in the slightest.

Undeterred, his boots strike the ground. He lowers himself into a crouch, spinning himself around and popping up again with one leg raised high. Stunned, Kimberly can only watch as the sole of his boot makes it way right to her face.

Her eyes close, her body flinching as it braces for impact. A burst of electric air rushes past her face, stinging her cheeks sharply.

But she still stands. The kick never connects.

Her eyes crack open slowly, one at a time. Her vision is filled with Electro's leather boot. It hovered a hair away from the tip of her nose, reflecting her heavy and panicked breaths back at her. Her legs shaking, she takes a step backwards.

He lowers his leg at last, revealing a very disappointed frown spread across his face. He finds some solid footing before slipping his hands back into his pockets.

“Not good enough,” he huffs.

Kimberly blinks, his comment slow to register in her mind. Not... good enough? That doesn't make sense!

“I-I'm the best in my class,” she stammers back in complete shock.

Electro raises a skeptical eyebrow, cocking his head. “Really?” he hums. His attention turns to the curved ice wall that rings the two wizards. He steps up to the wall, leaning in close to inspect it. Then, without warning, he gives it a solid punch. It shatters, exploding into tiny shards of ice.

Through the mist of dancing lights, he turns back to Kimberly, perplexed. He jabs a thumb at the new hole he just created. “It shouldn't be *that* easy.”

Anger begins to build in her chest, a howling gale that wraps itself around her heart and squeezing it tight. What does he know about gauging the strength of Ice magic?

He reaches out to the edge of the hole. Grabbing the ice as firmly as he can, he sets to work freeing a chunk of it from the greater whole. It doesn't take much effort for cracks to start spreading across the whole structure, bright white fractures stabbing through the cool blue. Another few tugs, and a chunk breaks free, another spray of ice being sent to the ground. He bounces the piece of ice from one hand to another, tumbling it through the air as he inspects every corner and face with scrutiny.

"It's so... grainy," he announces. He holds the ice up in his hand and asks, "Have you ever seen what your ice looks like?"

"Of course I have!" Kimberly answers in astonishment. How *dare* he imply that she doesn't know her own crystal structure! "It's supposed to be like that!"

He throws the ice to the ground, and it explodes into millions of white shards. The air fills with the shimmering waterfall of bouncing crystals.

"How long have you had your Blessing for?" he asks.

Kimberly has to pause and think about this one. She raises a hand to her face as she moves her lips silently, counting the years. It's been quite a long time since she was first able to summon snow. It always feels like it was just the other cycle off the top of her head.

"Almost nine years," she answers at last, looking up again.

Electro folds his arms, a troubled frown befalling his face. He taps his foot against the dirt. His head twitches as he keeps it from shaking. His brow furrows as he gazes at the remaining constructs around him. His tongue runs across his lips.

"In Jake's defense, there aren't many beings in Astria who are able to teach him what he needs," he says at last, his voice rising to fill the grand space. He wants to make sure that the others can hear his thoughts, too. His body shifts back to Kimberly. "With you, there aren't any excuses. You *should* be better than this." His eyes flicker up and down her form, searching for some kind of explanation to his thought process. "Ice isn't strong because it's thick or dense. It's strong because it's *woven* to be strong! This is fine for activities like sculpting, but not–"

"Oh, what do *you* know? You're not a Cryomancer!" Kimberly says, stamping her foot down in protest. She won't be lectured by *this* wizard on how her magic should be!

"I was *married* to one!" Electro retorts harshly. His magic dances around his body in an enraged flurry. "And if it weren't for Ryan I'd still be with her!"

"Well maybe you didn't deserve her then!"

"Kelsy was the *only being* I had!"

The thunderous roar fills the quiet night, reverberating across the stands and crashing back down on top of the two wizards in the pit below. Kimberly feels the color drain from her face, her stare unable to look anywhere else but the distressed wizard standing before her.

Electro jabs his arm at her, lighting jumping across the way to land at her feet. "You. Are *not*. Going. That's final."

Kimberly shakes her head. Slowly, at first, but it builds into a violent whip. It feels like the world around is spinning without her, shifting out from beneath her feet. "No. N-No! Wait– *What*?"

Electro turns his back to her, his head bowed. His arms rise to his front. His fingers wrap around the sides of his head, digging into his hair.

Kelsy... and *him*... That doesn't make any sense. Her father never mentioned anything about Kelsy having been with another being before him!

At last, he lets out a frustrated sigh as he turns back to her with a hard scowl. "I can't help you, Kimberly," he says, his voice deep with exhaustion. He waves a hand at her glittering ice. "This is too many years of lenience on you. You're probably better off using just your Blessing than your magic. This," he knocks against the edge of the hole, "is too fragile on its own to be of any use."

He's the one to walk off first. Kimberly's thoughts churn slowly. They're crowded by too many things, too many emotions. She yanks her arm out, closing her fist. Her ice shatters in an instant, disappearing back into the ether from whence it came.

"*WAIT!*" she yells, her voice sharp and demanding as she

feels her heart boil with heat. Electro falters, turning around with wide eyes as if she sounded to be in grave danger. She drops her arm to her side, though her fist tightens to the point where it trembles as she stares cold spikes of ice into Electro's distant gaze.

"No. No, you can't just *leave* like that!" she reprimands breathlessly. Her body shifts without direction, unsure as to what it should do despite knowing that it's incredibly *mad*. Her head swivels, not quite a shake but close enough. Her shoes claw at the ground beneath her. "You... Y-You and Kelsy... I... I'm her *daughter*. So what does that... What does this mean?" She takes a shaky breath to steady herself and her racing mind. "Please, just give me a straight answer. Just one. Just once."

Electro's hard scowl softens as he stares at her in this frantic state. His dark amethyst eyes hardly flicker as she feels his electric stare look her up and down over and over again. Then, with a sigh, he turns back around and slowly saunters up to her. He places his hands on her shoulders and their eyes lock together.

"Look," he says slowly, his tone calm and even, like he had been rehearsing what he'd say in a situation like this, "for all intents and purposes, we are complete strangers. You don't need to go this far to help me. You've done enough. Please," and he gives her a tight squeeze with his bony fingers, "don't go. I beg you. Don't throw your life away for my sake."

Kimberly can't help but stare back in stunned silence, her eyes searching his for a clearer answer. Something she can hold on to, that can help her make sense of all this insanity that he just won't tell her for one reason or another.

Her body acts before her mind can catch up, and she shakes her head slowly. The words follow soon after, "I'm coming. This is as much about me as it is about you, too."

Electro is the one to finally break eye contact, his head turning to the side as his eyes close to think, to process her answer. He still doesn't like it. Now she understands why. She *thinks*. It'd... be nice to have the confirmation come from him, though. That... she is his daughter. As ludicrous as it sounds in her head, it's the only explanation as to why he has been so irrationally adamant about her staying behind. *Only* her.

But how? *Why*? What happened between him and Kelsy? What about Jay? Who's her real father and who isn't?

At long last, Electro heaves a weary sigh, his shoulders visibly slumping as he turns back to her. "Fine. I won't stop you. You're almost an adult, after all."

"But what about you and Kelsy? And... me?"

Electro quietly mulls over his answer, his lips parting and closing in rapid succession as he picks his words carefully, appearing disappointed with himself the entire time.

"I promised your parents the chance to explain to you first," he finally says. "But... you *are* my daughter." He frees her shoulders from his vice-like grip at last. A small air of static rises between the two, making Kimberly's exposed skin tingle and itch.

"So when this is all over, you should go talk to them," Electro adds as he turns away from her. "But for now, what we need is a good rest. So let's not keep standing around here doing nothing."

***

Jake sits up on the couch as the other two return home from their training session. He would have gone to sleep if his mind wasn't so *awake*. There's just too much weighing on it for him to simply turn it off for one night.

They both stumble into view in strange dazes. Kimberly doesn't appear to be very present, her eyes somewhat misty with tears she seems to not be aware of. Electro looks a lot more physically exhausted, though his glassy eyes betray the weight of the thoughts stirring in his head. Thoughts he doesn't look all too happy entertaining.

The Electromancer throws himself down onto the mattress and heaves a heavy sigh, his whole body deflating as he relaxes as best he can.

Kimberly lingers in the doorway. “We didn't wake you, did we?” Her voice is small but not quite a whisper, concerned about him yet emotionally flat at the same time.

“No, I was awake already,” Jake replies with his own gravelly tone. He stands and makes his way over to her, pressing one of his warm fingers against her cold cheek as he takes a quick glance at her figure. Physically, she appears to be uninjured. But, of course, looks can always be deceiving. “Are you okay?”

Kimberly answers first with a shaky breath, her eyes briefly darting over his shoulder to the resting Electromancer behind him. “We... can talk in my room.”

Jake simply nods and lets her lead the way. She flicks the lights on and off as she sees fit, only half-bothering to consider the being behind her before ultimately deciding she's too tired to care. Jake doesn't mind. He'd do the exact same thing if he were in her position no doubt.

But she keeps the light in her bedroom off as she makes herself comfortable on the edge of the blanketed mattress. Jake joins her slowly, his eyes still adjusting to the dark after all the brightness of the stairs and hallway outside.

“Are you still going?” he prompts her gently.

“I am,” she confirms. Sharp, firm, already decided in her mind. She won't be backing down. So neither will he.

“But,” she quickly adds, “I don't know how much help I'll actually *be*.” She raises a hand out in front of her, staring down at her limp, half-curled fingers. She holds this position for the longest moment before letting it all drop, her head hanging and her body slouching forward.

“It's still... a lot,” she mutters. “What he said.”

"What did he say?"

Kimberly clasps her hands together in her lap. "Despite being the best in my class... I'm not actually as good as I thought I was."

Jake can't help but shift on the bed, leaning away from her out of surprise. Kimberly, a Blessed wizard, the top of her class... This doesn't make any sense.

"I might be able to cover you," she continues in that eerily calm, albeit weary, tone, "but I don't know what else I'll be able to do to help being... like... *this*."

Jake lets his face fall into sympathy as he places a hand on her shoulder to try and give her some comfort. Though his eyes wander away from her and down to the floor instead "I've... been wondering the same thing about myself, too. How useful I'll actually be."

"What do you mean?"

Jake takes a deep breath, steeling himself even as his gut churns with a thick ball of dread. This is far from how he envisioned Kimberly finding out about his failing grades. But now they actually matter. Now they might mean life or death and not just a breakup.

"I'm not doing too good in class either," he answers honestly, a little hint of shame underpinning his words. "I'm the worst in my class with magic and I just started learning how to use my sword properly. I... might get held back if my grades don't start improving soon. Or I'll get expelled."

Kimberly stares back at him quietly, processing his admission. Her gaze is cold, burning icy holes into the side of his head. She practically radiates disbelief with every bit of her being.

"How *long* has this been an issue for?" she asks at last.

"All year," Jake replies after a tense pause. He lets his hand drop from her shoulder back to his side, his fingers pressing down hard into the blanket beneath him. "Well...

actually it started last year, but I didn't think it was going to get this bad."

"And you never told me," she softly states.

"I... no, I didn't." He can't help but release a defeated sigh. He wants to make excuses for why he hadn't told her before – some already stir in his head – but knows that, in truth, all he had ever been was scared, unable to face his own shortcomings and the potential of a broken heart.

"I'm still coming with you," he adds, though he doesn't say it with much confidence. "I just... don't know if I'll be dead weight or not."

Kimberly places one of her hands gently atop his, drawing his attention back to her. Her eyes seem to shine with small white sparkles in the darkness. "Don't worry, Jake. I know you. You'll find a way to be helpful." She gives him a tight and loving squeeze to reaffirm her belief in him. It makes a small swirl of warm embers rise within his chest. He takes a slow, deep breath and nods back. He *will*. He needs to.

"Thanks," he replies. He licks his lips, parting them as if he were to speak more. Because there *is* more he wants to tell her – *everything*, in fact – but he doubts that now is the right time to bring it all up to her. Azna, his potential ancestry, Lukri, Ryan... there's a lot that stirs in his head. Some of the story he never talked to her about because he didn't even know the truth for himself. Now that he thinks he has all the information he had been lacking for so long, it's been difficult to reconcile with the conclusions he's been drawing. That he was unwanted and left to die while his "brother" was kept and grew up in luxury. But even Lukri didn't have a father, either, just like Jake.

Jake feels like he was a bit too harsh on Lukri back on the lift. Only a bit. He was not in the mood to talk about it then. He doubts he'll want to *ever* discuss it at all. It throws all that he's ever known into disarray, despite the fact that it's all already there. He can deny it all he wants, but Jake *is* a Serperas to a certain degree. And he is *also* a wizard.

But looking into Kimberly's tired eyes, he knows she isn't up for a conversation like that right now. Especially not since they'll be leaving Asandra at first light to combat Electro's Shadow and save the Font of Magic. The fate of Astria rests in their ability to stop it. There's little time for talk *now*, but whenever they succeed, they'll have all the time in the universe to discuss.

“You should try and get some sleep,” he announces at last as he stands from her bed. Kimberly releases a positive hum of acknowledgment, her wintery gaze following him as he walks over to the bedroom door.

“Good night, Jake,” she mutters. “I hope you get some sleep.”

Jake looks back at her and flashes her a soft smile. “Don't worry about me, Kim. We'll be fine.”

Chapter 19

Electro strolls up to the meeting point with Kimberly and Jake quietly in tow. None of them have spoken a word since waking up. The couple stride side-by-side, holding each other's hands in subtle support. He's still not happy that Kimberly's coming along. He'll have to have Jake stay back and guard her.

"Hey!" he calls out, raising a hand in the air. Ethan and Lukri stand by the lakeside, chatting with a Healer. The three turn to face Electro and the other wizards. The Healer readjusts his goggles to get a clearer look at the newcomers.

"Thanks, Blaze," Ethan says, giving the beings at his side a light wave.

"You *better* stop by when you're done," the Healer warns. He gives the three other wizards one last look, his mouth twitching uncomfortably. "You two, too."

"Okay...?" Kimberly replies, unsure as to what she's agreeing to. But it's enough for the Healer.

"Good luck!" Lukri encourages with a bright smile as the Healer extends an arm, lightly guiding the Serperas away by the shoulder. His other hand is buried deep into his pocket. The fabric around his fingers shifts as he fidgets with something stashed within.

"Alright, Fragment," Electro says, folding his arms. "We're here. Now where are we going?"

Ethan bows his head, one hand rising to pull down the brim of his hat as the other rests on his chest. Inside him, Shadow swirls with agitation. As the Husk feels the Shard within, an invisible breeze washes over the group, rustling Electro's hair.

"Down," he says at last, "to the center of Astria."

Kimberly and Jake look at each other, both exchanging wondrous and eager glances. They're going *beneath* the islands? To the center of the world? That's what they seem to ask each other in their shared silence.

"Are you all ready?" Ethan asks, drawing the attention of the wizards back to him. Concern glows in his dark eyes as he stares past Electro. "This is your last chance to stay."

Kimberly takes a deep breath and nods. So does Jake.

The Husk raises his arms. The darkness around them shudders and sharpens, stretching towards him as he calls it forth, bending it to his will. The shadows move like liquid as it washes the ground beneath their feet, blanketing them with its cold embrace, before rising up and over their heads. The light of the cycle is blocked out, leaving the four beings able to only see each other and a vast expanse of black.

"We're going down now," Ethan announces.

"Really?" Kimberly breathes in awe. Electro frowns and folds his arms. He doesn't want to be a skeptic – it's hard to be one anyway with everything he's been through as of late – but it really doesn't feel like they've moved from the lakeside at *all*. Even though he can't see the outside anymore, his body feels strangely still…

Ah, he thinks. That's it. The stillness doesn't feel quite right. Even though he's standing in place, his center of mass is shifting ever so slightly.

"I don't know how long it'll take to get to the bottom," Ethan adds. "Until then… try not to be too distracting."

Kimberly and Jake huddle close together, their hands joined as they whisper to each other. The occasional word grazes past his ears, but it's not enough for him to guess what they're talking about. Electro stands by himself with Shadow as his only company, though it sits silently in his chest, content with merely existing.

He keeps stealing glances over at Kimberly. She does the same back to him, so he doesn't feel too bad about doing it. He has been feeling a little guilty about the way he acted last night. He didn't really help her at all. He just exploded.

It's sad to see her magic in such a state. The strength of one's ice is the ultimate pride of Cryomancers. He knows that all too well. Though with her family lineage and her Blessing as such a young age... somewhere along the way, things changed to make her life easier. Jay never pushed her. Nor did her teachers, by the looks of it. Blessings are gifts from the Spirits to be rigorously nurtured to their fullest extent, not coddled and given free passes.

He raises a fist to his mouth and loudly clears his throat, though he tilts his head so that he doesn't have to look at the wizards. Out of the corner of his eye, he can see Kimberly shift her attention to him.

"Don't forget you still have control over your projectiles, Kimberly," he states. "You've got the right idea. Cryomancers would kill to be able to be able to summon their ice wherever they want. You just have to think a little more creatively. Your Blessing is your greatest strength, so use it as much as you can."

Kimberly is quiet as his words sink in. He doesn't know if she's processing or waiting for him to say more. Sadly, that's all the advice he can think of for now. He's left standing in the dark, waiting for something to happen.

"We're here."

Ethan's voice cuts through the eternal silence. He

gestures to the darkness and, following his movements, the dome opens once more after what feels like an eternity in its sightless embrace. The moment any light can pierce their protection, it streams down on the wizards with its blinding majesty.

It takes a while for Electro's eyes to adjust to the shining, blinking furiously to help the process along. Once he can make out shapes and colors in detail, his mind feels about ready to explode as it processes the incomprehensibly magical scene.

Astria's core is one gigantic hollow sphere – most likely a perfect sphere if the Spirits made this place – with half of its rocky face left intact and the other fractured into hundreds, if not *thousands*, of tiny pieces. Looking between the pieces, the surface is nowhere in sight. The early light of the cycle is nowhere to be seen. The black Void he spent all his life staring down into is now above him, an endless night that stretches on forever.

The edges of the divide between whole and fragments are aglow with golden sparkles that rain down from above, the little specks of starlight being drawn to the center of the world. The space is illuminated by some unseen source, painting the curved rock with all sorts of colors that swim and swirl together, forming new colors as they collide and diving into many different shades completely on a whim. The buzz of magic is strong here, almost overpowering, vibrating against his body so strongly that he forgets that he even has a body to begin with. He didn't even realize that he stopped breathing until he feels Shadow's cold numbness in his chest, forcing the air in and out of his lungs for him.

He closes his eyes to escape the bedazzling sight, only to find that it's burned itself into his mind. The colors still swirl in the darkness, refusing to give him respite from their indescribable dance. This is clearly not a place intended to be seen by just any regular being on Astria. With his eyes shut tight, he feels a pull against his body, both internally and externally. The magic wraps around him, trying to drag him forward, deeper into Astria's center. It invades him, hooking onto his limbs and tightening like a puppeteer's strings.

He opens his eyes again. A small white light has appeared in the middle of the arcane chaos, flashing at him invitingly. Its stable glow is a welcome sight in this place of overwhelming sensation.

Ethan flicks a hand forward, and the dark ground the group stands on slides forward through the air. It's hard to tell how fast they're going exactly; there's no air or wind down here to feel. But the sensation of magic, as bad as it was before, grows exponentially.

As they near the glow, it shrinks and turns into a black figure flying about Astria's center. What other being could it be but Electro's own Shadow? Waiting for them to arrive with the last Shard.

{*With two Shards, taking it down quickly might be… challenging,*} Shadow comments, trying to push past the tightness in its own voice to sound more confident than it feels. Electro pats his chest and nods, trying to give it whatever comfort he can provide.

The closer they get to the flying star, the golden sparkles from the Border Barrier above come together before his very eyes to form a large platform that slices the heart of the world into two. The tiny lights weave themselves into a transparent floor that floats in the air. With it, some sense of orientation within this impossibly massive space is regained.

Electro's Shadow slows its zipping as it finally notices the approaching beings, its figure sharpening into view. Around its body freely dances the two Shards it has already obtained, aglow with unspoken happiness at having been brought back to their home, all the while hovering close to their "protector."

"*Welcome!*" the Shadow greets them as the four land on

the golden light. It's warm beneath Electro's boots, filling him with part of its arcane strength. It courses with a strange sense of love and duty that stirs deep within his heart. Shadow swirls, reaching out to try and touch the distant emotions.

The Twisted Shadow above them grins with glee, its gaze trained solely on Ethan. It's sizing him up, looking for the Shard nestled within him.

He raises a hand before him, stating, "If you want my Shard, you'll have to rip it out of me."

The Shadow's smile doesn't falter, as if it were expecting him to say that. Instead, it rears its head back and bursts out laughing. Its body arcs so far that it spins around in the air, popping back up the other side facing the wizards once more.

"*I have a* better *idea,*" it replies ominously.

By the time any being realized what the Shadow was doing, it was already far too late to stop it.

Electro's Shadow bursts into smoke, turning itself into a long black arrow. The Shards elongate with it, curling themselves around its new form. But it's not returning to its rightful place at all.

The instant Electro's Shadow comes into contact with Ethan's body, his head snaps back in an instant. His hat flies from his head as his cape billows out violently, warding off any who dare try to approach the Husk. The lone hat, a black stain in the world of bright color, drifts away on some magical wind, growing smaller and smaller as it twists and twirls, reveling in its freedom.

Static fills the air. Bright bolts of white lightning jump from the Husk's figure, leaping out into the void and driving the others back. The two half-orbs that floated in the Twisted Shadow's hands bend and expand, wrapping themselves around Ethan's wrists like a pair of glowing shackles. His fingers curl and twitch uncontrollably as his body starts to shake. Bright cracks of white light begin to make their way across his body, even cutting through his clothes.

Electro's body falls away in a storm of blinding hot rage. His mind is being crushed by Shadow as it summons its weapon and rushes the Husk with murderous intent. A disjointed roar only a Fragment Shadow can produce leaves Electro's lips as it lunges, leaving his throat ravaged by the divine's rage.

But its sword only pierces the cape. In the blink of an eye, Ethan's body disappears into thin air. There was no fanfare. No glow. No noise. No obvious tell that it was going to happen. It simply *happened*.

Then a tremendous blast of magic blows from the right, threatening to knock Electro over with its gale. Ethan has reappeared as quickly and silently as he had just vanished, floating in the air above the present beings. Sprouting from behind are long strands of colorful light, each one humming with their own resonance which come together to form a strong vibration that rocks Electro's very core. They drift in the air aimlessly, a mass of tiny tentacles all clustered together, exploring reality around them.

Ethan gazes on the strings with twisted pleasure, one hand raised as if to feel them. In the presence of such overwhelming power, the air around him presses down on his body like a single massive weight. His chest seems to flatten as the air is forced out of him momentarily. Behind him, both Kimberly and Jake release alarmed gasps for air, much more severe than his. Shadow tries to keep Electro steady, even as its attention is fully enraptured by its possessed Husk.

The Husk's head turns, a distant yet mischievous smile across his face. His eyes gleam crimson red, alive with the Shadow now inhabiting his shell of a being. His chest pulses with the soft glow of the heartbeat within, the two Shards around his wrists following its rhythm.

"*For the first time since the Great War,*" the Husk speaks, the Shadow within using Ethan's voice with twisted pleasure.

The eyes linger on Electro, gazing inward to the entity within his own body, sensing and relishing in Shadow's ever-growing anger, "*the Shards have been reunited, and the Font of Magic returned to its rightful place.*" He lets out a triumphant laugh as he floats in the air, his body completely at ease.

{*Its guard is lowered,*} Shadow states. It rushes forward once more at alarming speed, moving through the Font's presence so fast that it feels like Electro's skin is going to tear from his body. Its gaze is trained on the beating Shard in the Husk's chest, sword at the ready.

Wait! Electro tries to stop it, but his thought is drowned out by the Fragment's icy presence. It pushes him away, not wanting to be held back.

Ethan's mouth twitches, bringing Electro's body to a dead stop. The point of Shadow's sword hovers a mere breath away from its target, but his body hangs suspended in the air, completely overtaken by whatever spell the Husk has placed on him. Try as Shadow might, it cannot force Electro's body to shudder even slightly.

"*You should be grateful,*" the Husk speaks, "*that your shell has become the living embodiment of all magic.*"

{*Ethan!*} Shadow cries out, unable to move Electro's mouth or even make his vocal chords quiver. Its broken voice is met with roaring silence.

Then, without word or warning, Electro's body is jolted to the right. It's so sharp and so fast that it smashes everything inside him to one side, squeezing all the breath out of his lungs and attempting to draw his eyes right out of his head. But he's not left this way for long, as he soon makes impact with the rocky sphere.

The world is spinning, too bright and out of focus to see. His body feels broken from head to toe. He can't move or breathe or even *think*. Did he feel his heart pop? Has his body been vaporized? How is he still *alive*?

Snap! Crackle, snap! Ba-dump, ba-dump…

He is forced to gasp for air as he hears and *feels* his body being pieced back together. Even with Shadow's numbing, he can still feel the pain ripple through him, reminding him that he, in fact, is still here. Somehow. A cry of agony escapes his coarse throat as he jolts and shakes uncontrollably. His heart is a small ball of fire pounding away. His lungs are forced to expand and contract, even as his ribs press into them painfully. His stomach burns. The rest of him feels about ready to fall out of his body, one way or another, with the only thing holding them in being the Fragment Shadow refusing with its whole heart for him to die.

His mind feels to float somewhere above him, spectating as it waits for the Fragment to finish working its magic. The center star glows and shifts, brought alive by the body and consciousness it has been given. The other two wizards that were brought down as well are so small that the Font's spectacle hides them completely from view.

An intense sadness hangs over his mind. He doesn't feel the need to weep just yet; it's bottled and ready to burst at any moment. It's soul-crushing defeat. An endless void with no light in sight, the lingering remnants having been already snuffed out.

His arms rise of their own accord, drawing his consciousness back. He emerges slowly from the hole his impact made in the rock. Shadow remains ever-present, but it's regressed to being yet a second mind to his limbs. It holds him right at its very edge, where he's able to still hold on as they stare down at Astria's glowing, corrupted heart.

{*Ethan…*} Shadow moans, its voice small, shivering, cracked beyond repair.

"Hey now," he breathes, attempting to offer it whatever comfort he can, "it's just occupying him, right? Like you are with me?"

The Fragment is sick with worry, and at the same time is making him feel ill along with it. {*I don't hear him, I don't sense him, I can't see, I can't... I-I...}* His breathing increases rapidly against his will. His heart launches itself from his stomach to his throat and back down again. His head is starting to spin. His magic thrashes against his body. Despite it just having brought him back from the brink of death, it feels like it's going to tear him apart from the inside!

"*Stop*!" he cries out. Shadow's swirling condenses into a pit of uselessness. Its other half is gone and it doesn't know what to do, but at least it's calm and he can breathe again.

So his Shadow got wise and managed to use their tactics against them. He's impressed that it came up with such a plan. It didn't need to fight them for the final Shard when it could simply possess the Husk that it's housed in. What worries him is that there was apparently no fight on Ethan's end. He was just... swallowed whole, becoming one with the Font.

He closes his eyes. If they're fighting Ethan and the Font now, they need to change their plan, too.

"That... *thing* you did back on Kendon. When we 'connected'. Do it again."

A pang of surprise rips through Shadow. {*Are you sure?*} it asks slowly.

He nods. He's more than sure. This is no longer the time to be of two minds and emotions. If they're going to get back in there and be *useful*, then they will have to become essence and body. They already had a taste. Now they have to finally commit. It's never going to be perfect, but it's the only thing they *can* do.

He feels Shadow's presence creep across his scalp, still somewhat hesitant. He doesn't blame it. Already it has had to get used to occupying a foreign Husk, but now for it to *connect* with him on such a deep level?

"I'm ready," he reassures it. To prove his point, his fingers dig deeper into the rock, his nails scratching at its surface.

He takes a breath, and he feels it follow along with him. It lets the air swirl around, feeling it weave in and out of its essence. Courage.

It descends on his mind, a cold yet comforting blanket being run over his thoughts. His head throbs, pressing against this new force as it attempts to sink its finger into him. His first instinct is to try and fight back against it.

He exhales, easing his fear as best he can. Just a crack is enough for the Fragment to worm its way inside. Electro squeezes his eyes shut and grits his teeth as the storm builds inside, trying to find an anchor to latch on to. Colors and noise, smells and sensations dance across all his senses, coming and going at their pleasure. Shadow's air whips them around chaotically, while simultaneously catching them in its embrace.

Every time he blinks, something new flashes in the dark. A duality of emotion and memory. The thrill of sparring, flames and lightning dancing in the air overhead. The longing for light beneath a starless sky. The squeeze of a comforting hand, walking aimless in the expansive city. The cold emptiness as forceful command pulls and warps. His free spirit clashes with its heavy chains.

Authority demands to be respected, but instead it is ignored. A fun time with friends is forsaken for a higher duty. The colors are blending together, the line between Asandra and Korodon blurring even further.

They breathe. They exhale. And they do it again. And again. And again.

The body shifts, and everything shifts along with it. Which one of them is it? Neither have been swallowed, but it's hard to tell which one commands– No, it should be *directs*. There are no orders given to either one. Just... an agreement.

So then they should agree who is going to take charge, shouldn't they? A committee will still be slower than a single mind. Only because Shadow can't ever see itself taking charge the way Electro does. Or Ethan.

It would only be confusing if Electro didn't understand. It

hasn't known the meaning of the word “free” for far too long. Shouldn't it have a taste of it in action now?

Later, perhaps, when there aren't beings in need of their help.

An eager smile once more creeps across Electro's face as he prepares himself to jump. If it insists so *badly*, he might as well.

Divine strength floods his limbs as they bend and flex. A pool of endless magic at his disposal, with his imagination being his own limitation. He leaps from the hole, lightning reaching out in his wake, sparking against the stone to push him forward with its energy. At the same time, a cold surge rushes to his feet, an invisible force kicking off from the rocky dome and adding to his speed. As hard as he can, he shoots through the air back towards Astria's heart.

They've come too far to give up now.

Chapter 20

"*Now*," Ethan says, his head turning to the remaining beings below him, "*how about we play?*"

It takes all of Jake's might to raise his sword, even as the magic emitting from the Husk's figure pushes back, demanding he kneel down and submit to its might. As much as he doesn't want to harm his friend, he can't fight the Shadow so long as it hides away.

Though, this is the Font of Magic he's staring down, too...

Before he can even begin to collect his thoughts, Ethan flashes forward, his hand wrapping around Jake's neck. He's hoisted into the air with little effort, the knuckles of his friend's fingers digging deep into the underside of his chin.

"Jake!" Kimberly cries out in alarm. A rush of cold air overtakes him as bright blue spikes rise around them, trapping the two inside of an icy canyon. Some of the ice breaks away, pointing inwards towards Ethan's form, stopping just shy of making contact with his body.

"*I remember you,*" he chuckles as Jake dangles from his grasp. "*From the Pyramid. It seems you still have a lesson to learn!*"

With all his might, Jake raises his sword arm, waving the blade in the Husk's direction. But all he does is sidestep his weak flailing with little effort.

From somewhere above, a large glob of white snow falls. It lands square on Ethan's extended arm with so much force that he reflexively releases Jake from his hold, finally rearing back. Jake somehow manages to land upright on his feet, though coughing and sputtering as his throat throbs with pain.

With an angry roar, Ethan turns his attention to the walls that box him in. He raises his arms, and with them the structure trembles and shakes. Cracks worm their way through the blue with ease, filling the air with its ear-splitting noise. It takes but a small twitch of his fingers, and the thing shatters completely, the jagged drift reduced to a series of sharp, floating shards. His crimson eyes are cast over Jake's shoulder, where Kimberly stands.

He draws his arms back, and the ice follows in a massive swell.

Jake kicks himself into action. He draws his foot back and raises his sword across his chest, his magic surging forward. He knows he has only just started learning how to use his skills properly, so he'll have to hope that he can rely on his improvisation for now.

Ethan pushes forward, sending the wave of ice on its way. At the same time, Jake throws his arm out, pushing the heat from within into the edge of his blade as hard as he can. He spins himself around in a wide arc, making sure to aim high as to not accidentally hit Kimberly with his flames. Red and orange mix with the white and blue, curling around as many shards as possible and feasting on their essence, with more losing themselves to the roaring flames.

Still, Kimberly lets out a scream of pain as she hides her face behind her arms. While Jake might have been able to melt a good portion of the shards, there are too many for him to handle completely. Small, bright red cuts appear across her arms, legs, and the sides of her face as the shards rush past her. Some manage to rip through her clothes and bounce off of her sides as she twists her body to shield her front.

He turns his ire back to the Husk. He sweeps his sword down low, resetting his swing as he leaps forward. It'll be wide. It might not even connect. But he's going to try anyway. *No being* hurts his girlfriend!

He brings his sword around, reaching out to strike the Husk across his torso. Ethan staggers back, just narrowly missing being cleaved in two. His gaze fixates on Jake once again, a dark scowl crossing his face.

He doesn't do much to combat Jake's swings other than twisting and turning, leaping and weaving. But Jake's better at keeping up now, thanks to Shadow. He keeps his sword close, careful not to overextend himself and flail wildly. Each swing brings him closer and closer to his target. With each arc, a burst of flame leaps forward, attempting to scar the Husk with its tiny yet sweltering might. Yet every time the tip of his blade comes within but a breath of the Husk it passes him by without fail. The flames, too, always seem to miss their mark, reaching for his face yet whirling away through the air at the very last moment.

"*Tenacious!*" the Husk laughs, finding their little dance amusing. The next kick of his feet springs him back far out of Jake's reach. He would still try to give chase, if not for the Husk raising a hand out in front of him, palm aglow with red light. A wave of intense heat blasts his face. He thought the lava lake on Kendon was hot, but at least it didn't make him feel like his body was going to spontaneously combust. "*I wonder how much of your own magic you will be able to withstand.*"

The flames surge forward, a powerful blast of Fire magic heading right for him. Aware of Kimberly standing somewhere behind him, he plants his feet firm and levels his sword at the oncoming flames. Blade aglow, its tip carves through the storm of red and orange, parting the magic so that it curves around them.

But the small gap of sanctuary he's created slowly starts to shrink as the intensity of the magic steadily grows. Even with the golden platform having a surprising amount of grip to it, he starts to slip backwards as he tries to hold his sword steady. All around him, the heat only intensifies as the color of the fire turns yellow, fading into scalding blue and blinding white. Where the tip of his sword meets the flames, sparks fly as it warms in the fire's presence. How much longer will his sword last before it begins to melt? Once his aid is gone, they'll both be blown away.

It takes all his might and willpower to hold the weapon steady as he continues to be pushed away from the Font, the burning walls close enough to where he can feel their embers nipping at his arms and legs. His entire body is engulfed in heat so intense that it feels almost as if he's become one with the magic around him. The only thing he has left to remind him that he's still alive and standing is his sword in front of him somehow holding back the Font's infinite power.

What happens next, he can't quite describe. It feels as if the Void above casts its impossible gaze down upon him. It reaches out, a single finger that makes his body tremble. Yet he doesn't falter as it worms its way inside. Though it's but a single finger, its endless size is more than enough to curl around his burning core, feeling his heat. It squeezes his magic as hard as it can, gathering the flames into one central point. The pressure makes it thrash as it grows smaller and smaller...

A flash of cold shocks his body. He sucks in a breath, bracing himself. The spark has been ignited.

A roaring inferno spills from his core, the flames filling his being with its unwieldy might in a single gust. New power seeps into his arms and legs, making his hairs sizzle with energy. His backwards sliding stops in an instant as this bestowed strength courses through him.

One tiny shift. One powerful slash. The flames around him disappear altogether.

His body moves on its own accord, dashing towards the surprised Husk with his flaming sword held at the ready.

He swings at the Husk with all his might, a vertical wall of flame spawning in the blade's wake. Even in his surprised state, Ethan still somehow manages to dodge the attack. Flecks of the fire leap to his robe, which burn briefly before fizzling out of existence. But Jake's already on the move again before the Husk can even start to process the sight before him. His last movements lead into his next as he closes the distance yet again, aiming for another strike.

Eyes wide, Ethan gives the blaze a sharp glare. The Font glows, answering his unspoken command, and in an instant he discharges a storm of electricity. The bolts leap out at Jake as he continues his forward flow, intent on stopping him in his tracks.

Calm and collected, he curls around the projectiles with ease, like a flame bending and shifting with the flow of the air. And similar to the flame in its perpetual state of motion, he leads into his counterattack with little pause or reduction in speed. His sword rises in another grand arc, leading into a forward spin and another rising sweep of the fiery blade. He feels the lightning before it can even leave the Husk's body, the air turning electric and cold in an instant, pushing Jake out of its way naturally.

He *is* the fire, bending to the will of the environment around him, dancing in his own indecipherable way.

The annoyance of the Husk is slowly starting to morph into panic as he watches as the flames continue to chase unhindered. Yet Jake still can't hit him, no matter how hard he tries. He just has to keep going. This standstill must end at some point.

He sees the Husk raise his hand again, a new haze glowing around his fingers. From it, Jake is blasted with a magic that he has never felt before. Something that finally forces him back, lifting him off his feet momentarily.

It's wind, but not the wind that he's used to. There are

traces of magic present, pressing against his body, but otherwise it feels much more crystal clear as it blows over his body with its cold breath. It stops his dance outright, pushing away the flames that make up his very being. He tries to step forward, only for his leg to be swept backwards, unable to do what he wants. He tries to lean forward into the wind, yet finds only pain as his fiery body is being ripped apart faster than it can ignite.

Reluctantly, he lets the wind carry him away from the Font to the point where it no longer threatens to snuff out the burning hearth inside of him.

Ethan smirks back, pleased with his new effort to repel the raging fire proving to be successful. Only for a moment.

A bright purple streak catches Jake's attention. It's moving fast, making it hard for him to determine the flying object at first. But a flash of white makes his heart jump for joy as an enraged roar echoes across the golden plane. It's Electro! He's okay! Or, at least, he *looks* okay.

He spins in the air, going for a kick from behind, a flash of crimson in his amethyst eyes. As he brings his leg around, there's a brief pause in his momentum as he is stopped but a breath away from the back of Ethan's head. But even though he doesn't land the strike physically, the sheer force of the swing blasts the Husk with a shockwave of energy, throwing Ethan to the golden ground. Lightning arcs from Electro's body, striking around the Font. The light bends and curves out of the way, unwilling to make contact with the Husk directly.

For but a brief moment, the Husk lies stunned against the sparkling floor.

Electro raises his arm high into the air, and from it a long black sword appears in his grasp. He wields it as Shadow would, elegant yet firm as he brings it down upon Ethan below him. It would have struck the Husk, but as he did before, his form blinks out of existence before the blade lands. Its tip drives itself into the golden ground soundlessly. In its wake, however, Jake feels the air shift, blowing his flaming body towards the distant wizard. In a blink, a black arc springs up from the ground, reaching high into the air and stretching on to the distant wall of rock that is one of Astria's distant islands. The void blasts the space with its cold gust, once more forcing Jake farther back as it greedily sucks in all the light around it.

Electro turns on his heel, just as Ethan blinks back into view behind him, sword drawn across his chest. Though he's nowhere near the Husk, he swings anyway. The air is blown from Jake's lungs as a cold, thin line of pain erupts across his chest and upper arms, shaking him to his core. The fire that is his magic is cleaved in half. The flames do their best to roar back in protest, but their energy has been severely hampered. He has been cut, but not physically. It's his own Shadow that has been struck.

The shock leaves him rooted to the golden ground as he watches Ethan extend a hand towards Electro, and from it bright ribbons of rainbow flow from his fingers. Lightning flashing around him, Electro weaves in and out of the ribbons as they pierce through the veil around him, looping back around beneath and threading back through the light. They follow behind him relentlessly, with only his lightning and his fast reflexes keeping himself from being skewered.

He arcs back around to face the hovering Husk, his arm bringing his sword across his chest once again at the ready. Once he's close enough, he leaps, a burst of gold rising beneath his boot as if to help him up into the air. The stiff black blade morphs and stretches around him as he twists his body, spiraling out into a grand circular arc like a whip. It thrashes at the Husk, though, just like before, each strike misses by a single hair.

As Electro lands back on the ground, something cold stings Jake’s flaming cheek. Surprised, he turns around.

Kimberly is standing, her glare sharp as her body is engulfed in a blue haze. White specks of snow materialize out of thin air, orbiting her figure with gradually increasing speed and density. The magic around her warps, joining her vortex of white flakes. Before any being knows it, an intense blizzard engulfs them all.

Even through his fire, he can still feel the cold of the snow and ice swirling around him, though the wind worries him more than the tiny specks that melt in his presence. Just like a fire, he is beholden to the whims of the world around him.

Never has he seen Kimberly use her magic like this before. For as long as she's had her Blessing, she's never used it to create a blizzard. The storm howls with rage, the soft snow gradually clumping together to form long needles sculpted out of the white and blue.

One of these spikes cuts across Jake's cheek, leaving behind an icy burn in its wake as it continues to travel with its other pointy friends. Jake raises a hand to feel the sore spot. Something wet and sticky smears itself onto his fingers. Pulling his hand away, he can see his skin through the dying flames stained with dark blood. It looks almost black with a tinge of red, though now that he thinks about it it seems closer to brown, as if two different colors have been mixed together. The burst of strength his flaming body provided is gradually ebbing away, and the weight of exhaustion is starting to take its place.

He grits his teeth and shakes his head, trying to stave off the early effects as best he can. *Not yet!*

He can't see through the blizzard. That's sort of the point to one, isn't it? But that means he doesn't know where Ethan could be. Or Electro. Or even Kimberly.

As if reading his mind, before his eyes, some of the snow breaks from the flow of the swirling wind, clumping together to form a powdery arrow. It points in a direction, and a single word appears next to it: *FIRE*

***

A bright burst of flame rushes past Electro's right shoulder, spiraling towards the dark figure barely outlined in the thick of the snow. It looks like the blast strikes its target, only to reveal that the Husk remains standing.

Sharp ice stings Electro's body, the worst of it only drowned out by the Fragment still inside. It'll take a lot more than a little cold for it to waver, though it can't completely disregard its shell's needs, either. Electro should already be dead three times over. It shouldn't need to do it again for a fourth time.

The dark figure ahead of him shifts, beginning to move through the storm. The wind alters itself in response, slowing to a crawl, stopping, and then speeding up again to follow the figure's path. Glints of red shoot past his eyes, bloodied crystals hurtling themselves after the Font.

He can't help but let out an impressed huff, pausing just briefly to stare at the magical wonder that now surrounds him. This is a *perfect* use of Kimberly's magic.

A cold hand emerges from the howling wind, causing him to spin around, his free fist raised high. Kimberly is looking quite worse for wear, her skin and clothes torn open, and small droplets of blood are starting to run down her face, making it almost look like she's crying rubies. Her eyes, however, have gone completely white as her Blessing consumes her. Her hands are plastered with soft snow, spots of which are gradually turning crimson from her injuries beneath.

There's a break in the storm around them as she opens her mouth to speak.

“Jake's going to collapse,” she warns him. “I'm trying to get it away from him, but... there's something wrong. I-I can't touch it.”

Electro presses his lips together, nodding back. He noticed that, too. The Font is protecting its host, or the host has found a way to use the Font to protect itself. Either way, so long as Ethan has it in his possession, he's untouchable.

"*Keep it busy,*" he says. "*I'll think of something.*" Her breath catches in her throat, her grip weakening. He flashes her a reassuring smile. "*I'm alright.*" He gently pulls his arm away and rushes off into the white whirlwind.

He follows the current of the air, even as it threatens to shred his body apart. It will lead him to his target. He does his best to protect his face as he pushes forward, deeper into the gale. Over the wind, he can faintly hear a frustrated roar as Ethan is surrounded by blinding snow. His black form gradually fades into view, along with the bright lights of the Shards wrapped around him. Electro raises his sword again. If he can't harm the Husk, he'll aim for the Font instead.

He thrusts his arm forward, and its point throws itself forward, elongating through the snow. Shards of ice spark against the blade as it pierces through the wind, aiming for the pulse of the light.

He feels the blade hit a break in the wind, where the storm is nice and still, piercing right where the little light glows. But there's no following strike as it slices through empty air. The light lifts out of the way and a dark hand appears through the gray mist.

At the Font's command, the snow and wind scatter, and the light of Astria's center rushes into the tranquil space. The storm hasn't ceased, only parted. He can see the white wind shudder and dance chaotically, trying to find its rhythm once more. A small flurry of particles are the first ones to start drifting back towards the Husk, leading the way for the others to follow.

Ethan raises a hand above his head and makes a fist in frustration. In an instant, Electro feels an impossible pressure rest itself atop his body, bringing all within the clearing to a halt. The snow rushes around outside, battering against this invisible force as whatever has drifted within trembles hopelessly in place.

Electro grits his teeth. It takes all his willpower just to lift his head, fighting back against the weight. He can feel the bones and muscles of his neck strain and grind, flooding his body with immense pain.

Just before the Husk can snicker back at him, a bright red figure leaps above the storm, flames trailing in its wake. Eyes aglow with red and body engulfed with roaring flames, Jake flies through the air with ease, bringing his sword crashing down upon the Husk. His figure appears to be made of pure fire, though flashes of his clothes and skin manage to flicker into view as the flames weaken bit by bit.

Like every attempt they've made before, his arc is brought to an abrupt halt just a breath away from Ethan's head. The fire pushes itself up and away from the Husk, being blown back by his presence. But at least it's enough to break his concentration. Ethan twists to Jake, extending his arms, while at the same time releasing his mighty spell from Electro. The blizzard crashes in, rising beneath his feet to help propel him upwards as he leaps back into the fray.

Jake is sent flying through the air as Electro rises, a fireball that disappears into the thicket of snow, crashing back down to the golden plane below. He thrusts once more, catching the Husk by surprise. Snow and wind burst up around the two, its biting chill cheering Electro on. He feels the blade snag on something hard and firm as the needle threads itself through the small gap between the spinning glyphs of the Shard.

But the momentary success quickly evaporates. The Shard's form gives away, turning to liquid light and freeing the sword from its teeth. It licks at the blade, shoving it aside. Thinking fast, Electro spins with the force, bringing his legs around for a kick instead. He knows it won't do anything, but it's better than being sent tumbling through the air.

He can *feel* the barrier that surrounds Ethan press back against his boot, its raw power making his whole leg tremble with its violent vibration. The Husk just lets out an amused laugh.

"*How much longer will you struggle?*" he wonders aloud. The barrier beneath his foot surges forward into a blast of solid energy, pushing him back through the wailing storm. Darkness consumes his sight as he flies, unsure where he is in space and how fast he's falling. His sense of direction corrects itself once Shadow reaches out, bringing the two to a halt as it presses its power against the ground below. It catches them before they're able to ram into the hard ground. The warm hum of the light presses itself against the palms of his hands. It seems to be swirling with encouragement.

Right as Electro straightens himself again, the wind of the blizzard shifts for the worst. The swirling snow is brought to an abrupt halt, bringing stillness to the space once more. The icy flakes hang in the air, waiting for a command to be given. A domineering force rests its invisible hand over Kimberly's magic.

"*I'm sick of seeing all this white,*" Ethan spits. It takes but a wave of his hand to wash it all away, blowing the flakes back into the ether. Kimberly lets out a sharp gasp as she falls to her knees, misty breaths bursting from her lips. She has gone completely white. A small swirl of flakes continue to dance around her, but it's clear that she is spent.

Nearby, Jake struggles to sit himself up, small embers rising from his clothes as steam drifts from his arms and head. He's doing his best to keep down his retching even as his body jolts violently in protest.

Ethan hovers in the air, oozing with glee as he stares at the two exhausted wizards. His arms rise from his sides, fingers curling. The air around him vibrates with another unknown power, this time a dangerous force that makes Electro's shell quiver.

Both their minds are racing, trying to think of something – *anything* – that they could do to land a blow on the Font. The Twisted Shadow within is beyond the reason of words. They can't defend the others forever, either. Though if they retreat, then it all might as well be over; Astria will be at the mercy of unbridled malice.

Electro knows nothing about Shadows to be of much use. But the Fragment *does*.

Its essence wraps itself tightly around Electro's mind as its thoughts withdraw from his. On its way out, he catches a glimpse of the plan it has in mind. A wild and crazy plan, one that might not even work. But a plan nonetheless, and it's determined to take the risk.

What are you doing*?!* he demands. His senses are numbing and he tries to thrash against it. But Shadow's presence overwhelms him as it stands firm. He's completely helpless as he watches his arm stretch across his chest, raising the black sword to his own neck. He feels the cold blade start to dig into his skin, along with his heart thrumming against it. He can't help but continue to panic as Shadow's form gently holds him back and forces him to breathe.

{*Trust me,*} it replies, its voice calm and determined. He wants to retort, but... well, it's not like he has much of a choice other than to go along with it.

Ethan's body whirls around in the air, his sadistic smile thinning as he lays his eyes on Shadow and Electro.

"*Hey now,*" he says rather cautiously, "*That is not a good idea.*"

Shadow tightens its grip on its blade, and Electro can only sit back and feel it cut deeper, making his neck sting as his skin is split open. It stares the floating Husk down with little emotion besides conviction.

Ethan does his best not to wince, but his crimson eyes betray the tinge of pain he feels within. They twitch uncontrollably.

"*FINE THEN!*" he roars, his hands rising to his own head. "*IF YOU ARE SO DETERMINED!*" It takes but a twitch of his fingers, one last triumphant smile spreading across his lips. A black line slides its way silently across his neck. Then... it falls.

Ethan's head lands unceremoniously beneath his feet face first. Now his body floats headless, black smoke billowing from his open neck. His body bends forwards, revealing the churning void within him, beneath a layer of skin thin enough to look like colored paper.

And... nothing else happens. Shadow isn't even fazed.

Let's see if it will be the same for you, Shadow taunts. Its arm starts to bend, dragging the blade down the side of Electro's neck.

With a sudden warbled screech, a headless Ethan flings himself forward, arms outstretched with smoke pouring from his head wound in a thick mass of angry vapor. Shadow surges into motion without skipping a beat. Its hand drops its blade as it throws its arm forward. Its essence swells, the anchors that tether it to Electro's body tearing themselves free. The final thing Electro sees is its fingers curling around the billowing smoke, its grip molding it into an all-too recognizable shape. Then Ethan's aimless body slams into his, sending him falling downwards, his floating sight filling with the light of magic.

***

Electro's Shadow hangs in the air by its throat, grabbing at Shadow's arm with barred teeth. Yet it stares helplessly as the Fragment glares at it. A burst of cold energy washes away the great swirl of magic around it, demanding the world's full attention as it holds firm on its prize.

Return, it commands. Its voice fills the impossibly large space, almost seeming to make it tremble.

No sooner is the word spoken than Electro's Shadow soundlessly bursts into formless black smoke. It hovers in the air, a small pang of relief and regret joining the Fragment's hot anger. It shifts around, not daring to travel too far from Shadow, its icy gaze falling Kimberly for a brief moment. Her skin prickles from its weight.

It turns to Jake as well before it takes off, heading towards its rightful home lying still not too far away. The smoke curls around Electro's arms and legs, creating a dusty gray film that is slowly absorbed into his body. Though even after the smoke is gone from sight, the Storm wizard remains stiff and lifeless.

Shadow steps across the plane of stars soundlessly, gliding along as if it were flying. It bends down and places its hands to the sides of Ethan's severed head. In an instant, Kimberly turns away from the sight, one hand flying to her mouth. Even though there's no blood or gore, she still can't believe...

Jake wraps his arms around her as she heaves, holding down her empty stomach. He pats her back awkwardly.

Though... at least it's all over now, right? She doesn't think she can go on anymore. Her magic is a quiet breeze barely able to blow. She's never used her Blessing so much before, and it's taken its toll on her.

Jake does his best not to wheeze on her, his dry retching sending splatters of a yellow substance across the golden ground next to them. His blood, no doubt.

"Jake..." she mutters, shifting in his embrace. She places her hands on his chest gingerly. Despite her deathly chill, her fingers still burn from the heat he radiates. She almost can't believe what she saw. Her own boyfriend, Blessed right in front of her.

"I'm... okay..." he breathes between coughs. He must be feeling the effects of magic sickness. Whatever magic he had going into this fight has been pushed too far.

You can look now, she hears Ethan's voice ring out. Slowly, cautiously, she raises her head again, braced to see the worst. She sees the Fragment standing quietly over Electro's body, head reattached without any visible mess. In fact, if she hadn't seen it for herself, she would never have guessed that his head had been removed in the first place. No seam is left behind of the cut that had been made.

Yet crimson glows in his eyes, making her heart leap into her throat in panic. But there's no need for her to be scared anymore. She *saw* Electro's Shadow return to his body.

“Ethan?” she asks tentatively.

Their friend shakes his head.

No, Shadow confirms with its forlorn expression. *It's... me.*

“How is he?” Jake manages to speak, though his heavy breaths betray the effort that it took.

Shadow is quiet for what feels like an eternity. The Shards are still wrapped around its arms, pulsing in rhythm with the heart beating inside its body.

I don't know, it admits. *He's... quiet.*

Kimberly takes a deep breath and staggers to her feet. The ground seems to sway beneath her as she staggers over to the Fragment Shadow and the Electromancer. As she nears, the gale inside her starts to pick up. A cool draft of air pushes it along gently, nursing it back to health. By the time she kneels beside Electro, the void in her chest has started to feel marginally better.

“Electro?” she asks, his name awkward on her tongue. His eyes are wide open, but to her relief they shift to look at her. His chest puffs with each deep breath. His gaze is full of unspeakable emotion. They finally sparkle with life all of their own, not of some other entity living behind them.

“Hi,” he croaks. His coarseness catches Kimberly off guard. How much of him was Shadow supporting all this time?

Tears spring to her eyes. At last, this insanity has been put to rest... mostly.

The soft strike of metal colliding with a firm surface rings across the space. Jake is up on his feet, too, using his sword as a crutch to carry his heavy body forward. He wipes his hanging hand against his pants, leaving behind a bright bloody smear in its wake. Though he, too, has color start to return to his pale face as he nears the Font.

He looks up at Shadow and wearily nods at its wrists. “What about those? What are we going to do with them?”

Wordlessly, Shadow looks down at its hands, at the Shards, with a blank expression. Even with it standing on the other side of Electro's body from them, its presence radiates a warm glow. Waves of magic pass over them, pressing against them with its sheer weight. She wonders if it’s trying to push them *away* from the Font, to protect itself from all beings unable to handle its power, but she feels no need to back away or that it’s actively trying to rid itself of her presence.

Almost like it knows she’s a friend now.

Shadow inhales and closes its eyes, contemplating. As it stands apart from the others, Kimberly glances back down at Electro still lying on the ground, immobile. She feels bad for wanting to rush it to reply, knowing full well that there’s a being here that *needs* to see a Healer.

Shadow finally approaches the group. Each step is taken slowly, methodically. Its gaze is lost in some other world, staring through the wizards like they weren’t even there to begin with. It crouches down by Electro’s head, extending a single finger to him. Its fingertip barely even connects with his forehead as a burst of warmth washes over them. The smell of dirt and blooming flowers tickles Kimberly’s nose as she feels her body relax, all her aches and pains from the earlier fight ebbing away.

A small orb of green energy forms between Shadow and Electro. The Fragment lowers its finger, pressing the orb slowly into the wizard’s body. The orb's light spreads across Electro's skin as it disappears, granting him a strange green hue. Before her very eyes, Kimberly watches in stunned awe as Electro’s frail body puffs up. His arms and legs bulge with muscle, veins popping and pulsing with his heartbeat. His ill-fitting clothes now look as if they're wrapped around him too tightly as they dig into his new form. Any scrapes and bruises are washed away in a flurry of white sparkles that rise into the air and wink at her before fizzling out of existence.

Shadow leans away as the light slowly subsides, giving Electro room to move. First, he bends his arms, stretching them above his head, rolling them forwards and back. He brings his knees up to his chest cautiously, seemingly fearful that if he moves too fast he'll somehow injure them. He holds the strange position for a moment, knees up and arms out.

Then, all at once, he's in motion. His arms swing themselves forward with so much force that his upper body rises from the ground. His legs kick into the air, taking with them the rest of his weight. The bottoms of his boots hit the glowing ground with a mighty *thump* as he pops up from the squat he landed in, arms throwing themselves into the air above, fingers laced together, rising up onto his toes.

The wizard stretches with a gleeful grin.

"*Ahhhh*!" he breathes, relaxing once more. The air around him buzzes with electricity as he turns to the others, his hands falling to his hips. He stands like he's ready for another fight, untamed eagerness glowing in his eyes.

His attention then turns to her, and a calm and comforting softness rounds out his jagged edges. He offers her a hand to help her up. It's not just the air that crackles with electricity, but his entire body. He shakes with it, energy pulsing up and down his arm as he grips her firmly and pulls her to her feet with little effort. Wherever he touches her, she feels herself tingle with that same electric pulse that fuels him.

"You did good," he says with an approving nod. Kimberly can't help but smile back.

He turns his gaze away from her and back towards Shadow. "The Font?"

Shadow blinks back, appearing startled that it had been addressed. Kimberly spots its fingers curl at its side, grabbing at its robe like it's a lifeline. One of its arms eventually bends, placing a hand on its chest, right where its beating heart glows. It doesn't speak, but the air of unease it exudes says it all. It's scared to part with its piece of the Font. It doesn't know what will happen.

"Well, we can't take it with us, either," Electro points out. "It belongs down here."

Ethan... it mutters.

He drops Kimberly's hand and strides right up to Shadow, clamping his hands down on its shoulders. Its gaze rises to meet his as he leans over it. "Hey, you know what we did? It'll be just like that. I'm sure you two can do it."

But he... it trails off, closing its eyes.

"It's not like he was going to be able to walk around without you forever, right? You're still his Shadow, and that isn't going to change." He gives Shadow an encouraging pat before standing back, giving it some space to think.

It presses its hand against its chest. Gradually, its fingertips turn dark, and Kimberly watches in silence as it starts to reach inside itself for its Shard. The color of its arm drains up to its elbow as it shifts around, searching. Then it suddenly stiffens and, in one swift motion, it yanks the Shard free. There's a flare of brilliant light as the Shard is brought out into the world for the first time in stars-only-know-how-long, bathing the gathering in its glow.

Kimberly blinks away the brightness slowly. The colors come back into focus, as does Shadow's solemn gaze as it stares at the little light in its hand. Though she had suspected what the Shard would look like, it still surprises her to find a pulsating white heart sitting in its palm. Shadow's crimson eyes reflect its glow, making them appear dull and lifeless.

Wordlessly, it opens its hand, and the Shard floats

upwards all on its own. The two disks wrapped around its wrists follow suit, opening and snaking up into the air, twisting and turning around the glowing heart. Then, in the blink of an eye, the three pieces fuse together.

The Font of Magic glows like a star, its presence erasing the cold of Shadow's magic. Energy pulses through the air in rhythmic waves, molding itself around the gathered beings gently. A small halo of color shimmers around the Font's perfectly curved edges, giving it the depth of a completed sphere.

The air is light and joyous. Kimberly finds herself smiling inexplicably at the little light that hovers before her eyes. Down at the very core of her being, she feels like it's thanking her and that it's happy to finally be home.

The only one that isn't smiling is Shadow.

Kimberly feels the ground jolt beneath her feet, dragging her attention away from the Font. Darkness gathers in a dense pool, and the void of Shadow's essence drowns out the gentle air. Its stare glows with magic and nothing more. There is no life to the crimson eyes.

Quietly, they rise up into the air...

Ceun.

Shadow flinches. Their dark platform comes to an abrupt halt, though it doesn't make any of the wizards stumble or fall. Slowly, it turns its head around, glancing over Kimberly's shoulder. Curious, she, too, turns around to find the origin of the new voice.

Peering over the edge, she sees a golden figure standing on the Border Barrier far below. Two white pinpricks stare back at her, carrying with them a noble aura. It dons armor made of the endless stars akin to what Shadow sometimes appears wearing. The only difference is that this figure holds a wide greatsword before it, its gauntlets folded over the butt of the hilt at attention. Just beneath its chest plate glows the orb of the

Font. Its heart.

This figure looks right, all the pieces falling perfectly into place.

Centi? Shadow breathes next to her. A beam of warmth falls over her face. It must be smiling at them.

The Knight lifts one of its hands, and from the Font a long strand of light flows to its fingers. The magic breaks into smaller strands that rise into the air, reaching for their perch high above. They twist and weave, binding themselves together as they dance. By the time the light reaches them, it has molded itself into the shape of a heart.

It pulses before their eyes, each flash of light exuding a different emotion. It cycles through happiness, loss, anger, love, annoyance, weariness, wonder... which calms as Shadow's hand wraps around it. It pulls the heart close, its eyes reflecting its glow as its shine stabilizes. It is... relief.

***

"Kim! Jake!"

Amber bursts through the curtain of the willow tree, her face alight with a wide smile. Lukri rushes along behind her. He's so close to her that there's a good chance he might manage to trip both of them up. It, thankfully, never happens.

Amber throws her arms around Kimberly, and the two exchange a warm embrace. Lukri's pace slows to a halt a few steps away, his smile wavering. He looks at Jake momentarily, but he quickly turns to Shadow.

"Well?" he asks, eyes wide.

A single drum pounds against its chest. Shadow nods back with a smile. *We did it.*

Amber breaks away from Kimberly, her cheery attitude faltering. "Ethan?"

Another beat strains its expression. *He's resting.* Still a void of empty space. Still no sign of his consciousness returning.

A third beat, light and fluttery. It rests its hand against its chest, closing its eyes. There's no sign *yet*. He will return. He just needs some time to recollect himself. Electro gives its shoulder a firm pat, reaffirming its hope.

But things won't be the same anymore. This gift – its new heart – doesn't beat the same way as the Shard did. It oozed with the gift of life. Life that Ethan will no longer feel. He will have to rely on Shadow to support himself again.

It steals a glance at Electro, who smiles at the young wizards as they stand around and chat. Jake has pulled Lukri aside, their expressions mute as the Pyromancer releases the words plaguing his mind. Kimberly, meanwhile, entertains the energetic Amber with the tale of Astria's center. Blaze has finally joined the group as well, though he stands at its edge, staring with a kind smile of his own. He fidgets with something small and red in his hand as his gaze appears to bounce between Amber and Shadow. He wants to approach it but doesn't know how.

The Electromancer's Husk and Shadow flow seamlessly as one once again. Something it hasn't done with Ethan in... quite a long time.

It took a big risk with Electro. Things could have gone much worse than they did. It could have crushed him with its will. It very nearly did.

The Electromancer's gaze shifts, sensing its stare. Despite its troubled expression, his smile doesn't falter. “Something wrong?”

What if he's gone? Shadow asks, its voice a haunting whisper.

Electro takes in a heavy breath as he closes his eyes, delving deep into the vast remnants of knowledge Shadow left etched into his memory. It takes him a while to find what he's searching for, to which he releases a light burst of laughter.

“Don't be so scared!” he reassures it. “You've already got

everything the rest of us have. You–" He points at its head. "–Ethan–" He raps his knuckles against its shoulder. "–and a heart." He plants his finger in the center of its chest. The heart within leaps in response, happy to have been acknowledged. "If I was able to hang on, he'll be able to bounce back, too."

Its head twitches, unsure if it should nod along or turn away. Its heart swirls once more with fleeting weightlessness.

"He'd be proud of you, you know," he adds. That makes it smile, albeit weakly. It knows he would.

So would Kelsy, it replies. Hearing her name makes his smile strain at last. He turns away from it as he reaches into his pocket, retrieving a stick of arcane.

"Yeah, well..." he hums back, popping one of the ends into his mouth and giving it a good twist with his fingers. He makes it sound like he has a point he wants to make, but once his eyes return to Kimberly, his words falter. He lets out a huff.

I think she'd want you to stay, Shadow tells him, following his gaze.

"That's a decision I'll leave for her to make," he replies. After all, she still doesn't even know the full story yet, only vague bits and pieces. There's still a lot for her to learn before she will be able to determine for certain if she'd want him in her life or not. For all intents and purposes, he's still a stranger to her.

He shifts the gold stick to one side of his mouth, taking a deep breath. "You lot did great," he speaks over the din of conversation. He gives each one of the present beings their own grin. "Three cycles ago, none of you knew who I was. But you helped me out anyway. So, thank you." He extends a foot forward, passing the wizards by with long, smooth strides. "Now that the drama's all over, I think I'll be off–"

"*Wait*!" Kimberly cries. The Electromancer halts, just as she ordered, and twists his head around just enough for her to catch a glimpse of his mouth and the tip of his nose. "About Kelsy–"

"That," he interrupts her smoothly, taking the arcane gold out of his mouth, "you should ask your parents about."

"But–"

"I promised them a chance to explain to you first." The corner of his mouth pulls upwards into one of his sly grins. "Come find me once you've done that." He bites back down on his gold as he starts striding away once again.

"Where will you be?" she calls after him.

"Eh, you'll figure it out!" he laughs. He throws a hand up in the air over his shoulder, fingers spread and sparking with lightning, in a parting gesture, as he wanders off deep into the maze that is the island of Asandra.

Epilogue

Electro staggers to his feet, battered and bruised from head to toe. But he forces himself upright. He *has* to stand. Sweat pours down his face, dripping off his nose and matting his hair. The skin on the back of his knuckles is split open, crimson red smeared across his fingers. Maybe he's overdone himself this time...

A gruff hand latches onto his wrist and yanks his arm high into the air. With it, the intoxicating roar of the crowd fades back into focus. “AND HE'S UP!”

He manages to clench his held hand into a victorious fist, a surge of energy jolting his body back alive. He straightens up and smiles at the crowd, his dazzling teeth visible for all to see. He can hardly manage make out the edges of faces as the beings jump up and down in the stands, pumping the air with fists of their own. It's a swarm of colors that fade in and out of the Firelight, backdropped by rocky walls. Closing his eyes, he can still see the magnificence...

What a show, he smirks.

The judge lets Electro go, giving him a hearty shove on his shoulder, both to congratulate him and to signal that his time on the floor is over. Laughing to himself, he makes his way across the burnt dirt, heading towards the stands as the next match is announced. A Healer will get him patched right up before the semi-finals take place.

Arms reach out from the stands as he hauls his heavy body up the stairs. Congratulations and wishes of luck barely manage to make it to his ears above the rest of the noise.

He leaves the crowd behind him as he waltzes back into the training grounds. A small medical corner has been set up nearby with a handful of Healers stationed within, caring for the fighters. One of the green robes hurries up to him, a towel and glass of water in their hands.

"Thanks," he breathes. He wipes his face clean first before taking a swig. Stars above, how good it is to feel alive again!

He's guided into a chair, where he's able to finally sit back and relax as the Healer tends to his wounds. The air buzzes with electricity as he gathers his breath again. The roar of the crowd leaks through the doorway each time they observe a new spectacle.

In the stillness, he feels something cold shift against the flow of his magic. He tenses, fingers curling, just as the Healer moves to place their hands on his arm. They hesitate, their eyes darting to the Electromancer with concern.

He turns to them and musters a calm grin. "Sorry! I'm good."

His head rolls back to the space in front of him, and standing before him is a wizard in bright blue. He'd be shocked if not for the shadow that she casts behind her. A pair of kind, crimson eyes stare back at him from over her shoulder as its form is stretched across the white fabric.

"Hey," he greets her.

"...Hi," Kimberly chirps back in a low voice. She casts a long glance over her shoulder, back towards the entrance to the arena, before returning to Electro's abused body.

"Come to see the show, huh?" he asks with a burst of laughter.

Kimberly's face contorts unpleasantly. "I guess..." she mutters back. Her hands run themselves along her skirt, meeting together in front of her. She clasps them together tightly, her quiet gaze full of thoughts and questions.

"I take it you talked to them?" he guesses.

"I did," she nods. "Ian... told me what he could."

He can't help but frown. "And Jay?"

"He's... in custody," she reveals. A dark shadow casts itself over her face, and she has to close her eyes and take a deep breath to keep herself calm and collected.

"I *tried* to warn him," he comments beneath his breath. He shakes his head sadly. Ian did the right thing. "I'm sorry, Kimberly." That "sorry" carries a lot more weight than mere sympathy for the one she *thought* was her father winding up in custody. He's sorry that he wasn't there for her. That he let their family break up all over one wizard's obsession. That he wasn't strong enough to resist Ryan. That all of this happened in the first place when it shouldn't have.

But he can't go back, either. Nor does he think that he'd want to. He wouldn't want to take away all that she has now. She still had a happy life without him, and she has a bright future. Reappearing in it now just feels... *wrong*.

The cold night air rolls over his hot head, making the wounds that remain open sting from its bite. There's been a noticeable shift in the mood of Asandra over these last few cycles since the Font was returned. The air is much more tangible than it has ever felt in his whole life. It's crisp on the tongue. Full of energy that it previously lacked. Bolder. More electric. It seems like every being can feel it, too. The crowd is much more enthusiastic than they had been all those years ago. The magic is palpable.

Kimberly's eyes open again. She appears to be much

more at ease with herself as she looks back down at the old Electromancer before her. Her mouth opens to speak again, but she's halted by the curtain to Electro's resting space being ripped open. One of the event organizers pops their face in. “Hey, you're up.”

“Right,” Electro confirms, holding up his thumb. The Healer lifts their hands as Electro rises to his feet. The splits on his knuckles are almost all gone, though they don't sting nearly as bad as they had before, and his exhaustion has been wiped away.

“You staying for the rest of it?” he asks Kimberly as they depart.

“Yeah,” she nods. Though she stops walking as she sucks in a sharp breath. He pauses and turns around to give the timid Cryomancer the fleeting remains of his undivided attention.

“I want to get to know you more,” she announces. Her eyes plead with him to stay and talk with her more, though they both know that he's got somewhere to be at the moment.

Electro places his hands on his waist, a smile stretching across his face. Despite all his doubts... he's happy. It's not a do-over. It's a start.

“Well, I ain't going anywhere any time soon!” he jokes, releasing a laugh. Kimberly's tense expression lights up with a hopeful smile. She releases a soft chuckle of her own.

“Wish me some luck, then, eh?” he proposes, stepping forward. He holds out a fist to her. She stares back at it, mildly confused. She raises her own hand, mirroring his, and gives his knuckles a tepid bump. He still gives her an approving nod. She got it.

He moves his arm to the empty space next to her. She blinks, confused, but he knows what he's doing. It takes a moment, but a black hand emerges from the dim light, also curled into a fist, and bounces itself off of his with a bit more spring. A jolt of electricity arcs between the two as a comforting chill works its way across his body.

"Enjoy the show!" he tells the two beings as he bounds off again. There's a bit more pep to his step as he springs down the stairs to the cheers of the crowd. His heart flutters against his chest; he hasn't been this happy since he proposed to Kelsy. At this rate, he feels like he can take on the whole world!

He takes a quick glance into the audience before leaving them behind. Picking Kimberly out of the expanse of faces is easy now. She works her way back into Jake's awaiting arms, smiling from ear to ear as she begins to shout over the noise the good news. Behind her, Ethan melts from the darkness, his hat and cape reclaimed. His onyx eyes meet Electro's, and he gives him a nod of encouragement.

That's about all he needs. He leaps from the stairs, his lightning propelling himself forward through the air. His boots crash down onto the dirt below, kicking up a brown haze that sparks with static as it shrouds his body in mystery. It's only the semi-finals, but that shouldn't stop him from making a grand entrance.

He plants his feet firm, raising his fists towards his opponent. He can't stop himself from beaming. To any other being, it's a wild grin that's looking for a fight. To him, however, it's for the beings that drive him forward.

"AND ON THIS SIDE, THE WIZARD WHO CAN'T BE KEPT DOWN – ELECTROOOO!"

About the Author

Miriya Greer is an American girl and third culture kid, the eldest daughter in a loving family of five.

In high school, Miriya was one of many writers that worked on a handful of student films for the American School in Japan, such as *Lessons for a Deity*. After graduating with honors, one of her short stories was published in No Bad Book Press' *The Mirror: A Cat Anthology* later the same year. In November of 2023, she self-published her first novel, *Shadowbound*, on Amazon.

Nowadays, Miriya curates two primary online profiles while she continues to work on her future novels and pursues her writing career. One is her YouTube, where she continues to develop her oral storytelling skills, and the other is her Substack, where she hones her writing style and shares her authors journey with her audience.

https://www.youtube.com/@seastorm1052
https://stormshorts.substack.com/

Miriya's sister, Elanor, drew the cover art for *Shadowbound* and *Bloodbound*. She loves anime, Japanese culture, sushi, and insists on being paid in chocolate bars. Find her art online at:

https://slhs-ecogirl.carrd.co/

www.ingramcontent.com/pod-product-compliance
Lightning Source LLC
LaVergne TN
LVHW010633110826
845149LV00014B/2838

* 9 7 9 8 9 8 9 1 0 6 5 5 4 *